Disheartened

The Spirit Quest Series
Book 2

A.L. Waddington

Cover Design by Scarlett Ink Publishing
Edited by Eric Staeheli

This is a work of fiction. Names, characters, places, brands, media, and incidents are either the product of the author's imagination or are used fictitiously. Any resemblance to similarly named places or to persons living or deceased is unintentional.

Hardback ISBN: 978-1-948143-29-5
Paperback ISBN: 978-1-948143-30-1
EPUB ISBN: 978-1-948143-31-8

Library of Congress Control Number: 2026904544

"Those who don't know history are destined to repeat it."

~Edmund Burke

Acknowledgments

I would like to thank my husband, Eric, for all his help with the research for this book. He is a born historian and investigator filled with the awe and wonderment of all the similarities between the two crisis periods in America.

For my beautiful grandchildren,
I pray my generation leaves you a better world
than the one we are living in now.
God Bless You

1

SATURDAY, JANUARY 25, 2020

I **STUMBLED OVER TO THE COFFEE** maker and pushed the button. I could still hear my live-in boyfriend, Landon snoring softly in our bedroom. Small drifts of snow had gathered on the narrow red brick ledge outside our kitchen window. I gazed sleepily out across our stamp-size backyard garden hibernating in winter haze. It appeared as barren as I felt.

It had been a hectic week. The spring semester was underway, and Landon and I had picked up extra shifts at the hospital trying to put as much money back as possible for school, rent, and everyday expenses. I was exhausted and felt like I was never going to graduate and have a life where I wasn't constantly worried about homework or studying because every time, I tried to enjoy life a little bit, I always felt guilty for not studying.

"Good morning darling," Landon entered the kitchen wearing flannel pajama bottoms, a thermal long-sleeved t-shirt, and his long fleece robe. His dirty blond hair was askew is a sexy way he pulled off effortlessly. The sound of his voice drew my attention away from the garden.

"Hey babe, I thought you would be sleeping in." I opened the cabinet and removed two mugs.

"I wish," he muttered rubbing the scruff on his chin. "I feel like I haven't slept in a month."

"Ditto," I poured each of us a mug.

Landon walked up behind me and wrapped his arms around my waist. I leaned back into him, closing my eyes and breathing in the faint smell of his cologne.

"I wish we could stay in bed all day." He leaned down and kissed me softly on my neck.

"Me too." I sighed heavily before handing him his mug. "But we can't." I added an ample amount of sugar and cream to my mug.

"Brunch with the folks." Landon raised his mug in a mock toast. "Can't wait."

"Hey. Don't give me any grief. This was not my idea." I reminded him with a smirk.

"That's hardly fair. They couldn't make it over Christmas and leave my siblings." He countered.

"My dad did," I teased.

"Not really," he pointed out. "He brought Ethan and Liang with him."

"We outnumber them."

"And they outnumber me," He rolled his eyes. "At least they got a hotel room and aren't staying with us."

"That was their choice. We offered." I took a sip of my coffee and leaned against the counter.

"They figured it would be too much with our schedules. Besides, it's only for a couple days." Landon kept ahold of his mug simply to keep his hands warm.

"What time are we meeting them?" I unconsciously glanced at the clock over the stove out of habit.

"Noon at *Theo's Cozy Corner*." He finished off the rest of his coffee and refilled his mug.

"Oh, I love that place." I moved in beside him and emptied the rest of the pot into my mug.

"I know. That's why I chose it." A sly smile slid across his shapely lips.

"Oh, really?" I raised an eyebrow and smirked.

"I figured it would be easier to get you to spend the day with my parents if I fed you from your favorite café." Landon laughed.

"You think you know me so well." I loved tormenting him.

"I know I do." He kissed me quickly on the forehead before taking another long drink of his coffee. "Come on," he playfully bumped into me. "Let's get in the shower."

The grey sky was filled with heavy clouds threatening to dump another round of snow upon us. The roads were heavily salted and mostly cleared by the dozens of snowplows traveling throughout the city but still held onto patches of black ice. The temperatures hovered in the mid-teens with a vague aspiration of reaching a whopping twenty degrees by late afternoon. It was typical weather for Boston in mid-January, and as much as I had grown accustomed to northern winters, I have never enjoyed them.

We arrived at the cafe just in time to catch Landon's parents before they were seated. They were removing their winter coats when we drifted through the door with a gust of bitter wind. Landon forced the door closed as I almost collided with them.

"Well, hello darling." Landon's mother, Diana, embraced me before I could even say hello.

"Good morning, Diana." I said when she finally released me.

"My dear, when are you going to start calling me mom?" She smiled warmly at me.

I rarely called my own mother mom and did not think overly fondly of the term.

"Hello mom," Landon turned and hugged his mother. "I'm glad to see you made it in one piece." He teased her because of her fear of flying.

"I slipped her a valium." His dad, Jim, beamed with pride.

"What?" Diana looked astonished. "You did not."

But Jim smiled knowingly at us and remained silent.

"Let's get a table." Landon quickly changed the subject and steered his mother over to the hostess podium.

We sat down in the booth along the wall and glanced over the menu the waitress set before us. We ordered four coffees to start with, and I scooted my menu over to the edge of the table. I already knew what I wanted.

"Did you have a nice Christmas?" I asked Diana while adding cream and sugar to my coffee.

"That depends on your definition of nice." Jim smirked at his son.

"What happened?" I raised an eyebrow at his mother who was rolling her eyes.

"I thought Lizzy and Holden were there when I called." Landon seemed confused. "Were they arguing again?"

"No. Nothing like that." Diana proclaimed shaking her head.

The waitress came by, refilled our coffees, and took our orders before disappearing once again. Everyone except Landon started adding more sugar and cream to adjust the additional coffee.

"Then what?" Landon persisted.

"Gabriella," Jim stated as if that explained everything.

"Holden's wife?" I didn't understand his meaning.

"It's nothing," Diana waved it off obviously wanting to change the subject. "She can be a bit difficult is all." Jim snorted, making Landon laugh. I was still confused but let it go. I would ask Landon about it later "Did you two have a nice Christmas? Your dad and brother flew out, didn't they Sidney?"

"Yes, and my brother's girlfriend." I added. "It was really nice to see them all."

"But you have family here, right?" Diana inquired.

"Yes. My sister and her husband and his family live here. Her sister-in-law is my best friend. Plus, my uncle is here as well. He's a history professor at BU." I explained.

"That must make it easier for you." She smiled sincerely.

"It does." I agreed.

"It's made the transition easier on both of us. Sidney's sister's in-laws have equally adopted us as well. I can't wait for you to meet them. They've invited us for dinner this evening." Landon boasted.

"I don't want to impose on them." Diana objected.

"Don't worry. It is no imposition. Emily loves entertaining." I smiled over at her. "And she is a wonderful cook."

"I'll say she is," Landon patted his flat belly as if he had something there. But it was enough to put a smile on both his parents' faces and ease their misgivings about having dinner with strangers.

"So," Jim asked as the waitress set our brunch down before us. "What are we going to do today?"

We spent the day shopping and visiting every little tourist trap around Boston. Jim and Diana were in great spirits despite the cold.

They had never visited Boston before and insisted on seeing everything as they put it.

Jim was a history buff and wanted to see the infamous site of the Boston Massacre between the British soldiers and townspeople. I had been there before and passed it countless times over the last several years. It had simply become another landmark that locals rarely heeded.

I had a wonderful time with Landon's parents. I had met them several times before we moved to Boston. It was not often since they lived near Peoria, Illinois and rarely came up to Chicago. Neither of them liked the city and avoided it if possible.

Diana was a short, round woman with a jovial face and stylish brownish gray hair. Now in her early sixties, she had retired last year from teaching English. Jim was a bit over six feet tall with salt and pepper hair, a full bushy beard, and a bit of a pot belly. With his glasses perched slightly on his large, rounded nose, he carried a strong resemblance to the images of Santa Clause I recalled from my youth. He also retired last year after spending his career running a security firm.

It was dark by the time we pulled into my sister's in-law's, Robert and Emily Chandler's driveway just before six o'clock in the evening. Their large Victorian home glowed with warmth in the darkness. We left our purchases safely in the trunk and treaded up the recently shoveled walkway. The bitter air was thick with the smell of wood burning from the chimneys of nearby homes. I held onto Landon's arm as we carefully navigated the winter wonderland. Emily had left all their Christmas decorations up, creating a festive atmosphere. Her exquisite taste in vintage décor enhanced the ambiance throughout their Victorian home.

"Good evening," Emily greeted us with a warm smile, stepped back and gestured to us to come in. "Welcome. I am so happy to see you." She embraced Landon and me warmly.

Emily was dressed in dark blue jeans, a cream-colored shirt, with a teal cardigan jacket and subtle but classy accessories. Her laced-up calf high boots perfectly completed her ensemble. Her long blondish-brown hair hung down loosely in soft waves over her shoulders. She was a very attractive lady who looked years younger than her true age.

"The temperature's starting to drop." Landon complained as he unzipped his coat.

"I hope it doesn't start snowing again" Diana chimed in removing her own jacket as well.

"Me too," Emily collected our coats and hung them in the hall closet. "Dinner is almost ready. Would anyone like a drink? I made some Hot Toddy's, and we have hot apple cider." She led the way into the parlor.

Robert greeted us warmly while we all took a seat near the roaring fire in the hearth. My sister, Jocelyn and her husband, Jackson appeared from the kitchen carrying trays with teapots and China teacups and saucers decorated in the *Old Curiosity Shop* based on the novel by *Charles Dickens*.

My three companions chose to partake in a Hot Toddy while I decided to warm myself up with apple cider. Jocelyn and Jackson sat down on the chase lounge opposite Landon and me and sipped their hot totties.

Jocelyn was wearing a hooded pink BU sweatshirt with oversized flannel pajama bottoms and woolen slippers. Her auburn hair was pulled up in a messy bun, and her cheeks were flushed red. Beside her, Jackson hovered over his Hot Toddy with exuberance. He was also casually dressed in an old sweatshirt and pajama bottoms with slippers.

"Please excuse the attire of our youngest and his partner in crime." Emily sat down in a chair near the fire. "They did show up in appropriate clothing, but apparently my daughter-in-law slipped pulling her husband down with her." I looked at my sister with confusion.

"How bad was the fall that you had to change clothes?" I asked.

"Your sister decided it was my fault for not catching her before she fell. In my defense, she was behind me and grabbed the back of my jacket pulling me down with her." A sly grin spread across his shapely lips. "So, I may have thrown a snowball or a few at her in return."

"More like a dozen," Jocelyn smirked back at her grinning husband. "I returned fire."

"By the time they made it into the house, they were soaked." Emily chuckled. "That's how they ended up in pajamas for dinner."

"Sounds like fun," Landon laughed.

"I can't remember the last time we had a snowball fight." Jim looked towards his wife.

"Not since our children were young." Diana replied with a casual shrug.

"I highly recommend it." Jackson beamed. "Definitely worth it."

"Quite satisfying," Jocelyn grinned. "Definitely worth hearing you squeal like a little girl and ducking behind the cars."

"You have a vicious aim," Jackson accused. "Too many years of playing softball."

"I was only the back-up pitcher," my sister defended. "It is not my fault you played short stop."

"This isn't over." Jackson's emerald, green eyes twinkled with mischievousness. "Just wait,"

"How was your flight?" Jocelyn ignored her husband's remark, changing the subject looking towards Landon's parents.

"As best to be expected, I suppose." Jim responded between sips.

"If you call dreadful the best to be expected, then I would agree." Diana smirked at her husband. "I am not a fan of flying simply because of all the hassle it involves and the cramp seats on the planes." She explained.

"I do not care for it myself." I agreed.

"You mean you hate it," Landon spoke up poking me playfully in the ribs.

"Yes, I hate it." I grinned back at him.

"We typically drive when we travel." Robert added sitting closely beside Emily. "We love to take back roads and see parts of the country with its small towns and rural landscape most never see from their seats thirty thousand feet above the ground."

"If we were able to, we would have loved to do that as well. But of course, this time of year is not idyllic for cross-country drives through the North." Jim concluded.

"Yes, that is true. October is our favorite time for those." Emily smiled. "I love Fall with the mild weather and changing leaves. It is simply breathtaking. We usually take a drive through the Blue Ridge mountains the second week of October when the leaves are typically at their peak."

"I cannot imagine living somewhere without the seasons." Diana spoke up. "That's why I could never live in the South and why we will never retire to Arizona." She looked pointedly over at her husband.

"I never said I wanted to live in Arizona." He rolled his eyes in a humorous gesture. "I only said I want to move out of Illinois."

"What?" Landon perked up. "Why?"

"Our liberal Governor is an embarrassing moron. He just took office and is already worse than the last one." Jim set his saucer and teacup on the coffee table. "With him running things, I hate to imagine where his ineptitude will have us in a year or two."

"Yes, I understand what you mean. Boston is not any better." Robert concluded.

"Excuse me for a moment. I need to check on dinner." Emily rose.

"Anything I can do?" Diana offered.

"No but thank you. Just relax." Still, my sister and I followed her into the kitchen.

We could hear the conversation continue with our absence as we put the final touches on dinner and set everything on the dining room table. Jocelyn and I carried the last of the dishes whilst Emily ushered everyone into the dining room and directed them to their seats.

Robert and Jim seemed to have reached a consensus on the direction our country was taking, and it was clearly one that neither agreed with. The ladies joined in occasionally remarking their two cents where appropriate, but the conversation was predominantly carried on by the men.

It was close to midnight before Landon, and I finally returned home. Both of us were exhausted but agreed it had been a success. Big fluffy snowflakes drifted outside out window when I turned out the light and climbed into bed. I snuggled against Landon and rested my head upon his chest. I let the steady strong rhythm of his heartbeat lull me into a deep peaceful sleep.

2

SATURDAY, JANUARY 28, 1860

THE DAY DAWNED WITH bitter cold winds whipping through our estate, Terrace Falls in Braintree, Massachusetts. The snow was knee deep making travel nearly impossible. I was in my seventh month of pregnancy and my husband, Keifer, had banned me from traveling outside of church and our small-town market.

Our estate rested on three hundred and sixty acres just outside the small town of Braintree directly off the Monatiquot River near the Weymouth Fore River just south of the city of Boston. My grandfather, Nathan built our home in the 1810's. It was a large brick two-story mansion with black shutters and large balconies across the lower and upper levels. The inside was detailed in intrinsic moldings, coffered ceilings, long windows, exposed beams and hardwood floors. Despite its size, it felt cozy and warm to me. It was home.

I pulled my shawl closer around my shoulders as I rested back against the chaise lounge. The blazing fire in the hearth crackled and popped, but even with the Afghan wrapped snuggly around my lower body, I dearly missed central heating.

I was working on another quilt knowing it would be greatly needed once the war began. My grandmother, Marissa, was sitting in the rocker across the hearth from me. She was stitching away while humming softly. The yards of fabric spread between us hovered inches above the hardwood floor.

Her long grey hair was pulled back in a low bun that rested at the nap of her neck. Her dark grey dress hung loosely on her thin frame. My grandmother had always been a petite lady, who kept herself active both physically and mentally. Despite her years, she remained sharp, spry, and aways quick-witted.

"You seem preoccupied this morning. Are you feeling all right?" My grandmother paused, looking over at me.

"I feel like a beached whale." I smiled over at her resting my hand on my ever-expanding abdomen.

"You are the picture of an expectant mother, absolutely glowing." Her eyes sparkled in the fire light.

"I believe that is the early stages of crow's feet." I smirked.

"You are beautiful and elegant, as always." My grandmother's eyes were warm and loving.

"You are kind," I chuckled.

"I was thinking of hosting a dinner party next month." Her words instantly erased the smile on face.

"Why?" I unconsciously pulled the Afghan higher up on my chest.

"With all this unpleasantness going on, I thought it would be nice to bring everyone together simply to remind us as to what is truly important — family, friends, and the ties that hold us together." My grandmother explained.

"Do you really believe that is appropriate?" I raised my eyebrows.

"Not only do I believe it is appropriate, but necessary. The tension arrives like clockwork on our porch daily and only serves to fuel the simmering fire that will soon erupt. We need to show solidarity with our neighbors and our community."

"But with me so far along," I hesitated.

"Darling, we are not living in Medieval times. Women have babies every day. That is no reason to shut yourself off from society." She smiled lovingly over at me. "Besides, you are barely showing."

"Fine," I took a deep breath and relented. "What exactly do you have in mind?"

"Well, obviously it will be indoors." A sly grin spread across her lips. "It is a bit too cold to spread out about the gardens."

"The snow can be such an inconvenience." I coyly remarked.

"Therefore," she gracefully ignored my comment. "We will use the parlor for conversation, set the dining room up in a buffet fashion, and clear the drawing room for dancing."

"You have given this a lot of thought." I concluded. "You have been planning this for a while." I pinched my lips together.

"Darling, you are not the first mistress of Terrace Falls." My grandmother's eyes danced. "Your grandfather and I used to host the most lavish dinner parties in years past. They were the talk of the town, and everyone loved them. I believe we are in dire need of one now."

"Very well," I shook my head in defeat. "If you insist."

"It will be grand. And do not fret, I will handle all the details." She rocked steadily in her chair looking very satisfied with herself.

It was nightfall before my husband, Keifer arrived home. He was cold, irritable, and hungry. He placed his medical bag on the table in the foyer, removed his gloves, jacket, and hat, and handed them to Ned with a slight nod. Ned quietly hung them on the coatrack beside the door and disappeared back towards the kitchen.

"Hello, my dear." I kissed him lightly on the cheek. "How was your day.

"Dreadful," he walked into the parlor and poured himself two fingers of bourbon before stepping in front of the hearth to warm himself.

I lingered in the doorway watching my husband closely. His sandy blond hair was beginning to curl around the ends indicating he needed a trim. His hazel-green eyes sparkled in the firelight, and I could see the tension in his six-foot, three-inch frame beginning to ease as he sipped his whiskey.

"What happened?" I stepped into the room and walked up behind him wrapping my arms around his waist and resting my head against his back. My five-foot, five-inch frame felt dwarfed beside his.

"Three broken fingers, a broken wrist, four knocked out teeth, and a broken jaw." He finished off the last of his drink, patted my hands pulling free of me and walking over to the canister to pour him another glass.

"What?" I was confused. "I do not understand." I remained in front of the fire because the heat was intoxicating.

"That damn *Fugitive Slave Law.*" Keifer slammed down another shot before refilling his glass. He returned to the hearth, but I did not touch him. "The bullheaded Samsons' decided they were going to go up against a couple Federal Marshalls who were taking a runaway back to Georgia. A fight ensued and now that I have patched them up, they are sitting in jail."

"I see," I sat down on the corner of the chaise.

"Hopefully, that will be the end of it, but I doubt it at least until next time. The Marshalls already boarded a train so," he gestured widely with his drink. "I hate all this anger and violence."

"It is going to get much worse before it gets better." My grandmother appeared in the doorway.

"Can it?" Keifer grunted.

"It will," she sighed heavily. "Much worse." Her eyes locked mine. "Dinner is served."

Keifer was restless the remainder of the evening. He barely spoke during dinner and afterwards took his coffee in his study. I found him buried behind the evening paper when I went to find him shortly before I retired.

The roaring fire had warmed his office nicely and it felt rather warm in comparison to the rest of the house. Keifer had his stocking feet up on the corner of his desk. He was so engrossed in the paper that he did not hear me enter.

"Darling?" I instinctively straightened the papers on the corner of his desk. "Are you coming to bed soon?"

"Yes dear," the corner of the paper turned inward, and his face appeared before me. "I was reading about the mess going on in Washington." He put his feet back on the floor and folded the paper and set it aside on his desk.

"What do you mean?" I inquired, taking a seat in the chair next to the hearth.

"The Democrat party is going to split." He got up and walked around his desk and sat down in the chair opposite mine.

"How do you mean?" I feigned ignorance to appease my husband.

"They cannot come to a consensus on a nominee for the Presidential election." He ran his fingers through his hair. "I cannot believe this is happening. Each day the news gets worse." He looked at me with mournful eyes. "Plus, I received a letter from Margarett today."

"Really? Why didn't you tell me earlier?" I questioned.

"It was waiting for me on my desk when I came in after dinner." He explained. "I guess Ned left it there for me."

Ned was the foreman of Terrace Falls, and I could not survive without him. Regardless of the opinions of my neighbors and friends, Marissa and I taught him reading, writing, and arithmetic. He was amongst the few free black men in our county who could do all three; his son, Duncan was another.

"What did Margarett have to say? How is your family?" I got along well with his older sister, Margarett, but not his younger sister Eugenia. We had a horrible visit with her when she came last year that did not end well.

"Worried. Stressed." Keifer leaned forward running his fingers through his hair. "There's a lot of talk about secession, mainly in South Carolina, but she says Savannah is buzzing with it as well. She wrote that Thad believes it may come to that, but she is hoping things will calm down after the election in November."

"I never thought Thad bothered himself much with politics." I said casually.

My brother-in-law Thad, Margrett's husband, was a Southerner in every sense of the word. Born the second son of a wealthy rice plantation owner on the other side of Savannah, his older brother inherited their family plantation upon their father's untimely death almost ten years ago. So, after Thad married Margrett, Keifer decided he wanted to go to medical school up North, much to the extreme disappointment of his father, David. Thad had stepped in to fill the gap left by my husband at his family's large rice plantation, Gable Garden. Now that Keifer's parents were getting older, Thad managed most of the daily affairs of the estate.

"I believe everyone in the country is watching closely what transpires in Washington right now." My husband raised an inquisitive brow at me. "People are getting nervous."

"And you?" Although we lived in Massachusetts my husband still held the South in his heart. His heritage also caused a great many of our neighbors to speculate about his loyalty if the South succeeded.

"I have told you before, I will not pick up a rifle against my kin or my home state of Georgia." Keifer rested his elbows on his knees and leaned forward with his hands locked together. "But I will use my education and skill to save as many of my countrymen as I can, on both sides."

"But which Army will you follow?" I tried not to hold my breath or consider the fallout from the men in our county if he decided to attach himself to a Southern army.

"I pray my family will forgive me, but Terrace Falls is my home. I will attach myself with the same unit as my fellow neighbors." I unconsciously let out a sigh of relief.

"Do you believe they will?"

"I guess we will find out?" Keifer raised an eyebrow.

"How so?" My stomach tightened.

"I know you want to spend the holiday season with your brothers in Chicago, but before we head West, I want to visit Gable Garden." I could not believe my ears.

"Do you think that is wise? It could be dangerous traveling that far south, especially for someone with a Boston accent and a new baby."

"Nonsense," a smirk spread across his shapely lips. "It has taken me years to lose my Southern drawl," the twang he'd had when I first met suddenly reappeared. "But I can bring it back whenever necessity dictates, ma'am." I laughed. "You will just have to speak as little as possible on the train and outside of my family's home."

"Oh, I am sure you will love that." I rolled my eyes playfully at him.

"This could turn into a very pleasant trip." He grinned before leaning over and kissing me on the cheek. "Let's turn in, darling."

3

MONDAY, JANUARY 27, 2020

I LEANED AGAINST THE COUNTER in the break room and filled my travel mug up with fresh coffee. I sighed heavily and closed my eyes for a long moment. It was my second twelve-hour shift in as many days, and exhaustion had set in my bones. It was just after three in the morning, and I prayed it would be quiet the remaining three hours of my shift.

The sound of shuffling feet behind me brought me back around. I opened my eyes and glanced over my shoulder. Natalie, a third-year resident, stood in the doorway looking dead on her feet.

"Hey Sid," I heard her weary voice though it was soft and low. "I didn't realize anyone was in here." She crept in quickly and closed the door behind her.

"When are you off?" I plopped down in the chair and rested my head in my hand.

"Tomorrow at six." She sighed heavily and removed her lab coat draping it on the back of the chair across from me. "Are you off at six?"

"Thankfully," I mindlessly added sugar and cream.

"Did you hear they confirmed a second case of coronavirus in Chicago?"

"Seriously?" I closed my eyes.

"Yep. That is one in Seattle and one in Chicago. Both just returned from China." She poured herself a mug of coffee.

"Wonderful. So, we've got at least two flights with possibly hundreds of people who have been exposed to this virus." I sighed heavily with disbelief.

"It looks that way. And there's no way of knowing how many of those people have already been exposed to others since they landed." Natalie remarked.

"This could quickly turn into a nightmare. What do we know about this virus?" I inquired, keeping my head resting in my hand.

"Not much. I tried to do a bit of research on it after I saw the report confirming the second case and I couldn't find much. I know it affects the respiratory system. I guess the elderly and those with compromised immune systems are particularly vulnerable." She shrugged.

"So, it's a more severe version of the flu?" I speculated.

"I guess, but I'm not sure. I suppose we'll learn more if more cases come about."

The room went quiet as we each became lost in our own thoughts. I had seen a brief news report regarding the case in Seattle almost a week ago, but I was not aware of the one in Chicago that had just been confirmed. I was hoping we would gain more information about this virus and quickly. I knew the implications could be particularly bad for those in the medical community as well as first responders because we were always directly affected and exposed to these things when they occurred.

Landon came home after the end of his shift. I slept most of the day and the sun was setting when I felt his lips on my forehead. I smiled before I opened my eyes and saw him leaning over me.

"Good evening sleeping beauty," he smiled back.

"Aren't you a sight for sore eyes." I stretched and rubbed the remaining sleep out of my eyes.

"I'm exhausted." Landon flopped down on the pillow beside mine. "I could sleep until Thursday." He groaned and kicked off his sneakers.

"But not before you take off those stinky scrubs and shower." I playfully shoved him away from me.

"Fine," he rolled off the bed and stumbled into the bathroom. A moment later I heard the shower turn on.

I yawned and stretched again before climbing out of bed. I threw on my fleece robe and slippers before heading into the kitchen. My stomach rumbled. I had not eaten since midnight the night before and I knew Landon was going to be hungry when he returned.

I put on some link sausages and scrambled some eggs. Once I poured them into the pan, I put a couple slices of bread into the toaster. I set the table and poured each of us a glass of orange juice. I was tempted to make some coffee, but I knew if I did, I'd be up all night.

I had everything set on the table by the time Landon entered the kitchen. His hair was still wet and plastered against his head as he did not dry it well before getting dressed. He was wearing pajama bottoms and a hooded sweatshirt which made him look years younger than his true age.

"Boy, something smells good in here." He kissed me quickly while passing before he took a seat and started spreading apple butter on his toast.

"I figured you would be hungry." I took a seat in the chair beside him.

"Starved," he grinned and picked up his fork. "That's why I love you."

"Because I made you scrambled eggs?" I chuckled.

"No, because you always take care of me." Landon responded before shoveling a bit of eggs into his mouth.

"Lord only knows why," I shook my head and took a bite of my toast. "Did you happen to catch the news?" I switched the subject.

"Yeah, Kobe Bryant died." The news completely shocked me.

"The Laker's star?"

"Do you know of another one?" Landon asked between mouthfuls.

"No," I smirked at the ridiculousness of both our statements. "How?" I finally asked after finishing my toast.

"Helicopter crash in California." He fiddled with his eggs for a moment. "Kobe's 13-year-old daughter was onboard along with seven other people. There were no survivors. Officials are investigating it, but it looks like fog may have been the cause."

"How horrible," I felt so bad for his family and the others who lost loved ones. "But that wasn't what I was referring too."

"Oh, the bar shootings?" Landon raised his brow.

"More shootings?" The news just kept getting better all the time.

"One in San Antonia and the other in Kansas City. I think two were killed in San Antonia and another five injured. And two in Kansas City were confirmed killed and fifteen injured if I'm remembering correctly." He shook his head slightly as if shaking off the disturbing news.

"This is insane," I muttered. "I cannot understand all this senseless killing."

"It's always been this way. It's just now with the internet news is instantaneous. But you look back throughout history, it's always been there." I knew he was right, but the knowledge didn't make me feel any better.

"I was referring to this Chinese virus. Natalie said they just confirmed a second case in Chicago." I told him. "Did you see anything on it?"

"I heard about it, but from what they are saying, they really don't know much."

"How is that possible?" I eyed him carefully.

"It isn't," he rolled his eyes. "They know exactly what they are dealing with. They just haven't told us the truth about it yet. Big shocker it came from China."

"Doesn't everything?" I smirked.

"Made in Taiwan," Landon chuckled. "Brought to you by the maker of SARS."

"I'm shocked," I huffed sarcastically. "Along with the rest of the free world."

"Exactly," he finished off his orange juice.

Jim and Diana stopped by as I loaded the dishes in the dishwasher. They were flying out on the red eye and wanted to spend some time with their son before they left. Landon and I felt bad that we could not change our shifts to spend more time with them, but they had been enjoying themselves with Robert and Emily.

I took their coats and hung them up in the hall closet. They left their travel bags by the front door as Landon led them into the living room where he had started a fire.

"Can I get either of you something to drink? Or are you hungry?" I walked into the living room behind his folks as they took a seat on our couch.

"Heavens no. Robert and Emily stuffed us over the last few days. I can't remember the last time I ate so much." Jim chuckled.

"That would be Thanksgiving, my dear." Diana teased him. "And then again on Christmas."

"I am sorry about our work schedules." Landon sat down on the recliner. I sat down on the arm beside him.

"Nonsense," his father waved him off. "We knew you would be busy when we arranged this trip. We are very proud of you, both of you for working so hard and balancing med school." I was touched by the pride in his voice.

"Thanks, dad. That means a lot." Landon looked down at his hands, obviously embarrassed by his father's sentiment.

"Do you know when you guys will be able to come home for a visit?" Diana shifted the mood.

"No. I doubt we will be able to get away any time before Easter." Landon shrugged. "Plus, with the second case of coronavirus confirmed in Chicago, who knows what awaits."

"Do you really believe it will be that bad?" Diana lowered her voice, which was filled with concern.

"If the news reports out of China are to be believed, then I would say it will be." Jim added.

"I admit, we rarely pay attention to the news. We're usually lucky just to find time to eat and sleep." Landon joked, but it was the truth.

"I suggest you start paying attention." His mother suggested. "I hope it doesn't spread here the way it has over there."

"It sounds like a heightened version of the flu." I remarked.

"I believe it shares many of the same symptoms." Jim added. "Have you guys heard anything about it at the hospital?"

"No. Nothing more than what was said on TV. And who knows how much you can believe that anymore. It has become increasingly biased based on political ideology rather than stating the facts." I spoke up.

"Don't get him started," Diana laughed. "Or we'll be here all night."

"I'm sorry if I'm fed up with all the BS on CNN and MSNBC. They are so far left and against our President that they will twist anything to fit their narrative regardless of the facts." Jim boasted.

"It is a complaint I have heard from Robert numerous times." I laughed and shrugged. "But I was raised a Republican."

"We need more young individuals who are. Most of your generation, these Millennials are downright lazy, worthless, and the most entitled generation of participation trophy ignorant assholes." Jim was abruptly cut off by his wife.

"I warned you not to get him going," Diana smirked.

"Very well," Landon chuckled at his father's tirade.

"Speaking of entitled ignorant assholes, what happened over Christmas with Gabriella?" Landon spat her name with obvious disdain.

I had never met this woman, thankfully. But I had seen pictures and heard earfuls from both Landon's parents and his younger sister Lizzy. It seemed his parents did their best to tolerate Gabriella for the sake of their son, but Lizzy held no affection for her whatsoever.

"I will say that her influence over Holden leaves much to be desired." Diana rolled in eyes in an evasive way.

"How so?" I could not help myself from asking.

"Apparently, she did one of those ancestry DNA tests after Thanksgiving and found out she is one sixty-fourth African. So, she was spouting all this Blacks Lives Matter BS and calling them 'her people'." Diana explained.

"She spent the entire dinner ranted about reparations and racial inequalities and victimhood." Jim rolled his eyes.

"And Holden just sat there parroting her ridiculous nonsense. It was absurd." Diana shook her head in disbelief.

"But Lizzy," Jim chuckled. "Well, you know how your sister is." Landon nodded with a smirk. "She finally dropped her fork on her plate and looked right at Gabriella and said, oh, will you just shut up. You are whiter than a freaking snowflake. Don't sit there and act like you have a freaking clue what it is like to be black. Do you have any idea how ridiculous you sound?" Jim couldn't stop laughing as he dabbed his eyes. "Lizzy went on spatting something like, you realize most people have a drop of African blood in them." Jim did the air quotes as he continued. "Lizzy then told her that she hoped she had saved the receipts from her tuition from Arizona State because the fact that she did not realize that there were white people in Africa too, not just black she should demand a refund because she obviously hadn't learned a damn thing. Also, it reasons that African blood does not necessarily mean black." Jim dabbed his eyes again. "Gabriella looked like she'd been slapped across the face. Her mouth hung open like a fish gasping for water. But then Holden stood up so fast he knocked his chair over sputtering at Lizzy to shut up and she didn't know what she was talking about. Lizzy just laughed in his face and told him he was a sad Beta man, and she was ashamed to call him her brother."

Landon and I burst out laughing. I could picture Lizzy saying that. She was the same age as my younger brother; Ethan and I adored her for her outspoken nature. I had met her several times, and she was very opinionative and strong in her convictions. She had no patience for BS.

"It was a disaster." Diana brushed a tear

"Now I am sorry I didn't make it home." Landon kept grinning.

"Me too," I tried to control my laughter and quickly changed the subject. "What are your plans when you return home?"

"Same ol' same ol'." Diana rolled her eyes. "Retirement is so much fun."

"Have you thought about substitute teaching part-time? At least it would get you out of the house a bit." Landon suggested.

"As much as your father cannot stand the Millennials, I am not up to dealing with the Gen Zs and worse than that, their parents." she adamantly stated. "My friends who are still teaching all want to walk away. They said the parents blame them for their kids' grades or if they fail a test. The kids are so disrespectful, and the school won't support their teachers."

"And on that happy note," I stood up. "Excuse me for a moment." I went over to the kitchen and turned on the kettle for some hot tea. I unboxed the coffee cake I'd purchased from the bakery on my way home and set everything up on a tray for our guests.

I could hear the conversation carrying on in the living room but could not make out what was being said. I leaned against the counter waiting for the water to boil, giving Landon some alone time with his parents. I recalled one of the things my father always told us growing up *'never discuss politics or religion in a social setting'*. I wasn't sure if this constituted a social setting, but the more passionate Jim spoke the more tension ceased in the room.

"Is everything all right?" Diana's voice broke my thoughts.

"Yes," I smiled. "I was waiting for the kettle to boil. I figured we could all drink some hot tea before you leave for the airport. The temperature is dropping again."

"Is it supposed to snow?" She leaned against the opposite counter.

"I have not checked the forecast today, but it would not surprise me." I shrugged. "Personally, I am sick of winter and the cold. I love white Christmas', but it could melt on the twenty-sixth and disappear until the following year."

"Ever think of moving?" Diana inquired.

"No. Not with all of my family here." I smiled.

"I understand, but besides your sister and your uncle, isn't it your sister's family that is here or rather her husbands?" She reasoned.

"Yes, but Robert and Emily are more like surrogate parents to me, especially Emily. Their daughter, Phoebe, is my best friend. And as you said, my sister is married to her brother. So, they are family to us. We have never considered them extended family." I said honestly.

"And your mother?" Diana tilted her head and eyed me carefully.

"My mother lives in Seattle and stays busy with her patients there. She has little time for me or my siblings." I said as politely as I could.

"Landon told me your parents had a nasty divorce, and she had moved across the country afterwards." She stated.

"Yes, that is true." Thankfully, the kettle started whistling and I poured it into the teapot.

"I did not mean to pry, dear." Diana reached out and touched me lightly on my arm. "I just wondered if you had spoken to your mother after everything you went through after losing the baby. I know it was so hard on you and Landon and sometimes a mother," I tried not to be abrupt, but I turned towards her and interrupted.

"My mother was livid when she found out about the baby. She flew out here just to yell at Landon and me. Then she not so subtly told me that having me when she did all but ruined her life." I swallowed hard, willing the tears not to fall as my eyes watered up. "So, I was not about to call her and listen to her say that my losing our child was the best thing that could have happened."

"Oh, I am sorry." She dropped her eyes and replied in a softer voice, "I didn't know."

"It's okay," I smiled over at her as I picked up the tray. "My family here took very good care of us." Diana nodded solemnly and followed me back into the living room.

His parents insisted on taking an Uber to the airport. Landon seemed upset, but I was happy not to have to fight the traffic around the airport, especially with the roads covered in snow and black ice.

Ninety minutes before their plane was scheduled to depart, we were gathered in the small foyer of our flat surrounded by their luggage. Diana was tearful, hugging each of us several times and saying how much she was going to miss us. She kissed her son on the cheek and clung tightly to him. Jim ushered her towards the door hugging each of us briefly.

"Please text me when you land so we know you arrived safely." I put my arm around Landon's waist as Jim picked up their suitcases.

"I will," Diana propped the shoulder strap of her carryon over her neck and touched Landon's cheek one last time before turning her eyes on me. "You take care of my baby."

"I will. I promise." I smiled as Landon opened the door for his parents.

"I love you guys," he hugged his mom one more time. "Travel safely."

"I love you, too." Diana brushed her tears aside and headed out into the hallway.

"Love you, son." Jim squeezed Landon's shoulder tenderly before following his wife out the door.

"I love you too, Dad."

With a final wave, Landon and I stood in the doorway and watched his parents drive away in an Uber. The cold breeze lifted my hair off my shoulders and kissed my cheeks causing me to huddle closer to Landon. He wrapped his arm around my waist as I rested my head against his shoulder. I knew he was going to miss them both. Hopefully, the next time we saw them it would be for longer than just a couple days and in better weather.

4

MONDAY, JANUARY 30, 1860

MY GRANDMOTHER WAS IN RARE form. She had rediscovered her passion and was bustling about giving our housekeepers, Marta and Wanda, various chores she wanted completed before the party. She went over the menu with our cook, Naomi, and spoke with our groundskeeper, Preston, about rearranging the furniture to make room for dancing.

It was humorous the way she had managed to cause such an uproar in such a short time. Keifer felt it was good for her and claimed she looked years younger than she had the week before. Although I was thrilled to see her so exuberant, I was still a bit concerned about my appearance and my ever-expanding abdomen and how it would look by the time we hosted the party.

"Do you not think this whole affair is in poor taste considering everything going on?" I asked Keifer over breakfast. "Not to mention how I look." I rested my hand on my belly.

"Darling," my husband reached across the table and placed his hand over mine. "You look radiant, and I am proud to show you off as my wife." Keifer grinned showing off his deep dimples. "Besides, I heard Marissa say the party will be on the eleventh of next month to celebrate Valentine's Day."

"My goodness," I chuckled. "I guess I know when I am defeated."

"Give her this one, Sidney. She needs it." He withdrew his hand and picked up this coffee. "I believe we all do."

Keifer left shortly after breakfast. The weather had cleared enough for him to make the journey to Boston and other patients who lived in between. I stood on the porch with my shawl wrapped around me and watched him disappear beyond the snow-capped trees around the bend.

My grandmother was sitting in the parlor when I returned. She was sitting at her writing desk staring off into space. I leaned against the doorframe and watched her deep in thought. Her hair was pulled back into a bun at the nap of her neck. Her ivory shawl was draped loosely over her shoulders and complimented her burgundy dress. She was picture perfect and I felt so blessed to have her in my life.

"Are you going to stand there all morning staring at me or are you going to come on in and have a seat?" She glanced over at me, and I giggled.

"You never miss a thing, do you?" I walked over and sat down in the chair by the hearth.

"Not in this house," my grandmother smiled.

"What are you working on?" I leaned a bit closer towards the fire to warm up my hands.

"The last of the invitations. I was going to ask Duncan to deliver them today. I only have a couple left to write out." She began scrawling again.

"Fine. I am going to read by the fire until I warm up a bit." I picked up my new copy of the Charles Dickens classic, *A Tale of Two Cities*. It was released in November and Keifer was so excited to purchase a copy for me for Christmas. I had read it a couple of times before in my *other* life, but that was not something I could share with him. Although my grandmother found it humorous when I informed her later that evening.

"That's nice, dear." She muttered under her breath, but I knew from experience that she was no longer listening to anything I said.

I lost myself in the words and the vivid images Dickens created and had not realized my grandmother had left the parlor, returned, and took up the seat across from me.

"I thought you said you had read that several times before?" My grandmother broke my concentration.

"I have," I closed my book and set it aside. "Sorry."

"I read it many years ago in my *other* life," she whispered in a low voice leaning towards me. "But I cannot say I remember much of it anymore." She sat back. "I will have to read it again once you are finished."

"Did you get the invitations sent out?" I adjusted my shawl around my shoulders.

"Yes, I sent Duncan almost an hour ago. We shall see who replies." My grandmother raised a brow.

"I would imagine most will welcome the distraction and chance to visit with those they most likely haven't seen since last fall." I reasoned.

"I hope so," she shrugged. "Either way I believe it will be a welcomed respite and hopefully dispel any misgivings about your husband."

"Keifer told me he will attach himself to the Northern troops." I recalled what my husband told me. "But I am aware of what some of our more colorful neighbors have been saying about him." It twisted my stomach every time I thought about it. "You will not believe what he mentioned to me the other night."

"What is that?"

"He received a letter from Margrett," I began.

"Oh, Lord." My grandmother groaned audibly.

"They are putting a lot of pressure on him. Now he wants to visit them before we go to Chicago." I sighed heavily.

"Certainly, he cannot be serious." She gasped. "It would be dangerous to travel so far South. I would not recommend you travel as far as Virginia, let alone Savannah."

"I know. I told him I do not believe it is a good idea."

"The idea of taking you and a new baby deep into the heart of the South is absurd." she stated, pinching her lips together.

"I want you to come with us as well." I pleaded. "Especially since we will be going straight onto Chicago from Savannah. I know you will want to see your grandsons."

"You know I do." My grandmother glanced over at the hearth, and sighed heavily before she continued. "But whether you were going straight from here to Chicago or from Savannah to Chicago, I will not be joining you."

"But why not?" I was astonished. "What about visiting with Patrick, Annabelle, and their children, your great-grandchildren, some of whom you have never met. And what about Monte and Nicholas? I know you adore them."

"I am needed here to oversee things," she began.

"No. Do not try that. Ned is more than capable of running this place while we are away, and you know it. He has done it many times before." I scolded.

"I understand that, but still," my grandmother fidgeted with the handkerchief she was holding.

"Please, be honest with me." Even though I was an adult and had been for many years, my grandmother had the tendency to always try to protect me.

"First, I do not wish to see Eugenia nor endure the pressure that Keifer's family is going to put on him about loyalty to his family and the state of Georgia. It is going to be extremely difficult for him and you, and I do not trust myself to hold my tongue. Secondly, I do not wish to see Bethany. I fear that if I do, I may tell her exactly what I think of her; how she treated you and robbed you of your father's and brother's love." She raised her brow pointedly. "And finally, I am almost seventy years old. I am no longer capable of holding my tongue nor do I care to try to." She smiled broadly at me. "Besides, I am too old to travel so far away from my home. I have a short time left on this earth and I do not care to be away from the only piece of your grandfather I have left."

"Not even to be with your son? He is a part of grandfather." I reminded her.

"I am very ashamed of my son and for what he allowed that wretched woman to do to you. It is the same as if he had done it himself." She said flatly.

"Granted, I do not care for my father's wife, but my love for my younger brothers outweighs my feelings towards her or my father. I am excited to see them and their families. However, I cannot say I am looking forward to another encounter with Eugenia. Hopefully, Keifer's mother and Margrett will be able to keep her in check." I smirked.

"A herd of wild boars could not muzzle that woman. It is no wonder she is still single. No man could tolerate her." My grandmother chuckled.

"Which is why I need you with me. Please do not make me face her alone." I begged her.

"You will do just fine. I have faith in you." She leaned forward in her rocker. "All you need to do is channel your *other* self." She grinned widely. "Then you will have the courage and strength to stand up for yourself."

"I wish I was more like Jocelyn." I leaned towards her. "She has more gumption in her little finger than I could muster in my entire body." I complained about my outspoken and strong-willed younger sister whom I truly adored in my *other* life.

"You have it, my dear. You simply need to tap into it. You and Jocelyn are cut from the same cloth." she noted.

"No. Jocelyn is more like our father, Shane. I resemble more of our mother, Amy." I reminded her.

"I am not referring to physical traits. Jocelyn may look more like Shane, but she has the head-strong stubbornness of Amy. And while you may physically resemble Amy, you are more tender-hearted like Shane. However, from what you have told me over the years, Shane is no pushover, and he can ruffle the feathers of the most steadfast rooster." My grandmother reasoned.

"Perhaps I should channel all three just to be safe." I laughed.

"Perhaps you should."

Naomi brought us some hot tea and ham sandwiches with potato salad shortly after one. The fire in the hearth was dying down so Ned added a couple more logs and stoked the fire back up into a blaze. This time of day he kept the fires burning in the parlor, the kitchen, and when Keifer was home, his study. However, it would be several more hours before he restarted the fires upstairs.

The room instantly began to warm up. I had not realized how quickly the temperature had dropped over the noon hour because of the bright sunlight pouring in through the bay windows. The reflection of the sun off the snowcapped lawn was almost blinding.

"And how are things at school?" My grandmother inquired after we were alone again. "How is Landon doing?"

"Landon is doing well. His parents came for a visit. They flew back to Chicago this evening." I took a sip of my tea. "It was so nice to see them. I know it is difficult on Landon being so far away from his parents and siblings."

"And you enjoy living in Boston?" She eyed me carefully.

"I do. I did not know Jocelyn well growing up. We never had much in common. But now, we are truly sisters; the way we should have been all along." I explained.

"I think that is wonderful and long overdue."

"Plus, being around the Chandler's and Uncle Nicholas has truly helped me deal with *E.V.E.* and make the adjustment to living dual lives much easier." I reasoned, picking at my potato salad.

"I know your initial transition was difficult. But you seem to be at peace with it now."

"I believe I am." I chuckled softly. "It has not been easy, but it truly is a unique life we lead." I poured myself some more tea and added a bit of honey to it.

"Sometimes I believe so. Other times I do not." My grandmother picked up her tea and finished it off. She reached for the teapot and began refilling her cup. "Knowing what is coming has been weighing very heavy on my heart." she admitted.

"So, the real motive for our upcoming celebration presents itself." I snickered.

"Partly, I suppose." My grandmother pursed her lips for a moment. "But can you say knowing all you do about what is about to come, that you are not the least bit apprehensive?"

"I am terrified." I answered honestly. "I have spent countless hours hiding away reading up on the war, talking to Nicholas, Robert, and Emily about it, but neither Nicholas nor Robert will tell me much." I confessed.

"And are you going to say anything to them when you go back there for the holidays?" She eyed me carefully. "You understand the dangers of that."

"I do. And I won't, I promise. But I am going to talk to Patrick about Annabelle and the kids staying with us because if he will agree, then Emily and her kids will join us as well." I could not help but be excited about the prospect.

"And you do not believe that will be strange?" My grandmother raised an eyebrow at me. "I mean, it is one thing to spend that time with Jocelyn, but have you considered what it will be like to also be with Phoebe and her brothers every day." She laughed.

"You know I was so focused on Jocelyn and eager to have Emily here with us, I had not thought about a young Phoebe and her brothers running around." I chuckled at the thought. "I guess I have been so worried about Nicholas and him being captured and sent to Andersonville Prison. If there is a possibility, I can prevent that," I reasoned.

"We have been through this countless times, Sidney. You cannot change the past." My grandmother reminded me sharply.

"But it is not the past, and Nicholas should be old enough to have his barrier down. If he is, there is no harm in warning him. If anything, just to be mindful, cautious." Nicholas was my dad's little brother and my favorite uncle. He was the first to explain the gift of *E.V.E* to me during our meeting over Spring Break in my *other* life and we had grown very close.

"Sidney. I know how you feel about Nicohlas. I feel the same way. He is my grandson and I love him. Do you honestly believe I want to see anything happen to him?" I shook my head honestly. "So, if you are sure, and I mean really positive that his barrier is completely down, then you may discuss it privately and discreetly with him." My grandmother relented.

"You have my word." I felt a weight lift from my shoulders. "If you do not mind, I think I will lie down for a while before dinner." I rose to my feet and set my cup and saucer on the tray.

"I will send Ned up to build you a fire." I leaned over and kissed my grandmother on the cheek.

"Thank you. I appreciate that."

Keifer arrived home as dusk settled across the back fields. I drew the drapes in the parlor and made sure Naomi had placed a fresh teapot on the side table when I heard his carriage descend across the bridge.

My grandmother was in the kitchen making sure everything was on schedule. She had invited Mr. Bennett to join us, and he was due to arrive within the hour. As much as she denied it, I knew she was every bit as fascinated by him as he was with her. I believe he was the main reason she did not want to take the journey with us later this year.

"How was your day, my dear?" Keifer kissed me lightly before removing his coat.

"My grandmother invited Mr. Bennett to join us for dinner." I took his coat and hung it up for him.

"I still say she is sweet on him." The corner of his mouth turned up in a grin.

"Do not tease her tonight," I warned him.

"Did you get the chance to talk to her about Savannah?" He headed towards the parlor with me directly behind him.

"I did," I poured him a cup of tea and handed it to him while he warmed himself by the hearth. "And she has decided to stay here."

"She believes it will be too dangerous to travel South," he sipped his tea and turned towards me. "Am I correct?"

"Maybe not for you, but for a Yankee woman and a new baby, I believe she may be right." I placed my hand on his arm and looked up into his soft hazel eyes. "I am scared, Keifer." I confessed.

"I would never let anything happen to you or our child, Sidney. But I am afraid that if I do not visit them now, I may not be able to depend on what comes next. South Carolina is already talking about succession again just like they did in 52′. When it did not pass then, I really hoped it would end there, but the fire for it has only been refueled and is spreading quickly across the Southern states due to the outrageous taxes being forced upon them." I hated the sadness that crept up behind his eyes.

"If the South succeeds, a war is inevitable." I pointed out. "If the Democrats split, they will divide the vote almost assuring the Republican candidate will win."

"The Democrats will not split. They are simply beating their chests, just like a bunch of gorillas trying to make their voices heard." He laughed at himself then looked coyly at me. "What have you been reading that would put such notions into your head?" I suddenly realized I had over spoken.

"I was browsing through the newspapers." I said, as casually as I could manage.

"I really wish you would not read those. You really do not need to worry yourself with such things, especially in your condition." Keifer rested his hand on my protruding belly.

A knock on the front door saved me from any further inquiry, for which I was grateful. Keifer patted my stomach lovingly and walked into the foyer where Ned was taking Mr. Bennett's coat and hat.

Mr. Bennett's wire glasses were perched on his slender nose hiding his bright and warm blue eyes. His white hair was combed back neatly and resting on his shirt collar. He was wearing a navy suit with a crisp white shirt and brown dress shoes. He must have come straight from the bank given his professional attire.

"Good evening, Edmund", Keifer shook his hand. "I'm happy you are able to join us this evening."

"My pleasure, Doc. I would never turn down an invitation to Naomi's fine cooking." He laughed heartily.

"Dinner shall be ready shortly," My husband led Mr. Bennett into the parlor. "Would you care to join me for a brandy beforehand?"

"If I must," he patted Keifer on the shoulder before joining me next to the hearth. "Good evening, Mrs. Marshall. You look positively radiant." He kissed my hand lightly.

"Thank you," I blushed.

"Here you are," Keifer handed our neighbor a glass a quarter filled with brandy.

"Thank you, kindly." Mr. Bennett tilted the glass towards my husband before taking a drink.

"How are things at the bank?" Keifer asked as he joined me on the chaise lounge while Mr. Bennett sat down in the chair across from us.

"Steady but slowing down. People are being more cautious as things become more uncertain." He shrugged half-heartedly.

"It appears that all this tension has only served to increase my practice. Men are fighting over every little difference of opinion." Keifer finished off his drink as my grandmother joined us.

"Good evening, Mr. Bennett." He took her hand and kissed it lightly. "I am pleased you were able to join us this evening." She smiled.

"You have discovered my greatest weakness, Marissa; Naomi's cooking." Mr. Bennett confessed.

"Then I am even more pleased to tell you that dinner is served." My grandmother waved towards the dining room. "After you, Edmund."

Keifer and I followed them into the dining room. Ned had started a fire around the time Naomi had started preparations for dinner, and it had warmed up the room nicely. Mr. Bennett pulled out a chair for my grandmother as Keifer did for me. As trivial as it seemed, it was one of the little niceties that I missed in my *other* world.

In the center of the table was a large, juicy roast beef with just a hint of pink in the middle. Large bowls of mashed potatoes, carrots, and corn surrounded it. Large golden yeast rolls and a gravy boat with little whiffs of steam rolling off it sat waiting for us. The aroma was intoxicating.

"How are preparations for your evening gala?" Mr. Bennett inquired as Keifer carved the roast.

"They are going well," my grandmother answered causing my husband and I to giggle under our breath. "Do not be so cynical." She shot us a quick scolding look.

"I would never," I stifled a laugh turning my attention towards our guest. "Let me simply say my grandmother is well on her way to ensuring our staff will need a long respite afterwards."

"I am intrigued." Mr. Bennett added some mashed potatoes to his plate before passing it on to my grandmother. "I am sure it will be a grand event."

"Yes, it will be." She glanced over at me with a sparkle in her eye.

"And how are you feeling, Ms. Sidney? I must say you are glowing." Mr. Bennett smiled over at me.

"Anxious," I passed the plate of yeast rolls to my husband. "I will be happy when I am able to sleep through the night again."

"I hate to tell you my darling, but that is not going to happen for several more years." My grandmother chuckled.

"When my first child was born, he refused to sleep more than two hours at a time." Mr. Bennett recalled. "It seriously made me reconsider wanting more children."

"But in the end, you did," I reminded him. "Four more actually."

"That was my wife's decision, not mine." He confessed. "But I am glad we did."

"Children are a blessing," my grandmother reiterated with a cautious smile towards our guest.

"Yes, they are." Keifer added. "I am excited for my family to have the chance to meet my son this summer." I almost choked on my tea seeing the look Mr. Bennett flashed at him.

"Are you mad, Doc?" He shook his head slightly in disbelief. "It is too dangerous to take your wife, a Northern lady down South, especially with a new babe."

"We have discussed it, and I believe we will be fine," my husband took a deep breath and spoke again with his thick Georgia Southern drawl. "I have cautioned her to speak as little as possible throughout our journey, and she will be perfectly safe at Gable Garden."

"Do you feel comfortable with that?" I wasn't sure if the question was directed at me or my grandmother.

"I do not." My grandmother answered before I could. "I believe our relationship with the Southern states will only worsen in the upcoming months." She eyed my husband carefully.

"Still, the very idea of a war between the states is absurd." Mr. Bennett half-heartedly shrugged.

"You do not believe there will be a war?" I curiously asked our guest.

"I am afraid there will be one if the Southern states leave the Union." Mr. Bennett did not hesitate before responding.

"I truly hope not," Keifer looked pushed his roast around his plate but did not take a bite. "I was born and raised in the South and as you well know, my kin are still in Savannah. Plus, the South does not have the resources or infrastructure to win a war against the Northern states." He looked at Mr. Bennett. "I pray calmer heads prevail."

"I believe it will come down to the Presidential election in November before anything is decided." I remarked without thinking and instantly regretted it as both gentlemen stared at me.

"I was not aware you followed politics." Mr. Bennett eyed me momentarily before shifting his gaze to my husband.

"I am afraid I left some Boston newspapers lying around and my wife let curiosity get the best of her." Keifer quickly explained as if he needed to.

"I see nothing wrong with a woman being well informed," my grandmother immediately defended. "I have always encouraged my granddaughter to read and be aware of what is going on around her. Afterall, it is our country too and if it goes to war, it will affect us all, not just the men." She held her head up proudly and I could not help but smile.

"My daughters never showed much interest in politics, nor did my late wife." Mr. Bennett raised his eyebrow at my grandmother. "Do you share your granddaughter's inquisitiveness?"

"I most certainly do." She answered proudly. "My late husband always strongly encouraged me to read both books and newspapers to stay abreast of current events as well as history."

"My late wife never learned to read." Mr. Bennett admitted. "And I admit at times I wish she would have so we could have discussed a wider range of topics. Unfortunately, every time I tried to teach her, she became very frustrated with me. As our boys grew up and started school, they tried as well, but did not have much more success than I. However, she was the most amazing cook and talented seamstress in the New England states. I was most proud of her." A tear slid down his cheek that he hastily wiped away.

"Iris was a wonderfully kind lady and a very dear friend." My grandmother reached over and patted his hand lovingly. "I miss her dearly."

"Every day," Mr. Bennett grinned sorrowfully. He cleared his throat and took a long sip of his coffee before he continued directing his attention back towards my husband. "Still, as much as I admire a lady's mind, I know there are some men who do not appreciate women who speak so freely."

"Yes, I am aware of that too." Keifer smiled, locking eyes with me across the table. "And heaven help the man who attempts to silence either of these two." He chuckled. "I have seen them outwit and disarm many who tried."

"I am sure it was well deserved," Mr. Bennett laughed.

"It was warranted and well justified." My grandmother declared with glee.

"Now back to your statement about the Presidential election," Mr. Bennett went back to talking between bites. "I think this talk of secession is simply a ploy to push the northern legislature into submission," he choked down some more of his roast before continuing. "Yes. I believe it is just like we saw in 54'."

"I pray you are right." Keifer sighed heavily. "The last letter I received from my sister expressed growing contempt towards Northerners."

"Well, I fear to say much of the feeling is mutual," I noticed the hurt look in my husband's eyes upon hearing Mr. Bennett's words.

"Do you expect the poor weather will continue?" My husband gracefully attempted to change the subject.

"I suspect we will have at least six more weeks of winter. Hopefully, not much more. With this much precipitation we are sure a wet spring will follow." Mr. Bennet projected.

The two men set forth on their discussion of the weather, seed prices, and Mr. Bennett's new mare. My grandmother and I exchanged knowing glances that conveyed thousands of unspoken words between us. The knowledge of the outcome of upcoming tragedies we held did little to ease our apprehension. A part of me desperately wanted to confide in my husband the truth about *E.V.E.*, but it was decided years ago when the barrier in my conscious mind between my two worlds was completely depleted, that I could never do that.

Keifer was an educated man. He was a Harvard graduate, highly skilled and sought after in his profession. He was an ambitious man who was extremely charismatic. He had the ability to charm the most cynical of people even while frustrating them to tears. But he had no ability to believe in something he could not see or touch. His belief was heavily rooted in science and any attempt to enlighten him to the heredity of *E.V.E.* would certainly give him an aneurysm, if not get me committed to the Boston asylum for the clinically insane.

The evening went smoothly and ended pleasantly with Mr. Bennett agreeing to join us for dinner after Sunday services. My grandmother immediately retired upon the departure of our neighbor. I held Keifer's arm and the corner of my hoop skirt as he led me up the stairs to our room. I was physically tired and mentally exhausted, and my husband looked much the same.

5

FRIDAY, FEBRUARY 7, 2020

JOCELYN POUNCED ON THE SPOT Landon had recently vacated abruptly waking me. She was dressed in jeans and a college hoodie from Boston University. Her long, light, auburn hair was pulled up in a simple ponytail, and she had almost no makeup on.

"Get up, lazy butt." My little sister bounced causing me to glare maliciously at her.

"What do you want?" I groaned rolling over and putting my back to her. I grabbed the extra pillow and pulled it over my head.

"Get up," she yanked the pillow off my head and hit me with it across my lower torso and buttocks. "I need to talk to you."

"What can be so important that you are interrupting my sleep on the one day I have off?" I growled.

"Valentine's Day." Jocelyn scowled. "I have been so busy; I haven't gotten Jackson anything yet. What did you get Landon?"

"Nothing yet." I pulled myself up into a seated position. "I haven't really thought about it."

"Well, you best think about it because you are running out of time." She smacked me with the pillow again. "So, get your happy ass up. We have some shopping to do."

"How did you get in here anyway," I growled yanking the pillow from her hands.

"Landon let me in on his way out." She grinned widely.

"Figures," I muttered putting my feet on the cold hardwood floor and making my way over to the bathroom. "Why aren't you at work?" I hollered through the open door.

"I decided to take the day off." My sister leaned in the doorway. "I needed a break."

"Is everything all right? Bad case?" I ran a brush through my hair.

"No," she shrugged and did not elaborate but I could tell something was off.

An hour later we were sitting in her SUV heading towards the mall. The roads were mostly clear, but the air remained frigid. About a half dozen inches of freshly fallen snow served to blind us glaringly when the sun appeared between the drifting clouds.

"I am so sick of this cold." Jocelyn began. "Someday, I am going to move south."

"Right," I laughed. "Like Jackson would ever leave his family."

"We did," she reasoned.

"We moved away from our dad and brother, but Uncle Nicholas came with us." I declared.

"That was his choice. It is not like we made him. He took it upon himself to find a position nearer to us." Jocelyn argued.

"I understand that. But you know how close Jackson is to his family." I raised my eyebrows at her.

"Robert, Emily, and Jackson moved to Chicago back when I was in high school, and Alex and Phoebe and their families stayed in Boston." She reminded me.

"I understand, but that was different. That was short-term and for a specific reason," I countered. "You." I smirked. "Have you even mentioned moving south to Jackson?"

"Are you kidding?" My sister rolled her eyes playfully at me. "I am just dreaming out loud. It will never happen."

"Never say never," I shrugged.

"You know how the Chandler's feel about Boston and their long history in the area." She navigated off the interstate and stopped at the light waiting to turn left. "And what about your ties? Do you think you could leave here?"

"I do not know. I believe my perception of the south may be very different than yours because of my current position *there*." I paused a moment flashing between my two eras, and the vast differences between them. "Keifer is wanting to visit his family this summer in Savannah." I said casually, still looking out the window.

"Do you think that is wise? Especially with a new baby." Jocelyn turned with the light following the row of cars before us. "You realize your accent will not go over well in Savannah?"

"I know," I sighed heavily. "But Keifer insists, and I do not know what to say. It is not like I can explain to him what is on the horizon."

"True," she pulled into the mall parking lot and parked in front of Macy's. "Still, I would find a way out of it."

"It is going to be difficult especially considering we are supposed to visit Chicago right afterwards." I opened the car door and hurried alongside her to the mall entrance.

"Hold it," my sister pulled me aside once we stepped through the second set of doors. "You are going to Chicago this fall? Who are you staying with?"

"Patrick and Annabelle." I admitted with a knot in my stomach.

"My family you mean?" Jocelyn's grip on my arm tightened.

"Well, yes." I confessed. "Annabelle invited us."

"When are you supposed to visit them?" She held on to my arm eyeing me closely.

"I told Annabelle we will arrive early to mid-October." I swallowed hard, understanding what she was just realizing.

"So, let me get this straight. You will be there when I am born?" She let go of my arm and raised her eyebrows.

"Yes, I guess I will be." I snorted. "How weird is that?"

"Um, yeah." she muttered, narrowing her eyes in disbelief.

"Don't act like it's that strange," I nudged her. "I was there when you were born *here* too."

"Yeah," she shook her head slightly. "You are my older sister."

"*Here,*" I smiled and put my arm around her guiding her through the clothing racks. "But *there,* I am your aunt."

"This is just too weird," She huffed and brushed it off.

"I agree," I chuckled. "Think about how I feel, especially between seeing you and Uncle Nicholas. He will be home for Christmas from West Point."

"Okay, that is strange." She laughed. "How old is he?"

"Um, 17 or 18 maybe — I don't know. Somewhere around there." I shrugged. "But it is going to be so odd seeing him as a teenager."

"That's priceless." Jocelyn laughed. "I wish I could see that too." She put her arm around me. "I envy you sometimes. Even though our other lives are linked, yours is far more interesting than mine."

"Don't." I told her. "I am terrified of what lies ahead."

My sister let it drop as we weaved our way through the racks and people until we reached the center aisles through the mall. Neither of us had a particular destination in mind so we just wandered forward considering the various shops with nothing particularly jumping out at us as something either of us wanted to purchase for Landon or Jackson for Valentine's Day.

"I hate this," I grumbled. "I never know what to get him. It's not like we celebrate this fictitious Hallmark holiday anyway."

"Boy, Jackson and I do." Jocelyn's eyes twinkled. "It has always been something romantic for us."

"Landon is not built that way," I shrugged halfheartedly. "I consider myself lucky if he remembers to get me a card and a box of cheap chocolates that I never eat."

"Perhaps I should have Jackson talk to him. He goes all out with a card, romantic dinner, flowers, and jewelry." A coy grin spread across her lips.

"I do not blame Landon," I casually shrugged. "With the long hours demanded of us between school and work, lack of sleep, and the stress it causes it is understandable."

"Still," Jocelyn continued. "I would think those things would make him want to do something special for you. Especially after everything you both have gone through this year."

"We don't talk about that," I was eager to change the subject. "Did you see President Trump was acquitted of the impeachment charges?"

"Yes. They were bullshit charges in the first place. I swear the Democratic party has lost its moral compass." My little sister rolled her eyes but looked a bit upset. "It scares me to even think about having kids with the direction this country is headed."

"How do you think I feel? My son will barely be a year old when the Civil War breaks out." I leaned over and whispered softly. "Don't you think I am terrified, and I already know what is going to happen."

"That is my point exactly." She flashed me a cocky look. "You know what is going to happen. You can prepare. You can verify exactly how close you are to danger, where the battles will be — everything."

"But" I started, but she quickly interrupted.

"I don't know," she shrugged and pulled me into *Things Remembered*. "I'm just rambling."

"What are we doing in here?" I followed her with no real interest.

"We can get them something engraved," Jocelyn started browsing through the decanters and watches.

"I am not sure that is Landon's style." I remained unconvinced.

"You could monogram a decanter for Landon," Jocelyn suggested pointing towards the display.

"Landon is not much of a drinker," I pinched my lips and wrinkled my forehead at the thought of him opening such a gift.

"What about a watch?" she shrugged.

"I believe Jackson topped all of us with that one on your 18th birthday." I smirked.

"True," Jocelyn beamed with pride. "That was pretty awesome."

"Which leaves us back at square one." I taunted completely over this shopping disaster.

"Okay," she stepped over to a row of luxury fleece robes. "What about these?" Jocelyn ran her fingers over the top one. "These are fabulous." she exclaimed, picking one up and holding it to her cheek. "I could definitely snuggle up to Jackson in this."

"I thought it was for him, not you." I reached out and touched it myself. She was right, it was heaven.

"It is for him, but that does not mean I would not wear it occasionally as well or snuggle up to him in it." My sister winked.

"We can get them monogramed." I suggested. "I like the navy blue." I selected a large one.

"Jackson would look so sexy in the smokey grey." She selected a large one too. "What do you think about getting them some engraved cufflinks too?"

"I think they would be a great gift for Jackson, but not so much for Landon." I smirked. "They don't quite go with his scrubs."

Jocelyn shrugged and picked out a beautiful rectangle sterling silver pair and handed them with the robe to the sales associate. She filled out the form with what she wanted, and I did the same. The middle-aged women told us it would be about 30 minutes to get them completed. So, my sister and I headed towards the food court.

We headed straight for Auntie Anne's Pretzels; a long-time favorite snack of ours. Jocelyn ordered a regular pretzel with nacho cheese dipping sauce. I ordered the sugar cinnamon one with white icing for dipping. We both ordered a hot caramel macchiato to go with them.

We found a table near the fountain and sat down with our treats. Jocelyn picked at her pretzel and looked like she was deep in her own thoughts.

"Jocelyn?" I tapped my fingers on the table.

"Huh?" she blinked.

"What is going on with you? You seem so distracted today."

"It's nothing," she shrugged and took a bit of her pretzel. "Just a lot going on at work."

"Like what?" I did not know much about corporate law that she, Jackson, and Robert practiced, but I was curious since this was the first time I could recall anything from work bothering her so much.

"You know Alex practices family law," I nodded. "Well, he had a father come in yesterday seeking help for his son to keep him away from his mother giving him hormone replacement therapy."

"How old is the kid?" I had heard this argument before between physicians at the hospital.

"Six." Jocelyn said flatly through gritted teeth.

"Six," she nodded. "A six-year-old can't even decide what cereal they want to eat for breakfast; let alone what gender they are."

"I know." She held her hands up in dismay. "Alex was telling us about it during our board meeting yesterday afternoon and it just made me physically sick."

"Is he going to take the case?"

"I know he wants to talk to you about it."

"Me? Why me?"

"Because you will be specializing in pediatrics, and he needs your expert opinion." She explained.

"I think one of my more experienced colleagues would be best suited for this." I began. "I could call mom and ask her about it. I am sure she knows more than anyone else. You know how she is."

"In court, yes. But for an initial consultation he needs to understand the full ramifications of hormone blockers and the long-term damage they do." Jocelyn continued to fiddle with her pretzel.

"Okay. I will call mom this afternoon and talk to her about it. Give Alex my number and I will talk him through it." I offered.

"Would you join us for dinner tomorrow? Everyone is going to be there."

"Yes, of course." I glanced down at my watch. "Our stuff should be done." I gathered up the napkins and empty cups and put them on the tray. I walked over and placed them in the nearest bin before my sister stood up.

"I hope they turned out well." she muttered as we wandered back towards the store.

"I am sure they did." I placed my arm around her shoulder and squeezed her.

"Are you sure you don't want to get another coffee for the road? Aren't you down a quart?" Jocelyn smirked, rolling her eyes at me.

"Do not tempt me little sister." I said with a coy grin.

Jocelyn dropped her bags on the island while I took a second to hide the gift-wrapped box holding Landon's robe in the back of our bedroom closet. She had already removed her coat and was starting a fresh pot of coffee.

"You don't mind, do you?" She glanced at me over her shoulder. "I'm freezing and wanted something hot."

"No, it sounds good to me." I sat down on the barstool and watched her.

"Is Landon staying at the hospital tonight?" She poured the water in and hit the start button.

"Most likely." I shrugged like it was no big deal although we both knew I hated staying at our flat alone.

"You know I am so proud of you and of Landon," I nodded. "But the demands of your schooling, and all the studying, not to mention the aggravation you must be dealing with daily *there*, must leave you feeling exhausted." She leaned against the counter.

"Yes, it does. But I cannot fathom doing anything else. I love it." I explained. "There is a great sense of satisfaction — and yes, frustration *there*. Especially when I know something that can help Keifer or perhaps treat or cure someone. I want to scream at the top of my lungs," I laughed. "But thankfully, I have learned how to be more tactful and have learned how to coax Keifer in the right direction."

"I don't know. To me it would be so frustrating." Jocelyn sighed heavily. "I mean, you know so much more than he does and yet you have to sit idlily by and watch some of the ridiculous practices of that time."

"At times, yes." I conceded. "But I interject when necessary. Unfortunately, I am more limited due to modern medicine than my husband. People in our region know I am a midwife and I have delivered babies when Keifer is not available. Plus, I have taken a liking to botany and that has helped many people and my sanity."

"I think that would be interesting." She shrugged casually. "You will have to show me."

"I can do that." I agreed. "So, what are your plans for the rest of the day?"

"I figured we'd put on a movie and veg out." She turned and fixed each of us a mug of coffee and handed one to me. "Do you have any plans?"

"No. Your idea sounds perfect." I sipped the hot liquid and instantly felt it seep deep into my bones and warmed my body. "Anything particular you want to watch?"

"Not really. Which streaming channels do you have?" She walked into the living room and picked up the remote off the coffee table.

"Not many," I followed behind her cradling my mug warming my hands. "We rarely watch television."

"I know what you mean," she had her back to me searching through the various channels on Roku. "Jackson and I have pretty much given up on anything new. Hollywood has turned to trash." She ran her fingers flipped through the names of each one. "Do you have prime?" I nodded as she clicked on the icon. "Let me see," she continued scrolling through titles and genres. "What about this one?" She turned towards me.

"*The Other Woman*?" I chuckled. "Perfect."

Jocelyn removed her boots and curled up on the couch. I sat down beside her and took mine off as well. I grabbed the big throw blanket I kept on the back of the couch and tossed it over us both. She wrapped it tightly around herself and snuggled back into the couch.

It was the perfect way to spend a snowy afternoon. Looking over at my little sister and thinking about how close we were now, it was hard to imagine that for the first couple decades of my life, I really did not know her at all. Now we talked nearly every day, and I was eternally grateful to her, Jackson, and his family for all they had done for me as I transitioned to living with *EVE*.

6

FRIDAY, FEBRUARY 10, 1860

MY GRANDMOTHER WAS IN HER ELEMENT. She was up at dawn rushing around trying not to bark but giving orders to our housekeepers Marta and Wanda in her pre-party day preparations. I found her in the kitchen with Naomi going over the extensive menu for the party.

"Good morning, ladies," I entered the kitchen in search of coffee.

"Koffee, eggs, bakin, an toast ar' on da table, Mizdress." Naomi heard me but never looked up from the tablet setting between the two women.

"Thank you, Naomi. How is the menu coming along?" I paused at the dining room entryway watching the two of them.

Naomi had joined our household before my parents were married. She used to tell me stories when I was little about my parents' wedding day, how beautiful my mother looked in her wedding dress and how happy my father was. I loved listening to her talk about them and the fairy tale love story they shared. It always made me feel so close to her.

"Never you mind. Your only job today is to rest." My grandmother rose from her chair and opened the swinging door to the dining room. "Eat and then rest. That is an order."

"Yes, grandmother," I glanced back at Naomi and winked at her smiling face.

"Now shush," she ushered me into the dining room pulling the door closed between us.

I picked up the morning paper and poured myself a cup of coffee. I sat down at the end of the table and nibbled on a piece of toast spreading out the paper before me. It seemed the investigation into the *Secret Six* involved in financing the late John Brown was ongoing. I was engrossed in the story when Keifer arrived at the table.

"Good morning, my dear. How are you feeling?" He leaned down and kissed me on the cheek before pouring himself a cup of coffee.

"Fine, darling." I smiled briefly before returning to the paper.

"Why are you reading that?" He rolled his eyes before sitting down opposite me. "You know how I feel about it."

"Yes, dear." I responded without looking up.

"Sidney?" My husband rapped his fingers on the table.

"Yes?" I smiled lovingly at him.

"What has garnered all your attention this morning?" He inquired with interest.

"I was reading about all these tributes and memorials to John Brown going on in the city. It seems though that not everyone is thrilled about them." I explained.

"Most notably the Irish community." Keifer raised his eyebrows. "I visited the McKenzie's yesterday, and Martin was in rare form."

"How are Molly and the baby doing?"

"Fine. Fine. They are fine." He waved off my interruption. "But Martin referred to Brown and his followers as terrorists. Then he went on about the insane tactics and rhetoric of the abolitionists and how freeing the slaves in the south would cause economic instability in the north by increasing the competition for limited jobs."

"And you consider that backward logic?" I raised an eyebrow.

"Not really. Not as much as you think." Keifer countered. "You must remember Brown was a protestant and a descendent of the English Puritans. Patrick Donahoe, the publisher of *The Pilot* has been theorizing in his paper that Brown was in cahoots with the British in a plot designed to undermine political power in the United States." I snorted accidentally at the absurdity of his words.

"I have never heard of *The Pilot*."

"It is the official newspaper of the Roman Catholic Archdiocese in Boston." Keifer explained. "After hearing all that speculation nonsense, it makes me question the likelihood of a war against the South. I have tried so hard to believe that our country could not possibly divide, but it almost feels inevitable." His expression turned grave.

"Did you know that Dr. Samuel Gridley Howe, and George Luther Stearns, along with several other prominent Boston men have disappeared since Brown's execution?" I glanced back to the section of the paper I was reading before he came in. "The paper says that officials believe they fled to Canada."

"Most likely," he shrugged. "They definitely did not go South." He laughed without humor. "Either way, no charges have been filed against anyone in the *Secret Six*. Officials said they only want to question them on how much they knew, if they knew anything of Brown's plans."

"But they financed him," I argued. "And these men sent Brown weapons when he was in Kansas where he massacred pro-slavers."

"I know," Keifer shook his head slightly. "And now many Northerners have martyred this lunatic without realizing the full ramifications or consequences of their actions."

"Hopefully the conservative groups and the anti-abolitionists voices will curtail the South's growing hatred of Northerners." I knew it was wishful thinking even as the words passed through my lips, but I felt the need to say it anyway.

"I am not sure anything either of these groups say now is going to alter the growing sentiment in the South. Southerners are tired of the overreaching federal government, the increasing taxes, and its impact on their daily lives." My husband stirred his coffee absentmindedly.

"You sound like a Southerner," I raised an eyebrow.

"I am proud of my heritage, and I will not apologize for it."

"Does that mean you have changed your mind? You would stand with the South?" I suddenly felt sick to my stomach.

"No. That is not what I said." He exhaled loudly. "I said I am proud of my heritage. However, I believe in preserving our country. I will do everything I can to provide medical care for any man fighting for their beliefs regardless of which side they fight for."

"And that is why I love you," I rose and waddled over to him. I wrapped my arms around his shoulders and kissed his forehead. "You are a good man, Keifer Lee Marshall."

I was sequestered to the parlor most of the day. Keifer had noticed me rubbing the small of my lower back and was afraid that all the commotion would be overly stressful on our baby. He kept an unnervingly close eye on me and rarely let me do anything other than reading or quilting.

Throughout the morning, I read six chapters, stitched three patchwork sections on the quilt my grandmother and I had been working on, and had no desire to start on the needlepoint Wanda had left in the basket beside me. I was bored to tears. I stared at the embers dancing in the hearth. What I wouldn't give for my laptop, I thought sarcastically. Or my cell phone, television, or ibuprofen. I rubbed my temples gently.

I could hear everyone moving around the house cleaning, cooking, bustling about, yet I felt very alone. I shifted on the chaise lounge and readjusted the pillow wedged behind my back. There was nothing I could do to get comfortable.

"Excuse me, Mizdress." I looked up at the sound of his voice and found Ned lingering in the doorway.

"Yes, Ned," I straightened at his appearance.

"Is dare anathang ah's kin git fo ya?"

"No, thank you. I am fine."

"Mizdress?" he slowly entered the room.

"What is on your mind, Ned?" I motioned to the chair across from me and he awkwardly sat down.

"Ah's balanced da nummers. Da vouchers ar on ya des waitin foy ya ta cign." He informed me in a low voice.

"Thank you, Ned. I appreciate your help." His awkward silence told me something else was on his mind. "Is there anything else? Something troubling you?"

"Yes'm, dar is." His eyes rested on the floor. "Ah's keep hearin' lots a talk bout da country splittin in two. Do ya tank dat'll appen?"

Oh, Ned," I sighed heavily and straightened myself up to better speak to him. "Unfortunately, I believe it will. Things have been put in motion that cannot be undone. Both sides feel very strongly about their position."

"But it peers ta me dath neether side kows wha da utter realie danks." He tilted his head to the side looking at me carefully.

"What do you mean?"

"Well, Mizdress," Ned rested his elbows on his knees and fiddled nervously with his hands. "Da ways ah's sees tis da white folks n' da Nor wan da South to frees dey slaves, but da South wants ta do it in dey's own way, n' dey's own time wifout bein told."

"Who told you that?" I was curious who he had been speaking to.

"Ah's herd a gentman frum Vergeenia talkin' wif Master Howard at da merkintile. He says dey's kows slavery's outdated but dey's don' believe the govment has da ight to tell em' when or how." Ned explained.

"I see." I considered his words carefully. "And what do you think?"

"Ya knows my pa n' ma is slaves in Alibama." I nodded. "N' ya knows ah's is born a slave too."

"Yes," I recalled him tell me when I was young.

"Mizdress Cameron gives us papers after Master Cameron died n' we com North. No one wod hir me pa n' da South. He tied da fin wook fo a ear. When we's com ere, Master Timmons give m' pa wook in da field n' ma wook n' da house. Mizdress Timmons ev'n taught me da read, rite, n' nummers." He smiled widely.

"Ned, you, and your family are valued and treasured employees here. You know how much all mean to us." I reached over and put my hand over his.

"Yes'm, ah's do." Ned nodded his head slightly. "Ah's dinks slavery is wrong."

"So, do I." I agreed with him.

"But freeing all da slaves at once wif no wook fo em', no homes fo em', no fud fo em' — dat is wrong too. Where's dey go? Whaddle appen to em'?"

"I do not know, Ned. I wish I had an answer for you. I do not believe that even those fancy politicians who serve in government can answer that." That was one thing I was positive about.

"Ah's don' understan' it." Ned continued to fidget with his hands.

"I believe it will be a difficult struggle for many of them. Very few know how to read or write. Even fewer will be able to support their families." I hated being so brutally honest with him.

"Dat's what ah's daught." He perched his lips together in a familiar fashion that I was accustomed to when he was deep in thought. "Da govment shood do some'in fo'em."

"Yes, they should. But I do not believe they understand the full ramifications of what is about to occur." I chose my words carefully.

"Ah's believe ya is ight, Mizdress." Ned stood up. "Ah's bes git bac da wook now." He stood back up.

"Please let me know if you need anything, Ned." I smiled.

"Ah's will. Dank ya, Mizdress." He bowed his head and left.

I spent a good deal of the afternoon lounging on the chaise watching the snow falling gently outside the window. Marta came in and draped a quilt over my legs and abdomen while Ned came in silently every now and again to stoke the fire and add a log or two to keep it going.

Our earlier conversation continued to haunt me as I stared at the grey winter sky. It was a horrible feeling knowing what was on the horizon and not being able to do anything about it. I lovingly and protectively ran my hand over my abdomen wishing I could change the world my precious baby boy was about to be born into.

Ever since grade school I had studied the horrors of the American Civil War. As my educational career advanced, so did the depth of my courses. During my bachelor's degree at Northwest University, I had taken my required classes on American history, but I had also taken a semester on the American Revolution and another devoted to the American Civil War. I wished I still had the same naivety I had back then. I had no clue that I was going to have to experience the latter firsthand.

The names of the battle locations, sieges, and the hellish conditions that plagued soldiers on both sides ran through my head. Lessons of the brutal ungodly prison camps, Sherman burning Atlanta along his journey to the sea, citizens being robbed by deserting soldiers, raping women, and burning their homes down. The atrocities committed by both sides were nothing short of abysmal.

I watched the sun burn away below the tree line and sink into the frozen fields. The clock on the mantle chimed five as darkness descended over the land. I listened closely for the sound of Keifer returning home, but none came. I could not recall if he mentioned he would be making any house calls today or would be staying in the office. As I watched the hands slowly note the passing of time, there were still no signs of my husband.

"I am sure he will be home soon." My grandmother stood in the doorway watching me. "Dinner is on the table. You should eat something. You must keep up your strength." Her smile was gentle and warm.

"I know," I glanced back toward the window one last time before I rose. "I really do not like him traveling alone after dark."

I followed her to the dining room and sat down in my usual seat. My grandmother sat opposite me and knelt her head for prayers.

"Thank you, gracious heavenly father for our bounty. Keep our family safe during these difficult times and prepare us for what is about to come. Bless us and keep us in your sight. In Jesus name we pray. Amen."

"Amen." I opened my eyes and looked over at the empty seat at the head of the table where Keifer was supposed to be.

"Do not look so worried. He will be here shortly." She reached for the yams and winked at me.

"I know," I reiterated with a heavy sigh. I glanced at the doorway to the kitchen to ensure we were alone. "My mind is exhausted. I hate watching our country disintegrate on two planes and there is nothing I can do."

"At least *here* you know what is coming." My grandmother shrugged slightly and began cutting her roast.

"Knowing, but unable to prevent it makes me feel even worse." I tore the corner off my yeast roll and dipped it into the gravy. "The idea of Keifer, my brother, may family and friends — all being involved in this makes me physically ill."

"But you know Keifer and Patrick will be on the outskirts. They will be safe." She reminded me between bites.

"But Robert, Monte and Nicholas," I brushed a tear off my cheek. "They will be on the front lines in the thick of it and Nicholas will be a prisoner at Andersonville. There must be something I can do to prevent that." I felt desperate.

"Sidney," she set down her utensils and reached across the table taking my hand in hers. "You know we cannot meddle with fate. You also know Nicholas will survive this. He is a strong young man, and I believe in him."

"How can you say that?" I choked through my tears. "Andersonville is a fate worse than hell. You have seen and read the same things I have about it. Nicholas is my little brother."

"And he is my grandson," she looked annoyed with me. "Do you think your love for him is greater than mine? I would sacrifice my life for any of my children or grandchildren. It rips my heart out to fathom what all those whom I love will have to endure throughout this horrific nightmare."

"I apologize," I reached for her hand and squeezed it gently. "I did not mean to insinuate. I know how much you love your family." I shook my head in despair. "I am just scared."

"We all are sweetheart."

Keifer joined me upstairs at half past nine. I watched him undress and change into his nightshirt by the glow of the embers in the hearth. I was still impressed by his muscular physique but had noticed that as he passed his 30th birthday the once light strawberry blond hair on his legs and chest had become a more prominent shade of red. When I mentioned it regarding his mustache and goatee, he immediately became overly defensive about it. This time I knew better than to say anything.

"Have things settled downstairs?" I inquired as he crawled beneath the heavy covers.

"Not yet." He sighed, settling in beside me. "I fear Naomi and Marta are in for a long night."

"I hope grandmother takes it easy on them. They have been working so hard over the last couple weeks for this gala." I snuggled up to my husband and rested my head on his chest.

"Knowing her, I doubt it." Keifer chuckled lightly.

"Ned overheard an awkward conversation earlier at the mercantile." I recounted our talk that afternoon.

"Ned is not alone. People are angry. I have never seen such open hostility. I see it daily in Boston." He kissed the top of my head. "The abolitionists want to keep people on edge. It is not that people on both sides of the Mason-Dixon line believe slavery is an outdated and inhumane system but not one of those fanatics nor the government, are offering a way to transition the slaves into civilian life. They basically will have no jobs, no homes, no way to support themselves or their families. They are setting them up for failure and no one seems to be concerned with the logistics." Keifer explained.

"I hate feeling like a helpless witness to the destruction of our country." I remarked. "I am so worried about what is to come." I squeezed him and closed my eyes feeling secure in his arms around me.

"I know, my love. Me too." He leaned down and kissed me lightly.

"I love you too. Sweet dreams, darling."

"Sweet dreams."

7

SATURDAY, FEBRUARY 8, 2020

I TRUDGED THROUGH THE SNOW IN the hospital parking garage. Fresh snow had fallen the night before and although the groundkeepers were doing their best to keep the area clear, high winds were making it challenging for them. My sneakers sunk into the snowdrifts. The wet snow seeped into my shoes and soaked my socks. I thought about what my sister said the day before about moving South and thought it was sounding better with each step.

"I hate this shit," one of the peds nurses I often worked with, Sara caught up to me carefully stepping in my footsteps.

"Me too," I smiled over my shoulder at her. "I cannot wait until spring."

"Just buy me a one-way ticket to the Bahamas and I'll be happy." She laughed. "Just sitting on the beach with my toes in the sand and a frozen alcoholic beverage with a little umbrella in it." She lost her balance and grabbed my arm pulling both of us down onto slushy concrete.

"Damn it," I dropped my purse in the snow and felt the freezing slosh seep through my thin scrubs.

"I'm so sorry," Sara apologized through her giggles causing me to laugh too.

"Don't worry about it," I sat up and brushed off my legs and jacket. "If you had not fallen first, then I was going too." I laughed.

"Are you alright?" She held onto the bumper of the car beside us and carefully stood up.

"No broken bones," I took her hand and got to my feet. "You?"

"Soaked, but in one piece." She picked up our bags and handed me mine. "I am really sorry, Sidney. Do you want to run back in and change? I'd hate for you to drive home soaking wet."

"Nah, it's okay. I live close and have to jump into the shower anyway. I have a dinner tonight." I explained.

"Are you sure?"

"Of course," all I wanted was to get into a hot shower. "Are you parked close?"

"Over there?" She gestured towards the other end of the garage.

We steadied each other about halfway down the row. My legs were freezing as my wet scrubs clung to them. My scrubs and panties were soaked and clinging to my butt in the most uncomfortable manner.

"This is me," I was thankful I reached my car. "Are you okay?"

"I'm fine." She held onto the car beside mine. "Be careful going home."

"Thanks, you too." I watched for a moment until I was sure she'd safely reached her vehicle before climbing into mine for the most uncomfortable ride home in history.

~

I peeled off my wet scrubs and noticed a wide purple bruise running down the outside of my thigh. Thankfully, the skin was unbroken, and it wasn't serious, but it was going to be painful for the next few days.

The bathroom filled with steam as I brushed my teeth and tossed my scrubs in the laundry bin. All I wanted to do was crawl into bed and put an end to this long hectic day, but I couldn't. I had promised my sister I would join her and her extended family for dinner.

The hot water rained down over my tired bones spreading warmth throughout my body. I was sore and exhausted. I was not up for a big family dinner, but I had given my word I would be there.

The subject Alex wanted to discuss literally turned my stomach and I had difficulty shaking it since Jocelyn first mentioned it. I had heard other pediatricians discuss the issue and about how its prevalence was gaining momentum due to social media influence. None of them believed in prescribing hormone treatments for minors due to the long-term effects.

I threw on some jeans and a cozy red sweater. I slipped into my boots and added some light makeup along with the heart-shaped necklace Landon had gotten me for Christmas. I spent the time blow-drying my long blond hair and pulled it up in a messy bun.

I knew before I left for the Chandler's I needed a bit more expert advice on the subject Alex wanted to discuss with me. I sat down on the plush corner chair by the fireplace wishing I could start a fire. But I knew I would be leaving shortly making it pointless.

I scrolled through my contacts list until I reached my mother's number. I had not spoken to her in several months and wasn't looking forward to reaching out to her now. But she was an expert in her field and a highly respected pediatrician. I took a deep breath and clicked on her name. Amy answered on the third ring.

"Sidney?" My mother's voice sounded suspiciously cheerful. "I was just thinking about you. How are you doing?"

"I'm good. How are you?" I swallowed hard.

"Busy," she chuckled. "How's the pregnancy going? You've only got another six or eight weeks, right? Did you find out the sex?"

"Yeah, about that." My throat went dry, and tears stung my eyes?"

"What do you mean?" she immediately sounded concerned.

"We had a criminal on PCP come into the ER and an intern loosened his restraints to move him from the gurney to the bed and he lashed out and attacked. It caused me to lose the baby." I mumbled as quickly as I could to get it over with.

"Oh, Sidney." She sighed heavily. "I am so sorry, darling. How are you? Are you okay?" She rushed. "Never mind. Of course, you are not okay. What can I do for you? Do you need me to come out?" For a moment I felt like I had my mother back — the woman who raised me, loved me, and was always there for me. And all I wanted at that moment was nothing more than for her to hold me and tell me everything was going to be alright.

"No. I know you're busy." I wiped the tears off my cheeks with the back of my hand. "I'm okay."

"Are you sure? I can be on the next plane." Her voice was filled with genuine concern.

"No. It's okay. I'm fine. I promise." I snuffled. "But I need to ask you about something else. Do you have a minute?"

"Of course," I heard a door close in the background. "What's going on?"

"Alex was approached by a divorced father recently who has a six-year-old son. His ex-wife is trying to put his son on hormone replacement therapy and transition him into a girl. The boy's father is absolutely against this and is seeking legal intervention to stop her and trying to get custody of the child. Alex wants a medical opinion on it and asked me. Unfortunately, I am not far enough along in medical school to know the critical details." I explained. "Have you come across anything regarding gender affirming care or hormone replacement therapy for minors?"

"Unfortunately, yes. It is the most absurd thing I have ever heard." My mother huffed. "We had a board meeting at the hospital last week about the topic. Needless to say, it was heated."

"I would imagine so," I could imagine my mother adding her two cents full of venom. "I believe it's only a matter of time before I have to sit through something like that here, which is why I'm calling you."

"And this child is six?" My mother exhaled loudly. "Jesus Christ. What in the hell is this mother thinking?" Amy's voice turned edgy. "Does she understand that she is sterilizing her child? Not to mention the psychological damage she is inflicting."

"I don't know all the exact details yet. I am meeting Alex over at the Chandler's for dinner in about an hour. I just wanted to pick your brain for a minute because to be honest, this whole thing makes me nauseated." I closed my eyes and took a deep breath.

"I truly do not understand what is wrong with these parents. A minor is not allowed to purchase cigarettes, get a tattoo, buy alcohol, or vote, but these parents think they can make life-altering decisions about their gender." Amy scoffed. "If you ask me, these parents have Factitious Disorder."

"I agree." I thought for a moment. "I believe Alex would be able to use that in his case. He should investigate the mother's medical and psychological history."

"If you would like me to talk with him more in depth, please let him know I would be happy to assist him. I am a true advocate against minors receiving hormone therapy unless it is medically necessary, and it should never be given to a healthy minor."

"Wonderful. I will let him know. Thanks mom."

"Please let me know how it goes."

"I will," I was just about to hang up when I heard her speak.

"And you and Landon, are you two doing all right?" Her inquiry caught me off guard.

"Yes, we are doing well. Busy with school and work. You know how that goes."

"Yes, I remember those days. Don't worry, it does get better." She sounded cheerful again causing me to think she was getting ready to drop a bomb on me which was typically her fashion. "I am glad you called. I was actually going to call you and Jocelyn this weekend." Here it comes, I thought. "Dane asked me to marry him."

"And you said yes." I tried to be cheerful, but I had never met the man.

"Of course, I did." Amy giggled. "And I want you to be my Maid of Honor."

"But I haven't met the groom, mom."

"Well, then I guess it's a good thing I'm not asking you to be the best man." She laughed at her own humor.

"Have you set a date yet?" I tried to sound interested.

"No, but as soon as we do, I will let you know. I realize the hospital will require substantial notice for you and Landon."

"Yes, they are delightful about time off." I chuckled.

"Fair enough. I will make sure you have ample notice."

"I appreciate that. And congratulations. I am happy for you." I surprised myself.

"Thank you," I swore I heard a sigh of relief escape her. "That means a lot. To be honest, I was nervous about telling you. I know we haven't exactly been as close as we used to be. But I am glad that you and your sister have grown much closer. I do miss my girls."

"We miss you too, mom." I said despite my true feelings.

"Well, I know you must be going. Please give Alex my number and tell him I would be happy to help him in any way I can — including testifying for the father to help save his son."

"Thank you, I will."

"And I will let you know as soon as we set a date."

"Oh, mom," I wasn't going to let her off the hook so easily. "You realize I am having dinner with Jocelyn tonight. Are you planning on calling her?" She hesitated for a moment.

"She would probably take it better coming from you." I knew she'd wimp out, but I wasn't going to let her.

"No, it would be best hearing it from you and you need to call Ethan also." I reminded her.

"Fine. You're right. I will." She sighed.

"When we hang up," I pushed.

"All right," Amy giggled. "Bye Sidney."

"Bye Mom."

I disconnected the call and tossed my phone in my purse. I figured it would take me about twenty minutes to get to the Chandler's if the roads weren't terrible, but I wondered if that was enough time for my mother to drop the bomb on Jocelyn before I arrived.

Jocelyn and my mother had a sordid history. Amy had been adamantly against Jocelyn and Jackson from the very beginning. She and our younger brother, Ethan held nothing back in making my sister's life miserable throughout her senior year of high school. Granted, I wasn't exactly thrilled about it either, but that was before I knew about *EVE* and the long history between my little sister and her new husband. Unfortunately, it was something my sister could never share with Amy or Ethan, and it had permanently damaged their relationships.

The roads had worsened a bit as the evening hours set in. I skillfully navigated the black ice covering the roads. I hated driving under these conditions but having lived in the northern regions of our country my entire life, I was accustomed to it.

Alex's wife, Leslie, answered the door. She was all smiles, but her eyes showed signs of exhaustion. Her two children, Lucinda, also called Lucy and Charles, better known as Charlie, were entering their preteen years, and were fighting for more independence by acting out. With the long hours Alex worked, the brunt of the parenting fell upon Leslie's thin yet strong shoulders.

"Hey Sidney," she stood back so I could enter. "How are you?"

"Good," I hugged her briefly. "Tired. How are you?"

"I'm smiling," Leslie chuckled taking my coat and hanging it in the hall closet.

"That good, huh?" It was the familiar sarcasm I heard almost daily from parents.

"You wouldn't have a pill to adjust their attitudes, would you?" She smirked.

"If I could invent one, I'd never have to work again." I followed her into the kitchen.

The kitchen was crowded with family members. The three Chandler children were all present along with their families. Jocelyn had dramatically improved her cooking skills thanks to spending long hours in the kitchen with her mother-in-law, Emily, who was a phenomenal cook. She believed in making everything from scratch and the women was a gifted genius.

"Hello," Emily wove her way through the crowd wiping her hands on her apron. "How are you?" She embraced me tightly.

"Hello, everything smells so good." I observed.

"Thank you," she smiled. "You are just in time. We were getting ready to set the table. Will Lanndon be joining us?" She motioned towards Leslie, Phoebe, and Jocelyn who started carrying steamy dishes into the dining room.

"I am afraid not." I shrugged. "What can I do to help?" I offered.

"Nothing." She led me by the arm, and everyone followed us. "Just take a seat."

The large family filed in around the extended elegant table. Everyone was talking all at once and I didn't believe anyone was listening except me. It was a wonderful sight and one I had only been exposed to in this welcoming home.

After several minutes of dishes being passed around, plates were full, and the noise level dropped considerably. The roast was divine, the mashed potatoes creamy, and the beer bread melted in my mouth as quickly as the butter melted over the top of them. The remainder of the sides were as spectacular. I lost myself in the pure delight of it all and had not realized that Alex was trying to get my attention.

"Oh Sidney," my brain finally registered someone calling my name. "Are you in there?" He laughed along with Jackson.

"Sorry," I apologized. "My mind was elsewhere."

"Jocelyn said she told you what I am up against." He raised his eyebrows across the table.

"She gave me the gist." I wasn't comfortable discussing this topic in front of his children. I did not believe Leslie would appreciate it.

"Let's wait until coffee to discuss this." Phoebe played the devil's advocate, saving me from having to do so.

"I agree," Robert eyed his son who reluctantly conceded.

"Mother's engagement wouldn't be what's on your mind, would it?" Jocelyn spoke up, changing the subject and shifting all eyes to her.

"I guess she did call you when she got off the phone with me." I smirked over at my baby sister.

"She asked me to be a bridesmaid." She said it like our mother had asked her to drive her car off a cliff.

"You got off easy," I rolled my eyes playfully. "She asked me to be her Maid of Honor."

"Are you serious?" Jocelyn choked on her tea. "We haven't even met the groom."

"Wait — what?" Phoebe interrupted. "Your mother calls you to say she is getting married, and you haven't even met the man she is engaged too."

"Exactly," Jocelyn smirked.

"What did you tell her?" I couldn't help but ask.

"I laughed," She looked pointedly at me and shrugged. "What was I supposed to do?"

"You laughed?" Somehow, I wasn't surprised.

"Well, seriously? I told her she doesn't talk to me for years and then calls me to say she is getting married to a man I have never met. Plus, has the audacity to ask me to be a bridesmaid for her when she boycotted my wedding. It is ridiculous." Jocelyn shook her head. "What did you tell her?"

"Congratulations," I shrugged. "She caught me completely off guard. I didn't know what to say."

"Are you going to stand up with her?" I felt all the eyes at the table shift to me.

"No. I've got classes. Besides, even if I wanted to, the hospital isn't going to let me off work long enough to travel to Seattle, not at this time anyway." It was the easiest out I could think of.

"Good," Jocelyn smiled. "Then I don't feel so bad skipping it as well. Do you think Ethan will go?"

"When was the last time you've seen your mother?" Leslie asked.

"Wow, um," Jocelyn stared off into space trying to recall. "Once since our high school graduation party, and that was only because she came out here to berate you." She looked over at me for confirmation.

"Pretty much." I shrugged.

"So, once in about five years," Leslie looked astonished.

"We are much closer to our dad," I piped in feeling guilty for no reason.

"Our parents had a nasty divorce shortly after Jackson and I were married. And our mother did everything possible to sabotage our relationship since we started dating. She made life at home a living hell and that pretty much ruined our relationship." Jocelyn offered a generic and lighter version of the nightmare my mother had inflicted upon her.

"I think it is sad how prominent divorces are today." Leslie stated with empathy. "It makes me feel so fortunate for my marriage." She reached over and squeezed Alex's hand with a smile.

"I agree," Robert smiled across the table at his wife. "The divorce rate in our family is zero. For that, I feel we are all blessed."

"Do you know anything about this man she is marrying?" Emily asked politely.

"Not really," I shook my head. "Only that his name is Dane and he's a pediatric surgeon. They work together at the hospital." I shrugged.

"I am surprised she would ever considering marrying again after the disaster with dad." Jocelyn said casually. "I cannot think of a time when the two of them were happy together."

"That's sad," Emily wrinkled her eyebrows. "It makes me wonder why they ever got married to begin with."

"I think at one time they were happy and loved each other very much. But their demanding careers, different schedules, and life in general simply pushed them apart." I added, wanting to dearly believe my words.

"It can be a difficult balance — juggling a career and homelife." Robert agreed. "However, a couple must be committed to growing together and meeting life's challenges together."

"Sometimes that is easier said than done," Phoebe pipped up raising her eyebrows. "Look how many of our colleagues are divorced."

"Hell, I make a living on divorces." Alex chuckled. "And a good one at that."

"That is why I went into corporate law. I do not know how you do it," Jackson looked over at his older brother. "I would go batty listening to couples bicker back and forth constantly." He laughed.

"That is why I would make the world's worse psychologist." Jocelyn said with a smirk. "You could not pay me enough to sit around all day and listen to people complain about their pathetic entitled lives and perceived injustices."

"Jocelyn, I am surprised at you." Emily chastised her daughter-in-law. "I would have thought you more compassionate than that.

"Don't misunderstand me. I have compassion for individuals who are suffering from actual mental disorders like depression, post-traumatic stress disorder, or any other true psychological abnormalities. But you take these bored, lonely housewives who come in and complain about their husband's long hours at the office, their unrelenting mothers-in-law, or the fact that their spoiled, self-entitled brat has no respect for them, and I would be fighting not to slice my own wrists just listening to them." My sister stated matter-of-factly.

"Ditto," I concurred, and the table laughed. "I know, I could not do it either. I hate to say this millennial generation, because I am part of it, but most are so freaking entitled. They want to blame everyone else for their behavior and they always play the victim. And my goodness, they are the most oppressed, sensitive bunch of whiners. I am truly ashamed to be labeled a millennial."

"I think many Gen-Xer's overcompensate with their children because of the way we were raised." Robert proposed. "Gen-Xer's were really the first generation who experienced working moms. Most kids were latch-key kids. Most went home after school to empty houses and when moms were home on the weekends, they were busy trying to clean and do laundry and get all the stuff done in two days that normally took a week to complete. So, they really did not want

to be bothered with their children and sent them outside to play."

The debate continued around the table with arguments being made from different perspectives. It was entertaining to listen to, considering Robert and Emily were the only two Gen Xer's present and everyone else at the table was considered Millennials. Still, since most were raised 'during a different time – at least partly' our perspectives must have seemed humorous to poor Leslie and Carson. For this group was definitely not what the world would consider typical millennials.

After dinner was cleaned up, the adults settled in the front parlor with a fresh pot of coffee. Leslie and Emily took the children into the kitchen for some hot fudge brownies with ice cream and kept them out of ear shot.

Jocelyn, Jackson, and Carson floated between the parlor and the kitchen until it annoyed Robert enough to send them into the kitchen to stay. Alex set a binder file folder on the coffee table centered in the seating area. I could not believe the size of it. It was stuffed full of papers, and I thought there was no possible way this could all be from one client.

But I was wrong.

Alex set up his laptop while Robert, Phoebe, and I fixed our coffee and munched on the angel food cake Emily had made for us. We were making small talk about Valentine's Day plans while Alex continued setting everything up.

"Okay, so I think I have all the pertinent documents." He mumbled to himself. "Sidney?" He turned towards me.

"Yes?" I mumbled trying to swallow.

"What can you tell me?"

"I know a little bit, but my mom said she would be more than happy to assist you with the specifics. She would even testify if you believe it would help." I told him.

"Amy would be an excellent witness." Alex rubbed his chin.

"She is highly respected in her field." Robert noted. "We could do a Zoom meeting with her next week."

"Do you know her schedule?" Alex looked over at me.

"No." I shook my head. "But I will text her." I took out my phone and texted my mother while Robert started browsing through the stack of papers piled in front of his son.

"I simply do not understand the mother's rational in this." Robert frowned with a furrowed brow.

"The father claims that throughout her pregnancy, his ex-wife had always dreamed of having a daughter. He said the nursery was pink and ruffled and the closet was filled with so much pink it looked like the tiny clothes has been hosed down with Pepto-Bismol." Alex chuckled. "Apparently she had been devastated when she gave birth to a son."

"She did not have an ultrasound at any time throughout the pregnancy." I questioned. "They are usually pretty standard these days."

"She had two, I believe." Alex flipped through the documents in front of him. "Yes, two." He confirmed. "But neither confirmed the baby's gender due to the positioning." Alex looked back up at me. "Still, his ex-wife remained adamant that the child was a girl – claimed she just 'knew it'." He sighed after doing the air quotes.

"Guess she was surprised." Robert smirked.

"That would be an understatement." Alex's eyes widened. "From what my client stated, when she learned of the child's sex when the doctor held him up after delivery was 'he has no clothes' and then turned her head away from the baby. He said she barely looked at him after he was born and placed on her stomach."

"That's sad." I said softly, thinking of my own son that I had lost on this plane.

"Afterwards, he said she rarely held the baby or interacted with him in any way. He claims his wife had always stated how important it was for her to breastfeed their child and the benefits it would provide for them, but she showed no interest in nursing their son. After several days of this when they returned home from the hospital, he called his mother-in-law and had her come stay with them since he was so concerned about his ex-wife's lack of interest in feeding or bonding with their son." Alex leaned forward resting his elbows on his knees before continuing. "My client and his mother-in-law started the baby on formula and constantly encouraged his wife over the next few weeks to engage with their son. But she remained distant – sleeping all the time, rarely eating."

"Post-partum depression." I reckoned, glancing over at Phoebe who nodded in agreement.

"Yes. This is what she was eventually diagnosed with, but it was more than that." Alex brushed his fingers through his hair restlessly. "My client said that after that first week, his ex-wife started dressing his son in all the baby girl clothes she had originally purchased. When he confronted her about it and changed his son back into boy clothes, she was furious." Alex shook his head. "His ex-wife's best friend that she had been inseparable with since elementary school was also pregnant at this time with her second child. Her first child, who was almost three at the time, had been a boy – which the father says everyone was thrilled and dotted on the little boy. But her best friend had found out during her ultrasound a week before my client's son was born, that her second child was a girl and she, of course, excitedly told my client's ex-wife. He said the two women spent the afternoon giggling on the couch about how their daughters would grow up together and be best friends just like they were.

"Oh, Lord," Phobe exhaled loudly.

"Yeah. Well, when her best friend showed up at the hospital after the birth, his ex-wife refused to see her. He stepped out into the hallway and explained that she had just gone through nineteen hours of labor and was asleep. But he took her friend down to the nursery to see his son." Alex admitted.

"Does he get along well with his ex-wife's best friend?" Robert inquired.

"Yes, they had a good relationship – still do." Alex smiled knowingly. "Over the next few weeks after they returned home from the hospital his ex-wife wouldn't talk to her best friend at all when she called. By the third week she had given up and came over to the house. My client let her in believing that she would be able to talk to his ex-wife and help her come out of this dark place she was in. Even his ex-mother-in-law thought it was a good idea and told the best friend how her daughter was struggling and dressing her son in girl clothes. But none of them expected the shitstorm that was about to be unleased on the best friend."

"Did she throw her out?" Phoebe asked.

"Yes," Alex nodded. "But not before going off on a tirade about how much she hated her best friend. My client said he and his ex-mother-in-law stood outside the bedroom door while his ex-wife screamed at her best friend. He said she was horrible claiming how it was not fair that her best friend was having the daughter she had always dreamed of, that she had a better house than her, a husband that made more money, and even screamed at her best friend for finishing her college degree after his ex-wife had dropped out of school."

"Good grief," I muttered. "She needs a therapist."

"Desperately," Phoebe agreed.

"Okay, so his ex-wife has a history of mental illness. Do you have documentation of it?" Robert asked.

"Yes." Alex shuffled through some papers. "She was diagnosed with post-partum depression and post-partum psychosis. I am not a hundred percent sure what that means but,"

"We need a psychologist or psychiatrist in the family." Phoebe laughed.

"You know why most avoid the medical field who have *EVE*." Robert pointedly looked my way with pinched lips.

"I understand that, but crazy is crazy regardless of the century." she noted.

"True," I reasoned. "Perhaps I will switch specialties and become Freud before Freud." I chuckled.

"You should," Phoebe shrugged. "You could change the entire face of modern psychology."

"Phoebe," Robert chastised his only daughter. "You know better."

"I am just kidding." She smirked with a twinkle in her eye.

"Anyway," Alex drew our attention back to him. "I believe we will not have any difficultly establishing my client's ex-wife's history of mental illness." He held up another piece of paper. "Three years ago, she was also diagnosed with manic depressive bipolar and borderline personality disorder. I also have documentation that she stopped taking her prescribed medication and quit counseling. Since then, she has been spiraling downhill with even more delusions of dressing her son as a girl and only buying him girly toys."

"Girly toys?" I questioned.

"Dolls, a kitchen set, baby strollers, makeup kits – girly toys." Alex shrugged.

"You should avoid saying that in court." I noted. "It makes you sound misogynistic and that will not play well before a judge."

"She is right," Robert agreed. "I would say something more along the lines of toys with more feminine attributes."

"That's worse." Phoebe argued looking over at her father. "Just say items typically found to be more appealing to little girls."

"Okay," Alex jotted down the phrase. "And what do you know about these hormone treatments given to children for gender dysphoria?" He looked directly at me.

"I know they are poison for kids – especially pre-pubescent children. Honestly, I am not aware of any studies that show the impact they have on a child's mental health, but the long-term biological impact is that it essentially sterilizes the children. This is medication the government uses to chemically castrate rapists and pedophiles. It is dangerous stuff."

"And you would be willing to testify to this?" Alex was writing down everything I said.

"I would if I thought my testimony would help you, but I am afraid it will not. I can talk with some of the pediatricians at the hospital and see if they would be willing to provide expert testimony. But I am only a med student. My testimony would not carry weight in a case like this. However, despite all her flaws, my mother is considered one of the best pediatricians in the field. I still believe she would be your best bet. Her testimony would make a huge difference." Robert nodded at my assessment.

"Is she willing to fly out to testify against hormone treatments?" Alex inquired.

"Either that or a video call in the courtroom." I gestured towards Alex's notepad. "Can I see that?" He handed me the pad along with a pen. "Here is her personal cell phone number, hospital number, and office number." I glanced down at the text she just sent me. "And her schedule for next week. She said she would be happy to help you with anything to protect this little boy. She is avidly against hormone therapy for children or adolescents."

"I cannot imagine how a parent, especially a mother could ever do something so horrific to their own child." Robert shook his head in disgust.

"This woman has completely brainwashed this little boy." Alex tapped his pen on the notepad. "They have joint custody of the boy and during his time with his mother she dresses him like a girl, tells him he was supposed to be born a girl and that God made a mistake by giving him a penis so, the doctors are going to fix him. My client is beside himself and has repeatedly told his son that he was not a mistake and God made him perfect the way he is. This poor child is so confused and has told his therapist that he is afraid his mom will stop loving him if he doesn't become a girl like she wants."

"This mother should be prosecuted for child abuse and child endangerment." I scoffed.

"I concur," Robert's brow wrinkled in disgust. "Parents like that are the ones who should be sterilized and not mentally deranging their children with their delusional ideology."

"Isn't there anything else we can do for this child?" I pleaded with the three attorneys sitting around me.

"Legally?" I nodded. "Win this case." Alex stated.

8

SATURDAY, FEBRUARY 11, 1860

BY MID-AFTERNOON, MY GRANDMOTHER had the entire household in a tizzy. The countdown had begun, and guests would be arriving within an hour. My grandmother was already dressed in an emerald, green velvet gown trimmed in ivory lace. Her ashen gray hair pulled up into a bun at the nap of her neck which showed off her sparkling emerald earbobs my grandfather had given her on their 25th wedding anniversary.

I had spent the last hour being poked and prodded until I was presentable, at least according to Marta. My expanding abdomen made me feel like a beached whale stuffed tightly into a corset. I was utterly miserable, and it was impossible for me to take a deep breath. Still, the dark royal blue dress did hide my current state well.

The natural curls in my soft golden crown highlighted my face. Marta had loosely twisted the sides up and back leaving a few soft curls to hang loosely framing my face. The combs she placed in my hair were embossed with blue sapphires and white diamonds. It was one of the few pieces I had inherited from my birth mother, and I cherished them, only wearing them on special occasions.

Marta tied my matching royal blue ballet slippers around my puffy ankles. Pregnancy was not nearly as glamorous as I had thought it would be. My body was rapidly changing in ways that were most unflattering. However, I was grateful that Keifer still told me daily how beautiful I was, how much he loved me, and how he thought I was even more beautiful carrying his child. His words meant everything to me especially since these last couple months, I was feeling anything but beautiful.

I navigated down the stairs carefully, finding Keifer sitting in the parlor beside the hearth enjoying a brandy before our guests arrived. My grandmother's voice drifted in from the kitchen as she delegated exactly how and where she wanted things. I smiled to myself joining my husband and taking a seat on the chaise lounge across from him.

"You look lovely, my dear." He leaned down and tenderly stroked my cheek before kissing me lightly.

"Thank you," I looked adoringly up at his handsome face. "I believe grandmother feels twenty years younger."

"I agree," Keifer held up his brandy to emphasis its necessity. "This is my third." His smile reached his eyes, and they sparkled in the glow of the hearth embers.

"You should be careful," I cautioned him. "I do not want you intoxicated before our guests arrive." My husband nodded slightly, indicating he understood but also informing me that he would do as he pleased.

Our closest neighbor and grandmother's admirer, Edmund Bennett was the first to arrive. Ned took his overcoat and hat before showing him into the parlor.

"Good evening, Doc," he shook Keifer's hand before turning his attention towards me. "My goodness Sidney, you look lovely this evening. Simply glowing." Mr. Bennett kissed my hand gently.

"Thank you," I blushed. "I am happy to see you looking so well."

"Can I interest you in a brandy, Edmund?" Keifer asked whilst making his way over to our wet bar.

"Yes, thank you." Mr. Bennett grinned heartedly and warmed his hands closer to the flames. "I keep hoping we will have an early spring, but I believe my wishes have been in vain." He chuckled.

"Perhaps so, but we won't know for at least another month." Keifer shrugged, handing the brandy to our guest. "Despite all my years living up north, I do not believe I will ever become accustomed to these bitter winters."

"Not much snow in Savannah," Edmund chuckled sipping his brandy.

"No," Keifer grinned. "Not that I have ever seen."

A commotion in the foyer drew our attention towards the front door. The McKendrick's arrived with their entire entourage in tow. Their boisterous voices echoed through the house as they shuffled about removing overcoats, caps, hats, and bonnets, and layering them on Ned's muscular arms.

"Good evening," the large frame of Stephan McKendrick filled the parlor's entryway. His wife, Judith, was barely visible as she stood slightly behind her husband. "Fine day for a gathering." He bellowed as he entered the room.

"Welcome, Stephan," Keifer shook his hand.

"I thank ye, Doc. We're glad to be here." His sons and their partners followed them into the room.

I greeted Mr. McKendrick as I stood up and made my way over to Judith. She was a pretty, petite lady with dark hair and almond shaped light brown eyes. Tonight, she was wearing a burgundy dress trimmed in delicate ivory lace. If someone did not know her, her appearance would give them the impression of a polite and gracious lady.

And I am not saying she was not one, but the Judith I knew so well was quick-witted and sharp-tongued. She stood at a mere five feet, two inches tall while her husband and four of her five sons towered her at well over six feet tall. Her youngest son, Cameron — affectionately nicknamed Runt, stood at a mere five feet, ten inches tall.

It was comical how her large sons, including her husband, feared the wrath of Judith's tongue and even more so, her reach for them with a well-placed riding crop when necessary. She was never one to hold her tongue or offer mercy after some offense.

And I loved her for it.

Judith's high spiritedness, quick-wit, and sharp tongue were what everyone – almost everyone, loved most about her. And all admired her ability to keep her large abode in check and humbled.

"Hello Judith," I leaned over and embraced her briefly. "I am so happy to see you."

"It is a pleasure to be here, Sidney." She took me by the arm and led me away from the men. "You are simply glowing. How much longer?"

"A couple weeks," I smiled. "Does it show that much?" I shifted my skirt around in embarrassment.

"Do not fear, my darling. You look as captivating as ever. I was inquiring because you are not showing." I sighed heavily with relief.

"What do you think it is?" Her eyes twinkled.

"A son," I beamed.

"Have you decided on a name?"

"After his father," I shrugged my shoulder lightly with a grin. "I hope he has his hazel eyes." I blushed.

"And your wit," Judith laughed. "And kind heart." She placed her hand on my forearm. "Plus, your gumption. It is something you and I share and so many ladies lack." Judith said in a low voice.

"I have to agree," I laughed. "I could not be so meek if my life depended on it."

"Don't think I do not know what people say about me and how I handle my family." She winked. "But they have no idea how difficult it can be to be the only female in a family of large, strong, bull-headed, men who tower over you." She leaned in and lowered her voice. "Still, even if I would have been blessed with all daughters, I would not be any different. I am simply not built that way." She laughed.

"Nor I." I confessed.

More people arrived and the foyer quickly became overcrowded. I glanced out the front window and noticed the porch was in the same condition and carriages were backing up down the pathway. I looked around the room for my grandmother chastising myself for not asking exactly how many people she had sent invitations to.

"Land's sake, Sidney," Judith leaned over my shoulder in awe of the sight before us. "Did Marissa invite the whole county?" She laughed. "The Morgan's are here, the Kirby's," she leaned a bit closer. "Who is that with the Beeler's?" My eyes searched through the crowd for the Beeler's.

"I do not know. They have so any children, how can you tell?" I smirked.

"Their boys are always hanging around our place with my boys. And I am telling you, those two," she nodded toward the edge of the porch, "aren't the Beeler boys."

"I heard your son; Cameron is courting Nadine Beeler." I raised an eyebrow at her before turning away from the window.

"Yes, I suppose he is." She placed her hand on my arm. "Please do not misunderstand me. Nadine is a sweet girl, but she seems too soft for Cameron. She is always so quiet and has her nose in a book.

But Cameron, he's full of spitfire and more stubborn than ol' man Johnson's mule." She shook her head slightly.

"Perhaps that is a good thing. She can calm him down and maybe keep him in line." I tried to sound optimistic.

"She would be the first." Judith snickered about her youngest child.

"Good evening, Ms. Sidney." Charlotte Morgan leaned in and hugged me gently. "You look so lovely in blue. It really makes your eyes shine."

Charlotte's beautiful, thick dark hair cascaded over her shoulders and down her back in large bouncy curls. It was pulled back on the sides with silver clips with small amethyst stones embedded in them. She was wearing a beautiful dark purple gown trimmed in white lace.

"I am so happy you and Evan came. I have missed you." Charlotte was the closest to my age and we have become good friends over the last several years.

"Well, I would have stopped by sooner, but Evan is rarely home these days. His cousin, Senator Wilson is constantly pulling him to Boston. I am afraid it is going to put Evan behind here as our county representative, but he assures me he had everything in hand." She explained. "And Mrs. McKendrick, it is so nice to see you again."

"Good evening, Charlotte. How are your little ones?" Judith asked politely.

"Levi is into everything since he is stuck inside with this bitter cold weather and Adelaide is trying desperately to walk." She grinned thinking about her adorable children. "I believe she wants nothing more than to keep up with her big brother." She laughed. "They are enough to keep Kezia and I running all day long. I do not know how you managed a household full of boys. You are a stronger woman than I."

"Boys are always more spirited." Judith smiled over at me. "You will soon find out."

"I hope so," I was not sure how to respond to that.

"Mrs. Marshall," Abigail Beeler made her way through the growing crowd toward us with two handsome young men beside her who appeared to be in their late teens or early twenties.

"Good evening, Mrs. Beeler, how nice of you to join us." I greeted her.

"It is such a pleasure to see you. I wanted to introduce you to my sister's sons who are up here visiting with us from South Carolina." She gestured towards the taller of the two young men who was dressed in a dark grey suite. "This is my nephew, Dalton Hindsley." Her hand waved to the younger of the two. "And his younger brother, Luke." Luke was wearing a dark blue suit with a white shirt. Both had blond hair and sparkling blue eyes. Luke had a little bit of freckles around his nose that gave him a boyish charm.

"Good evening, ma'am." They said in unison bowing their heads politely at me.

"Welcome to Terrace Falls, gentleman. Please make yourselves at home." I smiled graciously at the two nervous young men.

"Thank you," they responded together.

"Go find your uncle and cousins. And mind your manners." Their aunt warned them before she let them leave.

"Yes'am," they hollered before disappearing into the crowd.

"I am surprised your nephews chose to visit in the wintertime." Judith remarked. "This must be unsettling for them."

"They are not happy about being here. They have never seen snow before." Abigail smiled. "But my sister had little choice."

"What do you mean?" I asked.

"My sister, Amelia wrote me a letter before Christmas asking if she could send her boys up here for a spell because the governor in South Carolina has called up the militia."

"I heard about that." I looked over at Charlotte. "Evan and Keifer were talking about that back in November."

"Yes, I remember." Charlotte looked concerned.

"Of course, my nephews were eager to join, but Amelia would have none of it. So, to keep them from doing something stupid, she sent them to me."

"I thought you and your family were from here. How did Amelia end up living in South Carolina?" Judith asked.

"She married a Southerner who went to West Point with our brother, Conrad. Lloyd was in the same class as Conrad and he came home with him a few times over the years and well," Abigail shrugged. "After they graduated, Lloyd and Amelia were married, and she moved to South Carolina."

"I cannot imagine living in such a place." Judith mumbled.

"Have you ever been there?" I was curious.

"Well, no. Stephen and I visited the Capital in Washington once and I have seen New York City twice. It was unbelievable. I could not get over how large it was." Judith explained.

"But oh, it was so beautiful and exciting when Evan took me last year. We had the most wonderful time." Charlotte beamed. "Have you ever been?"

"Yes, it was lovely." I didn't want to tell her how dreadful and dirty I found it — or that it would only get worse in the future.

More people than I believe I had ever seen were piled into our home. I was feeling overwhelmed and suffocated. As I made my way from one room to another, each one felt stuffier and more crowded than the last. I believed not only was every person in our county present, but it also appeared everyone from the surrounding counties were here as well.

Judith and Charlotte were near me all evening. As close as I was to my due date, neither of them was letting me out of their sight. They feared all the commotion was going to cause me to go into early labor. While I truly did not believe the commotion would do it, the heat and stifling thickness of the air was a certain candidate.

The sound of broken glass from the dining room drew my attention from what Charlotte was saying.

"What was that?" I stood and headed toward the sound of loud voices followed by my two faithful watchdogs.

From the entryway I could see a large gathering of men in the center of the room. Judith's sons were around the parameter making it difficult to see who was at the center of it.

"What you do not appear to comprehend sir, is that our governor is simply tired of our great state being bullied by the Black Republicans. He does not care if they agree with slavery or not, but it does not give them the right to continually raise our taxes to pay for

Northern industries." Exclaimed the loud voice with an obvious Southern drawl that I knew did not belong to my husband.

"Oh, God." I whispered looking over at my companions. "I was afraid of this."

"Why in the world Abigail thought bringing her Southern nephews to a social gathering full of Northerners was a good idea, is beyond me." Judith sighed audibly.

"Exactly how many slaves do you own?" I recognized the rough voice of Martin McKenzie.

"Zero." Another Southern voice spat back.

"But your Pa does. How many does your Pa own?" The anger and tone of Martin's voice grew louder.

"Do you realize how ignorant you sound, Mr. McKenzie? My nephews, like our host, were born and raised in the South. What belongs to their father's or their families, is not them or who they are." Mr. Beeler spat as Mr. Bennett stepped forward between the men.

I was proud of Mr. Beeler's voice rising above the crowd. Our guests were gathered around the unpleasantness and tempers were beginning to flare. My eyes searched desperately around the room for my husband or my grandmother. Unfortunately, my stature made it difficult for me to see over the broad shoulders and heads of many of our male guests.

"But their families own slaves." Mr. McKenzie spat.

"I don't give a damn who owns what." Mr. McKendrick's voice boomed. "Mr. McKenzie, I believe you have had enough to drink, and it has impaired your rational thinking."

"I beg your pardon." Mr. McKenzie sounded astounded by the accusation. "Sir, I make no apologies for my convictions. Human bondage is wrong."

"I never said otherwise. However, you are making a spectacle of yourself, Mr. McKenzie and that is disrespectful to our host." Mr. McKendrick growled, lifting Mr. McKenzie by the arm to his toes due to his sheer height and large frame. "Come." He pulled him towards the front door. "Let the cold air sober you up a bit."

Hushed murmurs and disgruntled remarks settled over the crowd. I felt an unease pass through the center of my chest. I was afraid of something like this. It seemed everywhere these days conversations revolved around the deeper and growing resentment between the North and South. My heart broke as I looked over the faces of friends and family and wondered if any of them had an inkling of how bad this dispute would get before it was all over.

I navigated my way through the crowd and found my husband standing near the opposite door, leading into the dining room where everything had been moved away to allow for dancing. I placed my hand lightly on his arm to get his attention.

"Darling," but I was quickly interrupted.

"Beg your pardon, sir. I apologize for my outburst." Dalton stood before my husband with his head bowed.

"Thank you, Mr. Hindsley." Keifer responded politely. "Would you and your brother join me for a moment in my study?"

Luke and Dalton nodded and made their way through the crowd behind my husband. I glanced back at Judith and Charlotte nodding to them, letting them know I would return. I was not sure if I should follow the gentlemen or not, but my curiosity got the best of me, and I needed to know what Keifer had to say.

Keifer appeared startled that I followed but did not say a word as I joined him with the boys in his office. He closed the door behind us and gestured to the boys to have a seat. I heard music begin again as the musicians started playing a lively tune to lighten the mood. It was a surefire way of insuring everyone would be distracted by the dancing to care about some silly squabble amongst the men.

"Please, have a seat." Keifer gestured to the boys towards the chairs beside the hearth fire. "Did your aunt or uncle tell you anything about me before you arrived this evening?"

"Only that you are a doctor, sir." Dalton spoke up.

"Yes, I am. But what you may not know is that I was born and raised on a large rice plantation on the outskirts of Savannah. My family home is still there." The boys' eyes widened. "I understand how uneasy it feels to be in unknown territory."

"Yes, sir. It does." Luke agreed. "It feels like being in a foreign country." Keifer nodded in agreement.

"Yes, it can at times. I came up here for medical school at the university and stayed because of my wife, Sidney." Keifer nodded in my direction. "These are good people here. Still, it has taken time for many of them to accept me."

"My aunt said you are the best doctor in the state of Massachusetts." Dalton informed us.

"He is," I agreed proudly.

"I do my best." Keifer blushed. "But there are still a few in this county who continue to view me as a Southerner first and foremost. I understand how you both must feel, both here tonight and in general. The hostilities between the Southern states and Northern states, the Democratic party and the Republicans has been challenging for everyone."

"Your aunt said you gentlemen were sent here because you wish to join your state militia." I recognized.

"Yes, ma'am." They answered in unison.

"If the Southern states succeed, will you rejoin your family in Savannah, sir?" Luke asked.

"We plan on visiting them this summer so they can meet our child." Keifer reached over and took my hand. "However, my place is here with my wife. My brother-in-law is quite capable of running Gable Gardens on behalf of my family."

"But do you not feel you are betraying your kin?" Dalton asked hesitantly.

"No. I do not. My wife is my main priority. Still, I do miss my family, and we have had some heated discussions over the climate lately." Keifer half-heartedly chuckled. "But I feel strongly in supporting the family I am building here." He shrugged.

"Our Pa would never forgive us if we did not fight for South Carolina if it comes to it." Dalton quipped.

"But Ma will skin us if we do." Luke laughed.

"I understand how she feels." I looked sternly at both young men as Keifer smirked over at me.

"What I am trying to convey, gentlemen, is that you are not as alone as you think. If you find yourselves feeling frustrated and isolated here, please do not hesitate to stop by. You are always welcome at Terrace Falls." Keifer stood back up and walked towards the door. "Now, we should rejoin the party. There are plenty of beautiful Northern ladies here in need of a partner on the dance floor.

"Thank you, sir." Dalton and Luke expressed their gratitude with wide smiles and bowing their heads to my husband as they left his office.

"And how are you feeling, my darling?" Keifer reached for my hands as I approached him.

"Tired," I squeezed his hand before rubbing the small of my back. "I need to find somewhere to sit down for a moment." I leaned over and kissed him on the cheek.

"Please do not overdo it." He placed his hand gently on the side of my protruding belly.

"I promise," I kissed him once again on the cheek before exiting his study. He closed the door and followed me back to the party.

9

FRIDAY, FEBRUARY 21, 2020

RUMORS WERE FLOODING THE airwaves and social media about the potentially fatal COVID – 19 virus that was rapidly spreading across the globe. Most media outlets claimed it was released from a lab in China. The evidence was overwhelming, but who really knew the truth? It was nearly impossible to decipher the truth from the false narrative being released by the vultures on one side of the aisle in Washington D.C. It all felt like propaganda of some alternate universe.

Everything had to be taken with a grain of salt.

It appeared the Democrat party did not simply disagree with the Republican President Donald Trump — they loathed him with an unfettered vengeance. Their hatred seemed to be growing simply because he refused to play by their rules and was more interested in doing what was right for the American people rather than lining his own pockets like every other politician's false face.

I stretched my back and sighed heavily. My eyes were burning. I rubbed them tiredly. I had been studying all day after my morning classes. I was almost through my second pot of coffee and had only eaten a small bowl of oatmeal that morning before I left for campus. My head was pounding, and I was running solely on caffeine.

This term our university had decided to require all students — undergraduate and graduate to take a new Social Justice class. While undergraduates were together for their course studies, the graduate students working towards their masters, doctorates, or in medical school were all tossed in together. It became clear very quickly that I was going to have a lot of difficulties in this class — not because it was difficult — but because I was white.

The blatant racism and bigotry against anyone who was white, heterosexual, and conservative screamed off the pages of the course material. It was left leaning liberal nonsense. It made me cringe with disgust. I had already had a heated disagreement with my professor — a progressive liberal black lesbian. She had wanted — actually demanded that if I did not admit I was born with white privilege, that I am a white supremist, and that I am racist, I would fail the course. I had never been so insulted and disgusted in my life. I absolutely refused to do so.

So, she failed me on the assignment, and I appealed it to the Dean. Since the class, hence assignments were 'pass or fail' it was overturned. But her attitude towards me only grew worse. I tossed my pen down on my desk in frustration. I rested my head down on my desk and fought the urge to scream.

"Are you alright?" Landon walked through the front door and placed his keys on the side table.

"I hate this class." I sat up and finished off the rest of the coffee in my mug.

"Social Justice?" he rolled his eyes.

"How did you guess?" I snorted.

"Just write whatever bullshit you have to just to pass the class." Landon approached me and began to gently yet firmly rub my shoulders.

"It goes against every fiber of my being." I began to relax under his strong fingers.

"Mine too." He admitted. "But you must remember, this is one class and bigoted racist professor is not worth blowing your entire medical career."

"I just have a difficult time lying, especially when someone accuses me of something simply because I am white." I scoffed. "Tell me again how reverse racism, isn't racism?"

"Do you know what is worse than being a white woman these days?"

"What?"

"Being a white man," he retorted. "I had some Hispanic woman in the cafeteria today tell me I was eating 'white food' for lunch." Landon laughed and I joined in. "What the hell is 'white food'?"

"That is a new one." I kept giggling. "What were you eating?"

"Well, we were out of lunchmeat. So, I made me a peanut butter and jelly sandwich and packed it with some chips, an apple, and a couple chocolate chip cookies." He shrugged. "Who knew?"

"I didn't". I shook my head in disbelief.

Landon and I fixed dinner together. He turned on some music while I chopped up an onion and mushrooms for the spaghetti sauce. Landon was being goofy, singing along off key while putting the French bread on the baking sheet. He cut it in half and spread the butter across it. He playfully bumped into me grinning before he waltzed over to the refrigerator.

"You are such a dork." I laughed.

"You love me." He grinned over at me and grabbed the mozzarella cheese and closed the door.

"Yes, I do." I winked at him as I tossed him the garlic powder. "Go easy on it."

"Yes, dear." He mocked with an eye roll. "What time are your sister and Jackson coming over?"

"We have about 30 minutes." I glanced at the clock on the stove.

"Do you want me to make the salad?"

"That would be great." I wiped my hands on my apron and pulled the big pot from the lower cabinet. I filled it with water and set it on the stove. I added a splash of canola oil so the noodles would not stick together.

"Are they bringing dessert?" Landon started chopping the lettuce.

"Yes."

"Do you know what?"

"No clue." I shrugged, tossing the onion and mushrooms into the sauce before starting on the garlic.

"Hopefully, it's something Emily made, or she picked up at the store."" He snickered.

"Stop," I playfully smacked his arm lightly. "Her skills in the kitchen have improved greatly." I smiled at him.

"Emily has improved both your cooking skills." The smirk on his face was annoying only because it was well deserved. "When I met you, you couldn't boil water."

"Yeah, like I had a great role model for cooking." We both knew my own mother could not make toast. She was always focused on her career, and our childhood dinners were mostly frozen meals we could pop in the oven or fast food.

"But look at her career." Landon had always been impressed by my mother's credentials and skills. He viewed her as a perfect mentor. I completely disagreed. Yes, she was a highly skilled pediatrician and highly respected in her field, but she had failed miserably as a mother. In my opinion, Amy could not hold a candle to Emily in that area.

"Look at what it cost her." I stated the obvious.

My parents had gone through a nasty divorce after more than twenty years of marriage. My mother moved from our family estate in Chicago to Seattle shortly afterward. Our dad went through a horrible relationship that almost ended in marriage, but thankfully he saw her true colors at the rehearsal dinner and called the whole thing off. Since then, he has been extremely reluctant to trust any woman. I couldn't blame him.

"I did not say I wanted to imitate her life." He rolled his eyes with a smirk. "And I was referring to her professional accomplishments, not her personal ones."

"Because she has no personal ones." I snorted, tossing the crushed garlic into the pot.

"Oh, I don't know." Landon shrugged one shoulder spreading the cheese across the garlic butter. "Her three children are successful in their own right, and didn't she just get engaged to a pediatric surgeon? Most women would be thrilled at such a prospect." He snorted.

"I suppose so," I tossed the hand towel at him. "I guess I am one of the lucky ones, Dr. Harrison."

"Nah," he leaned over and kissed me quickly. "I am."

Landon put the French bread in the oven and checked the water for the noodles. It was finally boiling so he placed the spaghetti noodles in the pot. He leaned against the counter and watched me for a few minutes.

"I really am, you know." He reached out and took my hands pulling me towards him. He wrapped his arms around my waist and kissed me deeply. I melted into him.

"I love you." I whispered.

"I love you, too."

I leaned my head against his chest. I could feel the steady rhythm of his heartbeat through his hooded sweatshirt. It was strong and peaceful. I felt safe and secure in his arms. It was home to me and there was nowhere else I would rather be.

The doorbell rang, breaking my train of thought. I sighed heavily and patted Landon on the chest. I smiled into his eyes and kissed him lightly before letting me go.

"Stir the sauce." I teased on my way to the door.

"Yes, ma'am." He called after me.

The cold February wind rushed into our home like an unwelcome guest as soon as I opened the door. Jocelyn and Jackson had snowflakes scattered about their hair and shoulders. The temperature had fallen steadily throughout the day. Jocelyn handed me a covered cake carrier with a hearty grin.

"Hello darling," I hugged my sister and then her husband. "Good evening."

"It is freezing," Jocelyn said hurrying past me. Jackson smiled and closed the door behind them.

"It smells good in here." Jackson remarked taking off his coat and handing it to me. He wandered off towards the kitchen while I also took my sister's coat and hung them up in the small closet by the front door.

"How are you doing?" I asked as we made our way towards the kitchen.

"Good," she took my arm in hers. "I am glad it is Friday. It has been a long week."

"You are almost done." I encouraged her.

Landon was cutting up the tomatoes for the salad and Jackson had rolled up his sleeves and started slicing the eggs when we entered the kitchen.

"You don't have to do that," I attempted to take the knife from my brother-in-law and nudged him out of the way. But he refused and even pushed me back with his hip giggling at me.

"This is a knife, not a scalpel." He quipped.

"Is he always this brazen," I looked over at my sister for help.

"Yes. Always." She shrugged and rolled her eyes.

"So, what did you bring for dessert?" I set the carrier on the counter and lifted the top off it.

"It's a chocolate whipped cream cake." She boasted. "Emily gave me the recipe."

"But you made it?" Landon looked at her with a horrified expression making us all laugh.

"Shut up," my sister smacked him on the arm. "For that, you don't get any."

"Promise," Landon quipped with a sly grin.

"And you plan to marry this man?" Jocelyn shook her head looking at me.

"Eh," I shrugged. "He is kinda cute."

"Looks fade," Jocelyn stuck her tongue out at Landon.

"Ouch," he pretended to be offended. "That hurt."

"Truth usually does," my little sister piped back.

"Okay, okay. Everyone to their corner." Jackson – always the peacemaker, teased them.

I stirred the sauce and checked the noodles. Turning off the stove, I drained the noodles and poured the sauce into a bowl with a ladle. I placed it on our small dining table and let out a deep breath looking over at my small family in the kitchen. I listened to the three of them teasing and joking with each other and felt completely happy.

The four of us gathered around the table, passing the dishes and filling our plates. Jackson and Landon piled the spaghetti high on their plates and covered it with parmesan cheese. Jocelyn and I watched them in amazement, wondering how they could manage to consume all they did, and both remained trim and ripped.

It wasn't fair.

"So, what have you two heard at the hospital about this new virus?" Jackson inquired.

"Not much, really." Landon replied between bites. "I know they have started quarantining people who have tested positive for it."

"Really?" Jocelyn raised an eyebrow. "What does that mean?"

"I am not sure, but I believe this is going to get much worse before it gets better." I told her. "Last week they started making us wear surgical masks in the hospital."

"When around patients with the virus?" Jackson asked.

"No. Any time we are inside the hospital." Landon explained.

"You must be joking." Jocelyn looked disgusted. "Why? They do not stop germs or small particles."

"I know," I scoffed. "Believe me, many doctors and nurses have explained that until they are blue in the face, but the hospital board is adamant."

"That must be terribly uncomfortable." Jocelyn noted.

"It is." I assured her. "But after the first COVID-19 death occurred last week after that flight from Wuhan, people started to panic."

"This virus is said to have already killed hundreds in China, but who knows if that is true or not. You cannot believe most things you see on TV or social media." Jackson commented.

"Great," I muttered.

"Did you see that President Trump was acquitted on both articles of impeachment?" Jackson asked shifting the subject.

"I heard that." Landon tore off a piece from the corner of his bread. "They were ridiculous charges in the first place." He huffed.

"I know," Jackson agreed.

"What were the charges?" I rarely followed politics.

"What was it, abuse of power and obstruction of Congress?" Landon looked over at Jackson for confirmation.

"I believe so. I know he was acquitted by the Senate but is still considered impeached by the House." Jackson rolled his eyes. "The Democrat party is going to try everything to remove him from office."

"And stop his reelection." Jocelyn added.

"I would not put anything past them." Landon snorted. "They are delusional at best." He tore another piece off his bread. "Any party that would choose to have Schiff, Omar, AOC, Walters, and Pelosi represent them, makes me want to run in the other direction."

"Agreed." As little as I did know about politics, I knew those far left-wing nutjobs were perpetual liars, hypocrites, delusional, ignorant, and never to be trusted regarding anything and everything.

"Did you hear President Trump fired Lt. Col Alexander Vindman?" Jackson laughed. "Serves him right for testifying against President Trump during his insubordination trial — the damn turncoat."

"Did you hear about gas line rupture in southern Texas today?" Landon inquired.

"Wasn't there a shooting in Texas recently?" I asked. "I thought I saw something about it."

"No. You are thinking of Atlanta." Jackson corrected me. "One of those Real Housewives star's restaurant, I think."

"I heard about that." Landon remarked. "A couple people were shot, but nothing fatal, thank goodness."

"No. No." My sister chimed in. "The shooting in Texas about two weeks ago — at A & M, I believe. It happened in one of the residence halls. The gunman killed two people and injured a baby if I remember correctly. I only recalled reading about it because it was the same day as that shooting in California on that Greyhound bus. The shooter managed to kill one person and injured several others before the passengers took him down."

"At least there are some good people still in this world." I sighed wearily.

"Yes, it seems after they took the gunman down and got him subdued, they administered first aid to the wounded passengers until the first responders could take over." Jocelyn informed us.

"I do not understand what this world is coming too." Landon shook his head slightly before taking another bite of his salad.

"Oh, I don't know." Jackson sighed. "The violence has always been there, it's simply more publicized now due to social media. Instead of a half dozen reputable journalists that the country could count on for a mostly unbiased reporting of events, we are now confronted with hundreds if not thousands of unreputable influencers who do not have three working brain cells amongst them." He chuckled.

"The creation of social media has proven to be downfall of society." Jocelyn stated. "It has taken all the humanity out of being human as people hide behind keyboards spewing hate towards strangers and seem to have forgotten how to interact with civility in real life."

"I completely agree with you." I admitted. "People have no personable skills today."

"I could not agree with you more." Jackson reiterated.

"You all sound like my grandparents." Landon laughed. "One would never guess you all are in your twenties."

"Perhaps, we are old souls." Jackson smirked at his wife and then over at me. My sister and I both snorted accidentally at his words and giggled.

"What?" Landon looked around the table. "What did I miss?"

"Nothing, dear." I straightened myself up in my chair.

"Okay," Landon looked around at us with an odd expression. "If you say so."

Jocelyn and I cleaned up the dishes while Landon and Jackson settled into the living room. Landon had the fire burning brightly and warmly in the hearth and Jackson had selected a movie. Jocelyn had cut up the dessert and handed it out to everyone before joining Jackson on the couch. I curled up beside Landon on the loveseat and tossed a throw blanket over my legs.

"What movie did you pick?" I asked, cutting into my piece.

"An oldie but a goodie." Jackson grinned mischievously. "Something we have not watched in a long while." He fiddled with the remotes.

The first notes of music drifted from the television as the bright colors filled the screen, and I knew immediately what film he had put on.

"*Gone with the Wind,*" I chuckled. "My favorite."

"I know," Landon rolled his eyes over at Jackson.

"Really? You had to go there?" Jocelyn smirked.

"I could not resist." Jackson shrugged with his arm holding my sister closely. "I know it is also Jocelyn's favorite book and movie. I believe you over romanticize the era."

"Perhaps I do, but I do not believe you could claim the same about my sister." Jocelyn nudged him gently.

"Nonsense," I grinned over at her blinking back some unfallen tears. "I love *Clark Gable* as Rhett Butler. He's such a handsome scoundrel."

I snuggled against Landon as Scarlett tormented the Tarleton twins. My mind drifted back to another time, another place, to a small estate with a large porch very similar to the one on the screen. I could feel the heavy fabric against my skin, the awkward broad hoops of my skirts, and the sound of my grandmother humming softly while sewing next to the blazing hearth.

My hand dropped to my flat stomach. I unconsciously gripped the front of my sweatshirt and pinched my lips trying in vain to stop them from quivering. I felt empty. My precious baby, my round belly, my swollen ankles — were waiting for me in another time and place. I glanced over to see my sister eyeing me carefully. She mouthed 'are you okay?" I nodded with a painful smile. I knew she knew what I was thinking about.

The sound of Mammy yelling at Scarlett over her dress made me smile. She reminded me of Marta, our loving housekeeper and my personal attendant. She helped me dress, fix my hair, and attend to my baths. She was bold, kind, loving, and held a motherly figure in my life there. She was an amazing sounding board but never called me out the way my grandmother did when I was immature, or stubborn. Only Marissa or Keifer crossed that line, and I loved them both for it.

I lost myself in the film, hating to admit how much I could identify with Scarlett. She was strong-willed, sassy, and independent. All the things Keifer and Marissa had accused me of from time to time. I believe it was traits that Marissa loved about me, but qualities I am sure my husband wished I did not entail.

I chuckled to myself about how the various characters in the movie had certain traits of those I loved and cared for in my *other* world. The daring, honorable, yet sometimes foolish men. The sweet, often meek ladies and still others with a fire in their soul to reclaim their lives.

What would I be like after the war? How was I going to manage our estate through the war? How could I survive without Keifer beside me? How could I dare to bring my son into a world that was falling apart before my eyes? Were my shoulders broad and strong enough to be everything to everyone for the duration?

I had no answers.

10

FRIDAY, FEBRARY 24, 1860

THE EARLY MORNING LIGHT barely broke through the heavily clouded sky outside my bay window. My hands immediately carassed my enlarged abdomon. A sense of comfort and calm flooded over me as I felt my unborn son stretch his limbs to start the new day. I let out the breath I had not realized I was holding.

It was no longer a matter of the vast time differences between my two existences, the physical differences had become jaring as well. My flat stomach in the twenty-first century felt so bizarre in contrast to my eighth month pregnant body in the nineteenth century. What was once an occurance that could be described as an oddity, now felt like a catapult between my lives.

My mind was a blur as I ran my hand over my enlarged belly. Peace and calm settled over me. The dim light cast a soft warmth about our rustic yet elagant bedroom. I sighed heavily and tossed the quilted covers aside. I swung my legs over to the side of the bed and held onto the bedpost to ease myself over the side of the bed. I slid off the side as my stocking toes reached the small step stool beside the bed.

"Mizdress," Marta opend my bedroom door and quickly scampered towards me. "Pleas, be kareful." She cautioned taking my arm.

"Marta, really," I chuckled slightly with exasperation. "I am pregnant, not an invalid. I can certainly manage to get myelf out of bed in the morning."

"Mizdress." She took ahold of my arm and helped me step down. "Ya pains kin star ana' dime." The concern was evident in her eyes.

"Please," I attempted to wave off her concern while also acknowledging it. "I still have a few weeks to go."

"Well, less make shur dat lil angel stays where dey are til dey are reada ta meet us." She smiled lovingly.

"I shall do my best." I promised her.

Marta helped me dress and fix my hair for the day. The stays felt cumbersome and I could hardly breathe. A part of me longed for, even envied the loose flowing maternity clothes of the twenty-first century. This corset felt as if it was pushing my son up against my spine in the most uncomfortable way possible.

Naomi had a full spread of breakfast laid on the dining room table. The smell of hot fresh buttermilk bisquets and coffee hung in the air. My stomach growled in anticipation as I took my seat. My grandmother handed me a bowl of scrambled eggs.

"Good morning, darling. How did you sleep?" she sipped her coffee reading the morning Boston newspaper.

"As best to be expected considering I feel like a beached whale." I smirked fixing my plate. "I do not believe I shall ever be comfortable again."

"Only a short while longer." She assured me. "Would you care to ride into town with me after breakfast?"

"I would love to." I smiled. "It would be nice to get out of the house for a while." My eyes scanned over the room. "Has Keifer already left?"

"Yes. He went out to the Petraits' place this morning before dawn. Their youngest son, Caleb broke out in a high fever. Raymond sent his fieldhand, Harmond to fetch your husband." She explained.

The Petraits' lived on a small farm outside of Braintree. They were polite, but kept to themselves a great deal. Their abolitionist views had pushed the boundaries of tolerance with most of the families in our town. We lived in a free state, but that did not mean that the folks who lived here wanted free blacks from the South flooding the North. Most were adamantly against it. While blacks were accepted amongst our community, they were hired help and paid a fair wage. The Petraits' outspoken bluster over the last year had alienated them from most within our community.

The divide grew stronger as the anomosity, and hostility grew between the Republican's in the North and the Democrats in the South, the deeper the wounds cut. It was almost comical in a nonhumorous way how little things have truly changed a century and a half later. The only difference was the lines were not as clearly defined. Instead of a few border states, a century and a half later we were pitching cities against suburban and rural America.

"I hope it is nothing serious." I managed trying to bring my thoughts back to the present.

"I am sure it is simply a cold." She waved her hand dismissively. "You know how Paula tends to overreact whenever any of her children sneeze." She rolled her eyes.

Ned brought the carriage around to the front porch. My grandmother and I, wrapped in our woolen caplets and muffs climbed up into the carriage with Ned's assistance. I was thrilled to venture beyond my own gardens. It felt like Keifer had restricted my travel since Christmas out of fear for our child.

The cold breeze wrapped around us as we took our seat and adjusted the quilt across our legs. The sun continued to flirt with the clouds without making its strong presence known. I was eager for Spring to arrive. I was tired of these gloomy days and cold breezes that seemed to rip through my clothes despite the multiple layers.

Still, the overcast morning did not seem to hinder people in our town from socializing and completing their errands. The town square was bustling with activity. As soon as we reached the center of town, my grandmother said she needed to stop by the bank to handle a simple transaction — to speak with Mr. Bennet alone in my opinion.

I simply smiled knowingly at her as she smirked at me and crossed the street to the bank promising to meet me at the mercantile aftwerwards.

I had written a letter to my eldest brother, Patrick's wife, Annabelle and wanted to make sure it left with the afternoon post. I knew the afternoon carriage would be here around two and travel to Boston before it began its long journey by railroad to Chicago.

I handed the letter to Mr. Howard, the owner of the mercantile, and started browsing through the yards of new brightly colored Spring fabrics that had just arrived. I was considering which ones were most appealing for a new dress I was thinking about designing for me to greet Keifer's family this upcoming summer when I heard a soft voice from behind.

"Good day, Mrs. Marshall." I turned to see Charlotte standing behind me. "How are you feeling?"

"Hello, Mrs. Morgan," I addressed her formally due to the crowd in small store. "I am doing well. I was thinking of a making new dress to wear to my in-laws this summer." I mentioned casually.

"Oh, dear." Charlotte's face clouded over as she looked around. "Would you mind stepping outside for a moment. It is so crowded in here today." She waved her hand dismissively.

"Yes," I was a bit confused, but followed her to outside to the extended porch in front of the store.

"Is everything all right, dear?" I questioned stepping outside.

"Please tell me you are not still entertaining the notion of traveling South this summer, especially after what happened at the party. You saw what those boys were like. Can you fathom being surrounded by such hostilities with no escape? Not to mention traveling with a young babe." Her face was etched with concern.

"Charlotte," I lowered my voice and guided her over to the far corner away from others. "You act as if I have a say in this."

"Refuse to go." She said it like it was just that simple.

"As if you could do the same to Evan." I eyed her carefully. "Your husband is much like mine in that sense. They are the head of our households and while we can persuade them occassionally to our way of thinking, when it comes to their families they can be quite irrational." Charlotte, recalling her own struggles with her husband's family, his cousin in particular, simply nodded.

"But I am worried for you and the babe. It is not safe for either of you." Her voice was barely a whisper.

"I appreciate that," I took her hands in mind and squeezed them. "But I do trust my husband. I know Keifer would never put me or our child in harms way." She nodded in agreement.

"All the same." She smiled slightly. "You will write me a letter each week, even if it is only a few lines, you will let me know you are all alive and well." She squeezed my hands back.

"I promise. I will." I hugged her thightly.

"If I do not hear from you, you realize I will send the Union cavalry to Savannah after you." She released me with a smile, but I could also see the seriousness in her eyes.

"Good day, Ms. Charlotte darling. How lovely to see you." My grandmother crossed the street towards us. I had not noticed her until she was right beside us.

"Hello Mrs. Timmons. You look very happy today." I unconsciously snorted thinking Mr. Bennett to be the cause of my grandmother's smile and the lightness in her step.

"And how is Mr. Bennett doing today?" I grinned.

"Good," she playfully rolled her eyes in my direction. "He shall be joining us for dinner this evening."

"Wonderful. I shall inform Naomi upon our return." I glanced towards Charlotte tying not to laugh.

"Ms. Charlotte, how are your little ones?" My grandmother changed the subject gracefully.

"They are doing well, thank you for asking." She nodded. "I was just expressing my concerns about Sidney traveling to Savannah in the upcoming months with a young babe." I knew Charlotte was pulling out all the stops by playing on my grandmother's same fear.

"Yes, I share your concerns, Charlotte. I do not believe it will be safe for either of them, which is why I will join them at the end of summer before they journey to Chicago." She explained.

"Chicago?" Charlotte's head jerked around abruptly. "Sidney, why are you journeying to Chicago? And how long will you be gone?" I hated the sadness that rose in her eyes. She was one of my dearest friends and I would miss her terribly whilst away.

"We shall return after the new year." I carefully explained.

"What?" her eyes widened in surprise.

"I know," I reached for her hand. "But as we have agreed, I will write. The time will fly by." I promised.

Her eyes glistened with unshed tears, but she nodded squeezing my hand.

"Will you and Evan join us and Mr. Bennett for supper this evening?" I offered. "It will allow us to spend some quality time catching up." Charlotte's smiled brightened at the invitation.

"We would love to." She assured me. "Four?"

"Four would be lovely." My grandmother chimmed in before turning towards me. "Did you take care of your errands or do you need more time?"

"I mailed my letter to Annabelle. I was looking at the new fabics Mr. Howard recently got in, but I am unsure if they are what I want for my new gown for our trip." I explained.

"Certainly something we need to decide upon after the babe is born." My grandmother claimed. "But now we have other things to attend too." She turned back to Charlotte. "We look forward to seeing you this evening." I hugged Charlotte briefly before Ned helped me back into the carriage.

"I had not realized you had decided to join us in Chicago." I said as soon as Ned started down the bumpy road.

"Sidney my dear," she rested her hand on my arm. "I have given it a lot of thought and knowing everything that I do, I decided I wanted to see my grandsons." I noticed she didn't mention seeing my father — her son.

"Grandmother," I fought back the tears burning behind my eyes. "I am thrilled you will be joining us."

"I am glad." She chuckled softly. "I figure I have one last adventure in these old bones."

"You are not old." I said emphatically.

"Perhaps not in your other world, but in this one my journey is almost over." She reasoned. "Tell me," she patted my arm before straightening her shoulders defiently. "When is my doom's day."

"What?" I could not believe my ears.

"Oh, do not act surprised." She laughed heartily. "With all your fancy computers and how much you love research, have you not stumpled upon the date of my demise?" My eyes immediately dropped in shame. "So, you do know." I looked up at her and eyes widened. "It's okay," she patted my arm lovingly again. "I do not want to know." She nodded her head slowly. "Yes, it is best I do not know."

"Grandmother," I started, but she held up her hand.

"Life is a blessing and I plan to live every day to its fullest." The smile returned to her eyes.

"I suppose that is why Mr. Bennett is joining us for dinner then." I smirked.

"Yes, I suppose it is." Her smile widened.

Naomi cooked a proper feast for our impromtu dinner party. Keifer arrived home shortly before our guests arrived. He seemed relieved for the distraction after what appeared to be a long morning with the Petraits'. He quickly poured himself a brandy and warmed himself by the hearth.

"Are you sure you are alright?" I inquired watching him carefully.

"I will be," his voice was rough with a sharpe edge.

"I am sorry, darling." I approached his side and placed my hand on his arm. "I know they can be difficult."

"Difficult?" My husband scoffed and finished off the rest of his brandy in one shot. He walked over to the canister and refilled his glass.

"Keifer, we have guests coming. You may want to slow down." I regretted the words as soon as they passed my lips.

"Sidney, you know I love you." He slowly approached me and took my hand in his. "I am only here," he waved his glass hand about dismissively splashing a bit of brandy on the floor, that I pretended not to notice. "Because of you. I am a Southener, born and raised. I am proud of my heritage, just as you are of yours."

"Of course, my love." I whispered.

"And I will be damned if that low-life abolishionist scum," his words trailed off as my grandmother entered the room.

"Do not mind me," she waved him off and helped herself to a small brandy. "I cannot say I think very highly of those who force their views down another's throat."

"Evening, grandmother." My husband muttered before quickly finishing his brandy. He set his glass down on the small end table. "Please excuse me while I change for dinner."

Without another word he walked heavily out of the parlor. Neither my grandmother nor I said anything until we heard the heavy sound of our bedroom door closing upstairs.

"This should be a fine evening." My grandmother shot back her brandy and refilled her glass.

"My," I sighed heavily. "Sometimes I am envious of the women who are blissfully unaware of fetal alcohol syndrome." I muttered under my breath thinking how I could use a drink myself.

"Excuse me?" my grandmother arched an eyebrow.

"Nevermind," it occurred to me that the disorder was something she would not be aware of in either of her lives. "I hate seeing him like this. I was afraid he would come home in foul mood after visiting with the Petraits." I sat down in the rocking chair next to the hearth.

Mr. Bennett arrived about an hour later. He was in a joyful mood and his boisterous laugh echoed from the foyer as he laughed at something Ned had said. I smiled over at my grandmother as she rose to greet him. I prayed Mr. Bennett's mood would be contagious and help Keifer shift his before his foul mood tarnished the evening.

Heavy footsteps on the stairs alerted us to Keifer's reemergence from our upstairs hideaway. I was hoping his mood had improved during his respet of solitude.

"Good evening, Edmund." Keifer extended his hand with a smile that did not appear forced. I immediately wondered if he had hit the canister of brandy upstairs as well.

"How are you this evening, Doc?" Mr. Bennett beamed. "I hope you do not mind the intrusion, but I could not decline Naomi's good cooking when I received an invitation from Marissa this morning."

"We are happy to share your company, Edmund. As always." My husband guided him into the parlor and poured them each a glass of brandy.

"Thank you, Doc." Mr. Bennett accepted the glass and sat down beside the hearth.

"I extended an invitation to Evan and Charlotte Morgan this morning as well."

"Wonderful," Mr. Bennett beamed. "They are splendid company."

My grandmother and I left the men in the parlor excusing ourselves to go check on dinner. Naomi was bustling around with the help of Marta. Wanda was drifting between the kitchen and dining room setting the table and lighting the candles. Ned stocked the fire in the dining room and cleaned up some scattered ashes.

"Everything smells wonderful," I remarked peaking into the pot.

"Scoot," Naomi nudged me aside. "Ah's let ya no whin dis reada."

"Fine," I smirked ushering my grandmother out of the kitchen alongside me. "I guess we are not needed in here." I laughed.

I heard the sound of hoofs and carriage wheels approaching the front of the house. My grandmother and I stepped out onto the porch to welcome Evan and Charlotte. Evan emerged first and helped his young wife out of the carriage. Charlotte was a vision of beauty in her sage green gown.

"Good evening Evan," I greeted them. "Charlotte, you look lovely."

"As do you, as always Sidney." She smiled. "And Marissa, it is so nice to see you again."

"Charlotte, you are a dear. I enjoy your visits. You remind me of what it was like to be young and vivacious." My grandmother laughed taking Charlotte's hand ad leading her into the house.

"How was your day, Mr. Morgan." I took Evan's arm and followed his wife and my grandmother up the steps into the house.

"Tiresome," Evan chuckled. "But as they say, there is no rest for the wicked."

"I suppose not." I agreed.

The four of us joined my husband and Mr. Bennett in the parlor after Ned took Charlotte and Evan's cloaks and head covers. The two were more than halfway through the canister of brandy and feeling very jovial. The hearty laughter filled the room.

"Good evening, Doc. Mr. Bennett." Evan walked over to the canister and helped himself to a glass of brandy.

"Evan," Keifer and Mr. Bennett both responded with a raised glass.

Charlotte joined her husband on the chaise lounge while my grandmother and I sat down on the other. Keifer and Mr. Bennett's faces were already flushed with drink, but their spirits were high.

"The Doc here had a difficult morning tending to the Petraits." Mr. Bennett swayed a bit in his chair and I wondered if he would be conscious enough to join us for dinner.

"Tis nothing," Keifer belched softly. "Excuse me." He muttered with a grin.

"Nonsense. We are all aware of the disposition of Mr. Petraits and his kin." Evan joined in.

"Ah, they are quite disagreeable." Hiccupped Mr. Bennett. "I beg your pardon." He bowed his head towards us ladies. I tried to suppress a grin.

"What did Mr. Petraits say to you?" Charlotte inquired almost hesitantly.

"Charlotte," Evan looked at her sternly.

"Do not worry, Evan." Keifer pressed. "My wife is more outspoken than your dear wife could ever think to be." My grandmother laughed aloud and I felt my face flush in embarrassment.

"Perhaps," I shrugged nonchalantly not wanting anyone to think of me as anything less than a lady of high moral standing.

"Women should be allowed to speak their minds." My grandmother emphasized. "This notion that simply because we are females, we have no ability to think for ourselves or have an opinion is ludicrous."

"I could not agree more." I smiled over at my grandmother and noticed Charlotte smiling widely at her husband.

"We have a couple forward thinking ladies in our midst." Evan tried unsuccessfully to laugh it off, but it was clear he was not prepared to have a wife who spoke her mind or offered opinions.

"Petraits is a damn fool." Mr. Bennett declared. "He is constantly stirring up trouble when he visits town and I have seen people actively avoid him."

"That does not surprise me." My husband muttered. "I do my best to remain professional, but I loathe it when I receive calls for their ailments."

"And it appears they have a new one each week." I added.

"Mrs. Petraits is nothing short of a hypochondriac." My grandmother chimed in. "She always has been. She thrives on being the center of attention and her behavior only worsens with time."

"What a sad life." Charlotte's soft mouth frowned slightly.

"Sad?" my grandmother scoffed. "Nonsense. The vile woman thrives on her own discontent."

"I hope Mr. Petraits remain civilized during your visit?" Evan inquired.

"Hardly," Keifer took another long draw from his glass of brandy. "But as payment for suffering his intolerable behavior, I charged him twice as much as my normal rate."

"Keifer," I was genuinely surprised by his actions. "How could you?"

"Easily," he shrugged. "His behavior was insufferable. And doubling my charge was preferable to breaking his nose." He raised an eyebrow at me. I could not stiffle my laugh.

"Then I must inquire, what on earth did he say that upset you so?" My grandmother's brow furrowed.

"After I examined his son and assured Raymond and Paula that young Caleb had nothing more than a mere cold, Paula offered me a cup of tea. Feeling obligated, I joined them in the parlor for spell and it quickly escalated. Raymond asked if it was true that my family hailed from Savannah, which everyone around these parts are well aware of." Keifer's tone took on a sharp edge. "After I nodded he inquired as to whether my family owned slaves. I then announced that I had other patients that I needed to attend to, stood up and excused myself."

"As you should have," Mr. Bennett agreed.

"It should have concluded there, but Raymond was insistant. He asked if I thought it was right for one person to hold another in bondage. At that point, I simply demanded payment, took it and left. But not before he informed me that my family, myself included were doomed to hell for owning slaves and stated that I had irreparably tarnished the Timmons name."

"I am sorry, my love." I reached over and placed my hand over his.

"Sully the Timmons name? Ha!" My grandmother scoffed. "Son, we have always been proud to call you family. If Sidney had married someone as distainful as Raymond Petraits I would have disowned and disinherited her immediately."

"Indeed," Mr. Bennett agreed. "Thankfully, none of my sons found a woman as wretched as Paula Petraits."

"Well, thankfully our family members have much better taste and more sense." Mr. Morgan smiled attempting to lessen the tension that hovered over the room.

"I understand there are those whose marriages are arranged, or marry out of obligation. Thankfully, we were all fortunate to marry for love." I bargained.

The atmosphere shifted and the dinner party floated into an occasion filled with laughter, joy, and reminiscences of a time when we were all younger. My grandmother told tales of my father courting my mother and how smitten my father was with her. She talked about how radiant she looked on her wedding day and how the whole county had turned out for the glorious affair.

It was late in the evening before our company departed. Spirits had been rejuvenated and friendships strengthened. It was a bond I cherished in these troubled times. Although our companions had little inkling of how drastically our world was about to be flipped on its head, my grandmother and I dearly cherished these moments of peace and laughter shared with our closest friends.

11

WEDNESDAY, MARCH 18, 2020

THE NEWS BECAME MORE DREADFUL by the day. It was difficult to keep spirits up when everything around us — the entire country and world for that matter, was shutting down. Being essential workers, Landon and I were busier than ever, but on-campus classes were closed. Restaurants, gyms, all public buildings, and most stores outside of grocery markets were closing down for this global pandemic. Schools, athletic events, amusement parks, theatres, and malls locked their doors, many unlikely to reopen.

No one knew how people were going to survive and layoffs became commonplace. Money was rapidly becoming scarce. People were pouring into the hospital for every little sniffle, cough, or runny nose. Of course, we had to test everyone. Widespread implementation of wearing masks, social distancing of standing six feet apart from anyone near you, and rampant shortages became the new normal. Landon and I were running on fumes. Everyone at the hospital was running on fumes. Murmurs floated about the breakrooms that this was only going to get worse.

Robert had conceded and temporarily closed his law practice. Still, he kept his employees on remotely hoping to assist them in keeping their families afloat through this crisis. For how long, he was not sure. Especially with the courts closing down and nothing being filed, processed, or cases heard. It was almost as if the world had stopped. I rested my head down on the table in the breakroom. I had fifteen minutes to myself before I headed back into the dreaded jungle that had become my life. All I wanted to do was march up to human resources and turn in my resignation. But I knew I could not. "Are you okay?" the voice from the doorway startled me. I looked up to see Veronica standing there.

"Yeah, I'm good." I sighed heavily and took a long drink of water. "Only four more hours."

"Twelve hour shift?" I nodded. "Me too." She sat down beside me. "How long do you think it will take them to remove our chairs in the breakroom so we cannot sit next to each other?"

"Seriously?" I felt my shoulders slump in defeat.

"I heard several people — doctors and nurses mentioning it. I guess management is considering it." She rolled her eyes.

"Why am I not surprised? They have no backbone and could not care less about what we are dealing with."

"Is Landon still working in the lab?" Veronica asked cracking open some pistachios and popping them into her mouth.

"No. They closed it down last week and transferred him to the ER."

"Ugh. How does he like it?"

"He doesn't." I shrugged. "But what else can he do? We have bills to pay."

"I understand that. Both my parents have been temporarily laid off." She created air quotes in front of her sarcastically. If this lasts much longer, they are afraid of running through their savings and dipping into their retirement funds. They are middle class working people. They cannot afford to be out of work for long."

"My parents are both in the medical field, so thankfully, they are in the clear. But Landon's folks are not so lucky. My sister's father-in-law is an attorney and is meeting with clients and colleagues through Zoom, but of course the courts are shut down so nothing is being processed." I noted. "They are well-off, but even so this is going to hurt everyone sooner or later."

"Do you really believe all the calls for a global quarantine?" Veronica bit her lower lip nervously.

"Last Fall I would have said there is no way, but now." I shrugged. "Who knows?"

"This is going to get much worse before it gets better, especially for us." She remarked with an exhausted sigh.

"Unfortunately, I believe you are right."

Traveling home from work on the once packed freeways had now become laughable. Traffic was sparse. Even the police had given up pulling people over for speeding in fear of being exposed to the dreaded Covid-19 virus, leaving travelers to dictate their own speed of travel.

Landon was reheating some leftover lasagna from our dinner at Robert and Emily's over the weekend. He was lounging on the couch with his stocking feet propped up on the arm. His eyes were closed, but *Supernatural* was streaming on the television.

"You alive?" I dropped my purse and keys on the island in the kitchen.

"No." His voice drifted across the room as I opened the beeping microwave. I pulled out his lasagna with a pot holder and set it on the counter.

"Here, darling." I carried the bowl and fork over to him and placed it on his stomach. "Careful," I cautioned him. "It's hot."

"Thanks," he opened his eyes and shifted himself up into a seated position. "There's more in there if you're hungry."

"Thanks," I plopped down in the recliner. "Maybe later."

"How was work?" He muttered between bites.

"Long. Boring." I lifted the leg rest and closed my eyes. "I am beginning to rethink my entire career choice." I moaned.

"I'm right there with ya." Landon grumbled with his mouth full.

"Do you think this is going to be as bad as people around the hospital are saying it will?"

"Worse," he shrugged. "Honestly?" he turned his head towards me.

"Sure," I chuckled.

"I think this is just the beginning and it's going to get a hell of a lot worse."

"Seriously?" I grumbled. "This sucks."

"Okay, if you could change it. What profession would you switch too?" He tilted his head inquizitively.

"Oh, I don't know." I sighed and pushed the foot rest down. I leaned forward and contemplated. "Psychology, maybe." I chuckled lightly. "Perhaps then I could figure out what is wrong with all these freaking leftist liberals."

"If you can figure that out, you could make a mint." Landon laughed.

"What about you? What would you do?" I was curious.

"Hmm, I'm not sure. Maybe a chemical engineer or perhaps a tradesman like a plumber or something. People always need a plumber. Or maybe a farmer." He eyed me carefully. "I have always wanted a large plot of land to farm and raise animals. I dream of having horses someday and being able to ride about the pastures and through the woods. I love spending long days outdoors working the land just like my grandfather did." He confessed.

"Really?" I thought about it for a moment flashing to my other life on our large estate in Braintree. "I would love that."

Landon put his empty bowl on the coffee table and crawled over to me slowly edging his way up the chair until he was hovering over me. "You would like to be a farmer's wife?" A sly grin played upon his shapely lips.

"I would not mind. I love being outdoors and I like animals better than most people." I confessed running my hands over his shoulders and down his back.

"Old McDonald had a farm," Landon rattled off the silly children's jingle kissing my neck.

"You are such a dork," I giggled leaning into him.

Landon stood up and lifted me up in his arms. His lips brushed mine as he effortlessly carried me to our room. He gently laid me down upon the bed and hovered over me.

"I love you," his voice was barely above a whisper.

"I love you, too."

12

WEDNESDAY, MARCH 21, 1860

A **WARM BREEZE FLOWED** softly over the fields brushing lightly against my cheeks as soft as a sweet lover's kiss. The afternoon sun was starting to regain its strength with the promise of early spring. A cool breeze embraced me, lifting my hair gently from my shoulders. I unconsciously shivered and pulled my shawl closer around me.

"I brought you some tea." My grandmother walked out onto the front porch and placed the silver tray on the small table between the two rocking chairs.

"Thank you, grandmother." I smiled as she poured each of us a saucer and added a touch of honey. She handed me one before taking a seat beside me.

"The trees are starting to bud." She noticed casually.

"Yes. I hope spring will come early this year." I remarked, looking over the vast flowerbeds still amidst their winter slumber.

"This is a false spring." She assured me. "We will have at least one more bout of cold weather, perhaps even some snow before our true spring begins."

"Probably." I sipped my tea feeling its warmth spread through me. I readjusted myself again trying to get comfortable.

"Are you feeling all right?" Her eyes studied me closely.

"Yes, though I cannot seem to get comfortable." I complained rubbing my hand lightly over my protruding abdomen.

"Keifer should be home soon." Her eyes followed mine to the long entryway to our estate.

"I know. I had asked him not to go to Boston this morning." I glanced over at her with a sly smile. "I know he is needed at the hospital, but the way things are heating up around the train depot, it makes me nervous."

"Keifer will be fine. No one is going to attack a physician. They are in short supply as is." My grandmother continued watching me closely. "What else is on your mind? You seem troubled."

I glanced around briefly ensuring we were alone before I responded. "Do you remember me mentioning this coronavirus that hit the states from China?" I asked.

"Yes, I recall."

"It has officially been dubbed as a global pandemic. Now, there are talks about a national shut-down." I informed her.

"What is that supposed to mean?" Her expression looked inquisitive.

"Emily called me last evening. She has been on her book tour for the last couple of weeks promoting her latest release. She is out in Northern California and received a call from her publisher informing her that the remainder of her book tour was canceled. At first it was just the chain stores, but in the last three days even the smaller shops – the independent mom and pop stores – are closing." I shook my head in disbelief.

"I do not understand. How can everything simply close? It is not like now where people know how to survive on their own crops and cattle." My grandmother smirked. "I guess your skills will be extremely useful now."

"Unfortunately, I cannot grow toilet paper, which as of this week has become more precious than gold." I chuckled.

"Somehow, I believe that." She laughed. "How are people going to survive without grocery or hardware stores?"

"I do not believe anyone knows." I shrugged and sipped my tea. "There is talk of a national quarantine."

"Is that even possible? What about hospitals, banks, and all other essential things such as refineries, factories, skilled tradesmen." Her voice trailed off.

"Oh, I am an essential worker." I assured her with a hint of disdain and sarcasm as I snorted at my own air quotes. "Along with first responders, police, and such." I rolled my eyes.

"And what are your colleagues at the hospital saying about this virus?" My grandmother raised an eyebrow noting her curiosity.

"That depends on which ones you ask."

"Excuse me?" Her face marked her confusion.

"The pure evilness spewed by the Democrats is appalling. It appears their long game is shaping up as a desperate attempt to control the narrative — the media and the American populace. Something akin to communism." I explained not trying to hide my contempt.

"As in the ideology you told me about that will bring about the downfall of Germany within the next decade?" She visibly shivered as I nodded.

"Yes, exactly. The Democrats hatred, greed, and lust for power appears to know no boundaries." I glanced out at the long entryway again. "I have a horrible feeling that the nightmare in our country is just beginning."

"It appears neither of your lives are going to be peaceful in the foreseeable future." She sighed heavily.

"I know," I winced shifting my weight uncomfortably.

"Are you sure you are all right?" The concern was etched on my grandmother's face.

"Yes. I am fine." I awkwardly stood. "Excuse me for a moment. I need to use the water closet." I smiled and wobbled back into the house.

I crossed the foyer holding the underside of my oversized belly. I felt an urgency to make it to my room as quickly as I could possibly muster. It felt like my son was using my bladder as a trampoline. I grasped the stair rail with my free hand and pulled myself forward up the staircase.

"Oh, God," I gasped halfway up the stairs bending over as a sharp pain coursed through my abdomen. I felt warm fluid gush down my legs and over the stairs.

"Sidney?" my grandmother's voice called out frantically from the foyer.

Seeing me hunched over, she quickly rushed to my side in a movement so swiftly I would not have believed it had I not witnessed it myself.

"I am sorry." I gripped the rail until my fingers turned white. "I believe I just urinated on the stairs." I whispered to my grandmother in a weak voice.

"No, you did not my dear child. Your water has broken." She smiled tenderly brushing my skewed hair away from my face. "Your son is on his way." She turned her face to the vast space beyond us. "Ned!" She bellowed.

Ned's heavy footsteps were heard before he appeared looking flustered at the foot of the stairs.

"Yes'm, Misses." His normally casual and confident composure crumbled at the sight of me in distress.

"Ned, please carry Ms. Sidney to her chambers. Her child is coming." My grandmother barked orders in her near panicked state.

Ned took the stairs two at a time.

"Gab ahold m' neck, Mizdress" My grandmother steadied me as I reached up for Ned.

He lifted me into his strong arms as if my body was light as a feather. I visibly winced in pain with the sudden movement of my body.

"Ah's sorrie, Mizdress." His baritone voice sounded soft like he was talking to a child.

"It is not you, Ned." I attempted to smile. "My son appears eager to join us this evening." His soft eyes showed his concern, but his lips turned upwards in a gentle smile as he carried me into Keifer and my bed chamber.

Ned gently placed me on my bed. A stronger contraction ripped through my body. I groaned, turning my head and gripping the sheets so hard I was sure my fingers would break. I desperately wanted to scream. However, I had been told countless times that a lady does not scream during the throws of labor, only poor and uneducated women behaved in that manner. I had no choice but to lock my jaw tightly praying I didn't crack my teeth and endure.

"Ned," my grandmother sat on the edge of the bed and whipped my forehead with a wet cloth. "Run over to the McKendrick's and tell Judith that Sidney is in labor. Tell her Keifer is at the hospital and to come quickly."

"Yes'm," Ned scurried out the room closing the door behind him.

"I wish Keifer were here." I shifted my limbs, finding it impossible to get comfortable.

"I am sure he will be here shortly." However, I could see the uncertainty in her eyes. "Just breathe, Sidney."

My grandmother helped me out of my stays and gown. She held my hand helping me back into the bed in my chivy. I rolled to my left side and bent my knees up towards my stomach as far as I possibly could. My grandmother wiped my forehead again and stroked my hair away from my face. I wanted to scream from the pain, but my jaw remained locked with each contraction. Tears ran down my cheeks.

My grandmother stayed by my side, wiping sweat from my brow, stroking my hair, and murmuring comforting words of strength. Marla carried in a basin of fresh water and clean towels. She sat them on the small table beside the bed waiting impatiently for Mrs. McKenrick to arrive.

It felt like an eternity before I heard footsteps hammering up the stairs. I wasn't sure if I wished it were my husband or Judith. I was in so much pain I really did not care.

"How is she?" Judith rushed in and immediately began washing her hands.

"About ready, I believe." My grandmother answered, the tension lines evident on her face.

"The sheet." Judith turned around, her eyes scanning the room. "Where's the sheet?" she looked at Marla.

"Right here." Marla quickly handed her the folded linen.

Judith hastily shook it out and looped it around the footboard of the bed. She handed on end to Marla and approached my grandmother on the side of the bed.

"Marissa, help me roll her onto her back." My grandmother kissed my forehead quickly before she and Judith nudged me gently onto my back.

"Here." She placed the end of the folded sheet in my hand and Marla followed placing the opposite end in my other hand. "Pull on these when you push. It will help." Judith's voice was strong and sturdy.

Two long and excruciating hours later my son's cries filled the room. Judith, whose hair had become skewed from her neatly set bun with wisps falling along the sides of her exhausted face, was drenched in sweat.

"You have a son, Sidney." Judith held up my son triumphantly and placed him gently on my abdomen.

"Keifer," I let out a sigh of relief. Tears rolled down my cheeks as I smiled. "You're finally here." I wrapped my arms around my son.

"He's beautiful." My grandmother wiped his face with the wet cloth.

My son had his father's hazel eyes, round plump cheeks, and a crown of blondish brown hair. He was chubby with little dimples on his fingers, elbows, and knees. I guessed he weighed at least eight pounds. He had little fat rolls on his fat rolls. He was perfect.

"Let me clean him up." Judith lifted him from my arms and took him over to the basin.

"Marla, please fetch some more fresh water." my grandmother asked. The girl nodded and hurried back down the stairs. "Sidney," she turned her attention back to me. "We need to get you and this bed cleaned up. Can you stand?" I nodded, taking her hand and rolling out of bed.

My grandmother changed the sheets on our bed and piled the soiled linens by the door. Marla set another basin beside my grandmother as she helped me out of my chivy. She helped me carefully scrub clean and into a fresh chivy.

"Hold onto the bed post." She instructed me while she and Marla remade the bed.

My eyes drifted over to Judith who was drying my son after his first bath. I watched her skillfully diaper and dress my son with years of experience in her fingertips. Despite her haggard appearance, she had a contented smile on her lips.

"Sidney?" my grandmother touched my arm drawing my gaze away from my new son and dear friend. "Step up." She nodded towards the small stepping stool beside my bed.

Once I was settled, Judith handed my little bundle to me. He was sucking on his fingers with his eyes wide. I couldn't take my eyes off his precious face. My heart was so overflowing, it felt like it would burst from my chest.

"Marissa, you need to rest." Long shadows fell across the room as Judith lit a couple of oil lamps. "I will stay with Sidney until Keifer returns."

I glanced over at my grandmother sitting beside me. I noticed the dark circles under her eyes and the weariness was evident on her face. Her tired shoulders were resting against the mountain of pillows behind us. I instantly felt guilty for the long day and the stress she had endured because of me.

"I am fine, grandmother." I squeezed her hand. "Please rest."

"All right," she leaned over kissing me on the check and then kissed my little angel on the forehead. "Such a precious child. He looks like his father." She declared with a smile. "You get some rest as well." She got up and approached Judith before leaving the room. "I will have Ned bring the bassinet in here and Marta will bring you both some supper."

"Thank you, Marissa." She rested her hand on my grandmother's arm. "Do not worry, I will take care of them." My grandmother paused one more time at the door smiling over at us before exiting.

It was after ten o'clock when Keifer finally arrived home. Naomi heated up some supper for him but neither she nor Ned mentioned anything that had transpired that evening. Keifer must have assumed I was already in bed and did not inquire about my whereabouts.

Finally, after he ate and finished his nightly brandy while reading the evening paper in his study, he made his way up the stairs. It was just shy of midnight and the last thing he expected was to find his neighbor's wife dozing peacefully in the rocking chair placed next to his bed.

"Oh, good heavens," Keifer had walked in unbuttoning his shirt, shrieked and popped two buttons that rattled to the hardwood floor.

The sound of his loud deep voice in the silent room startled the other three occupants. I jerked awake and painfully sat up abruptly in bed. Judith leapt to her feet, knocking the rocking chair back against the wall. And of course, my little man howled at the sudden noise interrupting his sleep.

Keifer's wide eyes flowed in confusion in the candlelit room as he scanned over his surroundings.

"Doc, it's me. Judith." She regained her composure and spoke in a gentle voice as she swiftly moved towards the cradle. "Your son decided to make his appearance this evening." She lifted him expertly and handed him to his surprised father.

Keifer eyes widened and immediately softened as he carefully examined his new son.

"Five fingers, five toes. Perfectly healthy in every way." I assured him from the bed. Keifer's eyes turned toward me as if he had just realized my presence.

"My darling, how are you feeling?" My husband kissed our son's forehead and handed him to me. I adjusted myself and began nursing my son. His cries immediately ceased, and his low gurgles filled the darkened room.

"I am sore but feeling well." I confessed to my husband as he sat down beside me. "Judith came immediately after my water broke and took care of everything. Grandmother stayed with me. We sent her to bed a while ago. She was worn out from all the excitement." I smiled.

"I would imagine so." He leaned over kissing my cheek softly before looking at our neighbor. "Thank you, Judith." Keifer smiled with appreciation and respect towards my dear friend. "I am so happy you were here. I do not know what would have happened without you."

"Nonsense," Judith waved her hand dismissively. "Marissa could have easily delivered the babe by herself." She tiredly leaned against the bed's footpost. "She delivered all of mine."

"I am sure it was difficult for her seeing Sidney in such a state." My husband remarked, glancing between us. "I am grateful for you. I am sorry I was so late. I had four men brought to the hospital right as I was set to leave. Two of them were abolitionists stirring up trouble around the train depot and apparently a brawl broke out. The four men were in critical condition with gunshot and stab wounds. A half dozen other men were brought in with less serious conditions from the brawl."

"My goodness," Judith shook her head in dismay. "Is this ever going to end?"

"Not anytime soon." I muttered. "It is only going to get worse before it gets better."

"Do you really believe so?" Judith appeared apprehensive.

"Unfortunately," Keifer added. I was a bit surprised by his statement. He was typically the optimistic one between us, mainly because I knew what lay on the horizon and he did not.

"Judith, Marla made up the guest room for you. Please stay the night and Keifer will take you home after breakfast." I offered.

"That would be lovely. I appreciate it." She made her way to the door. "Try to get some rest, Sidney." I nodded in return. "I shall see you in the morning." She closed the door behind her.

"I am truly sorry I was not here, darling. I so wanted to assist in bringing our son into the world." My husband kissed me sweetly and then looked down at his contented son. "He is perfect." His voice was barely a whisper. "What shall we call him?"

"Keifer Lee Marshall, II of course." I giggled softly. "I told you I wanted to name him after you."

"I wanted to be sure you had not changed your mind." Keifer grinned. "My parents will be thrilled. I shall write them in the morning." My husband stood and finished undressing before slipping into bed beside me. "When should I tell them to expect us?" he asked, filling my heart with dread.

It was not that I did not want to visit his family. Truth was, I really did not know them well. Over the years, I have had very little interaction with them. I cared for them as his kin, but I could not say I loved them. Well, at least I cared for all of them except for his sister, Euginia.

But traveling South to Savannah made me extremely nervous. I was terrified of taking the train or sailing South, especially through South Carolina whose patrons were increasingly hostile towards Northerners. While Keifer could muster up his Southern accent upon command, my attempts were laughable at best.

"Do you really believe it is a good idea?" The fear was palpable in my voice.

"We have not seen my family in years, Sidney. Plus, I would like them to meet my son." Keifer reached over and gently stroked our son's chubby cheek. "I figure we will have Ned take us into Boston with our trunks and from there catch a steam liner to take us down to Savannah. And you will be able to do some shopping during our layover in Charlestown if you so desire." He smiled as if he had it all worked out.

"Keifer, I have not hired a nanny yet. And it may be difficult to hire someone who is willing to travel South given the current climate." I reasoned.

"Take Marla," he waved his hand dismissively.

"Marla is our housekeeper, not a nanny." I said pointedly. "She has no experience with babies."

"Ah, she will be fine. She will learn, especially by the time we leave." He shrugged casually.

There was no reasoning with him when he got like this.

"No. I want a proper nanny for our son and if he does not have one, then we will not go." I said flatly.

"Fine," he surrendered. "Hire who you please."

"Plus, we need to be in Chicago no later than the second week of October." I emphasized. I could not tell him I had to be there for Jocelyn's birth. I do not believe Annabelle even knew she was pregnant yet.

"Why so early? I thought we would arrive mid-November and stay through the New Year celebration."

"I know, but I would like to be there for the changing of the leaves." I took his hand in mine hoping he would buy my excuse. "You know Fall is my favorite season and I want little Keifer to enjoy it."

"I do not think he will be old enough to have a clue, but as you wish, my darling." Keifer chuckled and kissed my cheek. "Then I will tell my folks to expect us at the beginning of July."

"July?" I gasped. "Savannah will be a sauna in July." I groaned.

"Sauna? What is a sauna?" Keifer tilted his head looking at me carefully as I realized my mistake. I bit the side of my lip before responding.

"A sauna is a small steamy room that is very hot." I explained.

"Where did you learn that?"

"I believe it was from a book I had read." I shrugged casually. "It sounds like a fitting description of Savannah in July." I reasoned.

"True," he grinned. "But all the same, I believe going down in July would be best."

"But is that not a terribly long time to be absent from your practice and the estate?" I pondered aloud.

"Well," I could see his expression shift to the one he always wore when he was about to tell me something he knew would make me unhappy. "I spoke with Dr. Clayton about our trip, and he said he would be happy to cover Braintree during my absence two days per week. The hospital is fine with me taking a leave of absence." He explained.

"But?" I knew there was more that he was not telling me.

"But I am afraid Marissa is insistent upon not going to Savannah."

"But she must," I began only to be quickly shut down by Keifer's words.

"Now dear, she will meet us in Baltimore before we journey to Chicago."

"But."

"Ned will bring her, and he will look after everything during our absence." He declared.

"And how often will Mr. Bennett be dropping by in our absence to check on the estate?" I knew Keifer trusted Ned and my faith in him but that part of him that would always be Southern would not allow it.

"Weekly," he admitted. "I asked him to attend to the ledgers with Ned, the same as you have been doing. Nothing more." He confessed.

"And the numbers telegraphed to you weekly as well." I laughed, with disbelief.

"Well, yes darling."

"Very well, dear." I snuggled my sleeping son a bit closer to my chest, dreading the notion of spending the heart of the summer deep in the South.

A light breeze drifted through the cracked windows cool enough to raise goosebumps on my arms. Perhaps my grandmother was right, Spring was still a breath away.

"Darling," Keifer reached for our son causing him to stir a bit. "Let me put him in the cradle. You need to get some sleep before he is hungry again."

"Thank you," I barely whispered and snuggled against the mountain of pillows.

I closed my eyes and inhaled deeply. My body hurt and ached in ways I had never experienced before. I silently wished for ibuprofen, if not something stronger. Despite my physical fatigue, my mind would not rest. Terror of traveling South left a hollowness in my chest. I barely knew Keifer's family and their world felt foreign to me. How could I make him understand the possible danger he was inflicting upon me and our son?

The notion of a Southern plantation felt as foreign to me in this time as it did in my other. The stories that drifted through our community and from books Keifer had asked me not to read told various accounts of life in the Southern states. How much truth there was to any of it was anyone's guess. Uncle Nicholas' words rang in my ears, 'history is told by the victors, for only their perspective gets written'.

I was exhausted. As much as I wanted to continue staring at the little angel who finally graced our lives, my body and mind were completely drained. I barely felt Keifer lie down beside me before I drifted off into another world.

13

THURSDAY, MARCH 19, 2020

I AWOKE TO THE SMELL OF coffee drifting from the kitchen. Landon was already up, showered, and wearing his hospital scrubs. He was leaning against the island browsing the news on his phone and sipping coffee.

I stretched and ran my hands over my flat stomach. The odd sensation washed over me — I was filled with the vivid image of my beautiful son. I could still feel the weight of his tiny body in my arms, the warmth of his skin, the sound of his cries.

I choked back a sob that fought to escape. I reminded myself of where and when I was and that my son was no longer *here*. I closed my eyes and rubbed them roughly. I took a deep breath and kicked off the covers. The pain in my chest was overwhelming, but I could not let it eat at me. I had to get through this day.

"Morning," I casually poured myself a tall mug. "Are you going in early?" I turned towards him savoring that first long sip of heaven. "I thought you were not going in until ten this morning."

"Marcus was fired yesterday so I have to go in early to get a jump on the paperwork." He muttered with disdain.

"It's about time. He was worthless." Landon nodded. "What finally did it?"

"Besides his laziness, the no calls, no shows, tardiness, and pure stupidity — being the director's nephew couldn't save him once he started spewing his contempt for anyone and everyone diagnosed with Covid." He smirked.

"What? That does not make sense." I shook my head and sat down on a bar stool.

"He started off on his spiel about eugenics and natural selection."

"Really?" I raised an eyebrow and looked at him over the top of my mug. "Wow! That was brazen. Who was he spouting this too?" I wish I could have seen that moron get his just desserts.

"Everyone. Doctors, nurses, techs — I guess he was running his mouth to anyone standing near him for more than thirty seconds."

"Good grief. I am sure that went over well." I scoffed. "What an idiot."

"Yes, he is." Landon placed his mug in the sink. "I'm off." He leaned in and kissed me gently. "I'll see you tonight."

"Have a great day, darling."

"You too." The door closed behind him and the emptiness of the apartment enveloped me.

I slid down the cabinet and let out the sob that I could no longer suppress. The unfairness of it all — losing my son *here,* yet him surviving there in a world that was rapidly unfolding, spiraling out of control and running headlong into a war that would tear the country apart.

I don't know how much time passed, but it felt like a good long while that I sat there huddled on the floor sobbing uncontrollably. I felt spent. I knew there was no way I could handle going to work so I called HR and assured them I did not have flu-like symptoms but would not be coming in due to a horrific migraine. Sadly, I did not have to fake anything. I truly felt like hell.

After a long hot shower, I put on some jeans and a worn-out navy hoodie with my old converse high-top sneakers. I didn't bother with makeup but pulled my hair up into a messy bun just to keep it out of my face.

I grabbed my purse and keys and headed out to the small parking lot. The air was cool with a subtle breeze. The skies were gray and covered by a band of thick dark clouds that threatened rain. It matched my mood perfectly.

I drove straight over to Emily's house. She was the only person I knew who could possibly understand the heartbreak I was enduring. I knew as a mother herself she would understand. For a moment I considered calling Phoebe, but I did not think I could endure seeing her beautiful son, Wally, or seeing her belly rounding with the growing of her new child.

It felt selfish, but I could not help it. I wanted my son so desperately I could scream. I don't even remember the drive over there. All I knew what that I pulled into their driveway in one piece – thankfully. I shut the car off and a river of tears rolled down my cheeks.

The front door opened as I climbed out of the car. Emily stepped out and immediately ran to me. She wrapped her arms around me and held me tight.

"Sidney, calm down sweetheart." She whispered in a calming motherly voice.

"My son," I sobbed.

"What about your son, darling?" She tried to look at my face gently lifting my chin.

"I had my son last night." The pain in my chest ripped through me.

"Oh, darling." She gently guided me into the house.

We walked slowly, as I was leaning heavily upon her. Robert was standing in the front doorway with a concerned look etched upon his face.

"Robert, please make some coffee." He nodded and disappeared into the kitchen.

"Sit down, darling." Emily sat down beside me on the couch in the parlor.

My body felt numb, but my head was splitting apart. The pain in my chest was the only thing keeping me upright. I placed my hands in my lap attempting to keep them steady.

Robert returned with a silver tray adorning a silver coffeepot, three mugs and saucers and a plate full of scones. He sat it down on the coffee table in front of us before taking a seat opposite us.

"Is there anything else I can get you? Some aspirin, perhaps?" He offered.

"Yes, please." I tried my best to smile at him. "My head is killing me."

"Of course," he rose from his seat and disappeared once more.

Emily filled each mug and placed an apple scone on each of the little plates. She carefully handed each one to me although I had no appetite, I gracefully accepted it.

"Here," Robert returned and handed me a couple of Excedrin.

"Thank you," I popped them into my mouth and washed them down with the black coffee. "I am so sorry for dropping by unannounced and in such a state. But I did not know what else to do." I wiped my nose and tears with a tissue.

"Darling, there is nothing to apologize for. You are family." Emily reassured me.

"I thought I could handle it. I honestly did." I mumbled as the tears started flowing freely again. "I thought I was coping with the loss — that I was moving forward. But seeing him, holding him." Emily wrapped her arms around me and pulled me close to her.

"Sweetheart, it is understandable. You have every right to be so upset. I am sure it was surreal waking up this morning after giving birth there last evening." I saw Robert's eyes widen with her words.

"Oh, Sidney. I am so sorry. I had not realized." Robert apologized, leaning forward in his seat. "Is your son," he hesitated making eye contact with Emily before continuing. "Healthy?"

"Yes," I smiled and nodded. "Yes, my son is beautiful and perfectly healthy." I gushed.

"Good," I saw Robert visibility exhale with relief. "That is a blessing."

"I do not know why I am so hysterical this morning." I chuckled without humor. "It is a blessing. My son is perfect."

"Oh, I wish I could see him." Emily patted my arm.

"You will in a few months." I assured her with a warm smile.

"How are you doing — *there*?" Robert asked.

"Good," I nodded again. "Sore, but good. Keifer was not home, but my grandmother was with me and my neighbor and good friend, Judith, delivered him. She is still with us." I explained.

"Where was Keifer?" Emily inquired.

"He was in Boston at the hospital looking after his patients. My labor went much quicker than we had imagined. When my water broke, my grandmother sent Ned to fetch Judith." I took a bite of my scone feeling much better than before. "It was rough. I would have given anything for an epidural."

"You are a tough young lady," Robert smiled.

"But it was the oddest sensation," I sat back against the cushions. "As soon as I opened my eyes this morning my hands immediately rested on my stomach, and I felt this profound, overwhelming sense of emptiness." I said softly.

"That is perfectly natural," Emily reassured me.

"Did you experience the same thing?" I wondered.

"I am afraid my experience was different with my three pregnancies because I was pregnant on both planes." Emily locked eyes with Robert. "It was challenging and exhausting. You will understand the oddity of it with your next child." She smiled softly. "I do not know how to accurately explain it to you. It was surreal, because it was almost as if drifting across the planes from one period into the next throughout the labor."

"I did not experience anything like that." I admitted.

"It was jarring the first time I experienced it with Alex, but it was easier with Phoebe and Jackson. Thankfully, my mother and grandmother had prepared me." Emily took my hand in hers. "I also spoke to Phoebe when she was pregnant with Wallace, and I will explain it to Jocelyn as well when the time comes."

"I wish I could understand more about *E.V.E.*" I declared. "Sometimes I feel like I need an anchor to keep me grounded."

"We all feel that way from time to time. That is why, as a family with this unique gift, it is crucial we rely on each other." Robert pointed out. "It is not an easy life. I can only imagine how isolating it must feel for you at times. I mean, we all have each other on both sides, but you for now, must struggle alone."

"I am thankful I have my grandmother despite the distance of our *other* lives." I shrugged casually.

"Has she finally admitted her other period?" Emily grinned.

"No. Not concretely." I smirked. "I believe she loves being elusive."

"From my limited knowledge of Marissa Timmons, I believe she is a very spirited lady." Robert smiled.

"That is putting it kindly, sir." I laughed.

Phoebe dropped by in the afternoon after a phone call from Emily I assumed. But either way, she was in high spirits and a breath of fresh air blowing through the cloudy day. We talked about my son, and I described him to them — everything down to his tiny perfect fingernails.

I was absolutely in love with him and these long hours felt like an eternity as I waited anxiously to hold him in my arms once more. I paced, more than anything, that afternoon trying to keep my mind on anything else, but it simply was not working. I felt this constant void in the center of my chest like a vital piece of me was missing.

I tried. I tried hard to swallow my feelings, to join in on conversations, and not act like my world wasn't a confused emotional matrix of raw feelings. The lump in my throat would not disappear. I had no idea how I was going to manage this feeling going forward knowing that my precious baby boy was not with me for half of my life.

"Are things as bad at the hospital as what we are seeing on the news?" Robert leaned against the kitchen counter.

"If you mean is everyone freaking out over every little sniffle, cough, or runny nose? Yes." I appreciated the distraction. "The ER is overrun by everyone freaking out over this virus."

"It appears common sense is not that common anymore." Phoebe rolled her eyes with a smirk.

"I do not understand why everyone is buying into this propaganda." I climbed up on one of the island stools.

"The liberals and progressives in the Democrat party are doing everything to control the narrative." Robert explained. "I imagine it will get worse before the election."

"I am dreading this election. We are so screwed if President Trump does not win." Phoebe tossed a couple grapes in her mouth. "I know it is only gearing up, but ugh, I am so sick of it already. Some of this crap from the Left is utter nonsense."

"Can you believe some blue state governors have closed all restaurants, bars, casinos, and retail stores? Most office workers are now working from home for the foreseeable future." Phoebe muttered.

"I do not believe our economy can survive this. Thousands of people are suddenly out of work when most Americans survive paycheck to paycheck." Emily noted.

"Do you believe this threat is real?" I asked Robert.

"No," Robert shook his head. "People who buy into it fail to do their research. I will not be surprised if mandates and Marshall law follows, especially in blue cities. This is going to get much worse before it gets better."

"I feel like I am torn within two countries that are being torn apart. It feels like war is on the horizon in both my worlds and there is nothing I can do about it." I scoffed. "At least in the *other*, I know what to expect. In this one, I am blind."

"Do you really believe there will be a war in this time?" Phoebe asked hesitantly. I could hear the skepticism in her voice.

"I do," Robert answered first. "Although I believe it will not start for at least another five or six years, maybe a decade but make no mistake it is coming."

"But if President Trump is reelected," I started.

"President Trump will not be reelected. You mark my words. The democrat party is pushing a sociologist ideology across campuses, this DEI bullshit for corporations, and ESG shit." He rambled.

"Wait. What?" Phoebe interrupted.

"This division equity and inclusion — DEI bullshit and environment, social, and government — ESG rating nonsense. When a Democrat is elected, they will hire the most incompetent administration the likes this country has never seen." Robert scoffed. "The democrats are hell-bent on destroying this country."

"My Robert, I have never heard you talk that way." Emily took a deep breath. "At least, not on this plane. You sound like you did right before the Civil War broke out."

"And once again, history will repeat itself. The Democrats will be the downfall of America again." He rolled his eyes looking irritated. "They are greedy and power hungry. Just look at Maxine Waters, Nancy Pelosi, Adam Schiff, the Clintons, the Biden's, the Obama's — they are some of the most corrupt nastiest people in our governmental history."

"From what I understand of them, I cannot say I am a fan." I muttered.

"Me neither," Phoebe reiterated. "It is amazing to the me how they have accumulated such massive wealth during their time in office."

"Do you really think it is going to get worse than all these nonsensical lockdowns?" Emily asked.

"I believe this is only the beginning." Robert stated with a frown. "We, as white Americans, are in for a world of hurt, hate, and financial crippling when the Democrats steal this election. I saw it on the news the other night that the Democrat party are going to nominate Joe Biden officially at the DNC."

"I do not see how they can be." I shrugged casually. "Biden is a complete idiot. Even President Reagan called him a moron when he was in office. Plus, President Trump has done more for the American people of all ages and racial background than anyone else in recent history."

"Do you believe that matters?" Phoebe looked at me with skepticism. "I see it daily on social media how people – the democrats are constantly saying President Trump is racist and hates blacks and basically everyone of color."

"But he doesn't." I rejected.

"Do you believe that matters?" Robert asked. "It is the narrative the Democrats have been pushing simply to cause division amongst citizens."

"Why? What is the point?" I climbed off the barstool and fixed myself another mug of coffee.

"People divided, especially people who are angry and believe they are being treated unfairly, paid unfairly, disvalued, and disrespected because of the amount of melatonin in their skin, are easier to control and manipulate than a society that supports one another." Robert smirked. "You know this, Sidney. You are witnessing it firsthand *there*."

"True." I sipped my coffee and exhaled loudly. "I hoped our countrymen had evolved beyond it, that's all."

"Unfortunately, not. I hate to say." Phoebe rubbed her expanding belly unconsciously.

"I am astonished by this younger generations lack of knowledge about American history, let alone world history. Some of the claims they make on social media are absurd. I cannot understand their logic." Emily pursed her lips.

"Because they have no logic." I smirked. "I see it every day at the hospital and on campus — millennials are the worst offenders. It is as if they have rewritten history completely with delusions and fiction."

"I know," Emily chuckled. "Even I cannot write such absurd fiction, and I am a bestselling author."

"Those who do not learn from history's mistakes are doomed to repeat them." Robert shrugged.

"Who said that?" Emily eyed her husband.

"Winston Churchill. It wasn't an exact quote but close enough." He returned to the coffee pot and helped himself. "Still, no truer words have ever been spoken."

"If President Trump does lose this election, we are in for nightmarish term." The concern on Phoebe's face was evident.

I felt a dreadful knot form in the pit of my stomach. Something told me she was right.

14

THURSDAY, MARCH 22, 1860

THE HEALTHY LUNGS OF MY SON awoke me from a deep sleep. I felt exhausted. The room was dark with only the glow of the embers burning in the hearth as my guide. Keifer was snoring softly, completely oblivious to the cries from his son. I wish I had that option, but my son was insistent.

"Hey little man," I whispered lifting him out of the bassinet and kissed his plump cheek.

I quickly changed his diaper with a skill I was quickly mastering. I snuggled him close to me and got back into bed. I adjusted him and one of the extra pillows to nurse him. He latched on easily and made the sweetest little noises while he nursed.

"Sidney?" Her soft voice startled me.

"Come on in, Judith." I whispered to the silhouette standing in the barely opened doorway.

"Are you alright?" She entered the room silently, crossing over to my side of the bed.

"I am sorry. Did we awaken you?" I moved my legs so she could sit down on the edge of the bed.

"No." She shook her head. "It is four thirty. This is my normal time to start my day." Her voice was light and alert.

"My goodness, why?"

"With a houseful of men, the noise is deafening and most of the time I cannot think straight or find two minutes to myself. Getting up early allows me to enjoy my morning coffee, read the scripture, catch up on some sewing and find my own little piece of solace in this turbulent world." Judith smiled softly.

"I can appreciate that." I had to admit her logic was sound.

"I have a feeling this little one will give you plenty of long hours in the middle of night for the next several months." A smile played on her lips. "I am surprised this little one slept as long as he did." She gently stroked his head. "Such a beautiful baby."

"Thank you," I stifled back a yawn.

"Would you like me to start some coffee?"

"I would appreciate that. I do not believe I will be able to go back to sleep." She nodded and quietly made her way downstairs.

I switched sides and readjusted my son. He was not thrilled about it but soon started nursing hungrily once again. My little man was a good eater, and I hoped I would be able to keep up with him. I gently traced his plump cheek, and he reached up with his tiny fist and wrapped his tiny fingers around my index finger. My breath caught in my chest as my heart swelled with a love I had never felt before.

My husband continued to snore lightly beside me lost in a deep slumber I prayed was full of sweet dreams filled with the delights of becoming a new father. He looked so peaceful and beautiful. He had waited years for me to give him a child — a son. He dreamed of having a son, a namesake, a legacy to carry on long after our days on this earth were done. And his prayers had finally been answered.

Upon everyone's insistence, I stayed in bed. I was waited upon hand and foot. It was insufferable. I wanted to get up, move about. My muscles ached from lack of use. The few moments I was left alone with my son, I paced about the room rocking him gently in my arms. I held him constantly, savoring every moment with him and dreading the long hours I knew we would be apart as my soul drifted back to the 21st century.

Judith returned shortly before dinner. She carried up a basin filled with warm water to help me clean up. I wanted desperately to take a nice long hot shower, or a bath at minimum. But I knew in my vulnerable state of just giving birth, it was not idea. The possibility of an infection was greater do the less than idealized water.

I considered instructing Marta to boil enough water for a bath but that would have been a tremendous task for her, and it would require me to journey downstairs, which I knew my grandmother, nor Judith let alone Keifer were going to allow me to do.

I found it humorous, how much they coddled me like I was a piece of delicate and fragile China after giving birth when, in my *other* time, we were discharging women less than twelve hours after giving birth, maybe 24 after a cesarian section. Times have certainly changed.

"How are you feeling?" Judith sat down on the corner of my bed.

"Tired, but well." I smiled. "I am bored more than anything."

"Enjoy it." She patted my leg. "Trust me, it will not last."

"I am afraid of that too." I chuckled. "But I hate being confined to our chambers."

"But you need time to recover. Your body needs time to heal." She assured me. "You will be up and moving about before Easter."

"Easter? My goodness," Easter was weeks away. "I do not plan on being immobile for that long."

"Nonsense." Judith patted my leg. "Your grandmother is going to make sure you stay here at least that long."

"I will likely go stir crazy before Easter." I admitted.

"Do not fret, you and little mister Keifer Lee will be able to make his formal debut to the town at church on Easter Sunday."

"Do you think you could fetch me some parchment, quill, and ink? I would like to write some letters to my family." I straightened the coverlet and tried to prop myself up as best as possible.

"Of course, darling." Judith rose. "Would you like me to bring you anything else?"

"No but thank Judith. I do appreciate everything you have done for me. For us."

"I shall return in a moment." Judith closed the door behind her.

I could hear the soft gurgles of my son sleeping peacefully and I wondered how much time I had before he would demand to be fed again. I climbed out of bed and dipped the rag into the basin of warm water. I sponge bathed myself as best I could but still longed for a hot bath and to wash my hair. I felt disgusting.

Still, the warm sponge bath did help revive my spirit. I quickly brushed my teeth with baking soda and ran a brush through my hair. I French braided it away from my face in a long ponytail that hung over my shoulder. I tied it with a light blue silk ribbon and lightly brushed out the end before tossing it behind me. I had barely returned to bed when Judith returned with a tray and the writing utensils.

"Here you go?" She set the tray down on Keifer's side of the bed. "You look much better."

"I feel better. Thank you. I needed it." I sighed heavily. "I would love to take a long hot bath."

"Not yet, I am afraid." Judith walked over to the door. "I shall return tomorrow. Get some rest."

"I will. And thank you again, Judith." She quietly closed the door behind her.

I set the tray across my lap and balanced it carefully before opening the ink. I wanted to write to my brother Patrick's wife, Annabelle, and announce the birth of our son. I also wanted to confirm the approximate time of our arrival. It was strange to think that Annabelle was probably just a few weeks pregnant with my little sister, Jocelyn, and most likely was not even aware of it yet.

My Dearest Sister-in-Law Annabelle,

It is with great pleasure and happiness that I am writing to inform you of the birth of our son, Keifer Lee Marshall, II. He is blessed with good health, strong lungs, and resembles his father a great deal. We are truly blessed and are looking forward to introducing him to his extended family late summer. We intend to arrive in Chicago before the first signs of Indian Summer.

I pray you and the family are doing well. I am anxious to hear from you regarding my brothers and precious nephews. I am looking forward to a nice long visit with you all and spending the holiday season in Chicago.

The tension in Boston continues to build and I admit I am a bit apprehensive about our trip to Savannah, Georgia. But Keifer is adamant about visiting his family for fear of what may come with the next election. South Carolina as well as other southern states have begun to talk of secession again. Unfortunately, he fears this time it is much more than mere blustering and the vote will succeed. I am sure you are hearing and witnessing the same turmoil we are here. I pray for peace and solace for us all. Please be safe in your endeavors and know that we send you much love and peace. Give my brother and nephews a kiss for me.

Sincerely,

~Sidney

I folded the letter and stuffed it in an envelope. I scribbled down their address and set it to the side of the tray. I considered writing a letter to my father, Walter, about the birth of my son, but quickly decided against it knowing that his wife and my stepmother would most likely intercept the letter, and my father would probably never see it.

I set the tray aside, wishing I could write to Nicholas at West Point. But unfortunately, he really did not know me in this period and that thought was more than a little distressing to me. I missed his guidance, his caring smile, and his gentle words that always made everything better. I felt so alone *here*.

15

MONDAY, MAY 25, 2020

THE WORLD HAD STOPPED. THE state lockdowns continued and everyone was living in a suspended limbo. The bright skies that came with the burst of spring offered no joy. Even the luster of the spring sparrow's song left a lot to be desired. It felt like all the happiness had been sucked out of the world.

Cities had turned into ghost towns. Citizens were ordered to stay a minimum of six feet apart and had to wear hospital masks whenever they left their homes. Most stores and restaurants remained closed. Only large retail empires remained open, yet goods were becoming difficult to find. There was a rush on toilet paper, hand sanitizer, and cleaning supplies. People were stocking up as if they were expecting the apocalypse.

The number of Covid-19 related deaths rose exponentially. There was a peculiar reason for this. The hospital was issued orders to make every death, regardless of the cause to be marked as Covid-19 related. It did not matter if the person died of a heart attack, or a gunshot wound — if they tested positive for Covid-19, it was documented as a Covid-19 related death.

Most Americans had been laid off work. Some had taken to working from home. Only those deemed essential were allowed to continue their profession. The loss of income had hit everyone hard. People were dipping into their savings, canceling any little extras that were deemed unnecessary luxuries like streaming subscriptions, fast food, and vacations.

California governmental officials relocated the homeless into four- and five-star hotels at taxpayer expense and for the first time in more than a century, New York City shut down its subway system. Church preachers and ministers were being heavily fined for holding Sunday services in defiance of government orders against assembly.

The government was hell-bent on quarantine measures and began to arrest and fine anyone who defied their orders.

Time crept by and universities suspended classes until Fall and closed campuses nationwide. Civil unrest and domestic violence rates soared, as people struggled with the government's strict quarantine measures. Stimulus checks began arriving in the mail or directly deposited into American bank accounts. However, it did little to alleviate the financial strain being felt by every American. Hope was something not many were holding onto.

As hospital workers, Landon and I were deemed essential, but it felt like more of a punishment considering how insane it was. People were panicked, stressed, scared, and had no idea what was going on. The country and the world had turned into a pressure cooker, waiting to explode at any moment.

And it finally blew.

Civilian phone video footage began flooding the airways and every digital media platform of a black man who was being kneeled upon by a white police officer in Minnesota. Liberal democrats immediately started calling it a racially motivated murder of a black man by a power hungry racist white cop. The footage was covered by every social media and news outlet across the country at lightning speed.

I could hear my coworkers discussing it as I retrieved my purse from the locker room and clocked out for the day. I was exhausted from pulling a double shift and felt a constant feeling of suffocation. I could not wait to take this stupid mask off and be able to breathe freely again.

"Are you okay?" I noticed one of our ER nurses, Brandy, sitting on the bench looking bone tired as I slammed my locker shut.

"Yeah," she sighed and ran her hand through her hair. "I'm just worried, is all. Whenever something like this happens, people go after police officers making them the villains."

"Let's just hope that doesn't happen. No one knows the full story yet." I tried to sound optimistic.

"My husband works for Boston PD." The worry in her eyes was evident.

"Have you spoken to him?" I asked sitting down beside her.

"He texted. He's fine." Brandy looked back at me. "He's a homicide detective so thankfully he's not on patrol, but still. I worry." She shrugged. "He jokes that I worry for nothing because he arrives after the shit hits the fan." A weary smile could be made out beneath her surgical mask.

"He's got a point." I chuckled.

"I know. I just hope this isn't the match that lights this powder keg." She looked weary.

"Me too." I patted her lightly on the arm. "Be careful going home."

"You too. I'll see you tomorrow." I stood up and waved goodbye.

"Of course."

The warm evening air was refreshing against my sweat soiled scrubs. I ripped off my mask and tossed it into the back seat as soon as I closed my car door. I started my car, rolled down the windows, and headed towards the interstate. The roads were virtually empty, allowing me to make it home in record time.

Landon was lying on the couch with his stocking feet lounging over the arm when I entered our apartment. His eyes were closed, but the television was blaring reruns of comical crime series *Castle*. He didn't flinch when I closed the door or set my purse and keys down on the breakfast bar.

Taking advantage of his nap, I walked into the bathroom and started the shower. The small bathroom quickly filled with steam as I peeled off my scrubs. All I wanted to do was soak beneath the hot water and forget all about the events of today.

I threw on some sweatpants and a t-shirt after I dried off and ran a brush through my hair. I needed to start dinner but was so exhausted I wasn't even hungry.

I approached Landon slowly and sat down on the arm of the couch above his head. I brushed his sandy blond hair away from his face. I leaned over and kissed his forehead.

"Hello darling," I smiled down at his as he slowly opened his eyes.

"Hi, sweetheart." He kissed me briefly before pulling himself up into a seated position. "When did you get home?"

"About twenty minutes ago." Landon pulled me down into his lap and wrapped his arms around me. "When did you get home?" I wrapped my arms around his neck and snuggled into his chest.

"A little after six. I took a quick shower and thought I'd just relax until you got home, but I guess I fell asleep. What time is it?

"Almost nine." I informed him with a yawn.

"You hungry?"

"A little bit, but I do not feel like cooking. I just want to sleep." I complained.

"Did you see the news?"

"Yes, I believe everyone has." I closed my eyes and laid my head down on his shoulder.

"It looks bad. Can you believe they did that over a counterfeit twenty-dollar bill?" His expression was disgruntled.

"Does that sound right to you?" I looked up at him and raised my eyebrows. "Really?"

"I don't know. Some people," He shrugged.

"Well, I am not going to jump to any conclusions. I have seen multiple reports that he was high on fentanyl and had a criminal record a mile long." I countered.

"Still," Landon started. "Even if he was a criminal, it does not mean he deserved to die."

"I never said he deserved to die. I said he was a known drug addict and dealer with a long criminal history. How many times have we had patients come in high on fentanyl acting insane? How many family members have we seen whose lives were destroyed by these people's selfishness?" I stood up. "Hell, Landon. One criminal drug addict cost us the life of our son." My voice rose unintentionally. "So, do not ask me to feel sorry for some dead criminal drug addict because I won't. I can't!" I shouted and ran to our room slamming the door behind me.

I threw myself upon my bed and wept. The sobs from deep inside the gaping hole in my chest where the shattered pieces of my heart that belonged to my son would never heal, escaped from the depths of my soul. I was so angry at Landon and could not imagine how he could expect me to feel an ounce of sorrow for the dead criminal drug addict.

I cried to sleep in the darkened room. Somewhere in the recesses of my mind I felt for sure Landon would understand my sorrow and come in and hold me.

He never did.

16

MONDAY, MAY 28. 1860

N**ED LIFTED THE HEAVY TRUNK** and secured it with the others on the back of the carriage. My grandmother stood there holding my son tightly in her arms with tears in her eyes. Her bottom lip quivered as she kissed his forehead one more time.

"We really must get going." Keifer nudged me gently.

"I do not want to let him go." My grandmother kissed him again. "He is going to change so much before I see him again. He will forget me."

"He will never forget you. I promise." I leaned over and hugged her tightly. "I will miss you. You write to me."

"I will." She kissed my cheek. "You take care of yourself and my precious great grandbaby. I shall see you in October." I could feel her wet tears on my shoulder before she released me and handed me my son.

"I will gladly trade places with you." I leaned over and whispered. "At least you do not have to spend the summer with Eugenia."

"True," she smirked. "That is a blessing. The sweltering Savannah heat and months with Eugenia? No thank you."

"Coward," I muttered loud enough for her to hear me but low enough so as Keifer could not making her giggle.

"Keifer?" She pulled my husband aside. "You take care of my family and bring them home safely to me." Her voice was soft, but the seriousness of her tone was clear.

"You have my word, Marissa." Keifer hugged her briefly and kissed her cheek.

"I shall hold you to it." She cautioned him.

"I expect you will." Keifer smiled heartily before climbing into the carriage before Ned closed the door.

Ned climbed up into the driver's seat and picked up the reins. A quick jolt and the carriage lunged forward. I leaned over and waved goodbye to my grandmother standing at the bottom of the porch steps with Marta, Duncan, and Naomi waving back from the front porch.

"I am surprised she did not make you promise to write to her daily." My husband snorted with a final wave before turning back around in his seat. "You would think I was taking you off to the front lines of some war."

"Aren't you," I muttered adjusting my son in my lap.

"How can you say such a thing. They are my family." His eyes narrowed just a smidgen.

"I was not referring to your family," I glanced out the window. "I was referring to the rest of the Southern population."

"Perhaps, my dear," Keifer rubbed his chin thinking carefully of his next words. "If you open your mind, eyes, and heart just a little you may learn that, despite what the Boston newspapers have declared, Southerners are not Satan's children."

"Now Keifer be fair. I never said," but he cut me off.

"You realize I have spent our entire marriage crafting and molding myself to fit into your world. I am the one who has had to endure the snide remarks from our neighbors, our community — even my damn patients about my heritage and my loyalty be it to the North or my homestead in the South." Keifer leaned forward resting his elbows on his knees. "And never once did you ever offer to move South. Never once did you understand the loss I felt for my parents, my siblings, or my birthright in proudly running Gable Gardens." He sighed heavily. "I understand that you cannot comprehend the strong parental and familial bonds I walked away from, because you lost your mother and your father is a sad, weak man." His voice grew hardened. "But I know you understand the love of your homeland. Terrace Falls is your home. It is a part of you — your heartbeat. You thrive there. That is what I feel for Gable Gardens, and I walked away from all of it and them because of my love for you."

I had no response. There was no response because he was right, and we both knew it. He had given up everything to marry me. His birthright, his family, his home. I looked at him, but he had turned away. He sat back with his elbow resting on the windowsill staring out as the world slowing passed with the beating of the hooves on the dirt pathway.

I watched the deep green Northern fields drifting by, and my heart sank a bit deeper into my chest. I loved this land. I loved the smell of fresh jasmine in the spring fields. The feel of the soft rich soil between my fingers. The cool spring water from the river. The spectacular sunsets disappearing behind the tree line that could only be riveled by the peaceful bliss of the eastern sunrise.

A knot formed in the pit of my stomach. I feared traveling South. Open hostilities were now evident, and battle lines were being drawn. As silly as it sounded, I could not help but recall watching the *North and South* with Jocelyn a few years after we both learned about *EVE*. The scene where Patrick Swayze and Genie Francis' characters, Orry and Brett were traveling shortly before the start of the Civil War and how much trouble they had played on repeat in the back of my mind.

I knew it was ridiculous, but I could not help it. I looked down at my wide hoop skirt and felt the strong bindings of my stays. I stifled a laugh thinking of how completely ridiculous my life truly was. I do not know if Robert is right and this gift is a blessing or whether it was, as my sister referred to it, a curse. I wondered if she still felt that way after having years to adjust to it now.

I held my sleeping son closely to me and rested my head against the carriage beam. I closed my eyes and wished I could escape with my son to my *other* time. Still, I thought with a heavy heart I feared what was on the horizon there as well.

Was there no time that is safe where a person can live in peace and prosperity?

I was beginning to think not.

Houses appeared closer together and finally stretched out in rows as we entered Boston on the way to the harbor. It was hard for me to fathom, even in my *other* life, how anyone would want to live with neighbors so close to them. Despite living in an apartment due to financial reasons, I longed for the wide-open fields and the land I have in this life.

The carriage came to an abrupt stop. The sounds of the crowd and the bustling of people were almost deafening. The air was thick with sand and dirt and filled with the smell of salt and fish. Ned opened the carriage door and Keifer stepped to the ground. He took my hand and carefully helped us out of the carriage.

I stepped to the side as Keifer and Ned unloaded the luggage and transferred everything over to the ship orderly. Ned rejoined me by the carriage looking uncomfortable holding his wide hat in his hands.

"Mizdress, ya bes karful travelen dow dar." Ned looked at the ground but glanced at me. "Ah's don lik it."

"I will be careful, Ned. I promise." I reached over and patted his arm. "Just mind the books like I taught you." He nodded. "If you have any difficulty with them, please ask Mr. Bennett. He said he would help you and send me reports."

"Yes'm, Ah's will."

"And please look after my grandmother. I know this will be a difficult summer for her. But I believe Judith and Mr. Bennett will not leave her wanting for company in our absence."

"Yes'm," he smiled.

"I shall see you in a couple months. Take care, Ned." I gently squeezed his arm before turning towards Keifer.

"Here, dear." He held out his hand.

"Thank you," I took it and stepped up into the platform still holding my little boy close to my chest.

17

FRIDAY, MAY 29, 2020

THE STREETS OF BOSTON, LIKE MOST major cities throughout the country, had broken into utter chaos. There was no resemblance of law and order. Abandoned police vehicles burned, officers were being targeted and brutally attacked, and criminals ran unabated. Our democrat governor and mayor, in conjunction with all those of their political party, encouraged the rioting, looting, and civil unrest that was rapidly spreading without consequences.

The hospital where Landon and I worked was near the heart of the city. Within the last week our parking garage had been covered in Black Lives Matter, Antifa, and Pride graffiti. Many vehicles have been broken into, keyed, sprayed with graffiti, had their windshields smashed, headlights and taillights broken, and tired slashed. Most of the employees were now being escorted to their cars by security officers. Others had decided not to show up to work at all for their own safety and sanity. This left our limited employee roster even more crippled.

Still, nothing was done to alleviate the crisis. The liberal and progressive democrats appeared on every media outlet imaginable pushing their narrative and agenda. The lies rolled off their tongues with practiced efficiency. I had gotten to the point where I was avoiding social media and the news because it was too overwhelming and disheartening.

I arrived home after six in the evening. Landon was stuck in the ER until nine, if he got off on time, which hadn't occurred once this month. I took a long hot shower and collapsed on the couch flipping through movies on Amazon Prime. Nothing looked appealing so I settled on Outlander on my Starz subscription. My sister had turned me on to the books, and she and I had fallen in love with the series. In the last year, we had gotten Emily, Phoebe, and Leslie obsessed with it as well.

I was curled up with a blanket barely into the second episode of the first season when my phone rang on the coffee table. I considered letting it go to voicemail since I felt too tired to deal with anyone. But the name that flashed on the screen rarely called and I figured she must be trying to reach Alex.

"Hello mom," I answered on the third ring.

"Sidney, how are you?" Her voice sounded tense and off.

"Surviving. How are you?" I propped myself up and paused my show.

"The same." Amy sighed heavily. "I wanted to let you know due to this Covid mess Dane, and I have decided to postpone our wedding until we can have a proper one."

"I understand." I nodded even though she couldn't see me. "How are things in Seattle?"

"Have you seen the news?" Her voice piqued.

"No." I admitted. "I stopped watching it days ago. I couldn't take it anymore."

"Seattle is burning down and overrun with criminals. I haven't gone to the hospital in the last three days because it isn't safe. Dane, unfortunately, is stuck there and can't leave."

"Are you safe in your condo?" I had no idea where my mother lived in Seattle or how near she was to the chaos being unleased in that city.

"No, not really." Her voice sounded smaller than I had ever heard before. "I am surrounded by criminals and the riots. I cannot get to the hospital or the grocery store. The police are nowhere to be found. It's like they have completely abandoned the people in this part of the city."

"Jesus, mom." I exhaled audibly. "I wish I could do something." I didn't know what to say.

"I have been on the phone with Dane almost constantly. The hospital is overrun between patients and criminals. It isn't even safe there. I told him I have had enough — this is not what I signed up for."

"What are you going to do?"

"Well," she laughed softly without humor. "Being stuck here I decided to take matters in my own hands. I started making calls to colleagues and connections I've made throughout my career."

"Are you thinking of moving?" I was surprised.

"I received an offer this morning from a hospital in Tampa and one yesterday in the Florida Keys." Her voice brightened.

"Florida?" I couldn't believe it.

"Yes, well," her voice trailed off momentarily. "I believe Florida would be a much better fit for Dane and me."

"What does Dane think about this?" I was curious since I knew nothing about him nor the dynamics of their relationship.

"After this mess, he's a hundred percent on board."

"Is he from Seattle?" It was sad that I didn't know that small detail about the man who planned to marry my mother.

"No. He is from Tennessee. He moved here a couple years before I did, to accept the director of pediatric surgery position. He has never liked it here so he would be happy to leave." My mother explained.

"Tennessee is beautiful. Have you considered relocating there?"

"There are more opportunities and money in Florida."

"But housing and cost of living is also much higher in Florida." I reasoned.

"That is true," I could hear her wavering. "Plus, the mountains are stunning."

"Perhaps it would not hurt to reach out to some colleagues in that area just to keep your options open."

"I believe I will," I could picture the smile on her face. "I will let you know what I find."

"I believe you would be happier in Tennessee than Florida, although I do really like their governor." I admitted.

"As do I," she paused. "I suppose I should do some further research into Tennessee since for the first time since childhood, I have time on my hands." She laughed softly.

"True," I agreed.

"So, tell me, is Boston as bad as Seattle?"

"Almost, but not quite. The police are still fighting and arresting the so-called activists, but the DA and judges are just letting them go without bail or consequences. It's insane." My voice sounded as exhausted as I felt.

"The world has gone insane." My mother's voice sounded more vulnerable than I had ever heard it before.

"Yes, it has." I sighed heavily. "Common sense is not so common anymore."

"No. It's not." She paused for a moment. "I used to believe that everything happens for a reason. Now, it's like some people are just evil and have serious mental health issues that were never addressed. I am sure you are seeing more of this gender ideology BS in Boston as we are here." She laughed without any humor. "You know, I cannot recall one kid when I was growing up that suffered from gender dysphoria. Now you have all these parents insisting their children need hormone therapy and surgery because they were born in the wrong body."

"If you ask me, it's the parents who need their mental health evaluated." I said with conviction. "I am embarrassed to be a millennial."

"Honestly, I thank the good Lord every night that you three aren't typical millennials, especially you and your sister. I believe you are both old souls." I almost choked hearing her words — she had no idea how right she was.

"Jocelyn and I are more traditional, more conservative." I agreed carefully.

"Your father and I may not agree on much, but thankfully we raised you kids right. You all have manners, show respect, and take responsibility for your actions instead of making excuses. I am very proud of all three of you."

"Thank you," I squeaked. It was high praise from a woman who rarely acknowledged any of her children's qualities.

"My grandmother told me something at a family event when you were about eighteen months old. You had gotten into something you had been told several times to leave alone, and your dad finally smacked your hand. You wailed like he had killed you. I immediately picked you up and comforted you. My grandmother scolded me in front of the whole family." My mother recalled.

"And you let her?" I could not imagine anyone scolding the formidable force that was my mother.

"She was my grandmother and respect for our elders was ingrained in us from the time we could walk. My generation, or as you guys call us Gen Xer's, knew better than to ever talk back to an elder or any authority figure. We had a healthy fear of our parents, but we also trusted them. They never asked us about our feelings. They simply told us what was expected of us, and we did it without question."

"So, what did your grandmother say to you?" It was so rare that my mother talked about her past, I was intrigued.

"She told me that discipline without love will break a child but love without discipline will ruin one. Just another way to say, *spare the rod, spoil the child*."

"That is good advice. I think parents have become too afraid to discipline their children. So, children have become disrespectful and ungrateful with a victim mentality if they don't get their way. They no longer fear their parents but instead threaten them that they will call child protective services on them if they try to discipline them."

"I see it every day at work — parents who fear retaliation from their kids and their kids know they hold the power. These kids make ridiculous demands and expect their parents to give them everything their heart desires." Amy explained. "These morons on the evening news rioting, destroying, looting, and burning down cities across the country are a perfect example of kids who never learned consequences for their actions."

"I hope the police educate them where their parents failed."

"Dane's sister, Darline is a high school teacher. She and her husband, Jason, a police officer in Louisville came out for a visit last Christmas. The stories they told us were unbelievable. When I was in school, if a kid got in trouble their parents would ask what the kid did. Darline told us that parents now blamed the teachers when a kid got bad grades or misbehaved. She wants to retire even though she's only forty-eight because she can't take it anymore."

"Landon's mom retired from teaching for the same reasons. This whole notion of *gentle parenting* is ridiculous. Children need discipline and consequences. I don't mean beating a kid, but these young adults out there causing all this trouble are in dire need of a trip to the woodshed." I scoffed.

"Oh, but instead of discipline, parents are supposed to use *emotional processing*." My mother's voice dripped in sarcasm. "Parents don't even use time-outs anymore. My father took time out of his day to beat our ass." She chuckled. "Neither of my parents tolerated disrespect of any kind. And I know most of my generation feared their dad's — the whole, 'you just wait until your father gets home' narrative. Your grandmother never waited for dad to come home. That woman took care of things herself and let me tell you, she was much worse than our father."

"We were spanked as kids," I noted. "Ethan more so than Jocelyn and me, but still, we never thought we were abused." I rolled my eyes even though she couldn't see me.

"I think I've swatted you on the rear three times in your life." She confessed. "Jocelyn maybe a half dozen, but Ethan," she laughed. "Your dad used to joke that Ethan was born with certain frustrations."

"Ethan is stubborn." I giggled. "To put it mildly."

"Ethan is an asshole." My mother laughed wholeheartedly. "Ever since he was three years old. My sweet little boy grew mischievous and sneaky. By the time he was a teenager," her voice trailed off. "He was extremely difficult."

"Ethans changed a lot." I admitted. "We've never been close, but even he and Jocelyn rarely talk now."

"I'm sorry to hear that." Her voice was softer now. "They used to be thick as thieves."

"I remember."

"I am glad you and your sister are close now. I always wanted you to be."

"I guess we had to grow up first." I tried to sound casual.

"Either way, I am happy you two are close now." My mother sighed. "Have you and Landon discussed marriage."

"Yes," I appreciated the ease in which she changed subjects. "We decided to wait until we're finished with med school."

"Have you decided on your specialty or considered where you want to do your residency?"

"Landon is focusing on pediatrics." I bit my lower lip before continuing. "I am torn," I admitted.

"Between?" The question hung in the air like a lead balloon.

"Pediatrics and psychiatry." I held my breath.

"Psychiatry?" my mother exhaled audibly. "That's interesting." I could hear the tightness in her voice.

"I know you must be disappointed." I began, but she quickly interrupted.

"Nonsense, Sidney. A physician's specialty is a very personal decision. I want you to be happy. That's all I have ever wanted for you and your siblings." My mother's voice was calm and gentle, which surprised me.

"Thank you," I was at a loss for words.

"Well, I will let you go. Please be careful."

"I will. You too. And let me know what you decide about your new job offers."

"Of course. I will talk to you soon." She paused for a moment before she said in a small voice as if uncertain as to how I would react. "I love you, Sidney. And I am very proud of you."

"I love you, too."

I disconnected the call and set my phone back on the coffee table. I hit play on my television but was lost in my own thoughts. That was probably the most normal conversation I have had with my mother in years. It was strange and not something I was used to any longer. She had become so cold and distant since her divorce and pulled away from all three of her children. She moved across the country and started a life that none of us were a part of.

I heard Landon's key in the lock and realized it was later than I imagined. The door opened as I rose to my feet. His scrubs were smudged with God only knows, his hair disheveled, and there were prominent dark circles under his eyes. There were lines creased across his face from the mask he'd been forced to wear all day for the last several months that never fully disappeared — much like my own and every employee at the hospital and essential worker. He tossed his keys in the bowl on the entryway table and closed the door behind him.

"Hello darling," I hugged him briefly. "You stink." I pulled back. "Wow, you should take a shower."

"Sorry," he grumbled kicking off his sneakers. "I didn't think I was ever getting out of there tonight."

"Are you hungry?" I took a step back trying to clear my nose.

"Starving. What do you have in mind?" He peeled off his scrub top and headed towards the shower.

"Scrambled eggs and bacon?" I called after him.

"Sounds good." Landon hollered back before I heard the shower start.

I busied myself in the kitchen whipping up some scrambled eggs, bacon, and toast. I moved methodically without giving it much thought. I felt baffled by my conversation with my mother and was worried about her. Although she assured me, she was safe, it sounded like her condo was close enough to the riots that she couldn't even make it to work, and Dane couldn't return home.

"It smells good in here." Landon walked into the kitchen and poured himself a glass of orange juice before sitting down at the breakfast bar. "I am starved."

"Good," I buttered his toast and spread some apple butter across it. "Here you go, darling." I set his plate in front of him before gathering my own and taking a seat beside him.

"How was your day?" He asked with a mouth full of eggs.

"Hectic. I was happy to disappear as soon as I could sneak out of there." I smirked. "Guess who called me tonight?"

"Your dad?" I shook my head. "Ethan?"

"Nope," I grinned taking a bite of my toast.

"I give," he took another drink of his orange juice.

"Amy," I raised an eyebrow.

"Really?" I nodded. "How did that go?"

"Surprisingly well." I admitted.

I went on to recap my conversation with her. Landon listened intently while eating his food in record time. I watched the lines around his eyes and across his forehead deepen as I described my mother being trapped in her condo and Dane unable to reach her.

"They need to get out of Seattle. Now."

"They're trying. She has been reaching out to her contacts in red states and so far, they have two offers in Florida."

"Nice. Are they going to take them?" He raised an eyebrow.

"They are going to wait a couple more days and field other offers, but I believe they will accept the position in the Florida Keys."

"I hope they do," he grinned. "It would be great to have a place down there to vacation."

"You're terrible," I laughed, tossing a hand towel at him.

"Tell me I'm wrong," he held his hands up in surrender.

"Okay, you are not entirely wrong." I conceded with a smirk.

"All I am saying is once the world reopens again, it would be nice to have a vacation spot without hotel fees." The corners of his mouth twitched.

"But you're forgetting," I looked pointedly at him. "Amy will be there too."

"True," he wavered. "Still, that may be worth it, especially if they get beach front property."

Despite our fatigue, the conversation and teasing flowed in a comfortableness that only occurs when two people share an unconditional love. This man had stood by my side through our undergraduate years, the stress of my parent's divorce and its implosion of my family, moved across the country for me, and held me through the loss of our child. Even though he remained ignorant of *E.V.E.*, his love for me never wavered, nor mine for him.

I curled up beside him in bed. The lights were out; the doors were locked. The faint sound of the city outside drifted through the cracked window in our bedroom. The glow from the television in our bedroom provided enough light for me to see his strong profile in the dark. His eyes were closed, and his breathing was soft and even. I rested my head upon his chest taking comfort in the strong, steady rhythm of his heartbeat. His arm automatically wrapped around me, holding me closer to him. I said a silent prayer for us, for my family, for our country, for peace before drifting away into my *other* world.

18

FRIDAY, JUNE 1, 1860

THE SALTY SEA AIR KISSED MY CHEEKS as I stood on the sundeck. I had never been a big fan of ships and had almost no prior experience traveling on one. In my *other* life, my family would spend long summer weekends boating. My father, Shane, loved being on the water and taught all three of us children how to water ski. But those long sunny lazy afternoons on the water did little to prepare me for an extended voyage down the eastern coast.

It took me a couple of days to grasp my sea legs. I was fortunate not to experience sea sickness but experienced severe nausea until I got my bearings. Keifer and our son did not seem bothered and slept more peacefully during our journey than they did in their own beds at home. I felt envious.

After five long arduous days, the port of Savannah came into view. It rose in the distance appearing like a painting I had seen of small European towns — each home beaming like a picturesque cottage of a simple life long forgotten. The architecture was breathtaking and held an ambiance that northern cities failed to capture.

An endless sea of pale blue sky loomed overhead dotted with occasional fluffy white clouds. The spring flowers were in full bloom mixing the air with hints of lavender and jasmine. It was captivating to my naïve eyes as I absorbed everything.

Keifer's sister, Margarett and her husband, Thad, were waiting at the port when we arrived. I had not realized Margarett was pregnant once again, but she appeared to be heavily pregnant. I knew she had several children already, but I could not recall if this new addition would be her fourth or fifth. She ran up to her older brother and embraced him with tears in her eyes.

"Oh, Keifer. You're home." She kissed both his cheeks smiling through her tears. "You're finally home." I thought she would never let him go. It warmed my heart to see how cherished he was by his younger sister.

"My goodness, Maggie. I had no idea you were expecting again." Keifer laughed and stepped back holding onto his sister's hands, eyeing her for the first time.

"It was unexpected." Margarett laughed and embraced him again before turning towards me. "And Sidney, my dear." She leaned over and kissed my cheek. "It is good to see you again. This must be my nephew." She pulled back the side of the blanket a bit to view my son's face. "He looks like his father." She beamed.

"Yes, he does." I said proudly. "You are absolutely glowing, Margarett."

"Please, call me Maggie. Afterall, we are sisters." She took hold of my arm and started leading me towards the carriage. "Do not fret about your luggage. Thad and Keifer will make sure Otis fetches everything. He will follow us directly with the wagon." I turned and saw my husband and Thad talking with a large black man near the docks.

I had spent very little time in Savannah, or the South for that matter. Keifer and I had visited shortly after we were married, but our trip was cut short due to my grandmother becoming ill. She had not really been sick but sent notice anyway at my request because she knew how opposed I was to slavery and did not feel at ease at Gable Gardens plantation.

But now I had no choice. I was about to confront the good, the bad, and the ugly of American history that I had only read about it books. I was not sure what to expect, but I felt sick to my stomach and a weariness in my soul.

Maggie stopped shortly beside their carriage and looked back around at the crowd behind us.

"Did you bring your wet nurse?" She asked with a casual tone.

"Wet nurse?"

"Yes, for your son." Maggie smiled as our husbands approached.

"No. I am afraid we did not." I glanced over at Keifer who shook his head silently.

"Do not fret. Sadie, one of our house slaves, had another child last month and she can take care of little mister here." Maggie said casually as she climbed into the carriage, and I looked sternly at my own husband now beside me.

"Let it go," he whispered taking a hold of my hand and helping me up. "We will discuss it later."

"Is there a problem?" Maggie settled into her seat.

"No," Keifer answered before I could. "Sidney interviewed several but could not find a nanny she was satisfied with."

With the four of us seated and my son cradled in my arms, the carriage jolted forward through the heart of Savannah. My eyes were eager to absorb everything. But in my mind, all I could think about was General Sherman's march through Atlanta cutting a path of fire and destruction sixty miles wide all the way to Savannah and the sea. In such a short time from now, most of this beautiful peaceful city sitting on the banks will be destroyed.

I recalled that most of the city of Savannah itself would be spared from fire and destruction because General Sherman understood the significance of its large ports. But I also knew he would present the city off Savannah to President Lincoln on December 21, 1864, as an early Christmas gift and a sign that the war would soon be over.

The smell of magnolia trees and jasmine hung heavily in the twilight air. The evening sun was beginning its long descent across the tree line in the distant. The soft pink and pale purple hues across the sky looked different than what appeared from our Northern porch. The air was as thick as molasses, and I felt like I was covered in layers of dirt and sweat. I sighed heavily and leaned my head against the side of the carriage.

The tall, beautiful houses with their wide porches and black iron rails lined the street. The antebellum architecture was breathtaking and unlike anything I had ever seen up North. The majestic buildings were graceful and elegant in their structure and prominence. The ambiance surrounding us felt like I had stepped into a foreign world. Words cannot adequately describe the strange sensation that overwhelmed me as I watched the city streets drift away.

The canopy of trees overhead appeared to shelter us from the outside world. They stifled any reminisce of sunlight that had followed us beyond the blocks portrayed a time beyond a time I was familiar with leaving me with a sense of unease.

The ride lingered on through the stifling heat with only the occasional glimpse of various dwellings or homes tucked back beyond the dirt road. The dust kicked up by the horses and carriages hung in the air and clung to everything it touched. I felt the sweat on the nap of my neck and shifted uncomfortably. I removed the blanket from around my son. Thankfully, he was still asleep. I did not know how, but was thankful, nonetheless.

Tall brick pillars and an iron gate loomed before us. Gable Gardens was clearly scripted in calligraphy above in the expansive archway. Two young black boys scurried out from behind the pillars and pulled the iron gates open to allow our carriage and the wagon behind us to enter. I heard the loud crack of its lock once we were through.

The enormous antebellum, white-washed plantation house loomed before us. The red and sandy dirt pathway up to the house was lined with moss-covered trees, scattered benches, and small gazebos looking forlorn in the setting sun. The large two-story Corinthian columns were offset by the home's black shutters and oversize double front door painted to match the shutters.

A stone fountain with an angel statue in the center sat in the middle of a sea of flowers that marked the round-a-bout in front of the wrap-around porch. Taking Keifer's hand and cradling a now fussy infant son, I stepped out into, in my eyes, what appeared to be the set of Tara from *Gone with The Wind*. I had to stifle a chuckle that rose in the back of my throat as my feet hit the ground.

The front doors opened, and a flood of people came scrambling out. It had been almost a decade since I last saw my husband's family home and relatives. I had no idea who most of these people were. Of course, I immediately recognized his abhorrent younger sister, Eugenia, who kept to the back of the crowd and looked none too pleased to have me here. I had secretly wished she would have been off on one of her extended visits with some other poor suffering relative and save me the bother of having to contend with her this summer.

Keifer's mother, Angelina, was the first one down the steps. She was holding the sides of her wide hoop skirt rushing to greet her son. She was about the same height as me and had the same dirty blonde hair as Keifer. However, her eyes were so dark brown they appeared almost black. I quickly realized the adorable little dimple high on my husband's right cheek was inherited from his mother. She was thin and beautiful, looking much younger than her age.

His father, David, followed closely behind his wife. He was almost six and a half feet tall, a large imposing man with broad shoulders and salt and pepper hair. He had a full beard and the same hazel eyes as his son.

"Oh, Keifer." Angelina came bustling down the porch steps and threw herself into my husband's arms. "I have missed you so much," she kissed both of his cheeks.

She was quickly joined by his father, who hugged his son briefly and wiped a lone tear from his cheek. My husband's younger brothers and sisters all gathered around to where I stood off to the side unnoticed by all. And I was fine with it feeling extremely out of place and out of my element.

I expected the crowd to slowly disperse. My son was openly fuzzing for his next meal. I rocked him gently in my arms on the outskirts of the gathering trying not to be impatient but knowing he was well past his next feeding time. Still, more blacks came from around the sides of the house gathering behind the family all eager to greet my husband. It was a blur of faces of people I had only heard about in letters Keifer received from home.

"Sidney? Sidney?" I heard Keifer's voice rise above the crowd. "Darling, please come here." The sea of people parted, and my husband waved towards us.

I held my breath feeling utterly overwhelmed and very aware of the knot in the pit of my gut. I walked slowly towards my husband holding my son close to my body in almost a protective manner out of sheer fear of being in a strange new world.

"And this," Keifer lifted our son from my arms and held up our screaming son. "Is the next generation of Marshall's, my son Keifer Lee II." My husband's voice boomed with pride.

Angelina quickly retrieved my son from her own and smothered his little face with kisses. In turn, my son screeched loudly with his healthy set of lungs. No one seemed bothered by it at all, except for me.

"Sidney," Keifer turned towards me and took my arm pulling my attention away from our impatient son. "These are my younger sisters, Victoria and Caroline. My brother Lucas and this little moppet hiding behind mother's skirt is Oliver, one of Maggie's boys. That there is the other, Milo. Marina and Susanna also belong to Maggie. But this here is Beatrice, better known as Trixie. She's my youngest sister." Keifer continued to point to strangers and rattle off names that would take me most of the summer to remember.

But he was happy. Happier than I had seen him since the day I told him we were pregnant. He had a smile plastered upon his lips that appeared to stretch from ear to ear. It made me feel horrible that he had chosen to stay up North because of me and left a family whom he obviously adored dearly.

"You must be exhausted, my dear." Angelina smiled and hugged me gently. "We must get you settled and this one fed." She took my arm and walked up the porch steps with me.

In all reality we had probably been standing in front of the house for about ten minutes, but for me it felt like an hour or longer. I held up the edge of my hoop skirt and followed my mother-in-law up the steps and through the double doors.

The enormous tiger wood staircase ballooned out before us and divided to each wing of the oversized antebellum plantation house. It was elegantly decorated with furniture and paintings that were far beyond our financial reach.

"Otis. Leroy." Angelina hollered over her shoulder. "Carry our guests' trunks up to the east wing master room overlooking the pond."

"Yes,'m" a duo of voices answered in unison.

"Would you like a moment to freshen up before you eat?" My mother-in-law held onto my arm as she skillfully balanced my son with the other as we walked up the stairs.

"Yes, thank you." I smiled. "I know this little one is hungry."

"I am sure Maggie mentioned to you that one of our housemaids had a child several weeks back and she will be little master's wetnurse while you are here." Her voice was light and casual.

"I thank you, Mother Angelina, but that really is not necessary. I prefer to nurse my own child." She stopped and looked at me with a queer look at the top of the stairs.

"My goodness child," she shook her head in disbelief. "Perhaps that is acceptable in the North, but no self-respecting White lady would ever nurse her own child." Her lips pinched together in disgust. "Only po white trash nurse their own children, Sidney."

"Nonsense," I chuckled trying to make light of her remark despite how much it stung. "It is natural for a mother to nurse her own child. It creates a strong bond between a mother and her child."

"Well," she sputtered. "I shall speak to Keifer about it."

"There is no need. I am capable of deciding what is best for our child as far as feeding him. Besides," I placed my hand reassuringly on her arm. "Keifer knows I have been nursing our son since the day he was born. He is fine with it." I gently took my son for her arms and waited for her to continue escorting me to our room.

My mother-in-law appeared visibly upset by my words. With her lips pinched into a thin line, she led the way to our suite. She stopped in front of a large oak door, opened it, and stood aside.

"There is a fresh basin of water for you. Dinner will be ready shortly." She did not wait for me to respond but closed the door as soon as I was on the other side of it.

I smiled and shook my head at myself as I sat down on the edge of the bed and began to nurse my son. He latched on hungrily making me wince until he loosened his suckling a bit. I scooted back against the mountain of pillows piled at the headboard of the large canopy. I closed my eyes and let out a deep breath. It felt like the first time I had breathed easily since I left home.

"What did you say to my mother?" Keifer's voice interrupted my solace.

"Nothing," I answered without opening my eyes.

"Sidney?" His tone dropped an octave.

"What?" I was too tired to be irritated.

"She is upset about you turning down the wet nurse and said you are insisting on nursing our son yourself." He leaned against the canopy post eyeing me.

"I have been nursing my son since the day he arrived. Why should I stop now?" I narrowed my eyes.

"Because that is not how things are done here." He sighed heavily. "Can you please try to understand?"

"Keifer," I raised an eyebrow pointedly. "You married a Northern lady. Not some helpless Southern Belle."

"I am aware of that." A small smile tilted the corners of his lips.

"Then tell your mother to get over it." The words slipped out of my mouth before I realized what I had said and there was no way to put them back.

"Sidney?" My husband's eyes widened in shock. "You have never spoken to me that way."

"I apologize." I blundered. "I am so sorry." I felt so foolish. In my exhaustion, my *other* world had bled through in words.

"I understand. You must be so tired, my dear." Keifer sat down on the edge of the bed beside me. "Would you care for something to eat?"

"No, thank you." I shook my head before switching my son to the other side. "I honestly just want to sleep."

"All right," he leaned over and kissed me on the cheek. "I will let my family know."

"Thank you." I squeezed his hand. "Would you mind helping me change into my nightgown?"

My husband paused looking conflicted. "I could get," I knew what he was going to say and immediately shook my head. "Darling, Marta helps you dress every day. I do not understand what the problem is."

"I know, Marta, darling. I am comfortable with her." I tried to explain. "I do not know these women."

"This is their job, Sidney." He sounded exhausted with me.

"Keifer, I am not accustomed to slavery. You know how I feel about it." It was such a touchy subject with him, but I felt so strongly against it.

"I know," he nodded without looking at me. "But I cannot change my parents or my family's way of life. It is what it is."

"Please," I sighed. "Just help me this evening. I am tired and I really would like to get some sleep." I was too tired to argue with him.

"Fine," I shifted my son and patted him on the back until he burped. Then I laid him down in the center of the bed and climbed down. I turned my back towards my husband. He undid the eyelet buttons down the back of my gown and started loosening my corset. I felt like I could finally breathe. "You realize I cannot attend to you daily like this?"

"Yes, I understand." I muttered with clear discontent.

I washed my face and brushed my teeth in the basin before changing my son and cleaning him up from the long journey.

I placed him down in the small bassinet at the foot of our canopy, kissing him lightly on the forehead. "Sweet dreams, my love." I whispered.

"Is there anything I can bring you?" Keifer helped me back up into the bed and straightened the coverlet over me.

"No but thank you darling." He leaned over and kissed me. "And I do apologize. I did not mean to distress your mother." Keifer smirked back at me. "I promise, I will try."

"I would appreciate that, my love." He touched my cheek lightly before turning down the oil lamp and closing the door behind him.

The soft glow from the embers illuminated the large room. It felt so eerie and hollow. My eyes scanned each dark corner wishing I was back home in my own comfortable and familiar chambers. I missed my grandmother, the sound of servants scuffling about the house, the easy laughter that flowed up the stairs.

The silence engulfed me. Still, the room was beautifully decorated with a large canopy bed, a soft linen quilt, and light cotton sheets. A wash basin, vanity, and full-length mirror was arranged along the wall opposite the bed. A walnut armoire stood between the two windows along the wall on my side of the bed. The red-brick fireplace sat opposite on Keifer's side. In the center of the mantel rested a tall wooden and brass clock and flanked on each end by a vase full of fresh wildflowers.

Despite the attempt to make it feel cozy, it felt cold. The home was so enormous it sounded empty. There were no sounds drifting up from below. Just an unsettling silence that felt so uncomfortable and cold despite the warmth of the room. I closed my eyes and pulled the coverlet closer around me hoping to get a little bit of sleep before my son decided he was hungry again.

19

SUNDAY, JUNE 7, 2020

THE WORLD HAD GONE MAD. I had read about the protests and the riots that occurred throughout the 1960's Civil Rights Movement, but nothing could have ever prepared me to witness it. Major cities across the country were burning down. Stores were looted. People were murdered. It was complete anarchy with no end in sight.

After the death of George Floyd, a terrorist group under the guise of civil rights activism called Black Lives Matter led the charge in protests and riots. The center of the riots broke out in Minneapolis, Minnesota and the city, under the watchful eye of the incompetent governor Tim Walz, was burned, looted, and officers were brutally attacked and injured. People died.

Curfews were implemented in various cities nationwide. Chaos increased when a group of violent domestic terrorists known as Antifa joined Black Lives Matter protestors and increased the violence against every person in America. Groups of progressive liberal democrats went on a rampage calling every white conservative American a white supremist and spouting a nonsensical narrative about white privilege, social justice, and white supremacy.

Cries for defunding the police swept across America led by Black Lives Matter and Antifa activists. The racial division grew deeper amongst most Americans. Those who had never had a racist thought or behavior began to grow a deep resentment towards the black community as they watched their communities being destroyed under the hatred of the Black Lives Matter banner. The National Guard was deployed to squash the chaos but was largely ineffective.

The constant clashes with police only fueled Black Lives Matter's desire to dismantle police departments nationwide. Their hell-bent fury caused unprovoked and premeditated attacks and killings of numerous police officers. City councilmen, prosecutors, district attorneys, and even police chiefs turned a blind eye to the plight of the attacks on their officers and violent criminals ran rough shod in every city. The country was rapidly falling apart.

Most people were still out of work. Americans were struggling to buy food and essential household items. Black Lives Matter activists began marking their territories in every major city, including the capital with Black Lives Matter banners two blocks long across city streets. Hate filled messages geared towards white Americans flooded social media platforms and CEO's of America's largest corporations unashamedly took a knee beneath the Black Lives Matter banner.

The lines were clearly drawn.

I found Brandy sitting on the floor in the back corner of the locker room. Her hair was pulled up in a messy bun, and her head was resting on her knees.

"Brandy?" I approached her slowly. "Are you alright?" I knelt beside her and placed my hand on her shoulder.

"No," she looked up at me with red swollen eyes that held dark circles beneath them. "I worried sick about my husband."

"The riots," She nodded as I sat down beside her. "How is he?"

"Thankfully, home." She looked at me with sorrowful eyes. "At least for another two days. He has a broken eye socket from a frozen water bottle thrown by one of those peaceful protesters." Her voice was dripping with disdain.

"I am so sorry, Brandy."

"I was here when they brought him in." She let out a heavy sigh. "I have never been more scared in all my life seeing him lying there unconscious. I thought he was dead." She brushed a tear off her cheek. "Now we're constantly fighting because I want him to retire, and he says he can't walk away from his brothers."

"I thought your husband worked in homicide. Isn't he a detective?"

"He is, but when the riots started, they pulled everyone in from every unit and put them back in uniform on the streets." Brandy chuckled. "He called me and told me to dig out his uniform, wash and iron it. It's been almost twelve years since he wore it."

"How did that work out?" I smirked.

"About as well as you'd expect." She smiled for the first time. "His shirt wouldn't button, and he couldn't get the pants up over his thighs."

"Sounds about right," I laughed.

"He blamed my cooking before heading to the uniform shop."

"Figures," I patted her arm. "Do you think he will retire?"

"I hope so. I am going to do my damnedest to make him." She shook her head slightly. "I do not know how much more of this I can take. My nerves are shot. I am constantly worried, scared my husband will not make it home. My children are being harassed. Other children are calling their dad a murderer. My eldest daughter quit her part time job yesterday because someone posted a flyer on the bulletin board in the breakroom of a pig wearing a police officer's cap and the message beneath it said, 'All officers need to be roasted like the pigs they are.' She told her boss, a black woman, who just chuckled and said people are entitled to their opinions."

"That's horrible," I never thought I would see the day when calling for the death of police officers was acceptable.

"She quit on the spot and walked out."

"I don't blame her."

"I never thought I would ever see something like this. People burning our cities down and looting stores." Brandy scoffed. "These animals are throwing frozen water bottles, rocks, and bricks at our police officers. Several blocks around the state house are destroyed. Windows broken, merchandise stolen. They hit a Men's Wearhouse, some shoe store, a cell phone store, jewelry shop, Macy's and even a Walgreens. These savages have no shame, no conscience."

"I agree. It's inconceivable. I do not understand why they believe burning down their own cities and killing those who protect us from criminals is going to somehow make a difference. Their logic is so flawed, it simply demonstrates their ignorance and low intelligence." I scoffed.

"What irritates me most is the never-ending lies being perpetrated by the news and social media outlets. They twist the facts, fudge the numbers, and outright lie to fit their narrative. To hear them talk every white person in America is racist and born with a silver spoon up their ass." She spat.

"Yeah, well I have student loans I will be paying off until I die." I laughed. "And my parents were considered upper-middle class." It was true my parents did cover the cost of my undergraduate studies, as well as my siblings, but I was responsible for paying for medical school and even with supplemental income from the hospital, Landon and I were drowning in student loans.

"You and me both." Brandy mocked. "My parents are middle class. My dad worked at a refinery, and my mother was a bank teller. We were comfortable, but my parents had too much debt to pay for my college. I would like to go back and get my master's degree, but we cannot afford it with three kids and college approaching for them. We'll be lucky to help them out at all. But nothing has ever been handed to me or my husband. We worked our asses off for everything we have."

"I don't understand what this world is coming too." I said softly.

"Me neither," she looked at with worried eyes. "But I am scared for my children."

"Me too." I whispered and climbed to my feet. I reached down and took her hand helping her to her feet. "Come on, we need to clock back in. It's time to rejoin the circus."

"Oh, fun." Brandy muttered and followed me over to the time clock.

20

SUNDAY, JUNE 10, 1860

THE DAYS GREW LONGER. HUMIDITY enveloped us like a suffocating blanket and the temperatures began to rise. But each day twilight brought a peaceful respite. As the sun sank off into the distance, and the sky was ablaze with colors, I would sit out on the front porch engulfed in the warm breeze and rock my son.

My little man was growing and gaining weight steadily. He had found his voice, his giggles, and unfortunately, his temper. He was his father's son with Keifer's moody temperament, yet easy smile when his belly was full and his bottom dry. The dark hair he had worn at birth had almost been completely replaced with a blond crown. His eyes were the same hazel green as Keifer's and every time I looked upon his precious face, I felt overpowered by the immense love I have for this beautiful child.

An uneasy truce had befallen between me and Keifer's family since our arrival. I still did not feel comfortable in their home or surrounded by slaves. But I knew their status would soon change and my being disrespectful in any manner towards my husband's family would only harm him. So, I remained friendly yet distant and spent most of my time reading, writing letters to my grandmother and Charlotte, and tending to my son.

After church services and a quick bite to eat, little man had woken from his nap. I fed and changed him then decided to wander about the grounds before dinner. With my son on my hip and a lace parasol in my other hand, I walked down the long drive. I sang softly to my son pausing to point out various birds, butterflies, and small creatures. He was in high spirits and giggled and cooed his approval.

I was enjoying myself and the time alone with my son so much that I lost track of my bearings. Without realizing it, I had wandered off to the side corner of the grounds and found myself among the slave quarters. Dozens of little white board shacks laid out in rows before me. Little black children ran about chasing chickens, tending to small gardens, and washing clothes in half barrels filled with water. It was surreal to me. I paused in my steps suddenly feeling as if I had stepped into another world.

"Miss Sidney," a sharp voice from behind me startled me back to reality.

"Yes," I turned towards the voice and saw Keifer's twenty-year-old sister Victoria walking towards us.

"You should not be over here, Miss Sidney. Especially with the baby." She looked around quickly to see if someone else had noticed our presence.

"I was just out walking with my son enjoying the beautiful weather." I explained.

"That is fine, of course. But you really do not belong over here." Victoria looked nervous.

"I was not doing any harm." I protested as she took my arm and began walking us back towards the house.

"I understand that, but a lady should not be out here, especially with our young master who is set to inherit this great plantation." She smiled sweetly.

"What do you mean inherit this great plantation? My son will inherit Terrace Falls, our home up North near Boston." I explained as casually as I could muster.

"My sweet sister, if I understand correctly, you have three younger brothers who will inherit Terrace Falls before you. My dear brother is the eldest child; therefore, Gable Gardens belongs to him upon the passing of our father." She glanced over at me and playfully tickled my son. I had to fight the urge to jerk him out of her reach.

"My grandparents left Terrace Falls to me." I objected with more force than I intended. "Therefore, it belongs to me and my husband and will be passed directly to our eldest child." I swallowed back the bile in the back of my throat.

"Nonsense. Girls cannot inherit. Terrace Falls belongs to your eldest younger brother." Victoria stated as a matter of fact.

"You have a grave misunderstanding of estate law, Miss Victoria." I stopped and stared at her. "My son will never reside here outside of an occasional visit. He is a Bostonian."

"Your son is a Southerner by birth. His father is a Southerner."

"And his mother is a Northerner and his home and property rests in Massachusetts." I interrupted. "I do not agree with your lifestyle, but I respect my husband. Just because I have to be here, does not mean I have to like it." I left her standing there and walked back up to the main house.

I was not sure where my husband was, but I knew I was going to be chastised for what I said to Victoria. I was certain she was going to tattle to him and her parents the first opportunity provided to her. But I did not care. I was tired of being silent. I knew what was waiting for Southerners on the horizon even if they were yet too blind to realize it themselves.

I nursed and fed my son in the dim silence of the empty chambers assigned to our little family. Once he fell asleep, I laid him down in the basinet. I felt parched, but the only water in the pitcher on the nightstand was from this morning and had grown stale. I tossed it out the open window and headed downstairs to retrieve some fresh water.

As usual, I tried to keep my footsteps as silent as possible as they seemed to echo throughout the house. I wished to move about unnoticed as I was not in the mood for another confrontation. I felt like it was a constant battle since I arrived. The clashing of two worlds that went much deeper than an imaginary line.

"I was coming to fetch you, Miss Sidney." Maggie's voice reached me before my foot hit the first floor. "Supper is ready. The family is gathered in the dining room." She took the pitcher from my hands and gave it to the closest female slave. "Refill this with fresh water and bring it up to Master Keifer's chambers." She held out her arm with a false smile. I reluctantly took it and walked into the dining room with her.

David stood at the head of the table and said prayers as soon as we were all seated. Keifer reached for my hand beneath the table and squeezed it letting me know he had heard all about my encounter with his younger sister.

"Amen," the table responded in unison and an array of outstretched arms began passing around steaming bowls filled with delicious food. David stood at the head of the table and began carving the ham and passing it around. It was a chaotic mess the family had perfected.

"Are you alright, dear?" Keifer leaned over a bit and inquired in a low voice.

"Yes, dear. I am fine." I offered him a fake smile that I knew he would recognize as one telling him I did not want to discuss the matter.

I listened to my husband's family seemingly all talking at once with no one listening to what the others had to say. They laughed, joked, and teased each other just as every other family does. They were loving, respectful, and joyous. Yet, as I looked around and saw the dishes and glasses being refilled by slaves it made my stomach turn. I saw young black children probably between five to seven years old lined up around the perimeter of the room with huge ostrich feathers fanning off the family as they ate their supper. I could barely eat. I simply picked at my food and moved it about the plate.

"Are you feeling unwell, Sidney?" Angelina's voice caught me off guard.

"No, mother. Thank you. I am feeling well." I pressed my lips together in a faint smile.

"I heard you had an interesting conversation with Victoria this afternoon." David spoke up.

"A simple difference of opinion," I narrowed my eyes at my sister-in-law sitting across the table wearing a smug and satisfied expression.

"I understand you are not well versed in our customs, but it is clear there were some misunderstandings." My father-in-law's voice held an edge that I did not appreciate.

"No, sir. I do not believe so. Miss Victoria explained your customs and expectations quite well." Keifer shot me a disapproving look.

"I see. And from what I gather, you do not approve." His eyes narrowed a bit, and I could feel my husband's eyes boring into the side of me without looking over at him.

"Whether I approve or not does not matter." I answered honestly.

"How so," Maggie's husband, Thad joined in.

"Excuse me?" I wasn't expecting him to speak up.

"You stated that it does not matter whether you approve of our customs and lifestyle, but you married a Southern man." Thad tilted his head slightly, eyeing me as if he was truly interested in my opinion.

"Yes," I encouraged him to continue.

"Is that not a contradiction?" Thad smirked.

"How so?" I was beginning to enjoy toying with him.

"How can you be married to a Southern man, but not respect his customs and lifestyle?" Thad quipped.

"I never said I did not respect my husband's customs and lifestyle." I raised my eyebrows and fired back. "Did I?" I shot a look at Victoria. "Actually, I have the utmost respect for my husband, his heritage, and his family. To imply otherwise would be a great falsehood." I was becoming irritated by their insinuations.

"Granted, you did not say so in so many words, but the sentiment was obvious." Victoria responded coyly.

"No," I shook my head. "You are incorrect. I said nothing of the sort. I simply stated a fact. Apparently, you Miss Victoria are not familiar with Northern customs and estate law." I smiled sweetly and heard Thad choke down a laugh earning him a look of disapproval from his wife.

"And I do not care to." Victoria scoffed.

"Why don't you enlighten us, Sidney to your Northern customs and laws that differ from our own." My father-in-law seemed amused.

"What would you like to know?" I tried to hide my smirk.

"Sidney, please." Keifer cautioned.

"Now son, I am curious. Let your wife speak since she apparently feels free to speak her mind." The disapproval in his voice was obvious.

"I explained to Victoria that Terrace Falls was given to me by my grandfather in his will and therefore, does not belong to any of my brothers and will in time, be inherited by our son." I reached over and took my husband's hand in solidarity.

"I see," David looked towards his wife whose disappointment was evident.

"But Keifer inherits Gable Gardens. He is the eldest son. By right it belongs to him." David's voice was patronizing.

"Does that mean Thad and Maggie will inherit it?" Keifer's eighteen-year-old sister, Caroline, looked at her parents.

"No," my in-laws answered in unison.

"But why not? If Keifer rejects his birthright, as the second born, Gable Gardens should be ours." Maggie took hold of her husband's hand and pleadingly looked at her father.

"Plantations are inherited by son's, not daughters." David took a deep breath narrowing his eyes at Keifer.

"But Lucas is seven." Maggie huffed.

"While ideally Keifer would inherit Gable Gardens. The unfortunate passing of your bother Edmund and Keifer marrying a Northern lady has created some difficulties. We must keep our farm prosperous for Lucas when he comes of age." David stared a hole through my husband. "If Keifer decides to remain up North."

"Father, we have discussed this at length, multiple times." Keifer spoke in a low voice.

"And you know how I feel about it, son." David's voice rose an octave. "How can you turn your back on your birthright, your family?"

"Father," Keifer started but was abruptly cut off by his sister.

"You are a traitor to your family. Your home. Your heritage." Eugenia scoffed hatefully. "I do not understand why you bothered to even come home after all this time. Clearly, your wife does not want to be here. She looks down on us. She thinks she is better than us. She barely lowers herself to speak to us." She unleased her fury on me. It was the first words she had spoken to me since we arrived.

"That is not true," I defended. "Did you ever stop to think that perhaps I spend my time reading and alone with my son is because all of you have made me feel so unwelcome and uncomfortable. None of you have bothered to speak to me, to get to know me, or even inquire about our life." I turned towards Eugenia. "And you were so hateful and disrespectful to not only me and my family, but my neighbors as well throughout your visit that you made everyone around you miserable." I countered.

"You never wanted me in your house and did everything to make me uncomfortable. You and your wretched grandmother." Eugenia shouted back at me.

"I will not sit here and be insulted by your outright lies." I rose from my chair.

"Sidney, please." Keifer reached for my hand, but I jerked it away from him.

"It is your choice, your son and I or your family." I threw down the ultimatum without realizing the words fell out of my mouth. Keifer looked as if I'd slapped him. "I am going home tomorrow with my son." I tossed my napkin on the table. "Excuse me. Thank you for dinner." I directed my words towards my mother-in-law. "My apologies." I nodded politely before exiting, trying not to show them how livid I felt.

But I instantly felt regret as I climbed the long staircase. I felt horrible. The anger I felt melted away with each step and the knot in my stomach from the guilt seemed to grow with the same intensity. My husband deserved better, and I had let him down. I had disrespected him, humiliated him, and proved to his family that all Northern women were pushy, outspoken, and ill-mannered.

I considered turning around, returning to the dining room and apologizing for my outburst, but something deep inside me would not give Eugenia the satisfaction. Despite the guilt and remorse, my loathing for his sister was something I could not waver on.

My mind was racing with a thousand thoughts. I loved my husband more than life itself and I could not imagine ever living without him. The internal war raged within me with each step. I was so angry — with him, his family, with their Southern way of life.

This world that he belonged to had no room for me and I was fine with that. It was not a world I wanted to be a part of. Since our arrival I felt I was walking around in historical novels that I had read in college literature or history courses. But this was different. It was surreal.

I had never seen slave quarters before, except for ones that were vacant more than a century ago. I had spent little time exposed to slavery outside of Keifer's family and it felt wrong on every level. Granted, the Marshall's were good to their slaves and treated them fairly. But given the internal turmoil I felt from witnessing the riots, the looting, and the violence caused by Black Lives Matter and Antifa from my *other* life, resentment and hatred was building within me, and I felt horrible for it.

I closed the door to our chambers behind me and sat down on the bed. My son was still sleeping peacefully, but I knew he would be up shortly to have his own evening snack. I flopped back with my arm over my eyes wondering what the hell had just happened.

How was I going to get myself out of this one?

The room grew darker as the light outside faded behind the tree line. I climbed off the bed and wandered over to the open window. I stared out feeling the warm breeze drifting in the room. I closed my eyes and leaned against the sill. I could see my grandmother sitting on the porch sewing with a contented expression on her lined face. I missed her so much. I hated feeling so alone in this place.

"Sidney?" a voice followed by a soft knock on the door. "May I come in?" Angelina asked.

"Yes," I said without looking away from the view outside my window.

"May we speak for a moment?" I heard her enter the room and close the door behind her. "I apologize for my husband and daughter's behavior." She paused for a moment before approaching me. "And you were right. We really do not know each other well."

I chuckled softly to myself with my back still facing her.

"I know you and Eugenia had a difficult visit last year." She kept her voice low.

"That is an understatement." I glanced back at her over my shoulder.

"But I would like to move beyond that, Sidney." I heard her exhaling loudly behind me. "I can see how much you love my son, and it is clear he loves you too."

"We have been married almost a decade, and you have never seen the life we built in Massachusetts." I turned towards her and sat down on the edge of the windowsill. "You have never seen Terrace Falls, your son's practice, or how important he is to the community we live in. Your son is highly respected for his skills and his convictions." I explained.

"I am very proud of my son." Angelina declared raising her chin just a smidgen. "I always have been."

"I understand that. I am very proud of him as well. But I know you and the rest of your family did not approve of our marriage." I stated.

"Sidney," she pinched her lips together as if gathering her thoughts. "You must understand our position. We were concerned about how different your backgrounds are and how that would impact your future."

"Do you not believe my family held the same reservations?" Angelina shrugged with a slight smile.

"I suppose they did. I never really thought about it." She admitted.

"You can trust my words when I say they had the same reservations as yourself and David." I shook my head recalling the heated arguments I had with not only my grandmother, but my father as well after Keifer proposed to me. They were both adamantly against our marriage. "But once they got to know Keifer, they were able to see what a wonderful, kind and compassionate man he was. They understood why I loved him so much and most importantly; they saw how happy we were. After that, they had no problems accepting our marriage and fully embracing Keifer into our family."

"And we have never made that effort with you." Angelina said in a low voice with downcast eyes. She took a deep breath meeting my eyes before she spoke. "Well, I reckon there is truth in that."

"Perhaps," I was at a loss for words.

"Sidney," Angelina leaned against the canopy bedpost and held out a hand to me. "Is it too late? Because I would really like to get to know the woman who makes my son so happy and gave me a beautiful grandson." A soft smile played on the corners of her lips.

"I would really like that." I took her hand in mine and squeezed it. She surprised me by pulling me into a hug.

"Would you please join me in the parlor for dessert?" She asked as my little man stirred. She reached over and stroked his head softly. "Such a sweet blessing." Her face softened as she looked lovingly upon my son. "He looks so much like Keifer as a babe."

"I shall happily join you shortly." I reached down and picked up my son.

"Very well," Angelina stroked his head lightly before leaving our chambers closing the door behind her.

Fed and dry, I handed my son off to his Aunt Caroline. She loved spending time with her nephew. Of the numerous siblings belonging to my husband, she was my favorite. She had an easy smile and was quick to laugh. She had the same dark blond hair as her brother with soft waves. Yet, she had her mother's dark brown eyes instead of her father's green.

I stood outside the closed parlor door feeling apprehensive. I had no idea where my husband was or what he was thinking. I knew he most likely was not very pleased with me. But I wondered if he knew about his mother's visit to our chambers. I imagined he did. There was not much that ever slipped by him.

"Good evening," I opened the door and hesitantly stepped inside. Angelina was sitting alone on the chaise lounge. There was a silver tray with a kettle of coffee, mugs, and what looked like peach cobbler.

"Hello, Sidney. Please join me." She gestured to the love seat across from her.

"Thank you," I nervously took a seat.

"Again, I do apologize for dinner. I would like to move past it and have the kind of relationship with you that a mother and daughter-in-law should share." Her voice seemed genuine.

"I would like that too." I admitted.

"I understand that you are very close with your grandmother, Marissa and that she and your grandfather raised you. Is that correct?"

"Yes, ma'm." I fidgeted with my hands in my lap.

"Would you like some coffee and peach cobbler?"

"Please," I really didn't but it would give me something to do to settle my nervous hands.

Angelina poured a mug and added a generous amount of sugar and fresh cream. She handed it to me with a small China dish of peach cobbler.

"Thank you," I accepted them graciously.

"May I ask you something?" I nodded. "Why did you not move with your father and his new wife to Chicago after he remarried?"

"Bethany, my stepmother was very clear in her feelings towards me." I smiled nervously. "From what I observed and was told by others, my mother, Julia was the love of my father, Walter's life. He took her loss very hard. I was young when he remarried, but I bear a strong resemblance to my mother for which my stepmother deeply resented. She felt I was a constant reminder of Julia to him. So, she was eager to leave me behind and start a life with him without any traces of his previous life."

"I am surprised your father allowed it." Her lips pinched together in disapproval.

"Walter was never much involved in my life anyway." I explained. "My grandparents were my parental figures. They loved me dearly and always took care of me. Therefore, when he remarried and moved away, my life really did not change."

"You call him Walter, not father." She raised an eyebrow at me.

"Yes," I swallowed with difficulty. "I have always called him Walter, even when I was young. He was never a father to me.

"Yet, if I understand correctly, it is your plan to visit Chicago after your visit with us?" My mother-in-law eyed me carefully.

"Yes, the eldest of my younger brothers, Patrick, married an enchanting lady named Annabelle. When she and Patrick got engaged, she reached out to me. Since then, we have become dear friends. She keeps me abreast of my family in Chicago. I am very excited about seeing them all in September." I confessed.

"My son mentioned you will be staying with them through the holidays." I nodded.

"It will be the first Christmas with all my brother's. My younger brother, Nicholas, will be home from West Point as well. I have not seen my eldest brother since he was a baby and am eager to meet the younger ones." I finally took a bite of the peach cobbler. It simply melted in my mouth. I do not believe I have ever tasted something so good.

"Perhaps next year we will travel North for the holidays." Angelina smiled.

"We would love that." I said, knowing full well that it would never happen.

"I have not seen snow since I was a child." A soft smile passed over her face. "I would like to see it again. And it would be fun for the children as well." Despite my knowledge of the future, for a brief second, the very thought of Victoria at Terrace Falls made me nauseous.

"Our winters are much different than those down South." I cautioned her. "The snow can be dangerous, and the wind can tear through your clothes when it whips into a frenzy." Her expression showed a hint of fear. "Please, do not misunderstand me. It truly is beautiful. The world takes on a peaceful serine quality that unlike anything you have ever experienced." Her face softened again.

"It sounds lovely." She appeared reluctant. "How is your grandmother doing?"

"Quite well. Her arthritis troubles her when the seasons change, or the weather is damp. But it has not slowed her down. She is as spry, witty and restless as ever." I laughed.

"Do you have a foreman who assists with the daily running of the plantation?"

"Terrace Falls is too small to be a plantation. It is an estate." I explained. "I handle the daily running of the estate, along with the books since my grandfather passed. But I have a trusted overseer, Ned, who has been with our family since my father was a child. He was raised alongside my father. His wife is our cook and his eldest son; Duncan is a few years younger than I and will someday resume his father's role in our household."

"That must give you great comfort to have such a family in your service." Angelina helped herself with some more coffee. "Does his kin live nearby as well?"

"No. His father and mother were former slaves. He was also born a slave. They were set free upon the death of their owner at which time they moved north. His father was our blacksmith, and his mother was a seamstress." I explained nonchalantly.

"My Lord, you mean to tell me you have a negro overseer taking care of Terrace Falls in the absence of your husband?" she was clearly surprised.

"I do." I stated unashamed. "I have complete confidence in Ned to take care of our family and affairs in my absence. Keifer does not concern himself with the running of the estate."

"I cannot imagine." Angelina said in a low voice before meeting my eye. "Did you teach him to read and write?"

"Yes, of course. He is also quick with numbers, as is his son."

"And you feel confident in leaving the estate in his hands?" I could see her biting her bottom lip.

"My grandmother and our neighbor, Mr. Bennett who owns the largest bank in our community are there as well to ensure everything runs smoothly." I added to ease her apprehension.

"That is a blessing." She quipped.

"Yes, Mr. Bennett I believe has taken quite a fondness for my grandmother." I chuckled.

"Is she receptive?" her head tilted to the side a bit.

"I believe so, but to get her to admit it is another story." I laughed softly. "I believe she is intrigued. She enjoys the attention, and I believe she holds a great fondness for him as well. However, her heart will always belong to my grandfather, and I fear that she may never recover from his loss."

"I understand. I cannot imagine loving another man the way I love David. He is a good man." She nodded. "I have loved him since I was fourteen." She smiled. "He was sixteen. His father was a boyhood friend of my father. We stopped here for a visit on our way to the port in Savannah. My family lives in southern Virginia. My older brother runs my family's plantation there."

"That must be hard. You must be homesick. Is it not difficult to be away from your family?" I asked.

"It is. But they do visit each year or I them. And we write often." She shifted in her seat. "May I ask you something else?"

"Of course," I was curious, but I was not expecting the next words that came out of her mouth.

"I have read the sentiments from Northern papers and novels. And I have witnessed the growing hostilities." I nodded. "Do you believe our Union will separate?"

"Honestly?" I turned towards the parlor door to make sure it was still closed.

"Yes. You reside up North. Keifer has mentioned that he has friends in the federal and local government. What are your feelings on this growing resentment between the North and the South? I am curious about your take on it." Angelina eyed me carefully.

"My husband has become a prominent and respected man in our community." I informed her. "And yes, I have heard many things." I paused considering my words carefully.

"Please, say what is on your mind. You may speak freely." She encouraged me.

"I am hesitant to say." I took a deep breath and exhaled slowly. "My opinion holds no weight." I wanted to side-step this conversation.

"Sidney," she raised her eyebrows. "You and I both know we, as the fairer sex, know everything that goes on around us and in our homes."

"True," I laughed.

"Please. Be honest with me. What have you heard?"

"The Union will separate. There is talk that South Carolina will be the first to secede, and most believe the rest of the South will follow." She nodded slowly.

"If that should happen, I pray the North will let us go in peace." Her eyes cast downwards.

"I pray that as well. However, I fear they will not."

"But that would lead to war." Angelina whispered.

"I fear so," I agreed.

"Has my son indicated what he would do should that happen?" She swallowed hard and the fear was evident on her face.

"He has." I nodded. "And he had made his sentiments well known in our community. He has stated that he would attend to soldiers on both sides of the Mason-Dixon line."

"I am certain that ruffled a few feathers." My mother-in-law shifted uncomfortably but offered me a stiff grin.

"Yes, indeed it did." I chuckled softly. "However, it did not deter him."

"No. I suppose it would not. Southern honor is sacred and not to be trifled with." She mused sipping her coffee.

"I have learned as much." I took another bite of the peach cobbler. "Keifer is a strong, proud Southern man and I would not have him any other way." I answered honestly.

"But you condemn our way of life?" She raised an eyebrow.

"I believe slavery is an outdated notion." I admitted.

"As do we." Her answer surprised me. "But let me ask you something since you are familiar with your estate and numbers." She leaned forward. "Would you be able to run your estate, pay for essentials and things you cannot grow yourself, and pay your employees if the federal government was stealing eighty-six percent of everything you earn?"

"No." I shook my head. "It would not be possible. We would starve."

"Precisely." Angelina gave me a curt nod. "But that is what our federal government has done to us."

"What?" I had no idea.

"Yes," her lips pursed together tightly. "Last December they raised it to fifty-five percent. Five months later, in May this year they increased it to eighty-six percent. Do you know what that money is used for?" I shook my head. "To build Northern industries, railroads, and textiles — all of which will be used against us if we secede."

"Yes, Miss Sidney. We will be shot with ammunition and cannons our tax dollars paid for. Very poetic, do you not agree?" David stood in the entryway of the parlor with his hand still on the doorknob.

"No," I rose from my seat. "I do not."

"Your husband appears a bit more optimistic than you about the possibility of war if succession occurs." David entered the room followed closely by my husband.

"Yes," I acknowledged. "I know he does."

Keifer shut the parlor room door behind him as my father-in-law, and he joined us. They sat down with grave expressions.

"Sidney, I understand our way of life in the South is foreign to you." I nodded curtly. "I know many Northerners judge the South harshly, especially after the publication of the fabrication of lies bestowed upon the world in *Uncle Tom's Cabin*." David said the book title through gritted teeth. "But what Ms. Stowe failed to acknowledge in her lies is that less than five percent of Southerners own slaves and that a good many of them are indeed negros themselves. She also fails to recognize that there were many white Irish slaves in the South who endured harsher treatment than their negro counterparts. Did you know that?" He eyed me carefully.

"I have heard it before." I admitted but did not mention that it was learned in a college history class.

"Is it widespread knowledge in the North?" Angelina questioned me.

"No. I am afraid it is not." I confessed.

"I see," her eyes landed on her husband.

"I can tell you there has been great concern voiced by many in our community as well as around the North as to what would happen to the slaves if they should gain their freedom." I shrugged unintentionally.

"Meaning?" David raised an eyebrow.

"Employment within cities is scarce. Adding approximately five million uneducated and illiterate Negros to that would not only over saturate the market but set the Negros up for failure." I glanced over their concerned faces. "The freed Negros will have no property, no home, no ability to provide for themselves or their families." I stated the obvious. "Plus, they will receive no help from Northerners who, in general, despise them almost as much – if not more in many cases, than Southerners do. Southerners, generally, accept that Negros have a purpose for the economy of the South. Northerners, at least most, would happily donate funds to send them all back to Africia then see them flood across our Northern states."

"I had no idea you were so well informed." Keifer muttered with wide eyes and his astonishment clearly evident on his face.

"I pay attention." I answered nonchalantly.

"More than I realized," Keifer eyed me carefully.

"What would you recommend?" I turned my attention back to my father-in-law.

"This topic has been discussed for decades, and an adequate solution has yet to be discovered." David rubbed his chin thoughtfully. "This delicate balance in the South has been harshly judged, criticized, and ridiculed. Still, this does not stop the North nor Europe from purchasing Southern cotton, rice, or tobacco. The hypocrisy is staggering."

"Well, now," Angelina set her saucer back on the tray. "It is getting late, and we have much to do tomorrow." She faced me and held out her hand. "Thank you for spending some time with me this evening. Our conversation was enlightening."

"My pleasure," I smiled and squeezed her hand gently.

"Shall we," My husband rose to his feet and held out his arm to me.

"Thank you," I looped my arm through his and held onto his shapely bicep. I smiled as our steps fell together as we climbed the stairs to our chamber.

21

TUESDAY, JUNE 16, 2020

BARACK OBAMA'S VICE PRESIDENT, Joe Biden was officially named as the Democratic presidential nominee. After the rigging of the primary election when they pushed Bernie Sanders out again and Biden lost the first three primaries. Then magically won South Carolina after cutting a deal with Representative Clyburn. I believe the agreement was to choose a black vice president. The man was a career politician who had never accomplished anything and was an absolute liberal nutjob with maybe two functioning brain cells. Anyone connected to Obama was soiled and tarnished in vile pestilence that could never be cleaned.

Obama — arguably the worst hypocrite to ever be elected to the office of Commander and Chief had done everything possible within his power to drive racial division amongst Americans. I used to believe there was no person more vile and evil in politics than Hilary Clinton. But I quickly learned how dreadfully naïve I was. Maxine Waters, Adam Schiff, Chuck Schumer, and Nancy Pelosi had proven to be hateful spiteful creatures, the likes of which I had never imagined in my wildest dreams.

America was coming apart at the seams. Racial division was a prominent feature on the nightly news and in our everyday lives. The Black Lives Matter movement was tearing the country apart. If any white person did not openly support the terrorist group, they were immediately labeled a racist. Anyone who openly supported law enforcement officers were racist. If you were born white, you were racist.

Insanity ruled the day. Ironically, and sarcastically dubbed the 'Summer of Love' because it was filled with hatred towards every white American who ever lived. Resentment, betrayal, and loathing were evident amongst every liberal and democrat citizen. Most

Americans were tired of the lockdown, sick of the protestors, and fed-up with the government. One man drove his car through a crowd of protestors in Seattle injuring one person and was taken into custody.

Exhausted and receiving no support from their leaders, city council members, and most of their community, police officers in Buffalo resigned from the emergency units after two of their officers were suspended for pushing an elderly man in the heat of the protests.

I watched on social media outlets as liberal nutjobs, Black Lives Matter activists, and Antifa terrorists torched a police department in the dark blue leftist city of Seattle and then quarantined themselves off in several city blocks where stores and businesses were looted, destroyed and burned down. The media informed its listeners the occupants had named their stolen territory Capitol Hill Autonomous Zone or CHOP. Even more absurd was that democrat city authorities decided they were not going to use local, state, or federal law enforcement to take it back. The terrorists occupying the stolen property held free reign over it.

My stomach tightened as I watched the news in the breakroom. My mother was in Seattle. I had no idea how close or far away her condo was from this insanity, but I knew she was already struggling there. I pulled out my phone and sent her a quick text message praying she was safe. But the news kept getting worse.

The democrat-controlled city of Denver public school system announced that they would no longer allow police officers to serve as resource officers at any of the district schools. Police officers in major cities, both red and blue were resigning in record numbers due to ongoing protests. South Florida lost ten members of their SWAT team in one swoop. It had become advisable to take an anti-depressant and a shot of whisky before turning on the evening news.

I rested my head against my table in the breakroom and closed my eyes. I was exhausted. All I wanted to do was take a long shower and go to bed. I was sick of listening to people complain about everything from a sniffle due to a summer cold to a scratchy throat. Every paranoid person watching the evening news was coming out in droves.

It made me realize how uneducated and uninformed the general population was. The government, especially the democrat party and liberals worldwide in developed countries had instilled a deep-seated fear within the population that they were all going to die from Covid-19. If people had paid more attention in high school biology class, they would have realized it was all propaganda.

Six hours into my shift, Carson rushed through the emergency room doors with panic across his face. He was dressed in Bermuda shorts, an inside out polo shirt, and flip flops. His hair was disheveled, and his face was unshaven and unmasked.

"Sir," a hospital security guard stepped towards him with his hand up. "Sir, you cannot enter the hospital without a mask." He thrust a mask at Carson.

"Sidney?" Carson ignored the security guard's words pushing past him. "Sidney?"

"Carson?" I rose in my little administrative cubicle set off to the side of the emergency room sliding doors. "What's going on?" I asked as he rushed into view.

"Phoebe's in the car." He hastily pointed towards the doors. "She's in labor."

"Good Lord," I scurried through the backstage maze of barrios to reach Carson. "Get a wheelchair." I yelled at the disgruntled security guard rushing through the doors.

Carson had left their SUV idling under the awning in front of the emergency room doors. As I approached the vehicle I could see Phoebe panting, her knuckles white gripping the dashboard. Her face was contorted in pain with sweat visible on her brow.

"Sidney," she huffed as I opened the door. "My water broke forty minutes ago, and the contractions are eight minutes apart."

"Alright," I reached for her arm and helped her into the wheelchair with Carson guiding her from the other side. Once she was seated with her feet on the pedestals, I turned my attention towards Carson. "Please, park the SUV in the lot and meet me at my station. I will get Phoebe admitted." He nodded.

"I'll be right behind you." Carson assured his wife, taking her hand with a gentle squeeze. "I love you," and after a quick kiss on the cheek he scurried around to the driver's door, hopped in and drove towards the lot.

Phoebe gripped the armrests of the wheelchair breathing through the next contraction that ripped through her. She was doing her Lamaze breathing as best as she could, but it was clear I needed to get her upstairs as soon as possible.

It only took about three minutes for me to admit Phoebe to the hospital since I already knew her information almost as well as my own. She waited as patiently as she could giving me a worried expression as my fingers flew over the keyboard with precision speed.

I came around through the admin barriers once more and took the handles of the wheelchair and headed towards the elevator. Obstetrics were on the fourth floor. I pushed the button repeatedly and with more force than necessary.

Carson came screeching around the corner towards the elevator, a facial mask dangling off one ear, and tripping over his own flip flops in his eagerness to reach his wife. However, a middle-aged security guard stationed at the elevator put his arm out effectively blocking Carson as soon as the doors opened.

"Excuse me," Carson pushed the guard's arm aside. "My wife is in labor."

"Sir," the guard forced his way between Phoebe and I and the opened elevator door. "Hospital protocol prohibits all non-patients beyond administrative areas."

"My wife is in labor." Carson said louder with growing frustration.

"I understand, sir, but you are not allowed beyond this point." The guard insisted.

"Wait," Phoebe stuck her foot out blocking the elevator door from closing. "Are you saying my husband cannot accompany me to the delivery room?" Despite her pain, her eyes narrowed dangerously.

"Yes, ma'am, new Covid-19 protocols implemented by the city and adopted by the hospital prohibits non-patients due to potential spread." The guard looked indignant.

"You have got to be kidding me." I huffed. "When was this policy implemented? I work here and never heard of it."

"We were informed yesterday," the smug insignificant guard gloated.

"My day off," I muttered under my breath. "Carson, wait here. I will get her settled and be back down."

"He cannot wait here," the guard spoke up. "He can wait outside in his car."

"Seriously?" I said louder than I intended. "This is ridiculous." I glared at the pompous guard before meeting Carson's eyes. "I will text you once I get upstairs."

"Fine," Carson uttered through gritted teeth.

Phoebe looked at me with hurt and anger in her eyes, but she relented and placed her foot back on the chair's footrest allowing the door to close.

"This is complete bullshit." She spat as soon as the door closed. "If I would have known this, I would have gone to my parents' house and delivered this baby."

"Do you want too?" I leaned closer to her ear. "There is still time."

"You have delivered babies before." A sly smile crossed her lips. "Let's go home." She leaned forward and pressed the ground floor button.

I quickly pulled out my phone and texted our family group chat. 'Carson, please bring the car around. Phoebe has decided on a home birth at her parents' house. We're on our way'. I slipped my phone back into the pocket of my scrubs just before the elevator door opened again.

"Is there a problem?" The same security guard stepped forward.

"Not anymore. We're correcting one." Phoebe's knuckles grew white as she gripped the armrests.

"What are you doing?" the guard flustered. "Where are you going? This patient cannot leave. She is clearly in labor." He stammered.

"And I refuse to give birth in isolation without my husband and family." Phoebe said through gritted teeth.

"But ma'am," he followed us to the emergency room sliding doors just as Carson was pulling up.

He barely put the car in park before leaping out and opening the passenger door. We helped Phoebe back into the SUV. I carefully placed the seatbelt around her and clicked it. I squeezed the hand of my best friend and gazed at her.

"Don't worry about anything here. I will take care of it." I told her softly. "I'll meet you at your parent's house. Go quickly but be careful." I advised them both before shutting the door.

"Ma'am, I must protest." The guard stood with his arms crossed beside the sliding doors.

"I don't care," I brushed him off and hurried back to my cubicle.

I logged back into the system and opened Phoebe's file. I unclicked the admittance box on her file and closed the tab and logged back out of the system. I rushed down to my supervisor's station. She was buried behind her monitor with her glasses perched on the end of her nose looking annoyed.

"Excuse me, Mrs. Schmidt," I knocked lightly on her open door.

"Yes," she glanced up for a moment.

"I am afraid I have a family emergency and must leave at once. I am sorry." I waited anxiously for her response wringing my hands together.

"Ms. Timmons, we all have family emergencies, but you are scheduled to work until six. I cannot allow you to just leave, especially during a pandemic." She reset her glasses and turned back to her monitor.

"With all due respect, ma'am, my sister is in labor at our parent's home and I am her midwife. Her contractions are three minutes apart. I sincerely apologize, but I really must leave." The words gushed out before I could stop myself.

"Well, that is another matter." She removed her glasses and dropped them lightly onto her desk with a heavily disappointed sigh. "Fine," she said reluctantly. "But this will be documented in your file."

"Thank you," I nodded with a smile.

"Good luck," I heard her call after me as I rushed to the employee lounge and grabbed my purse from my locker. I clocked out quickly and ran out of the hospital. Once I was through the doors, I ran as fast as I could to my car.

I pulled out my phone and started my car. I had dozens of missed calls and messages waiting for me. I knew Emily could handle delivering the child without me due to her experience as a midwife in her *other* life, but I also knew it would be difficult for her since Phoebe was her daughter and every mother, regardless of the time, struggled with seeing their child in enormous pain.

I pressed on the icon to connect me with Emily and pulled out of my parking spot while the call connected.

"Sidney?" Emily's voice was an octave higher than normal.

"I'm leaving the hospital now." I said quickly, pulling out onto the main road.

"I just got her into bed. Her contractions are four minutes apart." I could hear Phoebe fighting through another contraction and Carson's soothing voice in the background. "Please hurry." Emily said in a rushed voice.

"I will," I disconnected the call and turned onto the ramp to the highway.

The only joy brought about by the national lockdown and restrictions was the lack of patrol officers on interstate highways. I pressed the gas pedal and drove faster than I had ever driven before towards Robert and Emily's home. Still, it felt like the miles crawled by as the roadside scenery blurred past my windows.

I pulled into the driveway twenty minutes later and leapt out of the car. I didn't bother knocking but threw open the door and flew up the stairs. Phoebe was propped up on a mountain of pillows in the bed in her childhood room. Carson was standing beside her timing her contractions and washing her forehead with a damp washcloth. Her mother crouched on the bed beside her, holding her hand, keeping her calm, and giving her encouragement.

"Oh, Sidney," Emily appeared exasperated and forlorn, rushed up to me taking ahold of my hands. "I am so happy to see you."

"Calm down," I chuckled squeezing her hands. "Everything will be fine." I assured her.

"I don't know why I am in such a state," she mumbled in a low voice. "I delivered Wally with no problems and remained completely calm."

"But wasn't that *there*, not *here*?" I whispered so Carson could not hear.

"Yes. He was born in a hospital *here*." Emily's lips drew into a thin line. "But there I felt more comfortable — accustomed to the expectations and skills." She audibly exhaled. "Things are simpler *there*."

"I know" I touched her arm lightly and smiled gently. "Right now, the only thing you need to worry about is supporting your daughter. I have this." I assured her with more confidence than I felt.

I returned downstairs to the kitchen. Robert, Alex, Jocelyn, Jackson, and the remainder of the family were milling about anxiously. I turned on the hot water and let it run until I could barely stand the heat of it on my skin. I thoroughly scrubbed my hands and arms up to my elbows just as I had been taught in medical school. I offered words of comfort and reassurance while being bombarded with questions from family members.

I took a deep breath and steadied my nerves. This was not the time for me to fall apart, and I knew it. I have delivered more than a dozen babies in my *other* life, but this was my first time *here*. I understood exactly what Emily was trying to express. Phoebe was my best friend, my sister, and a most beloved confidant. I could not fail her.

Phoebe delivered a seven-and-a-half-pound heathy baby girl. She entered the world after a total of four hours of labor, screaming and letting her arrival be known to the household. She had a head full of beautiful dark hair like her mother and Carson's dark blue eyes. She was destined to be beautiful.

I held her up, red faced, screaming and kicking. A broad smile spread across my face as I placed the little angel on Phoebe's stomach. Emily, Carson, and Jocelyn huddled around the bed in complete adoration at the new addition to our family.

"She's perfect." Phoebe's voice was raw and barely a whisper from exhaustion.

"Yes, she is." Carson agreed.

"What are you going to name her?" Emily gently touched the infant's cheek with her finger.

"Audry Harper Jade Adler," Phoebe's eyes met mine full of love and devotion.

"I love it," I choked back the tears. "Thank you." I whispered.

"Oh darling," Emily gushed. "How sweet of you. Thank you."

"We figured this way she will carry the name of two of the strongest ladies we know." Carson said softly.

"Yes," Phoebe kissed her daughter's forehead. "We agreed it was perfect for her." She reluctantly handed me her baby.

"Let me just clean her up, give her a quick exam, and get some measurements." I carried her over to the little basinet beside the basin of warm water.

I could hear them chattering behind me as I cleaned up and examined the newest member of our family. Little Audry was not happy about it. She cried and kicked, balling her hands into tight little fists in her indignation.

I handed her back to her mother and then returned downstairs to share the glorious news. The family was beside themselves with joy. I sat down at the island alone while everyone rushed upstairs to see the new baby and congratulate Phoebe and Carson.

I rested my head on my arms on top of the table. I closed my eyes and let out a deep breath I hadn't even realized I was holding. I was so lost in my own exhaustion that I hadn't heard the front door open, or anyone entering the house until I heard his voice.

"What were you thinking?" Landon dropped his satchel on the island beside me.

"What?" I straightened up and looked at him.

"Your little stunt at the hospital with Phoebe, telling your Ms. Schmidt you were a midwife, and conducting a home delivery." He looked at me with an expression I could not read – bewilderment perhaps.

"What about it?" I was too tired to argue with him.

"Do you realize how dangerous and irresponsible that was? You are not a licensed physician yet." Landon drummed his fingers on the island displaying his impatience with me.

"Not that you asked, but I delivered a healthy baby girl. Your new niece weighs seven and a half pounds and is twenty and a half inches long. She's got a head full of dark hair, her father's eyes, and a very healthy set of lungs." I narrowed my eyes at him. "It's all documented. Plus, I successfully delivered the placenta and stitched her up. Mother, child, and the rest of the family are resting comfortably upstairs."

"But why would you risk it?" He exhaled sharply, running his fingers through his hair.

"Because hospital policy now dictates that spouses and family are not allowed in delivery rooms or any rooms for that matter." I huffed. "This was Phoebe's decision, not mine."

"But you should have stopped her." Landon insisted.

"Seriously?" I laughed. "We are talking about Phoebe here. She is one of — if not the best criminal attorney in the state. Arguing with her on any given day is a lost cause. Arguing with her whilst she's in labor?" I tilted my head and eyed him carefully. "Right," I scoffed.

"I don't understand how you can be so blasé about it. Any number of things could have gone wrong, and it would have ruined your medical career." He continued with his rant.

"Landon," I sighed and put my hand on his cheek. "I love you but let this go. If I had to do it all over again, I wouldn't change anything."

"Don't patronize me, Sidney. This is serious." He huffed.

"Yes, darling. I am certain you think so." I shuffled off the barstool. "You can stand here and contemplate it by yourself, or you can join me and the rest of the family upstairs in celebrating the successful birth of Ms. Audry Harper Jade Adler." I kissed him on the cheek and headed upstairs.

Landon sulked downstairs for another ten minutes before he came upstairs. He leaned against the doorframe, silently watching all of us gathered around the bed, laughing, talking, enjoying the special day. Robert slipped away from the group and approached him.

"I understand you are not happy with Phoebe's decision to have a home birth." I heard Robert ask Landon.

"So many things could have gone wrong." He sighed and ran his hands through his hair once more.

"I understand, but my wife is an experienced midwife. She was here the whole time, and Sidney delivered the baby expertly." Robert boasted. "You should be proud of her." He clapped Landon on the shoulder. "Now why don't you come meet my beautiful new granddaughter."

Landon smiled and relented. He approached the bed slowly and stood beside me looking down upon Phoebe and the sleeping angel in her arms. His face softened.

"She's so beautiful." He whispered, taking my hand.

"You bet your ass, she is." Carson piped up, making all of us laugh.

22

TUESDAY, JUNE 19, 1860

THE HOUSE WAS A BUZZ WITH activity before I even rolled out of bed. The location of our chambers kept everyday activity and noise away from our ears. Yet this morning nothing could quelch the excitement that seemed to be infectious not only in the house but across the grounds. I pulled the sheer curtain aside and glanced out across the vast grounds.

The sun had yet to reach the top of the trees. The glow from the rising sun shimmered across the fields causing a mystical almost magical shine. Still, I could not help but think of how the early morning Midwest dew would have enhanced the view. I leaned against the glass surprised at how warm it already felt in this early hour.

My son squirmed in his bassinet and let out a holler letting me know he was ready to greet the day. My husband, however, was suspiciously absent. Not that it was particularly unusual for Keifer to be absent when his son and I arose, but given the obvious activity below, I was eager to investigate.

I changed and fed my little man; thoroughly enjoying my time alone with him before he was whisked away into the arms of one of his many extended family members. I dressed him in trousers and a little cotton shirt hoping to keep him cooler in this Southern heat. After dressing myself with some assistance from Tallie, I headed downstairs in search of breakfast.

My mother-in-law met me at the top of the grand staircase. She was beaming despite her hair being disheveled and wearing a kitchen apron that I had never seen on her before. She was wiping her hands and practically giddy in a way I had never seen before.

"Oh, good morning, my dear," I wasn't sure if she was referring to me or my son.

"Good morning, mother." I paused before descending. "How are you doing? There appears to be to be a lot of bustling about in the house this morning."

"Oh, my yes," she laughed. "Well, I suppose you slept through all the excitement last night."

"What happened?"

"Maggie had her baby just after midnight." My mother-in-law beamed.

"My goodness," I was astonished. "You could have awakened me."

"Nonsense," she waved me off with a smile. "We've done this so many times now." She laughed.

"How are she and the babe?" I adjusted the weight of my son on my hip.

"Fine. Fine," she waved her hand once again dismissively. "Both are happy and healthy. She had a fat little boy with her eyes and Thad's nose."

"How wonderful," I declared. "What a blessing."

"Indeed," she agreed. "A son is the highest blessing."

"Have they chosen a name yet?"

"Tobias Mitchell," Angela stated proudly. "Such a stately name."

"It's perfect," I agreed as she reached over and stroked my son's cheek. "Polly has prepared breakfast. It is waiting for you in the dining room."

"Thank you," I smiled before descending the stairs with my son.

The house was full of activity. Family members were running about all talking excitedly about the new baby. Tallie was carrying a stack of linen and rushing up the stairs. She nodded briefly as she passed me on the stairs.

The noise level from below was higher than normal and I could hear voices, dishes clanking, and laughter drifting in from the dining room. It reminded me of home and the meals we shared with my grandmother, Mr. Bennett, the Morgan's and the McKenzie's. I missed my friends and the comfort and ease at which we shared our lives.

Later that afternoon I was sitting on a rocking chair on the porch writing Charlotte a letter while my son slept on the make-shift bed I had created. It was a beautiful afternoon with a few puffy clouds lingering overhead. The sky was a soft robin egg blue, and the leaves rustled in the breeze.

The sound of hooves broke my concentration. I looked up and saw Caroline's beau, Phillip Rhoades riding up on his beautiful black stallion. Phillip was a handsome young man with dark hair, deep set brown eyes, broad shoulders, and a charming, crooked smile. He was unusually dressed for a Tuesday afternoon wearing a suit and tie. He appeared to be ready for Sunday services instead.

"Good afternoon, Mr. Rhoades." I rose from my rocking chair and greeted him as Otis held his reigns while he dismounted his steed. "How are you this afternoon?"

"Afternoon, Mrs. Marshall." Phillip tilted his Stetson with a wide, but nervous smile. "Is Mr. Marshall home?"

"Which one?" I was enjoying his discomfort. "There are several about the house and grounds." I smirked.

"Mr. David Marshall." He stumbled with obvious discomfort as he made his way up the porch steps.

"I believe he is in the study with my husband." I motioned towards the front door. "You can go on in."

"Thank you, ma'am." Phillip removed his Stetson, tucked it under his arm and disappeared into the house.

I smiled to myself and returned to my letter. I was describing to her the plantation with its various trees and flowers that grew in this region and were absent up North. I was starting on the second page of my letter when Caroline walked out the front door, appearing every bit as nervous as Mr. Rhoades had moments earlier. She was twisting a lace handkerchief in her hands and biting her lower lip.

"Caroline? Is everything alright?" I paused looking over at her.

"Phillip is asking my father for my hand." She replied in a shaky voice.

"Oh, Caroline." I rose to my feet and embraced her. "I am so happy for you."

"Thank you," she blushed. "You approve?"

"Yes," I clasped her hands. "He is a good man."

"I believe so too." Caroline's face was the perfect image of a young girl in love.

"You have done well. I know you will be very happy with him." I squeezed her hands. "So," I motioned to the other rocking chair for her to have a seat. "When are you thinking of getting married?"

"I was thinking," she continued to bite her lower lip as she sat down beside me. "I would love to get married while you and Keifer are here."

"This summer," I sat back in my rocking chair. "That does not allow for much time to plan a proper wedding and reception."

"I am afraid my mother will feel the same." Caroline paused for a moment thinking. "But I really want you and my brother there on my special day."

"We would love that too." I smiled.

"Perhaps we should do it next summer," she shrugged. "That way mother will have time to create the elaborate wedding she always dreamed of." She didn't even try to hide the smirk on her face.

"That is true," I felt a knot in my stomach knowing that there would be a slim chance of her having her dream wedding in the summer of 61'."

"I shall talk to her about it." Caroline said confidently. "If father gives us his blessing." She hesitated as a look of concern crossed her face.

"Nonsense," I squeezed her hand gently. "I am sure he will."

Keifer and Thad walked out onto the porch with coy grins written across their faces, but they quickly faltered when they saw us. They paused, each trying to transform their faces into blank stares.

"Why do you two look guilty?" I questioned.

"Guilty?" Thad glanced away and pulled a cigar out of his breast pocket. "We do not look guilty." He handed one to Keifer with a nod.

"What do you know?" Caroline narrowed her eyes at them.

"Nothing," Keifer immediately jumped in. "We do not know anything." He proclaimed passionately.

"That," I pointed at them before turning towards my sister-in-law. "I believe." I smirked making her chuckle.

"Very well," Thad lit his cigar and exhaled with a cough.

"Smooth," I rolled my eyes at Caroline who hid her smile behind her hand.

Caroline and I sat back down in the rocking chairs as the gentlemen leaned against the porch railing. The afternoon sun etched across the sky. The morning breeze died down, and the air settled into the sweet sticky smell that settles in mid-day. I closed my eyes curiously wondering what torturous interrogation David was inflicting upon poor Phillip.

Since my arrival, Angelina had been obvious in her favoritism towards my husband. David, on the other hand, despite having numerous children, showed a definite preference towards his daughter, Caroline. I believed it was because she looked like a carbon copy of her mother. She had Angelina's smile, the dash of freckles on her nose, and even the small dimple on her right cheek when she smiled like her brother. Plus, she embodied Angelina's personality — fiercely independent, head-strong, and beautiful.

My father-in-law and Phillip emerged from the house. Phillip's face was expressionless, but a sly smile played on David's lips, giving himself away. David paused beside his son and leaned against the porch post. I watched as his eyes scanned the four of us. Thad and Keifer were desperately attempting to suppress their laughter. David cleared his throat loudly drawing everyone's attention.

"Mr. Rhoades has come here today to ask for the hand of our beautiful Caroline." There was a devilish twinkle in his eye as David spoke as if he was truly enjoying making Phillip uncomfortable. "This young man has confessed his love for her and given me his word that he will provide her with a prosperous life full of stability, love, and happiness." He placed his hands behind his back and rocked back and forth on the balls of his feet.

"Well, father," Keifer quickly glanced towards Thad locking eyes for a moment of knowing. "What has this young man done to prove his ability to take care of our sweet Caroline?" I could see the struggle on my husband's face as he fought to maintain a serious expression as all eyes focused on poor Phillip.

"Sir, I," Phillip fiddled with the rim of his Stetson as he nervously stammered. "I give you my word as a gentleman and as the eldest son, I am to inherit Bella Ridge. I can assure you; it is a most prosperous plantation that will provide us with stability for the remainder of our lives as well as our children." He said with pride.

Phillip's words sounded so sincere, and I knew he earnestly believed them. Still, I knew within a year's short time that would no longer be true. But his words were heartfelt and genuine. I felt bad thinking of the wonderful life Caroline and Phillip would be robbed of shortly. I knew he would enlist as soon as Georgia seceded, if not sooner with the county militia troops.

"Father. Keifer," Caroline rose to her feet. "Stop." Her words cut through both men as she was accustomed to their antics.

"What?" my husband feigned innocence despite the guilty looks on the faces of three men of our household.

"Do not attempt to appear innocent," she eyed each of them carefully. "Any of you." A small smile played on her lips. "I have lived with all of you long enough to know the mischievous inclinations of your minds."

"Well said," I smirked.

"Very well," her father conceded. "I have already informed Mr. Rhoades that I wholeheartedly give my blessing to your union." A warm smile spread across his lips."

"Oh, thank you, father." Caroline rushed to hug her father who happily laughed at his daughter's delight.

Caroline released her father and grabbed a hold of Phillip's hand pulling him down the porch steps, their laughter trailing behind them as they galloped off towards the garden. I watched the two young people rush away to discuss the beginnings of their new life together. I envied their innocence and naivety. I wanted so desperately to protect them from the harshness of reality and the cruelty of what lay upon the horizon.

"That boy is so excited, he is likely to leave on his honeymoon without his bride." Thad exclaimed with a chuckle.

"No doubt," Keifer grinned with pride and adoration in his eyes as he watched his little sister.

Between the new addition of baby Tobias and the announcement of Caroline's engagement, the house was abuzz with merriment and activity. The joy was contagious and spread like wildfire through our small community. By evening friends from neighboring plantations began to trickle in to offer their congratulations to all parties. They brought various gifts for the baby and tokens for the new couple.

Mr. and Mrs. Rhoades and their other children arrived shortly before dinner time. They were in high spirits at the news of their son's engagement to Caroline and the joining of the two most profitable plantations in Savannah.

The arrival of so many had caused a flurry of activity in the kitchens. Polly had enlisted the help of three other female slaves to quickly prepare a buffet feast for all the well-wishers. I was amazed by their speed and efficiency. Tables covered in clothes appeared seemingly out of nowhere and were soon cluttered with various dishes.

I felt strangely out of place remaining on the fringes of activity. I held my son on my hip detached from the impromptu celebration. I was in awe at the genuine camaraderie, friendship, and bond between families and neighbors. Their compassion for their community was as strong as those I had experienced at home. It made me long for Terrace Falls, Judith, Charlotte, my grandmother, and even Mr. Bennett.

"Sidney?" Angelina waved from across the yard. "Please come here, dear."

My mother-in-law was standing beside two people I recognized from church as Phillip's parents. His father was an imposing figure well over six feet tall with dark hair and broad shoulders. His mother was a stoutly woman with her hair pulled back in a severe bun at the nap of her neck. She had kind eyes and a gentle smile. Both were immaculately dressed in the latest fashion.

"Good evening," I approached with a happily squealing son in my arms.

"Sidney," my mother-in-law eagerly relieved me of my son who was reaching for his nana. "I would like to introduce you to Phillip's parents, Leo and Alice Rhoades." She turned towards her guests, adjusting my son with seasoned proficiency. "Leo and Alice, I would like to introduce you to my son, Keifer's wife, Sidney from Braintree."

"My pleasure," I bowed my head respectfully.

"Braintree?" Mr. Rhoades appeared confused. "Where abouts is that? I am not familiar with the name."

"It is near Boston, Massachusetts. Keifer and I run a large estate called Terrace Falls." I said proudly.

"I was under the impression that Dr. Marshall had returned home to accept his rightful inheritance of Gable Gardens." Mrs. Rhoades looked over at my mother-in-law for confirmation.

"It does not appear so," Angelina pressed my son's chubby cheek to her own. "Thad will continue to run our plantation until Lucas is old enough to take over." She offered a tight smile in my direction.

I shifted uncomfortably looking about the grounds for my husband. I found him standing near the picnic tables with his father and Thad helping himself to another plate of food. It seemed he could not get enough of Southern cooking as he put it and had gained a bit of a pooch since we had arrived.

"Is this your first time in Savannah? I am sure it must be a great change for you." Mrs. Rhoades said shifting uncomfortably.

"No, my husband and I visited once years ago shortly after we got married." I fidgeted with my fan in the stifling heat. "It is beautiful and I am enjoying spending time with my husband's family." I smiled warmly at them.

"Are you an abolitionist?" Mr. Rhoades eyed me suspiciously.

"Leo!" Mrs. Rhoades scolded him harshly.

"I am simply asking," he shrugged. "She is from the North, dear." He lowered his voice.

"No." I chuckled lightly. "I am not an abolitionist."

"My apologies," Mr. Rhoades looked ashamed. "There has been a lot of tension." He shrugged his shoulder.

"She is married to a Southern plantation owner. She could not be an abolitionist." Mrs. Rhoades scoffed, rolling her eyes at her husband.

"I am sure Sidney appreciates our way of life in the South." Angelina cleared her throat and kissed my son again. "And we are so happy to have them here and the chance to spend some time with our handsome grandson." She attempted to change the subject.

"Now Angelina, that is hardly fair." Mrs. Rhoades tickled my son who squealed eagerly in his grandma's arms. "You are covered in grandchildren." My son wrapped his chubby little hand around Mrs.

Rhoades' finger. "I cannot wait for Phillip and Caroline to start their family."

"Darling," Mr. Rhoades placed his hand on the small of his wife's back. "We have a wedding to plan first."

"Perhaps they will want a fall wedding." Angelina noted. "The colors would be stunning."

"Plus, the weather would be more amenable." Mrs. Rhoades remarked.

"That is true." Mr. Rhoades agreed.

They continued their banter when Caroline and Phillip approached us. She had her arm looped through his and both were glowing with happiness. Her pale pink gown complimented his suit well and they looked like the perfect couple. Her fair complexion balanced his rugged brutal nature.

"Good evening," Caroline said in a giddy voice. "I am delighted to see so many of our friends."

"We are blessed." Her mother agreed.

"Indeed," Mrs. Rhoades waved her hand dismissively, moving on to more important topics. "Have you two considered when and where you would like to get married?"

"I would like to get married before my brother and Sidney leave for Chicago." Caroline said hopefully.

"That soon?" Angelina glanced over at Mrs. Rhoades with fear on her face.

"Darling," Mrs. Rhoades touched her son's arm gently. "I am not sure we would be able to put together a proper wedding that quickly." She nervously bit her lower lip.

"We do not need anything fancy." Caroline spoke up immediately.

"She is right," Phillip joined in. "As long are our families and friends are there, that is all that we care about." Caroline nodded in agreement.

"But darling," Mrs. Rhoades still looked apprehensive. "We were wanting," But the look on the faces of the young couple stopped her short. She sighed deeply looking back at Angelina who nodded. "We will figure it out."

"Of course, we will." Angelina said assuredly, but I caught a glimpse of apprehension in her eye.

"We shall all work together to make it perfect." I squeezed Caroline's arm lovingly.

"Yes, we shall." Mrs. Rhoades chimed in with less enthusiasm and a look of genuine fear.

"When are you scheduled to leave?" Mr. Rhoades turned towards me.

"The end of September, early October." I shrugged nonchalantly.

"I am afraid that does not leave us much time." Mrs. Rhoades said more to herself than anyone in particular.

"Nonsense," Angelina tried to sound optimistic. "We have plenty of time." The worried look in her eyes said otherwise.

"It will be beautiful." I tried to sound convincingly.

"Yes, it will be." Mrs. Rhoades concluded, patting her son on the arm.

"Sidney, did you meet Phillip's siblings?" Caroline offered me a tight smile and took a hold of my elbow stirring me away. "I apologize," she said once we were a safe distance away. "Mother can be a little intense."

"Mine or yours?" Phillip smirked.

"Both," Caroline relented with a raised eyebrow.

"They were both endearing." I gave Caroline a coy look. "Trust me. I have met some challenging mother-in-law's and neither of your mother's apply."

Keifer approached us carrying a whisky in one hand and a smoldering cigar in the other. The blush on his cheeks had nothing to do with the summer heat. The broad smile on his face and the glint in his eye told me that he, and most likely his brother-in-law, Thad had been knee deep in the whisky since before the impromptu celebration.

"Hello darling," my husband flung his arm around my shoulders. "Isn't this a joyous day?" He took a long drag on his cigar.

"Where did you get that nasty cigar?" I glared at him.

"Thad was handing them out to celebrate Tobias' birth." His glassy eyes sparkled.

"Of course, he was," I muttered under my breath.

"What dear?" Keifer slurred leaning into me.

"Can I get you anything else?" I said sweetly but Caroline snorted stifling a giggle while Phillip pretended not to hear her.

"No," he looked around sheepishly. "No. I was looking for," he let go of me and wandered off staggering towards his father.

"He is going to be in top shape tomorrow." Caroline snorted.

"I am happy he is enjoying himself." I shook my head but continued smiling watching Keifer try not to make a fool of himself and failing miserably. "He truly appears at ease here." I said more to myself than anyone else.

"He's home," Caroline offered me almost a pityingly look. "Sorry."

"No," I shook my head nonchalantly knowing she was right.

And I hated that she was right. I watched him standing there with his father, Leo, and Thad, laughing casually and easily. It made my heart ache realizing how different he was between this place and the life we had built in Terrace Falls.

Caroline and Phillip got distracted by other guests congratulating them on their engagement. It gave me a moment to slip away from the crowd and collect my thoughts. I wandered back into the house and found myself alone in the parlor. I needed a moment to myself. A moment to breathe. A moment to collect my thoughts. I gazed out the front window at the cluster of family, friends, and neighbors. All were smiling, chatting, children were running around giggling and sneaking an extra helping of dessert while their parents were lost in various conversations.

I sighed deeply and leaned against the glass. Observations throughout the evening had shifted amongst the guests. While the women primarily focused on the joy of the birth of Tobias and speculated about the upcoming nuptials, the men focused on and contemplated about the secession and what it may bring.

I wanted to warn them. I fought the urge to tell them they were walking into a fight they couldn't possibly win — that after thousands of lives were lost, their world, their culture, the foundation of their lives would be shattered forever and everything they knew, trusted and believed would be lost to faded history books.

But I couldn't. I unconsciously bit my lower lip, dreading what was to come for all of them. I closed my eyes for another minute, then plastered on a fake smile. I walked back out into the courtyard, past the fountain and rejoined the festivities.

What else could I do?

23

FRIDAY, JULY 3, 2020

I STOPPED TURNING ON THE MORNING news as I made coffee and got ready for work. Mainstream media was becoming more concerned with political agenda and correctness rather than unbiased reporting of facts. It had become mind numbing and outrageously ridiculous. I had given up on all major networks, and the newspaper outlets were ten times worse. Even though traditional newspapers were almost obsolete, their online presence was annoying on social media sites.

Instead, I turned on a classic music station realizing the influence my dad, Shane had on my taste and danced around the apartment. Landon had left for his shift a couple hours earlier leaving me a vacant apartment. It was nice having some time all to myself without Landon laughing at my horrific dance moves. The years of cheerleading competitions had left me with the ability to dance choreographed dances, but not the ability to translate to typical dance moves.

The music lightened my mood considerably. I put on my scrubs, added some light makeup, and pulled my hair up into a messy bun. I sang slightly off key and fixed myself a travel mug of coffee for the road. I was dreading spending another twelve-hour shift suffocating behind a worthless surgical mask. I reluctantly flipped off the stereo, picked up my purse, and begrudgingly set off for another miserable day at the hospital.

"Are you alright, Sidney?" Brandy slumped down in the breakroom chair beside me.

"No," I grumbled.

"I wish I could take a vacation," Dr. Erica Grant approached us dragging along looking at bad as the rest of us. "But of course there is no place to go."

"Do you think this will ever end?" Brandy rested her head in her hand.

"Not anytime soon, I fear." Dr. Grant rolled her eyes. "I've actually seen noted physicians on the news warning people and such. I guess common sense is not so common anymore." She rubbed her eyes.

"That is for sure." I mumbled. "Ignorance appears to be running amuck these days."

"It's so ridiculous to me how people can't seem to comprehend that this is simply another variant of the freaking damn flu." Dr. Grant leaned against the counter. "Each year, hundreds of people die from the flu, and no one freaks out about it, but give it a fancy name, add a bit of propaganda and bam . . . everyone panics."

"Dr. Grant," An ER nurse I recognized as Tammy, came around the corner. "I'm surprised to see you in here."

"Yes, well I was looking for Brandy actually." She shifted her attention. "Do you happen to recall what time the patient in exam room six was discharged?" Brandy wrinkled her forehead in thought. "The one with the sprained wrist, fat lip, and black eye from falling down the stairs – with the help of her husband, I daresay."

"Ah, yes. She signed out against medical advice around five, I believe." Brandy told her. "After she did, I called social services to do a wellness check on the children."

"Good." Dr. Grant nodded. "I wanted to make sure someone followed up with them."

"The spike in domestic violence has gotten out of control since they implemented lockdowns." I noted. "More than a third of the people who come in here are a result of domestic violence."

"Being cooped up 24/7 is wearing on people. It's almost like everyone I see wants some sort of antidepressant or anxiety meds." Dr. Grant shrugged and glanced at her watch. "Another two hours." She sighed heavily. "Back to the lions den. Have a good evening, ladies."

"You too, Dr. Grant." Brandy said.

"Thanks, you too." I called after her.

"I don't know how she does it. She's not had a day off in the last three weeks." Tammy shook her head before grabbing her things off the counter. "Have a great evening." She waved as she disappeared.

"How is your husband doing?" I asked Brandy once we were alone.

"Coping," she got to her feet. "I keep begging him to retire. He hit his 20th year last April and is eligible to retire now with fifty percent of his pay from his top three years earnings."

"That's not bad." I admitted.

"No. Plus, he would be able to find another job. One that he enjoys and doesn't put his life at risk." She stated.

"That would certainly put your mind at ease." I remarked opening my locker.

"True, but he was diagnosed with PTSD last year and it's only gotten worse. I'd really like him to take some time off and work on managing the symptoms before doing anything else. Between his pension and my pay, we'll be fine."

"Hopefully, you can convince him." I grabbed my purse and slammed the locker shut. "Be careful going home."

"You too. Roll the window down and turn the radio up. Stay awake." She cautioned me.

"Thanks, you too."

I followed Brandy's instructions, rolled the windows down and turned the radio up. I ripped off my mask and tossed it into the back seat. I pulled out onto the main road and relaxed as the warm evening air floated through the car caressing my face and lifting my hair off my shoulders. It felt invigorating.

I noticed my Uncle Nicholas' car in the driveway as I pulled up in front of Robert and Emily's house. I was not expecting him to be here but was excited to see him. It has been more than a month since I saw him due to my heavy work schedule at the hospital.

I entered the house through the side door without knocking. This had become a second home for me, and Robert and Emily were like a second set of parents. I found everyone milling about the kitchen. It appeared dinner was getting underway. Emily was setting out the chopping block and the vegetables. Robert was on the back porch lighting the grill.

"Hello everyone," I called out setting my purse on a barstool.

"Hello, darling," Uncle Nicholas hugged me. "I was hoping you would stop by after work."

"Landon is working a double so, I thought I would come by." I smiled and hugged Emily. "I hope that is alright."

"Of course, sweetie." She smiled.

"What can I do to help?" I offered.

"You have worked all day." Emily patted my arm. "Relax. We will have dinner ready in about an hour."

"Would you like to take a walk before dinner and enjoy the evening air?" Uncle Nicholas offered.

"I would love too."

"Shall we?" My uncle held out his arm with a joyful grin.

"Enjoy yourselves," Emily smiled as we left through the kitchen door.

The sun was fading off in the distance as twilight set upon us. The temperature hovered in the mid-80s, and a light warm breeze embraced us. It was refreshing to be outside without a stupid facial mask covering half my face. The lines from the constant wearing of one at the hospital were etched upon my face. I unconsciously rubbed my hand over my face.

"It's nice not to be suffocated for once, isn't it?" My uncle smirked.

"Yes, it is." I agreed.

"So, I am curious." He glanced at me briefly. "How is your summer going in Savannah? I haven't spoken to you since you arrived."

"We had a bit of a rough start," I chuckled. "It seems Keifer's younger sister Victoria is a lot like Eugenia." I rolled my eyes. "And the humidity is unbearable." I complained.

"And how is life at Gable Gardens?" He raised his eyebrows at me. "What?" he shrugged. "I've always been curious. I had some friends at West Point from the South, but I never had the opportunity to visit a true Southern plantation before the war."

"It is strange," I looked out over the horizon but not seeing what was in front of me. My mind was back on the porch in Savannah. "But I must admit it is beautiful." A thin smile passed upon my lips. "It is almost serene. At first it felt like I stepped onto the set of *Gone with the Wind* or something. I can say I understand the majestic tranquility of it."

"The first time I saw the South was after the war had broken out. What I saw was not very majestic at all." His eyes widened with emphasis. "It was sad, really. And I cannot say I had or have fond feelings for the South."

"I can understand that. But surely, your feelings have changed since the end of the war." I glanced at him.

"Do you know many World War II veterans, or Korean war veterans, or even Vietnam war veterans?" He inquired.

"A few," I nodded.

"And have they gotten over what their enemies did during those wars?" I shook my head. "I know many World War II veterans who fought on the Pacific front who continue to hate Japanese people. The same can be said for most veterans, even our current Iraq and Afghanistan veterans. Those who have endured such atrocities rarely get over them. They may in time be able to forgive their transgressors, but they can never forget what was done." My uncle explained.

"I would imagine that would be difficult." I sympathized.

"After spending a year in Andersonville, I cannot say I am very fond of Southerners." He confessed.

"You realize my husband is a Southerner." I raised an eyebrow.

"I know," he ran his hand through his hair absentmindedly. "But Keifer is more Northern than Southern now."

"You know we will be traveling to Chicago in September. We will be together for Christmas this year." I took hold of his arm and gently squeezed it. "I only wish I could say something to you, warn you as to what is to come."

"But you cannot." He gently shook his head. "Our experiences, both good and bad shape us, mold us, and define who we are."

"Still," I objected. "Some experiences we could definitely do without." I tried to laugh and make light of it, but we both knew there was no humor in the years to come.

"Even so, you must not meddle." We continued down the sidewalk in silence for a few minutes each lost in our own thoughts.

"How old were you when your barrier started to dissipate?" I tried to ask as casually as I could.

"Nice try," my uncle chuckled. "But it was much later, I am afraid my barrier did not come down until I was in my early 20s."

"Damn," I smirked.

"So, tell me. What do you think of being on a Southern plantation," his voice lowered an octave. "In its original state?"

"Can I confess something I feel horrible about?" I chewed on my bottom lip nervously.

"Of course. You know I would never judge you. You already know my horrid secrets." He chuckled.

"Well," I led him over to a bench on the side of the small lake at the park at the edge of the neighborhood. "When I first arrived at Gable Gardens every fiber of my being detested the very notion of slavery." I began. "Now, all this Black Lives Matter bullshit, the violence Antifa brings everywhere they appear, constantly being called a white supremacist, a colonial, and this social justice nonsense at school. I just," my voice trailed off.

"I understand," my uncle patted my arm. "It made resigning my post rather simple." My head whipped around.

"You did what?" I could not believe what he just said. "You resigned?"

"Yes, I did." He chuckled softly. "I cannot tolerate this woke garbage. I refuse to apologize for something neither my ancestors, nor I, did. And for one race to demand accountability for the actions of people who died more than a hundred years ago is absurd. To me, it is the same as us blaming every Japanese child for the attack on Pearl Harbor. The logic is ridiculous."

"How convenient for Blacks to forget that more than a thousand Blacks owned slaves in the South." I spat. "Every race has been held in bondage at some point in history. There is not one race that is immune. Yet, all whites are apparently responsible for slavery?"

The sun had faded into a soft glow of streaks of pink and orange across the evening sky. I was not sure how long we had been gone, but I had a gut feeling it was almost time for dinner. However, I was not quite ready to head back yet.

"I feel bad because I," I sputtered.

"Because you are not a racist person, but find yourself harboring resentment towards all the people causing this bullshit?" He asked.

"Yes." I admitted. "And I feel horrible for it."

"Has it changed your opinion of Ned, Duncan, Naomi or the others you have lived with all your life?" my uncle asked.

"No, and I have a lot of black and gay friends at the hospital and at school. They do not act that way, nor do they believe what these fanatics do. But I cannot help but feel horrible that some of the stereotypes have proven themselves to be true." I confessed.

"I was raised to define people based on their character, not the amount of pigment in their skin. You cannot lump everyone together by the actions of a few. If you do that, it makes you no better than they are." My uncle emphasized.

"I know. I was raised the same way." I shook my head with exhaustion. "I just hate the division Black Lives Matter, Antifa, liberals, and the freaking alphabet people are causing in our country. It's like waiting on the cusp of another civil war to break out." I explained. "I do not know how to explain it without sounding horrible."

"You are fine," he laughed softly.

"You know I had a talk with Ned before I left for Savannah. He had overheard some gentlemen talking at the mercantile." I hesitated.

"And?"

"Well, they were discussing what was going to become of the slaves if they are freed."

"What did he think about it?"

"Ned said the men talked about how there would be millions of blacks, most who cannot read or write, or have a way to support their families and no ability to purchase land or a home will be left with little more than the clothes on their backs." I explained.

"He is correct." My uncle nodded. "We both know how the years following the war — the reconstruction years, were in many ways worse than the war itself." He pointed out. "I recall the blacks in the South fared worse than those that ventured North, but not much.

They were universally disliked, and most Americans blamed them for causing the war and all that happened after it." My uncle shrugged slightly.

"Didn't Lincoln want to send them back to Africa?"

"Yes, he mentioned it more than once and many people agreed with him. However, you are forgetting that it was their own people who captured them and sold them to the slave traders to begin with. Lincoln had some reservations about how they would be received if they were sent back. Plus, there was the additional problem of gathering them up to send them back." I nodded. "You have to remember, there were literally millions of not only slaves, but free blacks as well. Therefore, is it right to only send back the ones who were slaves or also those who were free? And at that time, neither free nor former slaves were considered American citizens. There was a great deal of turmoil about what to do with them after the war."

"I think about what is happening right now, and I wonder if perhaps Lincoln was right — send them all back." I grumbled.

"You realize this is all government propaganda meant to cause racial tension and division."

"But why? It makes no sense."

"It makes perfect sense, Sidney. You of all people who have studied history extensively over the last several years understand that people who are divided are easier to manipulate and easier to control. Think back to the 1930s. What does that tell you?" He raised his eyebrows. "Let's not forget Lincoln abused his powers by suspending Habeas Corpus and imprisoned the entire Maryland State Legislature throughout the Civil War on a Northern Warship in the Bay just to keep Maryland from voting to secede as well because he did not want Washington D.C. to be surrounded by seceding states. It would have placed the Union Capital in the Confederacy."

"You do not think they are trying to turn the United States into a Communist country, do you?" I was surprised to hear his implication.

"A Marxist Communist country controlled by socialism? Yes, I do. And I believe this is just the beginning."

"But why?"

"Money. Greed. Power." My uncle shrugged his shoulder again. "The usual suspects."

"Who?"

"Whoever is controlling the Deep State and the Democrat Party."

"But President Trump?" I objected.

"Have you noticed how they," he looked me in the eye. "And by they, I mean every Democrat and RINO in D.C. and every RINO has done everything possible to impeach him and make him powerless. I guarantee they will never allow him to be reelected because they cannot control him. President Trump refuses to play by their rules. And he wants to get rid of corruption in Washington. He is a threat to the establishment."

"President Trump has done a lot of good for this country and all the people in it." I stated, "And people will vote him back for a second term." I said with confidence.

"Never happen," He scoffed at my insertion. "I am being serious. Mark my words, the Democrats will steal this election and put someone they can easily control and manipulate into office. Joe Biden is a mere puppet in their game."

"But why?"

"Biden is a useless career politician. He is a far-left extremist and the exact opposite of President Trump. The Deep State can easily control him and will be able to destroy the country from within."

"So, we are screwed." I huffed.

"Pretty much. The next four years will be hell. It would not surprise me if they do not try to implement martial law before the end of his term just to cancel the next election."

"Seriously?" he nodded. "Do you really believe the American people will tolerate that?"

"Initially, most will. But it will not take long before many will stand against governmental policies."

"It feels like we're on the verge of another civil war." I rolled my eyes.

"It's possible. But this one will not be split like the previous one. It will be Liberal Democrats against Conservative Republicans." My uncle tilted his head a bit. "More like blue cities against the rural and suburban rest of the country." He chuckled.

"You realize we live in a blue city?" I scoffed. "Not very comforting."

"Let's not think about that tonight." He put his arm around me and pulled me to my feet. "Come on, I am sure we are late for dinner."

24

FRIDAY, JULY 6, 1860

MAKING THE EFFORT TO GET TO know my mother-in-law and the rest of my husband's siblings made a world of difference. I learned that despite our initial impressions and differences we had a great deal in common. I grew closer and fonder of my mother-in-law, which left me feeling even worse knowing what was to come. I knew Sherman would spare most of the city of Savannah due to its port, but the area outside the city would not be spared. I could only hope and pray that Sherman and his troops would spare Gable Gardens.

The thought of it being burned to the ground broke my heart. I had taken to spending my days leisurely rocking on the porch with my son, taking long walks with him about the grounds, or sitting on a blanket spread across the vast lawn under my favorite oak tree watching my son playing beneath its wide canopy.

I had grown to love this plantation. I began to feel at home here. I loved how relaxed my husband was. The sound of his laughter was a welcome reprieve on my tired soul. He appeared so at ease in this place. It was a part of him. I could see that now. Just as Terrace Falls was a part of me. It made me feel horrible to take him away from it again. It was his home. His birthright.

But I also knew it was existing on borrowed time — just like the rest of the South.

My heart wanted to be honest with them, to bring Keifer's family back to Braintree with us where I knew they would be safe, cared for, and well-feed throughout the duration of the war. But I knew I could say nothing. I knew I could not save them from what was to come. And if Gable Gardens was taken, destroyed, or burned down by

Sherman and his troops, I knew Keifer, nor his family would recover from the devastation.

My only solace was that I hoped I could plead with them after Lincoln's Emancipation Proclamation was issued. Knowing food and provisions would be scarce in the South, perhaps I could encourage them all to come North and seek refuge at Terrace Falls. I knew it was a longshot, but perhaps I could keep them all safe. I prayed I would be able to keep them all safe. They were my family now too.

The long days were filled with warmth and laughter. Each Saturday we would visit neighboring plantations for barbeques, dances, and mingling with friends. Each Sunday we would attend church services as a family and then share dinner, discussions, and laughter. I fell into the easy rhythm of life here and understood how it was treasured. The tranquility of it. The beauty of the gardens. Afternoon tea on the porch. And evening suppers filled with the voices of family and friends all gushing about the latest news and gossip.

It amazed me how all the men talked about with excitement was possible secession and the war that would inevitably follow. They spoke of it as if it were a child's game laughing about how they would surely lick the Yankees within a month.

During these times, I would bite my lower lip and remain silent. There was no point in trying to discredit their arguments with fact. None appeared to realize the South's lack of factories, iron mills, industrial railroads or navy. It appeared *Rhett Butler* was correct in saying the South only had an abundance of cotton, arrogance, and slaves.

The afternoon sewing circles with neighboring ladies from church held a similar sentiment. They would express their concerns about the possibility of their husbands and sons having to fight. They gossiped about who was courting whom. Who was getting married. Who wore what gown to what party or heaven forbid a lady was seen wearing the same dress twice in a season. Or whose party was the grandest. But never once did these Southern ladies discuss seeds for planting, harvest tables, or money. They literary left every decision in the hands of their husbands and fathers. They knew nothing of the day-to-day operations of their plantations.

It amazed me how some stereotypes were true. Some of these ladies were empty vessels. However, it was obvious that some were very intelligent but purposely downplayed it. I could never fathom why they felt it necessary to do so, especially in the company of men. It seemed to be backward to me, but perhaps that was just the influence of my *other* life shining through.

I had befriended a young married lady, Bonnie, who resided with her husband Randall's family at the neighboring plantation. She was two years younger than I but already had three children and was expecting her fourth around Thanksgiving. She was a delightful girl with a headful of bright red hair and scattered freckles across her face. She had the most beautiful and striking green eyes I had ever seen. Each of her children had her character traits and prominent features.

I would visit her place at least twice a week and she would drop by ours the same. I was dearly going to miss her once September rolled around. She had offered to come up next summer for a long visit to Terrace Falls. I happily agreed simply because I could not tell her by then we would be living in a different world.

I was sitting on the front porch drinking lemonade and writing letters to my grandmother and Charlotte when Bonnie rode up. She was alone today, which was unusual for her. Normally, she arrived by carriage accompanied by two or three of her daughters. Her horse kicked up dust as she drew closer to the porch. I arose from my seat and approached the steps.

"Bonnie is everything all right?" she appeared disheveled with her hair falling out of its braid and dirt smeared across her cheek.

"Oh, thank goodness Sidney. Is your husband here?" She pulled up the reins but did not dismount the horse.

"Yes, he is in the office with his father." I turned to motion behind me when the front doors opened. Keifer and his father stepped out on the porch.

"Mrs. Farwell, are you alright?" My father-in-law descended steps and steadied her horse.

"Mrs. Farwell, you really should not be riding in your condition." Keifer stood beside me and chastised her.

"Nonsense," she bellowed back dismissing him with a hasty wave of her hand. "I need your help." She paused to catch her breath. "My father-in-law is ill. His speech is slurred, and he cannot move his left arm, and he is experiencing numbness in his left leg."

"A stroke," I muttered without thinking.

"Excuse me," Keifer glanced at me.

"Nothing dear," I looked back at Bonnie quickly. "We will be right there." I told her dragging my husband towards the house.

"Otis, fetch the carriage. Tell Leroy we must make haste." My father-in-law shouted behind the black man running towards the stables.

I passed Keifer in the hall and ran into the parlor. Angelina was reading on the chaise lounge. I quickly explained what had happened and that I would be going to the Farwell Farms plantation with David and Keifer. I asked her if she wouldn't mind looking after my son when he woke up. She agreed telling me to let her know if she could do anything else for them before I rushed out to the carriage.

The afternoon sun beat down relentlessly upon us on our short ride. The air was heavy with humidity with no trace of a breeze. Beads of sweat lined my forehead and made my corset and gown stick uncomfortably to me like a thick coat. Bonnie had left only minutes before us and the traces of her dust clung to the heavy air. It was clear she had pushed her horse to its limits, especially on a hot day such as this.

Farwell Farms plantation was grand. It also had a long dusty pathway leading to the home. The house was somewhat smaller than the one at Gable Gardens, and it was built with red bricks. It had black shutters across the front windows and a balcony across the second floor. It was a beautiful home.

The porch was littered with slaves milling about concerned about Mr. Farwell. It was obvious they respected the man. I had met him several times. He was soft-spoken man, a kindhearted family man who took great care of his family and those who resided on their plantation.

"Where is he?" Keifer hollered before jumping out of the carriage before it came to a full stop.

"N' dar, sir," a smaller black man pointed towards the front door. "Ms. Bony ges run in." Keifer bolted up the steps with David and I closely behind him.

A small houseboy sitting on the lower step in the foyer immediately leapt to his feet and pointed up the stairs when we entered the house. The air stood still even with the windows open. The lack of a breeze made the house stifling, and I immediately thought of how nice it would be to have central air conditioning. I sighed to myself and followed my husband up the grand staircase.

The shades were drawn in the master suite. Mrs. Mariam Farwell was seated on the side of the bed. Their children, spouses, and grandchildren were scattered about the room and lingering in the hallway outside the room. I felt horrible for them.

"Good day, Mrs. Farwell." Keifer approached the bed. David and I hung back by the edge of the canopy. "How long has he been this way?"

"Thank you for coming Dr. Marshall. Remus was fine this morning. He spent some time with our overseer, Franklin. He came inside midday saying he was not feeling well. I tried to get him upstairs to rest, but he collapsed at the top of the stairs."

"Randall helped him into bed." Bonnie told us about her husband.

"Would everyone please step out for a moment so I may do an exam?" Keifer stepped closer to the bed, nodding and checked his Mr. Farwell's pulse.

"Of course," Mrs. Farwell stood and gestured to everyone out of the room.

"Sidney, would you mind assisting me?" Keifer asked over his shoulder.

"Yes, dear." I touched David's arm lightly. He nodded and followed everyone out into the hallway.

I waited patiently while my husband conducted his initial assessment. I knew exactly what had happened but was racking my brain on how to explain it to Keifer in a way that he would understand without him being overly curious as to how I knew what I was talking too. Robert's words of caution suddenly flashed into my mind about why individuals with *E.V.E* do not go into the medical profession.

Keifer listened to his chest with his stethoscope, took his pulse, and checked his extremities. I remained silent but wanted to check the degree of Mr. Farwell's paralysis. When Keifer turned to retrieve the thermometer from his bag I approached Mr. Farwell and sat on the edge of the bed. I took his hand in mine and tried to make eye contact with him.

"Hello Remus, can you hear me?" His eyes tried to focus on me. "Blink if you can hear me." He did. "Good," I smiled in reassurance and took his other hand in mine, holding each of his hands in mine. "Can you squeeze my hands?" He firmly squeezed with his right hand, but his left hand was noticeably deficient. "Good," I praised him.

"What are you doing?" Keifer hovered behind me.

"Just a moment," I turned. "I am checking him for paralysis. I have seen this before. I believe he has had a stroke."

"A stroke?"

"Yes, a blood clot that travels to the brain. It causes dizziness, weakness, confusion, blurry vision, partial paralysis, and/or slurred speech. The damage can be permanent." I almost said if not treated early but caught myself.

"And you say you have seen this before?"

"Yes," I turned back to Mr. Farwell. "Can you smile for me, Remus?" He tried and while the right corner of his mouth lifted into a grin, the facial muscles on the left drooped and refused to smile. "That is good," I smiled at him reassuringly and lightly touched the side of his face. "Can you bend your legs for me?" The right one bent obediently but the left refused. "That was good. Thank you."

I felt horrible. I knew there was nothing I could do and that his condition was unlikely to improve much even with extensive therapy.

"May I speak with you privately for a moment?" I stood up and took Keifer's hand.

We walked over near the hearth away from Remus. I glanced at the photos of his family. It had become common in recent years, but the contrast to modern photography was drastic. The images still looked foreign to me with the faded black and gray features and lack of personality displayed.

"A blood clot traveled to Remus' brain causing him to have a stroke. He has pronounced weakness and paralysis on the left side of his body. His mobility and speech are impaired. They may improve over time, but he will not return to his previous state." I explained.

"Are you sure? I have seen similar conditions at the hospital and some people do improve." His optimism was touching.

"I do believe he will improve, but it will be minimal I am afraid." I explained.

"I have to talk to Mariam." My husband looked upset as he did when he had to deliver news he did not want to.

"I will stay with Remus." I patted him lovingly on the arm.

The afternoon faded into evening. The shadows along the wall grew taller and more imposing. Miriam had drifted in and out of the master chambers throughout the day, but she was struggling. The realization that her husband would likely be partially paralyzed, struggle with even the smallest of things, and would likely never return to his former self was devastating to her.

Bonnie came in shortly thereafter to sit with me and her father-in-law. Randall appeared to be struggling with his father's condition as much as his mother was, for both the same and different reasons. With his father unable to take care of the daily operations of the plantation, as the eldest son all the responsibility rested on his shoulders.

Bonnie's husband was not always the most responsible young man from what Keifer had told me. He had been expelled from multiple Universities before he got involved with Bonnie. Randall was a strikingly handsome man with dark wavy hair and deep-set brown eyes. He was quick to laugh and usually had a mostly unlit cigar hanging out of his mouth, and a drink in his hand.

Bonnie evened him out. She provided the stability he desperately needed in his life. She was light-hearted, fun, and had the ability to keep Randall in check. She was strong-spirited and strong-willed. The color of her hair was an apt indicator of her personality.

I joined her beside the hearth in the front parlor for some late supper. It was almost eight in the evening, and I was ready to return home. I was concerned about leaving my son for so long and was concerned about feeding him. I knew in my absence that Angelina would rely on Tallie to feed him, and I felt terribly uncomfortable about that.

"How is Randall doing? I have not seen him for a while." I picked at the ham and sweet potatoes on my plate.

"He is hiding out over at the Coffman's with George and Bryan." Bonnie appeared annoyed.

"I am sorry." I had no idea what to say to her.

"I expect he will turn up in the morning nursing a headache and feeling regretful." She took a bite and swallowed before she continued. "I know he is hurting, but you know how men are. It is not like they can have an intelligent conversation about it. Instead, they drink whisky and are most likely sitting on the back porch firing shotguns at some haystacks or grain barrels." Bonnie snorted.

"I understand." I honestly did not because Keifer was not that sort of man, but then again, I could imagine Landon reacting in a similar way.

"I know you enjoy reading and have assisted your husband for more than a decade. Is there a chance Remus will improve?" The concern was etched on her face.

"I can show you some exercises you can do with him to help him regain some of his mobility and speech. He will improve, but he will not be able to speak or perform his old work-related tasks as he did before." I wanted her to be optimistic but still wanted to keep her expectations realistic.

"I would appreciate it." Bonnie's face looked somber.

"I know it is not going to be easy. But I will help you in any way I can." I tried to sound reassuring.

"Thank you," she offered me the best smile she could muster. "I am worried about Mariam. She is walking around in a daze."

"I imagine she will for a while." I sympathized. "The adjustment will be difficult, and expectations must be kept to a minimum."

"It is going to be a long summer." Bonnie exhaled audibly. "I hate that you will be leaving in a few weeks."

"Six weeks," I corrected her. "And it is not like we will not be returning." Although a part of me hated the fact that it would be more than four years before we would see each other again and our lives and country would be a very different place.

"You simply must return next summer so you can meet our new addition." She smiled halfheartedly and patted her stomach.

"It would be my pleasure," I reached over and squeezed her hand.

25

SUNDAY, AUGUST 9, 2020

LANDON AND I FINALLY HAD A Sunday off together. We had requested it four weeks ago to celebrate Robert and Emily's anniversary. Going against the city ordinances, we had planned a special party for them. It was an amazing feeling belonging to a family. Leslie and Phoebe were like two more sisters to me. I loved how close the four of us had become. We had conspired to throw a surprise party for the parents we all loved.

Alex and Leslie had invited Robert and Emily to their home for brunch while the rest of us had decorated and prepared the food at their home. Leslie had promised to keep her in-laws out of the house until half past two, so we had time to get everything set up. Landon, Carson, and Jackson were hanging out on the back deck drinking beer and trying not to blow up the house while starting the grill. I paused by the window watching the three men in their mid-twenties behaving with the collective age of twelve.

"I do not believe they will ever grow up." Phoebe's voice startled me from behind.

"Me neither," I asked Phoebe as I took Audry from her arms. "How are you feeling?"

"Good," she smiled wearily. "Just tired. Little Miss here still does not understand the difference between night and day."

"I cannot believe she is almost a month old already." I lightly touched her chubby cheek making her appear to grin in her sleep.

"Me neither," Phoebe climbed up on one of the bar stools and rested her head on her hand.

"How is Wally taking to having a little sister?" Jocelyn joined us.

"He thinks Audry is his little pet." Phoebe chuckles lightly and sighs. "He is so cute with her."

"That's wonderful," I smirk. "I guess I was really jealous when Jocelyn was born."

"Yeah, but you were a little mother hen when Ethan arrived." My sister taunted me.

"I guess that explains the dynamic of your relationship." Phoebe speculated.

"I guess it does," Jocelyn looked at me closely.

"Perhaps," I shrugged.

"I am going to put little Miss down before everyone gets here." Phoebe took her daughter back carefully from my arms and headed towards the stairs.

"Do you think that is why we were never close?" Jocelyn asked me once we were alone.

"No," I shook my head. "I was always Amy's daughter, and you were Dad's. They, especially Amy made that very clear throughout our childhood."

"And Ethan was always Dad's too." Jocelyn noted. "I believe Amy only ever wanted one child and the fact that you look like a carbon copy of her — blond hair, blue eyes, very feminine, was just the cherry on top." She looked down at her hands. "That did not leave much for Ethan and me." She said in a whisper.

"I am sorry," I pulled her into a tight hug. "But in all honestly," I let her go just enough to see her face. "She did you and Ethan a favor. Shane was a much better parent than Amy."

"True," Jocelyn eyes glistened with tears. "Our Dad truly loved us despite his flaws." She smiled slightly.

"At least we had one parent who wanted us and accepts us as we are and not for who they expect us to be." I grinned. "And who still does."

"And knows the truth about us." Jocelyn raised an eyebrow with a coy smirk.

Uncle Nicholas arrived shortly after one and brought this amazing red velvet two-tiered cake with butter cream frosting. He hugged me and handed me a bag of fresh fruit and vegetables from his home garden. I smiled and eagerly unpacked all the delicious items and arranged them on platters.

"How is retirement treating you?" I playfully nudged him at the island whilst arranging the fruit platter.

"I am loving it." He grinned. "How do you feel about classes starting back up next week?"

"Um," I stepped back and leaned against the counter. "I wanted to talk with you about that."

"Okay," his eyes narrowed a bit. "What is on your mind?"

I glanced out the kitchen window over sink at the three semi-intoxicated men laughing on the deck. None of them were paying attention to what was going on in the house.

"I am not sure what I want to do." I whispered.

"What do you mean?"

I went on to explain what had happened over the last month with Remus Farwell, his stroke and the painful rehab I was helping Mariam and Bonnie with. I explained how frustrated I was with the differences in the medical field and medicine between the two times. It was mentally exhausting knowing more as a med student than my husband who was a practicing physician due to the limited knowledge in the nineteenth century.

Unfortunately, I had pent things up for a long time and I rambled on unnecessarily. I droned on about how worthless it made me feel. I told him about how frustrated I was knowing that if I had had access to modern medication, Mr. Farwell's condition would not have been so severe and debilitating.

"But do you not see what a difference you have made not only for Mr. Farwell, but for his entire family?" he asked. "Physical rehabilitation is nonexistent in the nineteenth century and yet, you introduced it to Mr. Farwell and have steadily improved the quality of life for him and his family."

"I suppose," I signed heavily. "He is walking again. Granted, it is not the steady gait of a strong man, but he is mobile. And he is speaking again and has regained limited use of his left arm." I did feel immensely proud of that.

"Imagine where he and his family would be without your intervention." Uncle Nicholas smiled. "You did that. You took what you learned *here* and used it to create a better outcome *there*. I am proud of you."

"Thank you," I hugged him. "That means a lot."

"I know it may be difficult. You are a strong, passionate, and intelligent lady. I strongly encourage you to continue your studies. You may not be able to fix everything, but you can make a difference in the lives of many people."

"Okay," I felt a weight lift from my shoulders.

"Hey darling, when do you want us to throw on the ribs? They're going to take a while to cook." Landon leaned in through the back door and hollered.

"Put them on in about fifteen minutes. I will bring them out." I waved back and turned to get the marinating ribs out of the refrigerator. I set them on the island and turned towards my uncle. "Would you mind helping them with the ribs? I do not believe any of them know how to grill." I smirked. "I am surprised they got the grill going without blowing up the house."

"You have a lawyer, a doctor, and a," he wrinkled his forehead. "What does Carson do?"

"Anything he wants from what I can tell." I laughed.

"Well, I am sure they can manage, but just to put your mind at ease, I will go supervise." My uncle chuckled and carried the platter of ribs out to the back deck.

I finished arranging the fruit, vegetables, and cookie platters. I carried them into the dining room and set them down amongst the potato salad, baked beans, deviled eggs, chips and dip, and other goodies we all pitched in to create an elaborate spread. Phoebe and Jocelyn came in with wide smiles and were wearing beautiful sundresses. It was hard to believe several years ago I could rarely get my sister to wear a dress. Spending time around Phoebe and me had really rubbed off on her.

Phoebe opened a bottle of white wine and poured each of us a glass and herself some ginger ale. Then we joined the guys on the deck. It felt like it had been a lifetime since we had all relaxed, laughed, and talked about something other than our failing country, economy, and the heated presidential election campaigns. It was like we had an unwritten agreement today to leave certain topics at the door.

We lost track of time and instead of us surprising them, the other half of our family showed up surprising us. They appeared at the French doors after our third glass of wine and multiple beers for the men. The look on their faces was nothing compared to the look on ours when they showed up.

"Happy Anniversary," the seven off us sounded off in an off half-drunken unison.

"Thanks," Robert laughed. "What is going on here?"

"Oh, just a little celebration behind the governor's back." Jocelyn giggled and refilled her glass.

"We were just talking about that at brunch." Emily sat down in one of the patio chairs.

"How attached are you all to Boston?" Robert stood behind his wife and leaned against the chair.

"What?" Phoebe, Jocelyn and I spoke out in unison. Those were the last words I ever expected to hear from his lips.

"You love this place." Phoebe looked shocked.

"We still do." Emily took her husband's hand.

"However," Robert steadied himself. "With the direction this state is going, we have a lot of concerns about Wally, Audry, Lucy, and Charlie. This woke ideological bullshit has infiltrated every aspect of our lives here, especially in the school systems. This transgender, gender identity, LGBTQAXYZ+ nonsense — the boy's on girls' sports teams, in their bathrooms, locker rooms. This insanity about gay pornography books in school libraries, drag shows for children." He glanced at his three eldest grandchildren playing on the small playground in the corner of the backyard. "Alex and Leslie agree that perhaps it is time to consider moving to a safer state."

"One that reflects our personal and family values." Emily added.

"Which state?" I asked still stunned by his words.

"Well," Emily poured herself some wine and took a small sip. "Robert and I have been casually looking at different states and researching their laws."

"And?" Jocelyn urged.

"We considered North Carolina, Florida, Alabama, Mississippi, Tennessee, Arkansas, or perhaps Texas."

"So, basically every Southern state." Landon smirked at me and then went into the house to get another beer.

"Well, not New Mexico or Arizona." Robert sighed heavily.

"Those are considered Southwestern states, not Southern states." Everyone's head turned towards Carson in stunned shock.

"New Mexico is controlled by the Democratic party and Arizona is heading in that direction due to some corrupt politicians." Robert pressed on trying to ignore the awkward stunned moment.

"What we found there was quite disappointing." Emily admitted. "It seems Arizona is getting flooded by people fleeing California and its impact on the state is devastating."

"What do you think?" Robert looked over at my Uncle Nicholas for help.

"Well, given the way things are in Massachusetts and every state surrounding us, perhaps it is something we should consider." He shrugged.

"You would consider leaving New England?" Jocelyn looked surprised.

"Hey, I am a Midwesterner just like you. Not a New Englander." My uncle defended himself. "Besides, I expect to be a great uncle in a few years and for them," he gestured towards the kids. "They deserve to be raised in a sane environment. And that is no longer possible here."

"And what do you propose we do about school? Our residencies?" Landon returned and flopped back down into his chair. "Not to mention our jobs. Our careers. The life we spent building here." He looked exasperated. "I agree that the children are not safe here any longer. The schools around here suck. Hell, our university is so freaking woke I'm hated for being a white man," he gulped his beer down. "Excuse me, a cis white male." Landon scoffed.

"Landon," I reached over and touched his arm. "You need to slow down."

"I am finally relaxing and just being realistic." He shrugged me off. "But it would be impossible for us to change universities right now." He took another large gulp of his beer and looked directly at me. "Are you telling me that you believe this freaking bullshit the hospital is pushing on all of us."

"No," I admitted. "I have taken microbiology and genetics, same as you and every physician in the place. I do not trust anything that is being pushed through digital media and propaganda news outlets."

I was jealous of the rest of my family. Since they all worked together at the law firm, they were surviving better than most. Landon and I were on the verge of exhaustion, and we knew it was only a matter of time before our bodies fought back against the lack of sleep and constant stress. Neither of us were independently wealthy nor the loss of either of our incomes would be devastating.

"Then perhaps this is something we should consider."

"Okay." I muttered looking down hoping he wouldn't see the look in my eyes. "I'm going to grab another bottle of wine." I finished off the bottle and carried the empty one into the house to dispose of it.

"Hey," Jocelyn followed me into the kitchen. "What is up with you? You got awful quiet after Landon's little rant."

"Oh, tis nothing." I opened the little wine refrigerator built into the island and pulled out another bottle.

"You really are a terrible liar, you know that." My sister leaned against the counter across from me. "You never make eye contact when you lie."

"Thanks," I used the corkscrew and opened the new bottle. "More?" She nodded and I poured a decent amount into each of our glasses.

"What is up with you?"

"What do you mean?" I feigned ignorance.

"You know damn well what I mean." She smirked and took a sip. "You are hiding something, and you have been for a long time." I raised my eyebrows. "Spill it already."

"Okay, fine." I took a deep breath and glanced over at the French doors to make sure we were alone. "But this stays between use. No one knows," I shook my head. "Well, dad and Landon know, but no one else."

"Okay," she wrinkled her forehead in confusion.

"When I went back to school after our Spring Break in New Orleans, my life changed in more ways than one." Jocelyn nodded along in agreement. "Well, I did some digging when I returned to school after Uncle Nicholas talked about how most people with our gift avoid the medical field. After a bit of research, I discovered many of the classes I was taking in premed overlapped a lot with the nursing courses."

"Okay, and?" she took another sip of her wine. "That is kind of a given, isn't it?"

"Well, as things became more clearer across the planes, I was not sure how I was going to feel with the whole lack of modern medicine, tools, procedures, and such, so I talked with my advisor and decided to do a dual major." I shrugged casually.

"Dual major?" She looked a bit surprised but not really fazed. "So, did you get a second bachelor's degree that I do not know about?" Jocelyn smirked.

"Yes," I smirked back. "I took a few extra classes over the summer, did my clinicals at the hospital, and am a licensed registered nurse in both Illinois and Massachusetts."

"Seriously?" My little sister smiled a shit eating grin before throwing her arms around me and hugging me tightly. "I do not understand why you would hide this. You should be proud. That is amazing. I am so proud of you."

"Thanks," I felt a huge relief. "That means a lot."

"But I don't understand why all the secrecy around it." She let me go and stepped back.

"You know how our mother is. I mean, she went ballistic when you chose law school over med school. Can you image the fallout if I told her I did not want to follow in her footsteps either?"

"Please let me be included on that conference call." Jocelyn started laughing. "That might just kill the old bat."

"Phoebe told me she has been very helpful with Alex's custody case. Apparently, she has agreed to fly out to testify on behalf of the father." I informed her.

"At least she is good for something." She smirked.

"Are you ever going to make peace with her?"

"I am not at war with her." She playfully scoffed. "I just do not like her as a person."

"When did like become a thing? I love her because I am obligated to, but I cannot say I like her either." I admitted.

"You know, I used to think you were so much like her." Jocelyn laughed.

"Nope," I shrugged. "Despite her best efforts I think you and dad rubbed off on me more than she likes."

"It took long enough." She teased. "You certainly gave a good impression of being mom's doppelganger through high school."

I ignored her jab because I knew she was right. We both knew that the only thing that turned me around was learning about *E.V.E.* My world did a complete 180° and changed me in many ways, especially when the barrier completely dissipated, and I had a clear memory of my *other* world.

"Can you keep a secret for now?" She nodded. "I don't want to finish medical school. I think I would rather become a physician's assistant. What do you think?"

"What does that mean for this semester?"

"I don't know." I took another sip of my wine. "But I need to talk to Landon about it and the hospital."

"Are you wanting to switch from administration to nursing?" she smirked.

"No way," I scoffed. "Not right now, especially. I do not have a death wish. I have seen firsthand the impact this craziness has had on the nurses and doctors at the hospital. I have no desire to participate in that."

"Understandable," she giggled. "What do you think about moving?"

"I cannot deny what Robert says is spot on. I know Chicago is even worse than Boston. The riots and crime there are completely unchecked and without consequences." I finished off the wine in my glass and added some more to both our glasses. "Perhaps it would not be such a bad thing." I shrugged. "I would hate to raise a baby in this place. Wouldn't you?"

"While I do not plan on having children any time soon. No. I would not want to raise my children in this mess. More importantly,

I do not want Wally, Lucy, Charlie, and Audry growing up in this mess."

"Me neither, but do you really want to move South?"

"I could live without the snow." Jocelyn admitted.

"Have you spoken with Dad or Ethan recently?" I had been so busy I hadn't checked in with them lately.

"I spoke to Dad a few nights ago and Liang last night." She finished off her glass and added a little more. "Dad said he is considering retirement and weighing his options about the house."

"Retirement?" I gasped. "He is much too young for that."

"I said as much to him, but apparently, he said he made some wise investments years ago and can retire comfortably." Jocelyn shrugged. "Who knew?"

"I didn't," I pursed my lips together in thought. "Do you find it strange that he brings this up after his younger brother recently retired?"

"Are you saying Dad is envious of Uncle Nicholas?" I chuckled.

"I would be if I were him." My sister acknowledged. "How happy would you be if I retired before you?" A smirk danced upon her lips.

"I think you and I can agree that we will be old and grey before we ever consider retirement." I raised my eyebrows.

"I'm sure I'll be working until noon on the day of my funeral," she conceded.

The French doors opened, and Landon and Jackson loudly entered the kitchen. I was not sure how many beers they had consumed, but from the way they were acting they were more than half lit.

"Did you guys get lost?" Jackson teased setting the platter of ribs on the table.

"Yes," I rolled my eyes at my brother-in-law who put his arm around my little sister and kissed the top of her head.

"The ribs are done." Landon stated the obvious. "I am starving." He grabbed a plate and started piling food on it.

"Save some for the rest of us." Jackson picked up a plate and followed Landon's lead. Jocelyn laughed as she and I stood back watching our men in awe.

The family staggered in. It was not long before everyone was seated around the large table on the deck enjoying the warm sun of a late summer afternoon. Everyone was talking at once, laughing, and discussing the constant barrage of political nonsense from both sides of the aisle.

It never ceased to amaze me how tight knit the Chandler's were. I knew the gift of *E.V.E.* strengthened their bond, but still, having grown up in a family dynamic that was more than less traditional, it still felt surreal to be adopted as one of them. I could never imagine my father and Amy sharing Sunday dinners with me, Ethan, and Jocelyn with our significant others. Jocelyn and I barely spoke to Amy, and we talked to Ethan's girlfriend, Liang more often than we spoke to our younger brother. Thankfully, our dad remained consistent with his weekly calls to Jocelyn and me.

"Did you see that they are going to force us to wear masks all day at school?" I heard Lucy complain. "I would rather be homeschooled."

"Me too," her younger brother, Charlie added.

Lucy was set to start the third-grade next week, and Charlie was entering first-grade. Neither seemed to be hyped about school considering they had spent the last semester doing classes online. It had been ineffective, stressful, and psychologically stunting for children across the country. Students were now essentially a year behind.

"Sweetie, you cannot step outside now without a worthless mask." Alex said sarcastically.

"Do we have to go? I can't breathe in those things." Charlie complained.

"Do you want to do the online schooling again?" Leslie asked with raised eyebrows at her children.

"No," they responded in unison.

"I wish there was another option, but I don't believe there is. You two hated doing online classes." Leslie pointed out.

"We learned more from you than those computer classes." Lucy pouted.

"I appreciate that sweetheart, but I am not a teacher." Leslie explained, looking uncomfortable. The spring semester of lockdown had been extremely difficult for her as well as the kids.

"I do not understand how states can make it mandatory when President Trump refuses to make it a mandate." Landon spoke up.

"I thought federal law trumped state law." I questioned.

"It is supposed to." Alex chimed in. "But the Democrats disdain for President Trump threw the playbook out the window."

"Don't you mean the Constitution?" Robert scoffed.

"Pretty much," Jackson joined in. "Okay explain this to me." He smirked. "If the federal government still lists marijuana as a Schedule 1 narcotic, how is it now legal in varying degrees in over half the states?"

"The federal government is still trying to figure that out." Robert remarked.

"Okay, then let me get your take on this." Jackson was waving his fork around for emphasis. "I had a zoom meeting Thursday with a girl in her 20s who went on vacation in California for two weeks where marijuana and edibles are 'legal'", he made air quotes. "She did partake while on vacation, but a girl who has an axe to grind with her that works in human resources decided her name was up for random selection for a drug test when she returned to work."

"She failed," Phoebe rolled his eyes.

"Obviously," Jackson playfully shoved his older sister. "Now she wants to sue them for illegally terminating her because she only participated," he grinned at the kids sitting close by. "In California where it is legal and therefore, cannot be terminated for it since she was not only off the clock but across the country. She even provided lab results that showed she only had trace amounts in her system which line up with her recounting of events."

"Can she sue them?" Jocelyn inquired. "I mean, it doesn't matter that she participated in a state where it is legal, if her employer has a zero-drug tolerance policy, then they have every right to terminate her if she failed a drug test."

"I do not know. I spent all day Friday with two associates and four paralegals pouring through every law book and case file we could think of but came up with nothing." Jackson explained. "There is no precedence for this."

"What is your approach? Or are you going to turn down the case?" Alex leaned forward intrigued.

"We have a partners zoom meeting," Jackson rolled his eyes. "On Tuesday. I swear it feels like the Muppet Show opening credits every time we do these stupid things."

"I think we all feel that way." Phoebe scoffed. "It appears these lockdowns and forced mandates are going to continue for a while. Every time I turn on the news it gets worse."

"I swear if I hear the name Dr. Fauci one more time I am going to scream." Jocelyn said with a venomous tone. "That man is a corrupt moron."

"I agree, but honestly I am more shocked and confused by Biden's vice-presidential pick." Landon paused long enough to take a long pull on his beer.

"Wait a minute. What did I miss?" I rarely paid attention to the news these days and only glanced occasionally at social media to post stupid memes about the insane antics of Black Lives Matter, Antifa, and other crazy liberals.

"Biden announced his VP pick as Senator Kamala Harris." Emily rolled her eyes and scoffed — an action she only did when something or someone truly disgusted her.

"I've never heard of her," Jocelyn appeared confused.

"Harris is a radical leftist who was loathed as a District Attorney in San Francisco. She was raised by a Marxist professor and is known for sleeping her way to the top, not showing up for work, aggressively prosecuting black men for marijuana, and being a homewrecker." Robert explained.

"She sounds lovely," I noted with wide eyes. It was unusual for Robert to speak of someone with such disdain.

"Kamala is an idiot. She could not even pass the California bar on her first try. She is loathed in the state of California. She is nothing more than the Whore of Babylon." Robert said through gritted teeth.

"Okay," Emily smiled. "On that happy note. Who would like some dessert?"

"I would," Phoebe rose from the table.

"I will help." Jocelyn jumped up beside her and followed Emily into the house.

The silence that fell over the deck was deafening. It was rare for Robert to get so railed up. His reaction caught me completely off guard. He was always such a gentle and loving soul.

"Regardless of who Biden selected, I can guarantee you the Democrats will do anything to regain control of the White House." Uncle Nicholas said as a matter of fact.

"Meaning?" Landon inquired.

"The majority of Americans are against the fascist Marxist ideology pushed by Obama." Robert scoffed.

"Don't you mean Biden?" I questioned.

"No. I mean Obama. Biden is merely his puppet. Make no mistake about that." Robert's voice had an edge that concerned me.

"What do you believe they will do?" Jackson joined in.

"They'll rig the election." I blurted out without thinking and everyone turned to look at me.

"Most likely," Uncle Nicholas agreed.

"Or they will attempt to assassinate President Trump." Robert shrugged. "They have already impeached him and failed. What is going to be next?"

"Jail." Uncle Nicholas stated. "They will find the most corrupt prosecutors with no morals, values, or integrity to bring some ridiculous bogus charges against him and his administration. I guarantee it. They will weaponize every federal agency to go after him."

His words hung in the air with a thick tension that could be felt and seen by all those at the table. None of us knew how to respond. There was a profound eeriness in both his tone and words that put a knot in the pit of my stomach.

"I hope everyone is hungry." Phoebe returned to the deck carrying the oversized cake with Jocelyn and Emily behind her with dessert plates and silverware.

"Happy anniversary," a chorus rang out from everyone as Phoebe set the cake in the center of the table.

"Excuse me," Alex rose from his seat and tapped the side of his beer. "I would like to say a few words as the eldest child of this wonderful couple." He made a goofy face making the three children giggle. "I am one of the few millennials that grew up in a two-parent household unaffected by divorce. I was fortunate to have two loving parents who set a great example of what marriage entails. They showed their children what it was like to put your trust in another person, love unconditionally, and build a life of honor and unselfishness." He raised his beer just a bit. "So, happy anniversary to my parents. We love you and thank you for not being another statistic." Their son offered them a shit-eating grin before sticking his tongue out at his siblings before taking a long swig of his beer.

"Very nice," Phoebe mocked her brother. "Happy anniversary, mom and dad." She raised her ginger ale and rolled her eyes at her brother.

"Boy, you guys are full of class." My little sister rose to her feet. "If it is all right with everyone, I would like to say something as well."

"Of course," Emily smiled.

"First, I would like to wish my in-laws a very happy anniversary. Secondly, I would like to thank you both for welcoming me into your family. You both know Sidney and I did not exactly come from a functional family," she raised her eyebrows in my direction making me laugh. "But you both have shown me the strength of love and family and for that, I am forever grateful. I pray that Jackson and I will always emulate the kind of relationship you two share. I love you both. Happy anniversary."

Landon and I took an uber home later that evening. It had been a beautiful day but also offered us plenty of things to consider about our future. I had come to love Boston, the university, the architecture, and the hospital despite its politics. However, I had great concerns for my niece and nephews and the education and influences they were destined to encounter due to the extreme ideologies being forced on them by delusional liberal democrats.

"Would you really consider leaving Boston?" Landon stared out the side window and not looking in my direction.

"I don't know," I turned and looked out the window as the passing buildings. "I can understand why Alex and Phoebe want to, even Robert and Emily, but I just don't know."

"You realize if they go, your sister and Jackson will follow. And most likely, your uncle Nicholas too." Landon reached over and placed his hand over mine. "It may be worth considering."

"But school?"

"We're almost finished. We can apply to residencies wherever we land."

"But," I interjected.

"But what?" Landon smiled at me. "I know how much family means to you. Besides, interest rates are really low right now. With our credit, we could possibly buy a house."

"Don't you believe we should wait until after," my voice trailed off with words unsaid.

"I think we should look into it." What he was referring to, I wasn't sure, and I was afraid to ask.

26

SUNDAY, AUGUST 12, 1860

THE LATE AFTERNOON SUN SHONE one through the trees casting long shadows across the lawn. My little man was supposed to playing with his aunts on a blanket in the plush green grass. However, he had recently learned how to scoot on his stomach. He had not mastered crawling yet but keeping him in one spot was proving challenging. I sat on the porch in a rocking chair watching them with Keifer's mother and loved how wonderful it felt to be here.

We had a short time left before we departed for Chicago and a part of me truly did not want to leave. I thought about the amazing people I had come to know here, the neighbors I had befriended, and the city I had grown to love. It weighed heavily on my soul. I knew by the end of the war most of what I was looking out upon would be ashes. It broke my heart to know that essentially my neighbors would be responsible for it.

I wanted to scream. I wanted to holler. I wanted to tell Keifer's family and friends everything that was coming just over the horizon. I wanted to gather up everyone I loved and bring them all to Terrace Falls for the duration of the war to keep them safe. I was terrified. I felt helpless.

"Trixie, please be careful." I bit my lower lip watching my 10-year-old sister-in-law pick up my chunky son.

"I have him," Keifer's thirteen-year-old sister, Edith took him from her little sister.

"Edith is going to be a wonderful mother someday." Angelina gazed peacefully at her daughters, carefully watching them scurry about laughing and playing with their nephew.

"Yes, she will." Hoping she would have the chance to experience love, marriage, and family.

"I wish you and Keifer would reconsider." My mother-in-law's face appeared peaceful and contented. "I realize I am selfish, but the thought of my grandson growing up so far away from me." She cut her sentence off, but I understood what she meant.

"Perhaps you can all come up to Terrace Falls in the Spring. March is beautiful." I exaggerated hoping to get them there safely before the fighting began at Fort Sumter.

"March is cold in Boston, is it not?" My mother-in-law appeared hesitant.

"You will love the Northern Springs." I sidestepped her question hoping I sounded convincing. "The cool air, the crisp morning sun rising over the river. It is breathtaking."

"We shall see." She smiled softly, but I knew they would never make it. "How is Mr. Farwell recovering?"

"He is improving daily." I assured her. "His progress is slower than he would like, but that is to be expected."

"Will he ever be like his old self?" Angelina raised her eyebrow.

"No." I shook my head slowly. "Unfortunately, that is not possible. His mobility, strength, and vocal skills will improve, but a full recovery is not possible."

"Have you told Miriam?"

"I did not have the heart." I gazed out at my son. "I explained it to Bonnie."

"You and she have grown close this summer."

"Yes. I hate to leave all of you." I turned my head trying to keep the tears from spilling over.

"I do hope it will not be for long. I really do want us to come to Terrace Falls in the Spring. I would love to be there for my grandson's first birthday." Angelina sighed heavily with a peaceful expression on her beautiful face as she gazed out at her daughters and my son.

"Lil' Keifer has grown a great deal since we arrived. My grandmother will hardly recognize him." I said casually.

David, Thad and Keifer approached from the South side of the house. Their skin was kissed by the sun and Keifer's hair was shades lighter than it ever was back home. The truth was he flourished down here. That little dimple high on his right cheek that was long absent from our daily life in Terrace Falls, was now constantly present since our arrival at Gable Gardens.

A smile crept across my lips as I gazed lovingly at my husband. But a wave of guilt washed over me. I realized how selfish I had been keeping him up North and away from the land that was clearly a part of his soul. The transformation in him since our arrival was evident. Keifer's face seemed to always adorn a smile. He laughed easily. His shoulders relaxed and the swagger in his step that I loved about him when we first met but long gone, had made a reappearance.

"How are you ladies doing this afternoon?" David stopped at the foot of the porch steps with one foot on the bottom step as he leaned heavily on the stair rail. A bead of sweat glistened on his brow, but his smile was warm and hearty.

"Very well, thank you dear. Would you like some iced tea?" Angelina gestured towards the pitcher on the small side table.

"Yes ma'am, I am parched." David removed his wide-brimmed hat and wiped his brow with a handkerchief before climbing the remaining steps.

"It is hotter than a June bug out here." Keifer complained, fanning himself with his own hat following his father up the porch steps. "May I have a glass too?" He sat down on the railing across from his mother and me.

"Of course, darling." Angelina poured a glass for her son and handed it to him. Keifer gulped it down quickly. "Slow down, son. There is more. No need to upset your stomach by drinking so quickly." She laughed taking his glass and refilling it. "You never change." She shook her head slightly with a distant look in her eyes as if she was remembering the boy she once knew in the man before her.

Thad greeted us with a smile and a nod of his hat before he disappeared into the house. I assumed he was looking for his wife or seeking out some food. The man ate nonstop. Granted, he was a hard worker, but I had never witnessed someone consume the amount of food he ate and still not have an ounce of fat on him.

Sadie crossed paths with Thad hurrying down the steps and lifting my son from Edith's arm. Both girls followed on her heels back into the house. It was darling how infatuated the girls were with their little nephew. Sadie paused on the porch before crossing the threshold into the house.

"Misses', Ah's gunna fead lil mister tis suppa." Sadie curtseyed slightly while balancing my son on his hip.

"Thank you, Sadie." Angelina nodded before turning her attention back to us. "Son, your wife has invited us to visit Terrace Falls this Spring, around March." She raised an eyebrow.

"I thought it would be wonderful for them to be there for our son's first birthday." I said quickly before my husband could respond. Keifer glanced at me with a confused expression and all I could do was pray he would keep his mouth shut.

"Yes, it would." Thankfully Keifer did not remark on the cold March weather in Boston and frighten her off.

"Boston in March sounds cold." David wiped his brow again. "But right now I could go for some cold weather." He laughed.

"I have never been a fan of cold weather." Angelina remarked furrowing her brow at her husband. "Still, I do not want to miss my grandson's first birthday. Plus, the children would enjoy the journey." She turned her attention towards me. "Are you sure you want all of us? That could quickly become overwhelming for you."

"Yes," I glanced at my husband and added. "I believe it would be very beneficial for you both and the four youngest children to come to Terrace Falls for a nice long visit." I purposely excluded my husband's sisters Eugenia and Victoria. Even with the Civil War looming down upon us, I could not and would not open my home to those vile creatures.

"Thad and Margaret are more than capable of running things here. Plus, Eugenia and Victoria could help." David did not miss my subtle exclusion of his daughters nor the lack of love between us.

The three of them began discussing the details of the trip and my mind began wondering what I had just stepped into. In my determination to save my husband's family, I had completely forgotten about convincing my brother's family along with the remaining Chandler's to stay with me and my grandmother at Terrace Falls. Our home was sufficiently large, but not quite equipped to host close to twenty additional people plus the servants they would inevitability bring with them. We would need to add on to the existing house or build separate guest cottages.

Time was short. I had eight months before all hell was to break loose across the country. That was going to be barely enough time if I contacted Ned and got him working on things immediately. In addition, the cost of materials was going to increase rapidly in the near future so supplies such as lumber, nails, and furniture were going to need to be purchased immediately.

"Please excuse me for a moment," I rose from my seat. "I shall be right back." Keifer gave me a quizzical look as I hurried past him into the house and rushed up to our room.

I took a seat at the desk, pulled out a sheet of parchment, ink and a quill. I inhaled deeply and tried my best to think of how to word this letter properly.

Dear Grandmother,

I pray this letter finds you in good health. I am missing you terribly and wish you were here. We are doing well, and your great grandson is growing daily. He began scooting last week and appears determined to figure out how to crawl. There is nothing he does not wish to explore. Also, the transformation in Keifer is nothing short of astounding. He is carefree, relaxed, and laughing. The constant smile on his face is contagious.

I am pleased to inform you that Keifer's parents and four youngest siblings will be joining us in March to celebrate our son's first birthday. As you may recall, whilst in Chicago I am hoping to persuade Annabelle and Emily Chandler, along with their children, to stay with us as well given the upcoming events on the horizon. I believe several in their charge would accompany them as well.

My concern is how to host them all. We could build an addition onto the existing house, or we could build guest cottages near the main house. I believe the plot on the west bank near the maple trees would be lovely. It would provide a barrier for privacy but is adjacent to the house for protection. I am anxious to hear your thoughts.

I was pleased to hear in your pervious letter that the new storage shelter has been completed and is being put to good use. I believe now would be idyllic to purchase the necessary supplies for the addition. I fear prices will increase soon. If you or Ned have any questions, I am sure Mr. Bennett would be happy to assist in any of the details. Please ask him to oversee the project whilst we are in Chicago through the holidays. I shall also write to him as well.

I look forward to hearing from you. My love to you and all.

Sincerely,

Sidney

I reread the letter a final time and folded it properly to address it home. I scurried down the stairs and found Tallie dusting the parlor. She was humming softly to herself and appeared oblivious to my presence. I watched her for a moment thinking about how graceful she was in her movements and light on her toes. Had it not been for the soft melody she hummed; I would never have known she was in the room.

"Oh, misses," Tallie jumped when she noticed me. "Ahs sorry. Ahs wuz jus kleenin'." She stammered.

"I apologize, Tallie. I did not mean to startle you." I tried to explain. "Do you know if anyone is heading into town today? I have an urgent letter that must go out today."

"Musder Tad sed e tis goin' da git sum dangs et da murgents afta suppa." She said with a wide smile.

"Wonderful." I returned her smile. "Thank you."

"Wood ya lik a to give it to em?" Tallie held out her hand as she approached me.

"That would be most helpful, Tallie. Thank you." I handed her the letter as she hurried out of the room.

I returned to the porch to find it vacated except for my husband. Keifer was still half-sitting on the railing with one foot on the porch. He was staring out over the vast grounds with a look of contentment on his face. His wide-brimmed hat covered most of his profile, but from what I could see; he appeared completely at peace.

"Penny for your thoughts." My voice barely above a whisper.

"I do not believe my thoughts are worth that much." He chuckled, turning his head in my direction. "I would owe you change."

"I do not believe you." I walked up to him wrapping my arms around his waist.

"Where did you disappear too in such a hurry?" His eyes softened.

"I had to write a letter to my grandmother. I wanted to let her know we are doing well since it has been a couple weeks since I wrote to her. Thad is heading into town shortly and I wanted him to be able to drop it by the post." I explained without going into detail.

"I know you miss her." I leaned my head against his chest.

"Yes, I do. I cannot wait to see her." I admitted.

"I would not be surprised if she marries Mr. Bennett in our absence. We may return to a new grandfather." Keifer laughed heartily.

"Do you honestly believe she would do that?" I smirked.

"Mr. Bennett wishes she would." His laughter was infectious.

"Honestly, me too." My eyes met his. "I want her to be happy again and I believe Mr. Bennett would make her very happy."

"Have you told her that?"

"Yes, many times." I rolled my eyes. "She has a million excuses, mainly centered around her age." I scoffed.

"Mr. Bennett is older than your grandmother, is he not?"

"I believe so. Although I have not confirmed that." He nodded silently.

"I am surprised you invited my family to Terrace Falls this Spring; and in March no less." Keifer raised an eyebrow.

"Your son was born in March." I defended.

"I understand, but my parents have never been exposed to cold weather, especially not the extreme cold of Boston winters." He explained.

"Yes, but March is Spring." I reasoned.

"March is winter according to the calendar." He defended.

"Please, be optimistic about this. I would love for your family to be there for our son's first birthday."

"My family except for Maggie's family, Victoria, and Eugenia." Keifer snorted.

"Maggie and her family are always welcome at our home." I batted my eyelashes playfully at my husband.

"You, my dear, have a devilish streak in you." He leaned his head back laughing loudly.

"That is not fair," I playfully argued. "You know how close I have gotten to your family this summer."

"I do." My husband admitted. "Please do not misunderstand me. I am thrilled that after years of marriage you and my family have finally built a relationship. Still, it only makes leaving more difficult."

"Yes, it does." I answered solemnly.

The evening passed with a lively dinner, animated discussions, engraining more happy memories into my brain. Angelina was going on about how excited she was to visit Boston in the Spring and said she wanted to travel over to New York City to do some shopping. She gushed on and on about how envious the ladies in her sewing circle were going to be. I smiled enjoying her romantic notions of New York City and its grand ambiance whilst trying not to think about how disappointed she was going to be with the reality of it.

It appeared everyone was in a lively mood, even Eugenia managed to smile when she learned only the younger children would be traveling North with their parents and she was not expected to attend. It was exactly as she and I preferred it. I knew Angelina and my grandmother would become fast friends, but I nor she, could endure another season or perhaps longer with Eugenia under our roof. War or no war, I believed I would rather spend my time on the front lines than dealing with Eugenia and Victoria any more than I absolutely must.

As the evening wound down, we made ourselves comfortable in the parlor enjoying tea and peach pie. Caroline graced us with her exceptional talent for the piano. A soft breeze drifted through the open windows barely stirring the curtains. The humidity clung to my skin like a thin film of dust making me long for a hot bubble bath. Unfortunately, I knew the feeling would return immediately upon drying off and climbing back into these stifling layers.

My son dozed peacefully on my lap with his little head snuggling into my chest. I stroked his chubby cheek lightly and a small smile appeared across his lips. He was such a sweet dear child who filled my heart with an overwhelming love I never imagined before. I leaned against Keifer's shoulder wanting to hold onto this moment forever. As I gazed upon the happy and contented faces of my husband's family, the thoughts lingering in the back of my mind still haunted me.

The sound of scattered gravel, pounding hooves, and the neighing of multiple horses approaching flowed through the front windows. Every head turned at the interruption. David, Thad, and Keifer rose to their feet.

"Wait here," my husband squeezed my hand following his father and brother-in-law to the foyer.

The crash of heavy boots on the porch steps reached us as we heard the front door creak open. Lucas ran over to the large window and peeped through the curtain.

"There is a group of men on horses," he whispered to his mother. "They have rifles and torches."

"Lucas, come away from there. Do not be nosey." Angelina chastised her young son. "That is your father's business."

"But mother, Keifer and Thad are out there with father. Why can't I?" he questioned.

"When you are a bit older." She reassured him lovingly.

"Good evening, Mr. Stewart." David's deep voice echoed from the foyer and through the open windows from where he stood on the porch flanked by his son and son-in-law. "What brings you here at this hour?"

"Evening, Mr. Marshall. Doc. Thad. My apologies for interrupting your evening, but we need your help." His deep winded voice flooded the room. The parlor fell silent as our ears strained to hear the voices outside. "There's a slave uprising at the Cameron plantation." He explained in a rush. "Grab your rifles and guns."

"Right." My eyes met with the concerned ones of Angelina. I could tell she was struggling to remain silent. "Otis, you and Leroy saddle some horses for us." David commanded before we heard the pounding of feet towards the stables.

I rose to my feet and handed my son as gently as I could to Caroline. Angelina nodded at me, and I followed her to the foyer. Maggie and her daughters followed behind us. Keifer and Thad were walking out of David's study carrying three rifles with gun powder horns slung over their shoulders and pistols on their sides. I bit my bottom lip to restrain myself from speaking.

"Do not wait up, dear." Keifer paused in front of me adjusting the pistol in his belt on his hip. "I may be late."

"Please be careful," I cautioned him. "I love you." I attempted to smile but it was difficult.

"I will," he leaned over and kissed me quickly. "I love you, too." He hurried out to the courtyard after his father.

We followed the men outside but stopped on the porch. I reached for Angelina's hand as I watched Keifer skillfully climb into the saddle and adjust his rifle. She squeezed my hand in reassurance, but it could not squelch the knot forming in my stomach. We stood in silence watching our men ride off into the dark night with the large group of other men from across the county.

"Is this common?" I said with my eyes lingering on the now empty driveway.

"Unfortunately, it has become more so recently." Angelina sighed heavily. "Ever since John Brown's raid on Harper's Ferry, many slaves have become emboldened and insolent."

"Many negros have become arrogant. Some have managed to learn to read in secret and begun preaching about God's freedom being their right, twisting bible passages to their narrative." Maggie's voice was low and almost eerie on the warm porch.

"Talks of secession and the possibility of war continue to spread adding fuel to the discord amongst the slaves." Angelina finished Maggie's train of thought. "We have heard multiple reports of negro insurrections where plantation owners and their families were murdered."

I nodded towards my mother-in-law but did not verbally respond. I knew this misinformation was widespread throughout the South and greatly exaggerated but not entirely unfounded. There were a few documented cases where the family was killed, and the plantations burned. But I knew after John Brown's Raid, the fear of a negro uprising in the South was very real and terrified women and children.

"Shall I call for some more tea?" Angelina patted my hand as we walked back into the house.

"That would be lovely. I fear it is going to be a long night." I smiled weakly over at her as we walked into the parlor.

I paced across the floor in front of our bed. The small brass clock on the mantel in the bedroom told me it was half past one in the morning. I walked over to the window and pulled the sheer curtain aside. The red glow miles away in the distance from the Cameron plantation was barely visible now. Several hours earlier it was quite distinguishable against the black sky. Billowing smoke had risen above the tree line filling me with a sense of dread in the pit of my stomach.

I rested my forehead against the window wishing the glass was a tad cooler. The night air was still thick with humidity and the breeze we had earlier vanished. I knew this situation was common. I had read about multiple accounts of such happenings, but somehow that did not make me feel any better.

Race relations were a heated topic, even in the twenty-first century. From my understanding, race relations were decent, if not good throughout the latter half of the twentieth century, but once Obama was elected to the White House, racial division had intensified. The Black Lives Matter cult had been increasing racial division and sowing the seeds of hatred over the last several years.

It was disheartening to think about how little things had progressed in a century and half despite the civil rights movement in the 1960s, Martin Luther King, Jr.'s struggles and inspirational words, and all the lives lost before them in the name of equality. I knew I was witnessing the cusp of a nightmare that was only going to get worse in the upcoming months and last for years. I said a silent prayer for all those involved and cursed my inability to know what was going on.

Most of the time I truly enjoyed the lack of technology in this era. It was peaceful and provided a solace that I have never experienced in my *other* life. But at times like this when every fear I ever felt from the dangers of this era, I felt utterly helpless, and I hated it. I was not some damsel in distress who needed to be protected from the outside world. Being a member of the fairer sex, it aggravated me to no end how Keifer and the male members of the family treated females as fragile creatures.

I turned away from the window, glanced at my tiny son, sleeping peacefully in the bassinet, and continued my nervous pacing across the floor. The small clock on the mantel chimed softly, drawing my attention. It was now two o'clock in the morning. I sighed heavily, trying to let go of the tension that weighed heavily on my chest.

Finally, at a quarter after, the sound of hooves on the gravel grew louder and closer. I rushed to the window and pulled the curtain back. I could see three dark figures galloping towards the main house. I threw protocol out the window and rushed down the front staircase. Angelina, Maggie, Eugenia, and Caroline were directly behind me.

"Keifer," I called for him in a rush to open the front door.

"I am fine, Sidney." I heard his voice before I could clearly see him as I stepped out onto the front porch flanked by his family.

"What happened? Is everyone alright?" Angelina nervously asked watching our men dismount their horses.

Otis and Leroy took their reigns and led the horses towards the stables. The men slowly approached the porch. The soft glow from the lanterns illuminated their tired and soot covered faces as they approached the porch. Keifer barely reached the bottom step before I jumped into his arms, hitting my shoulder roughly against the butt of his rifle. But I did not care. I was back in his arms, and he was safe. Nothing else mattered.

"I am fine, Sidney," my husband reiterated with a weary expression. "Just tired." He kissed me on my forehead. His steps were stiff, and I noticed he winced when I squeezed him.

"What's happened?" Panic washed over me.

"He'll be fine." My father-in-law's commanding voice boomed through the darkness. "It is barely a scratch."

I noticed quickly all three men were moving with a bit of awkwardness. As they reached the porch, I saw how badly the three of them looked. Their faces were covered in a mixture of blood, sweat, and soot. Their dreary eyes conveyed their exhaustion through their ashen appearance.

"How are the Cameron's?" Angelina asked when David reached the porch.

"Not good," David muttered softly leading us all into the house.

Angelina led the way through the bottom floor through the walkway to the back mud room next to the kitchen. Talle and Nala were rushing about warming up water over the large inlet fireplace that I could almost walk into.

Sadie handed Angelina, Margarett, and I some clean towels and set down large basins in three of the four corners of the room. Dividing screens were placed between the men. Amidst the groans and the grunts, the men slowly undressed. I could not see the other two men, but from the hushed words drifting around the room, I imagined they looked somewhat like my own husband.

Keifer removed his torn shirt that looked barely above a rag. The front and back of his torso was badly bruised and covered in scratches. There was a large deep gash on his left side beneath his rib cage. I put a clean cloth in the warm basin of soapy water, rinsed it out, and lightly cleaned my husband's torso.

"Talle, can you please bring me a thread and sewing needle?" I asked.

"Sidney, do you know how to do that?" Angelina stepped around the divide to face me with concern in her eyes.

"Yes, I do. I have done it many times." I offered her a weak smile.

"Mother, Sidney knows what she is doing. I taught her well." My husband reassured his mother.

I smiled silently to myself recalling the long hours I spent mastering the art of suturing – those silly little pin cushions, pig's feet, and cadavers. But truth be told, I got more practice in suturing in this facet of my life than the *other* due to the shortage of individuals with the skill and the abundance of accidents that appeared to be a common occurrence here.

But it was sweet and somewhat humorous of my husband to believe he was solely responsible for my skills. In truth, my suturing skills far surpassed his own. I could create stitches that left almost no scar, whereas my husband's typically left a prominent raised red scar.

"Sadie," Keifer took a deep breath. "Fetch me the canister of brandy." He smiled weakly at me. "I believe I am going to need it."

"I imagine so," I said softly gently washing the wound while he flinched in pain.

Once I had his torso, face and hair cleaned, I waited a few moments while he gulped down some of the brandy. He nodded and turned his face away from me grunting as I carefully stitched the gaping wound. Victoria stepped around the divide and was watching me carefully. I hadn't noticed her there until her mother chastised her whilst pulling her away.

"Are you going to explain to me what happened tonight?" I tried to keep my voice low.

"It was bad." My husband winced as I added another suture and took another swig of brandy. "Thankfully, it is over now. You have nothing to worry about."

"But what happened? Are the Cameron's alright?" I pushed.

"Nothing you need to concern yourself with." He muttered, clearly being as dismissive as possible.

"Keifer Lee," I stood up directly in front of him and looking him in the eye.

"Well," he ran his hand through his hair as he often did when he was agitated. "Some negro had been squatting in the slave quarters. Mr. Cameron nor the overseer had any inclination he had been hiding on the grounds. I can only imagine the garbage he must have been preaching because the Cameron's have never had any difficulties with their slaves. And they are so kind to them and treat them very well." He sighed heavily. "Which is why their behavior was so shocking."

"What did they do?" I went back to suture his wound.

"They began by setting the barn ablaze. Then they attacked the main house with torches. They set the porch and front parlor on fire before they physically attacked Mr. Cameron and his overseer." His eyes dropped and I noticed the entire room had gone silent. Everyone was listening to his rendition of the night's events.

"And Mrs. Cameron and the children?" I choked out barely above a whisper.

"They were not spared either."

"Oh, my God." Angelina gasped. "Are they alright? Were they hurt?"

"Yes," David responded before his son. "They were badly beaten and one of the girls – Carolanne," his eyes dropped to the floor. "One of the field hands tried to have his way with her." The disgust in his voice was evident.

"Please tell me he did not succeed." Maggie gasped.

"No. He did not. One of the house servants intervened. But Carolanne was badly beaten, and her night dress was torn off her." Thad said through gritted teeth.

"They also tried to assault Sylvia." Keifer spoke up through gritted teeth. "Young Ronnie hit the field hand with a vase. The field hand broke his neck. At least Sylvia managed to escape."

"Little Ronnie is dead?" Angelina's hand covered his mouth in astonishment.

"He's only ten, isn't he?" Maggie asked looking back at her mother.

"Yes. He turned ten in May. He is a month older than Trixie." Silent tears ran down Angelina's face, and I noticed her hands trembling.

I quickly realized who they were talking about. I met Ronnie at a barbeque hosted by my in-laws right after our arrival. I recalled a little blond boy with freckles on his nose and sun-kissed cheeks. He was an adorable little boy who followed Trixie around like a lost puppy. I remembered Keifer joking about them getting married someday and uniting the two families. Ronnie was the fourth child of the Cameron's and the first son. His father's pride and joy.

"I remember him." My voice was barely a whisper. I choked on the words, seeing this small child clearly in my memory.

"He was such a sweet boy," Angelina's voice was barely audible.

"Where are the Cameron's now?" Maggie asked softly.

"Home." Her husband placed his hand on her shoulder.

"The funeral?" Angelina's eyes rested on her husband.

"I am not sure." David's lips pinched together in thought. "Probably tomorrow. I thought we would ride over this afternoon after I get some sleep. I am exhausted." Angelina nodded.

I finished up the last couple of sutures on Keifer's abdomen. But I could not shake the image of little Ronnie in my head. My greatest fear was losing my son. I could not imagine the pain his parents were suffering.

It was almost four in the morning before we retired to our beds. Keifer stood in front of our son's crib watching him peacefully sleeping for several minutes before crawling in bed beside me. He winced from the pain and finally closed his eyes. Within minutes, he was snoring softly.

I stared up at the ceiling. My mind kept racing and the fear in the pit of my stomach would not subside. Regardless of Keifer and his family's reassurances, I felt terrified. I could not dismiss the overwhelming imbalance between the number of slaves that lived on the property verses the number of family members.

All I could think about was my desire to flee North as soon as possible. My chest felt tight, and I could not breathe. I closed my eyes and concentrated on my breathing trying to slow my heart rate. I had never experienced such fear before. Never in my life had I ever felt uncomfortable, let alone fear with any of the black people in my life up North. I considered Ned, Naomi, Marta, Duncan, Preston, and Wanda as dear close friends. And all those who worked on our estate had always treated me with kindness and respect.

But this. This was different. The dynamics were different. For the first time in my life, I was acutely aware of it. My ears listened to every slight movement in the house. Every creaking floorboard, every fluttering distant sound brought a new sense of unease.

Exhaustion was taking a hold of me. I could hear the ticking away of the clock on the mantel counting down the long hours of the restless night.

I just wanted to go home.

27

MONDAY, AUGUST 10, 2020

I WALKED INTO THE BREAK ROOM after being on my feet for the last ten hours. I was so exhausted I could not see straight. My head was pounding, and my feet were killing me. My lower back was screaming as I pulled out a bottle of water from the refrigerator. I twisted off the cap and lowered the suffocating facemask I had been required to wear since I walked into the hospital. I took a deep breath loving the feel of unfiltered air flowing into my lungs before I quenched my thirst.

"Is there any coffee left?" Brandy walked in looking as bad as I felt. Her scrubs were wrinkled, and her messy bun was barely holding up with loose strands falling around her face.

"Some," I glanced over at the half full coffee pot on the counter. "I don't know how long it has been sitting there."

"I don't care as long as it's hot and has caffeine." She half smiled, exhaustion clear on her face and in her posture. She poured the stale coffee in her oversized mug adding sugar and cream.

"What time are you off?" I slumped down in the nearest chair and chugged half the water bottle.

"Eleven," Brandy slumped down in the chair across from me. You?"

"Nine, and then I am out of here for two weeks." I rested my head down on the table. "I am so freaking tired of these twelve-hour shifts that always turn into fourteen or sixteen hours."

"How did you manage time off?"

"Landon and I scheduled it last February and it was already approved."

"Damn. It's a shame travel is restricted." She leaned back in the chair and put her feet up on the chair beside her. "Are you planning on going anywhere?"

"I guess I should say no since the hospital would make us quarantine if they found out we left the state." I smirked.

"True," she smirked. "So, where are you two not going?"

"To look at some property in North Carolina and Florida with my sister, her husband, and in-laws. They just bought a beautiful RV for the trip." I rested my chin on my hands looking over at her.

"You're really going to leave Boston?"

"Between the riots and the liberal bullshit allowing criminals to control the city, it isn't safe anymore." I reasoned.

"I know. My husband, Jeff, is talking more and more about retiring. I wish he would. He's put in his twenty, and then some. He said something the other night about making a lateral move to a department in Florida or another red state since there's a nationwide shortage of officers right now." She sighed heavily. "I am happy he has options and is thinking about what's best for his career and our children. I don't even feel safe going to the grocery store anymore."

"He'd be an asset wherever he decides to go." I offered.

"I would love to move to a much smaller community. Some place where this destruction and liberal nonsense is handled before it gets out of control."

"Is there such a place?" I raised my eyebrows.

"Isn't that what you're seeking on your vacation?" The corners of her mouth twitched.

"Absolutely," I sighed. "I'll let you know if we find it."

"Perhaps we'll join you there." Brandy laughed. "Wouldn't that be something." She shook her head as if clearing her thoughts. "Oh, my gosh, I've got to tell you something." She perked up with a sudden twinkle in her eye. "You will never believe what happened yesterday at the grocery store."

"What?" I sat up, leaning forward, intrigued.

"Jeff got off work early and went with me to the store to grab a few essentials and things for dinner." I nodded stretching my arms above my head with a yawn. "So, we stop at Kroger's before picking the kids up from school. Both of us put on our face masks as we step out of our car. Jeff was in his street clothes that he wears every day to work — dress pants and button-down shirt. He was still wearing his badge on his belt and his gun in the holster on his hip."

"Okay," I imagined the scene.

"I am used to wearing these suffocating things, but Jeff hates them. When I am not at work, I typically wear it under my nose because it fogs up my glasses. He's fidgeting with it as we walk into Kroger's. I grabbed a cart and started walking towards the produce. Jeff wandered off like usual." She rolled her eyes, and I chuckled.

"Landon does the same thing." I told her. "I keep threatening to tie a balloon to his ass when we go to the store so I can find him because I am tired of searching for him with an armload of things."

"I know what you mean." Brandy rolled her eyes again before continuing. "So, I'm standing there picking up a bag of apples when this older lady, probably in her sixties comes storming over to me and deliberately runs her cart into mine. This older man, who I assume was her husband is staggering towards her. She looks at me and says, 'you're face mask is supposed to be over your nose.' I tried to be polite and told her it fogs up my glasses and I'm fine. She then gets louder saying, 'it's selfish people like me who carry this virus that compromises the lives of everyone else.' People were now stopping and staring at us. I couldn't believe it. I said, 'lady, how I wear my mask is none of your business.' So, she pulls her phone out of her purse and announces that she's going to call the police on me and have me arrested for endangering lives during a pandemic."

"Seriously?" I scoffed. "What a liberal Karen nutjob."

"Oh, it was perfect." Brandy howled with laughter. "Jeff, completely oblivious to the encounter comes waltzing around the corner — police detective badge fully displayed on his belt, gun on his hip, and his face mask — wrapped beneath his chin — his nose and mouth completely exposed." I started laughing, picturing the Karen's reaction. "I pointed to Jeff and told Karen, 'you're in luck. The police are here. Let's ask him.' Her face went white and she aggressively pulled her cart back and stomped away in a huff with her husband still scuffling along behind her. I tell you; it was absolutely priceless. Jeff had no clue how perfect his appearance had been. He said he wished he'd had the chance to talk with her. I'd hate to think of what he would have said."

"You should have let him." The liberal Karen epidemic was spreading faster and was more out of control than Covid-19.

A mid-sized recreational vehicle arrived on time typical of Robert and Emily. Landon had spent ten minutes tossing clothes and toiletries into a duffle bag and called himself ready. However, I was still sorting through outfits when they arrived. I was attempting to zip my suitcase when there was a sharp knock on the front door.

"I got it," Landon looked at me with disbelief and left me in the bedroom.

"Hey Jocelyn," Landon's voice drifted across our small flat.

"I was sent up to get you and my sister." She stated like it was obvious. "Everyone is waiting downstairs. Where's Sidney?"

"In the bedroom trying to zip her suitcase." Landon chuckled.

"Figures." I heard her sigh heavily. "I will get her," Jocelyn muttered suddenly appeared in our doorway. "Good morning." I glanced up hearing her footsteps approach. "Let's go."

"Okay," I put more weight on the final corner and got the zipper closed. "Done." I announced straightening up and turning towards her.

"I am so ready to get out of this town." She bounced over to me. "The entire world is on hiatus. Jackson and I could really use a change of scenery."

"It is going to be great." I grinned.

"Yes, it is." Jocelyn reached for my suitcase and pulled up the handle. "I am glad this thing has wheels. What in the world did you pack?"

"I wasn't sure what I would need." I shrugged.

"Yeah, because wearing jeans and t-shirts on a road trip would be unthinkable." She rolled her eyes and headed out the door.

"You think you know me so well." I muttered grumbling behind her back.

I locked the apartment and double checked everything. I always felt nervous leaving our home unattended for an extended time.

Fortunately, this was one of those times when having a curtain twitcher for a neighbor pays off. The old bat across the hall never let anything slide. If a squirrel farted in the tree outside the building, she was on the Facebook neighborhood group letting everyone know.

"Come on," Jocelyn's voice carried from the parking lot.

"Excuse me," Ms. Curtain Twitcher cracked her door open. "Are you and your young man responsible for that RV blocking the parking lot?"

"My apologies, Mrs. Fincher. We were just leaving." I smiled politely.

"Very well. Please tell your guests not to block our parking lot again." Her lips pursed together in a scrawl. "It's rude and inconsiderate. I was about to report the RV to the police. It is double parked."

"My apologies. I will let my family know," my smile broadened. "Have a lovely day." I waved and trotted towards the RV.

"What took you so long?" Landon was waiting patiently holding the door to the main cabin open for me.

"Ms. Curtain Twitcher," I rolled my eyes with a smirk.

"Oh, did you send her my love?" He loved tormenting the old hag across the hall.

"Always," I smiled coyly.

I climbed aboard and was pleasantly surprised. The RV was beyond luxury. It was like a mini, yet spacious apartment on wheels. Jackon was lounging in a recliner with his feet up and sipping a Dr. Pepper from a bottle. He grinned and tilted the bottle in greeting. Robert sat behind the wheel and Emily looked comfortable in the passenger seat.

"Welcome aboard," Jackson pulled his wife down into his lap. "This certainly beats driving across the country in that CRV." He was referring to our long road trip during spring break, their senior year of high school when we had driven from Chicago to New Orleans.

"Yes, it does." I looked around. "This is gorgeous."

"We figured it would be more comfortable for all of us." Emily turned around towards us.

"This is great," Landon nodded looking around.

"Everyone ready?" Robert hollered and a loud chorus affirmed. "Alrighty then." Robert turned the ignition over and pulled out onto the highway.

The hum of the tires on the highway lost their charm after we reached the hundred-mile mark. We played multiple road games — slug bug, license plates, I spy, 20 questions until we were bored to tears. I finally dug a paperback out of my purse and settled down on the sofa.

It wasn't long before the four of us in the back were dozing on and off, picking on each other, tossing pillows and acting like a group of elementary-aged children. Emily turned around more than once to playfully chastise us.

We arrived in Bath, North Carolina to view a property on the Pamilco River. The town of Bath looked like it was a set of a Hallmark movie. It was adorable in a simplistic sort of way. The four of us sat in the back with our faces pressed against the windows observing the ambiance completely mystified by the storybook setting.

We passed through the tiny main street and headed, what I assumed was towards the river. A couple of miles down the road, the sun was glaring off the asphalt, and the houses were becoming more scattered apart. Robert slowed down and then turned onto a dirt road. My eyes widened as I noticed the ram-shackle house where an old living room furniture was sitting on the front porch. There were old tin trailers – tornado magnets sticking out of the thick tree line. The RV was stirring up a cloud of dust behind us.

"I think I hear the banjos." Landon smirked over at Jackson.

"I think I'd slit my wrists if I had to live here." Jackson muttered low enough so only the four of us could hear.

"I would join you." Landon's eyes widened.

We made a right turn, and the road became asphalt again. The thick forest around us showed herds of deer, and other small creatures scurrying about. The thick smell of pine trees hung heavily in the air. The difference in making one turn was mind boggling.

The house was a beautiful Victorian home on twelve acres. It had a boat dock with a lift, an inground pool with pool house, and a gazebo. The house was four bedrooms with a wrapped-around porch complete with swing. The yard was full of mature trees and gorgeous flower beds. Robert was most excited about the oversized RV garage and workshop that sat about an acre from the main house. He was talking about building a woodshop and learning how to build things. Emily thought it was cute in a comical way whenever he talked about it, rolling her eyes behind him with a smirk.

The local realtor was already waiting for us when we arrived. He looked surprised to see our abode as we all clambered out of the RV. The house was picturesque. It was exactly like the home I had always dreamed of owning someday.

"Wow," Jocelyn whistled lowly stepping down from the RV. "This is beautiful."

"Yes, and spacious." The pudgy little realtor's face lit up.

"It would be great as a vacation home, but there is no way we could live here year-round." I looked over at my sister.

"How close is the grade school?" Emily stepped up beside us.

"We have a small elementary and middle school combined, but the high school age children are bused over to the next town. We just don't have enough population of teenagers to have our own." The realtor explained nervously.

"Well, let's take a look around." Robert ushered us all towards the house.

The four of us followed the realtor into the house. Jackson and Landon hung around outside exploring the huge barn, pool, gazebo, and dock. The house was beautifully decorated, but we were all disappointed by the small kitchen. Knowing how much Robert and Emily loved their home-cooked meals we all knew it wouldn't suffice. There was barely room for two people to move around. The bedrooms were also very small. There was a full bathroom in the master suite and a second that was to serve the other three bedrooms.

Still, there was a balcony off the master that looked out over the water. It was a breathtaking view. The master bath had a claw tub that stood in front of an oversized window that looked over the river below. The view was almost worth the other inconveniences of the home. However, the glaring issues would have made it nothing more than a vacation home.

We thanked the realtor and followed him to the second property a couple of towns south. It was somewhat larger than Bath, but not as impressive. As soon as we arrived, we all agreed it was a waste of time. Out of courtesy to the realtor, we toured the house and property. It left a lot to be desired. The renovations alone would cost more than the value of the property.

Back in the RV, the six of us debated on where we wanted to have dinner. We made our way to South Carolina before we stopped for the night. Robert pulled into an RV park within walking distance to Myrtle Beach. I had not been here since middle school on a family vacation and neither had Jocelyn.

We grabbed dinner at a beachside diner sitting out on the deck. We ate steamed lobster, shrimp, and crab legs. The garlic butter rolls melted in our mouths. I had forgotten how incredible the seafood was down here. We certainly did not have a lack of it in Boston, but it was somehow different down here. The salty ocean air enhanced the atmosphere and everyone's spirit.

Emily pulled out a file from her purse of several other homes they were considering. She had organized them by state and made multiple notes about political ideology in each state.

"I never thought we would be house hunting based on politics." Emily muttered crumbling up a listing for a home in Georgia.

"I never thought I would witness a criminal become a martyr, thugs take over a police precinct and half of a city, and government officials sponsor nationwide rioting." Jocelyn smirked. "The second summer of love has been anything but."

"I never thought I would have a front row seat to the disintegration of our country." Emily said, catching herself before adding *again* at the end of her statement.

"The irony of it all is not lost on me." I muttered with a smirk in the direction of my family leaving Landon a bit baffled.

"Have you heard from your mother?" Emily asked.

"Yes," I nodded. "She and Dane accepted positions in Florida — The Keys. They put in their notice at the hospital in Seattle. She said the hospital begged them to say, offered them more money, and even a research lab. But they turned it down."

"Good for them," Robert added.

"They will be out of there before the end of the week. She said they are very excited about the move." I told the table.

"I hope the transition goes smoothly." Emily smiled softly. "Still, I think it is sad that those who believe in traditional Christian values — the same traditions and values that our country was founded upon, are forced to flee their homes, communities, and states because of the rampant mental illness that is running amuck within the Democrat party." Her eyes looked forlorn. "I hate the thought of leaving Boston. It is my home and has been for most of my life. But I no longer recognize it, nor do I feel safe there." Robert took her hand in his.

"We have survived worse, my love." His eyes met hers and held them. "We will survive this too."

"I know," she whispered, still holding his gaze.

After dinner Robert and Emily decided to relax on the small patio with a bottle of wine while the rest of us went down to the beach. It had been years since my sister, and I went to Myrtle beach. I was a freshman in high school, and my siblings were in junior high – back when our parents pretended to be happily married. It was around that time that the cracks were starting to show in their marriage enough to where we could see it.

"Do you remember the last time we were here?" Jocelyn and Jackson were walking alongside Landon and me.

"I was just thinking about that." I admitted holding Landon's hand and carrying my sandals in the other.

"Do you remember how annoying Ethan was?" my sister chuckled softly. "God," she sighed heavily. "He was such a brat."

"You go it worse from him than I did because of the closeness in your age. He ignored me most of the time." I shrugged.

"No," she looked at me with a coy expression. "You ignored us." Jocelyn mockingly flipped her long auburn hair over her shoulder and laughed. "You were too perfect to have time for your little siblings."

"That's not true," I defended but both men laughed. "I was not a snob." I spat, which only made the three of them laugh harder.

"Ah, it's okay." Jocelyn threw her arm around my shoulders and gave me a condescending hug. "You know I love you. And more importantly, now I like you."

"Gee, thanks." I rolled my eyes in her direction. "Life has a way of changing you in unexpected ways."

"True," Landon spoke up. "I never thought I would ever witness mass hysteria, but here we are."

"I know what you mean." Jackson joined in. "I would love to check out the antique shops and stores down there." He gestured towards the make-shift boardwalk. "But it's ninety-six and if we go up there, we will have to put on these ridiculous worthless masks. I do not feel like suffocating any more than I absolutely must."

"I swear, all these politicians who believe they are experts in every facet of reality think these things work and social distancing is going to restrict the spread of this flu." Jocelyn's voice took on a harsh edge. "I feel like we are not living in a free country any longer. People are losing their jobs, businesses are closing permanently, you cannot attend church, but hey – if you want to protest, riot, or loot, the corrupt government officials are completely behind you and will even bail you out of jail if you get arrested." She threw her hands up in exasperation. "Nothing makes sense anymore."

"Do you believe it's going to get worse?" Landon looked over towards Jackson.

"Yes," Jackson muttered. "A lot worse. I agree with my dad. I think the democrats are going to steal the election from President Trump and, at minimum, the next four years will be hell. They will do everything to destroy this republic and implement a Marxist doctrine. This so-called global pandemic is simply a springboard to start the process. It is going to get much worse."

"Great," I added sarcastically. "I understand why your parents want to leave Boston. Our governor is an absolute moron with no common sense, puts criminals above victims, and couldn't care less what anyone thinks."

"Where are we headed next?" Landon tried to lighten the subject.

"I think there's a property in the panhandle in Florida that my parents want to look at. That may be our next stop." Jackson kicked the sand with his bare feet.

"Nothing in South Carolina?" I thought that was why we had stopped here for the night.

"No," my brother-in-law shook his head. "Not that I am aware of."

"What about Tennessee? They're a deep red state and man, Tennessee is gorgeous. I would not mind living there. My parents took me to Gatlinburg when I was in my teens." Landon's face brightened.

"We talked about looking in Tennessee." Jackson nodded in agreement with Landon's assessment. "But my mother was adamant, if she was going to leave her beloved home, she was moving somewhere warm." He chuckled. "She says the older she gets, the more she hates the cold and if she never has to shovel the driveway or drive on black ice again, she will be happy. But she is insistent on Fall," he rolled his eyes in mockery. "She loves Fall and all the colors of changing leaves. She insists it is the warm days and cool nights that inspire her to write. So, my father is trying to accommodate her wishes — as always." A wide grin spread across his lips.

"I think it's sweet." I confessed. "Your parents seem to have an ideal marriage."

"I do not know if I would call it ideal, but they get along well. My dad has no ability to say no to her, or Phoebe, his daughters-in-law, granddaughters, or you two." Jackson playfully bumped Jocelyn with a smirk.

"That is not true," Jocelyn tried to sound offended but failed spectacularly.

"Name one time when he said not to you." Jackson challenged her, and I smirked because I could not recall one either.

"Okay," My sister pursed her lips for a moment. "Our senior year, you disappeared, and your dad would not give me your contact information." She tried to be vague since Landon was there and did not know anything about *E.V.E.* or the obstacles my sister and Jackson had had to contend with early in their relationship.

"That was different." Jackson exclaimed clearly not expecting my sister to recall that difficult time. "He was following my wishes." His facial muscles tensed.

"But clearly, your father followed your wishes over my pleas so therefore, you cannot say your father cannot say no to the women in his life." My sister looked proud for making her argument.

"Always the lawyer." I muttered loud enough for the three of them to hear and gave my sister the side eye.

"I learned from the best." She playfully poked at her husband who finally relented with a grin.

"You are impossible." Jackson shook his head at his wife.

"Honestly, my family is the exact same. My dad pretends he's the head of the house, but my siblings and I know it's my mother who calls the shots and makes all the decisions." Landon laughed lightly trying to ease the remaining tension away. "It's comical to watch them. My dad is a big, burly guy, but when it comes to my mother, he's like puddy in her hands."

"Just because he loves her and wants to see her happy does not mean he is weak." I noted.

"My father is anything but weak." Landon looked pointedly at me. "You've met him. You know how he is." I nodded. "He just adores her and therefore, gives in. Not always, but I would speculate mom wins ninety percent of the time." A full smile spread across his shapely lips reaching his eyes.

"As it should be," I smirked.

"Oh, you think so, do you?" Landon kicked some sand with his bare feet in my direction.

"Stop," I screamed and kicked some back at him before sprinting off closer to the water's edge laughing uncontrollably.

"Oh, you're going to regret that, missy." Landon screeched chasing after me.

He tackled me in the sand momentarily knocking the wind out of me. I wiggled beneath him laughing and trying to catch my breath. He pinned my arms down in the sand sitting on my abdomen. I kicked my feet into the sand while my sister and her husband stood by laughing at us.

"Say you're sorry," Landon teased me quickly kissing me all over my face as I squirmed beneath his weight.

"Never," I retorted as I continued struggling and squirming attempting to free myself from his iron grip.

The tide washed over us, and I screamed loudly, getting completely soaked. Landon laughed climbing up off me and sitting down in the sand beside me. I playfully smacked his thigh rolling towards him and sitting up.

"You deserved that." He continued laughing loudly along with Jocelyn and Jackson.

I could have gotten mad. I should have been irate. My hair and makeup were ruined. My clothes were soaked through. I had sand in my hair, stuck to my skin and in places I didn't even want to think about. I was a hot mess, and most likely, looked even worse.

But I laughed — a full belly laugh poured out of me until my sides hurt. I needed this. The combination of the stress from school, the hospital, our finances — everything had been weighing heavily on my shoulders for months. The release felt incredibly freeing.

"I did not," I playfully shoved Landon away from me. "You are such an ass." I could not stop laughing.

"You look like a drowned rat." Jocelyn said as she and Jackson approached. To my horror she snapped a picture with her phone. "This will look perfect on Instagram." My sister stuck her tongue out at me.

"Go ahead," I returned her childish gesture with a giggle. "I don't care."

"You're still beautiful." Landon leaned over and kissed me on the lips. "The most beautiful woman in the world."

"Oh, please," Jocelyn mocked with an exaggerated eye roll. "Talk about a kiss ass." She leaned into her husband.

"Seriously," Jackson mimicked her sarcasm.

The wind kicked up as we made our way back towards the RV park. The previously clear sky took on a grey hazy appearance as if a storm was creeping up on us. The late summer heat ensured I wasn't wet for long. My clothes dried but also became stiff and quickly uncomfortable due to the salt water. I kept messing with them trying to smooth them out as they grew itchier with each step.

"Problem?" Jocelyn mused.

"Shut up," her slap-happy grin only made me more miserable.

"If you start digging, I'm crossing the street. I don't want people to think we know you." I could see her fighting a laugh as she tormented me.

"If you do. I will chase after you in the most exaggerated fashion, calling your name loudly so everyone will stare." I quipped back with a coy smile.

"You would too," she eyed me carefully as if weighing her options.

"I dare you," I challenged when Jackson snickered.

"No one knows me here." Jocelyn must have caught the mischievous glint in my eye. "I will embarrass you to no end."

"I believe you." She shook her head and held up her hands in a surrendering manner. "Truce."

"Truce." I smirked with guilty satisfaction.

I couldn't sleep. Not because the small sleeper felt cramped, which it did. My mind had shifted to what was awaiting me once sleep found me. I thought of the insurrection at the Cameron plantation, the young boy's death, the assault and attempted assaults on the women and young girls and my heart ached. I felt like screaming, crying, and hitting something — hard.

I could not get comfortable. Despite the luxurious décor in the RV, the little sleeping quarters left a lot to be desired. Landon and I were sleeping in the equivalent of a twin bed. He was spooned up behind me snoring softly in my ear. I could feel his breath on the back of my neck and the steady rhythm of his breathing against my back.

At home we share a queen-size bed but have the habit of entangling ourselves in each other as we sleep. But being forced to share such cramped quarters, it felt suffocating rather than comforting. My restless mind could not find peace. I feared what awaited me on the other side once my eyes opened to the dreadful aftereffects of the slave insurrection.

I gently slid out from beneath Landon's arm and leg off the side of the small bed. He stirred gently but did not awaken. I stood in the dark, unsure what I was doing but feeling immensely restless. I heard the low but distinct voices of Robert and Emily just outside and noticed the soft glow from an oil lantern resting on the folding table between their lawn chairs beneath the RV's awning.

I stepped outside quietly trying not to startle them or awaken the others. The stars shone brightly against the black ink sky. The cool air was refreshing and heavy with the smell of saft and marine life.

"Sorry, I couldn't sleep." My voice felt loud in the quiet night.

"Pull up a chair," Emily gestured towards the folded lawn chairs stacked beside the RV. "Is the bed to small?"

"No, it's fine." I lied setting up a chair beside her. "I cannot seem to calm my mind." I sighed heavily, keenly aware of both their eyes on me. "I am dreading what I will awaken to *there*." I admitted.

"I thought you were enjoying Savannah and getting along well with Keifer's family." Robert's voice was low.

"I am and I do. Last evening Keifer, his father, and his brother-in-law, Thad, were called out to help with a slave insurrection on a neighboring plantation." I fidgeted with the loose tag on the arm of the chair.

"Was anyone hurt?" Emily looked astonished.

"Yes," I nodded and explained what Keifer, and the other two men had told us upon their return.

"We heard similar stories of small insurrections occurring across the South." Robert admitted. "Although it was hard to know what was real and what was fabrication. Even then, the news was extremely one-sided and dependent upon which side of the Mason-Dixon line you resided on."

"What caused it?" The concern was evident upon Emily's face.

"A mole," I shrugged. "Almost like a sleeper cell agent of a modern terrorist group. They infiltrate. Lie. Promise victory and freedom. Then disappear when it does not go as planned."

"And move on to another plantation where it will start all over again." Emily and I nodded in agreement with Robert. "There will be a hanging tomorrow."

"Keifer said there would be." I noted. "I just," I shook my head in disbelief. "I am so angry." I unintentionally balled my hands into fists. "I just want to go home. I no longer feel safe in the South. I jump at every little noise in the house." Tears rolled down my cheeks. "After all the Black Lives Matter and Antifa violence this summer, the Diversity Equity Inclusion bullshit, the demand for reparations, I understand why such stereotypes exist." I hastily brushed away my tears.

"I understand." Emily reached for my hand squeezing it gently.

"I hate it because I never felt this way. But now." I said angerly. "I don't think I will ever look at Ned, Naomi, Marta, or any of the others in our household the same again."

"Don't let this harden you, Sidney. You are better than that." Emily words were soft.

"I get it." Robert's voice was harsher. "It feels like all the work done over the last sixty years was for nothing. The racial division has grown intense. The victim mentality has become the accepted norm and accountability, common sense, and lawfare are fading memories."

"Robert," Emily's voice was barely a whisper.

"No." He raised his hand slightly. "I agree with her. "When you have people like Al Sharpton spewing hatred, victimhood, reparations, and racial division as easily as he breathes." He spat. "And this hypocrite has the audacity to call himself a Reverand. It is utterly shameful."

"I am not disagreeing with you, dear." Emily interjected. "I was trying to say that we should be careful to not lump them all together. If we do that, then we are no better than they are."

"I am not saying they are all the same. They aren't. I know that. But there is a reason stereotypes exist. There is enough truth to them to create a stereotype to begin with." Robert shrugged. "I have friends of every shape, race, and ethnicity, and not one of them agrees with the direction this country is headed. The only ones I have seen embrace it are weak-minded liberals."

"I do not know what to do. It doesn't seem to matter which time I am in; the tension is always there. Just waiting for the smallest of spark that is going to ignite us into war." I exclaimed.

"Well, at least one you know when and can prepare." Emily offered a weak smile. "As for here," her voice trailed off.

"Here, it is like sitting on a powder key wondering which spark will be the one." Robert exhaled loudly. "The thing is when the silent majority get pushed too far, that is when all hell is going to break loose."

"Yeah, but can we survive long enough for the silent majority to take a stand?" I raised my eyebrows.

"We will do what we can to hold on until then — such as fleeing the insanity of Democrat run cities and states." Robert observed.

"I never thought I would leave Boston." Emily said solemnly. "Its historical nature always make it feel like home regardless of which time we were in."

"We will make a new home with new memories." Robert took her hand in his with a gentle smile. "It is the people and love that you fill a house with that make it a home, not its geographical location."

"I know," Emily whispered.

The three of us sat in silence lost in our own thoughts. My mind was consumed with stress and fear of what awaited me when I awoke to a new day in Savannah. I lifted my eyes towards the stars and wondered if these were the same ones resting over my little family sleeping beneath the swampy Spanish moss trees in Gable Gardens.

"What about Texas?" I asked in a low voice. "Have you considered looking there?"

"Not Austin." Robert said sharply. "To many progressive left-wing liberal Karen and Kevin's migrating there from California." He looked at us with raised eyebrows. "I also do not want to live somewhere that I have to watch tumbleweeds blow across the front yard." He smirked.

"Well, we can look around Northern Texas perhaps on the outskirts of Dallas." Emily shrugged.

"Northern Texas is green, isn't it?" I had never been to Dallas, so I wasn't sure, but I knew Louisiana was.

"Yes," Emily nodded with a smile. "Well, the northeast corner of Texas is green."

"I don't think I could live without the seasons." I considered. "Especially Fall."

"I have to agree with you on that." Emily chimed in.

"Okay, hold on." Robert was already typing on his phone. "Let me see what we're looking at."

"What are you doing?" Emily leaned over trying to peak at his phone.

"Searching," he mumbled back. "It seems Jefferson, Fredericksburg, and Nacogdoches are historical locations in Texas. Jefferson is the furthest North. It might be worth looking into." His eyes met with his wife.

"Perhaps," Emily glanced over at me. "Tomorrow." She rose from her chair. "As for now, it is late and way past my bedtime."

"Thank you both for listening." I got to my feet. "I appreciate it." I leaned over and gave Emily a warm hug. "Good night."

"Night dear," She squeezed my arm with a gentle smile.

"Sweet dreams," Robert said before I closed the RV door behind me.

I could still hear their muffled voices outside as I climbed back into the small bunk beside Landon. His arm instinctively found me pulling me closer to him. His breathing was steady and hot on my neck. I squeezed his arm and closed my eyes. I said a silent prayer that peace and level heads would prevail in both my lives and that I would find a way to understand my place in each.

28

MONDAY, AUGUST 13, 1860

THE SOUNDS OF MY SON'S HUNGRY cry woke me from a restless sleep. He was never shy about his demands and had inherited his father's temper. Keifer, oblivious to his son, continued to snore loudly beside me. I pushed the sheet and thin blanket covering us aside and slid out of bed.

"Good morning, little man." My son immediately ceased his racket upon spotting me. His bright hazel eyes, exactly like his father's, sparkled up at me and a big smile spread across lips. "You are just like your father," I smiled picking him up and kissing his cheek. "Impossible not to love."

I changed his cloth diaper, missing disposable diapers once again. My little man smiled and squirmed kicking his little plumb legs. I smoothed down his dressing gown and picked him back up. He had grown so much over the last couple of months. I carried him over to the rocking chair beside the window, sat down and began nursing him.

The sun was just beginning to rise over the horizon. The hazy sky let me know we were in for another hot and humid day. I watched the sun creeping over the tree line with a heavy sense of dread in my chest. I saw the field hands making their way across the vast green rows. The knot in my stomach tightened by the sheer number of them verses us.

My mind immediately turned to thoughts of going home. I knew our time here was drawing to a close, but in my mind, I could not get out of here fast enough.

"I believe our son loves watching the sunrise." Keifer mumbled rubbing his eyes and stretching.

"Every single one since the day he was born." I smirked. "How are you feeling." I asked after I saw him wince in pain. "How are the stitches?"

"Sore," he grumbled and tossed the covers aside. "It's going to be a long day."

"When is the funeral?" I asked softly.

"Tomorrow or Thursday, I imagine." Keifer sighed heavily, rising to his feet. "Dad Thad, and I will head over to the Cameron's after breakfast."

"What for?" My face crumbled as I shifted my son to the other side.

"The County Sherriff will be out there, and we will need to give statements about last night." I nodded.

"What will happen to them?" I met my husband's eye.

"For those involved," he looked down at his hands uncomfortably. "They will hang."

I remained silent as my husband got dressed. I did not know what to say because I did not know how I felt about it. But then I gazed down upon my little angel's face and thought about the unimaginable pain little Ronny's parents were waking up to this morning. I squeezed my son a little tighter and fought back the tears ready to spill over.

No, a hanging was the bare minimum they deserved. I felt no sympathy, no empathy, no remorse. These men had chosen to violate innocent girls and take the life of a small innocent boy for a culture they were impervious to change.

"Can I go with you?" I brushed the tears off my cheeks and covered myself up.

"I do not believe that would be a good idea." Keifer paused buttoning his shirt.

"Why not?" I set my little man back into the bassinet so I could get dressed myself.

"Sidney, I really do not want you to be exposed to," his voice trailed off.

"To what?" I challenged him, narrowing my eyes. "I want to check on the Cameron's and their daughters." I explained. "I believe they could use all the support they can get right now. I cannot imagine what they are going through." I ran my finger softly over my son's check as he smiled brightly up at me. My heart broke as I fought back tears.

Keifer shrugged but did not reply. Instead, he finished getting dressed and left our room without saying another word. I looked at the door for a moment before turning back to the armorer. I flipped through the gowns I had brought down with me and there was not a black one in the bunch because it was the last thing I thought I would need. I grabbed a dark navy-blue gown with a little black lace and not very stylish. It would have to do.

The atmosphere around the breakfast table was somber. Everyone picked at their food, but never really ate anything. Thankfully, the coffee was strong, and I was not the only one in dire need after the unexpectedly long night the night before. Angelina, Maggie, and Eugenia were wearing black mourning gowns. They had made it clear in their intentions to join the men on visit to the Cameron's.

We left the house shortly before nine. The men saddled up as the ladies, and I climbed into the carriage. My eyes were hypervigilant as I continuously kept darting across the landscape. I could not help it. I was genuinely frightened. It did not take long before my mother-in-law noticed.

"Sidney," she drew my attention away from the window. "Slave insurrections are very rare. You can calm down." She reached for my hand and squeezed it gently.

"No one is going to jump out of the bushes and kidnap you." Eugenia said, rolling her eyes.

"Eugenia, hush." Maggie chastised her sister harshly.

"I was simply explaining to someone from the North that she needn't be so scared of every shadow around the corner." Eugenia huffed.

"Eugenia," Angelina narrowed her eyes. "I will have none of that."

"Her fear is absurd." The whale of a women rolled her eyes once again. "Northern women are so soft and naïve."

"Really, Eugenia?" I almost laughed as she smirked. "You think Northern women are soft? When was the last time you cooked a meal by yourself. When was the last time you sewed a dress or the jagged edges of torn flesh together. When was the last time you were responsible for balancing the family budget and making sure everyone was paid, fed, and clothed? When was the last time you started your own fire to stay warm, milked a cow, or even gathered the eggs from the chicken coop?" I scoffed. "Don't you ever call me or any Northern lady soft because all you have is unfounded arrogance, jealously, and bitterness. I take great pride in being a Northern lady and knowing that I am self-sufficient and independent. Something you can never claim."

"I will never understand for the life of me what my brother sees in you." Eugenia spat back at me. "You are no lady."

"If the measure of a lady is being what you are, I would proudly agree with you." I smirked, causing Maggie to cover half of her face with her fan to hide her giggles.

"Eugenia," a smile twitched at the edges of my mother-in-law's mouth. "You owe Sidney an apology. She is not familiar with our culture, and it is unfair of you to dismiss her feelings, especially after last night's events."

"I will not apologize to her. You heard her insult me worse than anything I said." Eugenia, like an unrulily child, stuck out her chin in defiance.

"Very well," Angelina tapped on the window behind her to get the driver's attention.

I glanced over at Maggie, confused as the carriage slowed to a stop. The men walked their horses up to the carriage to inquire what was going on. The wide fields with scattered trees surrounded us. The morning sun glared down upon us like we were ants under a magnifying glass.

Angelina unlatched the side door on the carriage door and swung it open. She held onto the bar and stepped down without any indication of her intentions.

"Is everything all right, Momma?" Keifer asked, halting his horse next to the carriage.

"No," Angelina's face was calm and collected. "I do not believe Eugenia is in the right frame of mind for a visit today."

"What?" Eugenia shrieked from inside the carriage.

"I believe it would be best if you headed back home, Eugenia." My mother-in-law looked indifferent.

"Then turn the carriage around if you do not want me to attend with you." Eugenia huffed.

"We are halfway there. I will not waste more time backtracking for your benefit." Angelina said calmly.

"You cannot expect me to walk home alone." Eugenia's mouth hung agape.

"Since you believe in the superiority and strength of Southern women and the silliness of Sidney's concern, then you have nothing to worry about." Angelina's mouth was pursed into a thin line. "Please step out of the carriage."

"Mother, no. Please." Eugenia looked at Maggie and I, her eyes pleading for either of us to speak up on her behalf. Neither of us said a word.

"Exit the carriage, Eugenia." Angelina repeated, but her daughter did not move.

"What is the hold up?" David trotted up beside his son. "It's not getting cooler out here." He wiped off his brow with a scowl on his face.

"Mother is being cruel because I was being honest with Sidney." Eugenia poked her head out of the carriage but refused to step outside.

"What did you say to my wife?" Keifer's eyes narrowed at his sister.

"We will discuss that further once we return home." Angelina turned towards her son. "Eugenia, I will not ask you again to step out of the carriage."

"Eugenia, now!" David's voice carried across the open field making all of us jump.

Eugenia scrambled to her feet and squeezed herself through the carriage door. "Father, please."

"I am not going to argue with you. You heard your mother." David's voice left no room for argument.

Angelina took one final look at her daughter before climbing back up into the carriage. She closed and latched the door rapping lightly on the window to signal the driver. No one said a word for the remainder of the trip.

I was not sure what I expected at the Cameron's plantation, but it was worse than I had imagined. Charred splintered wood rested in a smokey grave where their large barn had once resided. The surrounding trees and grass were scorched with black streaks. A portion of the main house's roof was charred and collapsed on the west side where the ballroom and dining room previously stood. The whitewashed brick was streaked with shards of black soot. It reminded me of the faded pictures of Europe during World War II.

The air felt heavy and still. The lack of breeze amongst the ruins provided an apoptotic atmosphere that felt difficult to breathe in. I inhaled sharply stepping out of the carriage and looking over the destruction and devastation inflicted upon this once beautiful and peaceful plantation.

The men climbed off their horses and tethered them to a large hickory off the main pathway. They joined us beside the carriage with disbelief and grief written across their faces. I reached for my husband's hand and squeezed it gently. I needed to gather every ounce of strength from him I could get before entering this once happy home that was forever altered now by the absence of little Ronnie's laughter.

"Are you alright?" Keifer whispered.

"No." I answered honestly.

"Sherriff Mitchell is already here," Thad nodded towards the horse tethered to a tree near the porch.

"I am sure he has been here all night." David placed his hand on the small of his wife's back and let her up the front steps.

The front door opened before we all made it up steps to the porch. A young girl who I suspected to be in her early teens answered the door. She had visible bruises on her neck, black eyes, and busted lips. There was a prominent dark bruise on the side of her jaw. Her eyes were bloodshot clearly from crying all night.

"Evelyn," Angelina stepped forward and wrapped the young girl in her arms. "I am so sorry. The flood gates reopened, and the young girl sobbed in her arms.

We all stood in silence for several minutes letting Evelyn cry in Angelina's arms. It was awkward. Painful. Heartbreaking. She had been terrorized, viciously attacked, beaten, and almost raped. She had witnessed the murder of her little brother who gave his life to protect her virtue. It was a heavy burden for anyone to carry, let alone someone so young with such slender shoulders.

Crossing into the parlor felt surreal. The room was dark despite the bright cloudless sky above us. The mirrors were shrouded in black, the shutters drawn tightly, and a single candle glowed from the mantel offering no comfort to those within.

Mrs. Cameron was standing beside the empty hearth, eyes vacant as if she was looking but not seeing anything before her. Her blond hair was pulled up in a bun at the nap of her neck covered by a shroud of black lace. I was not sure exactly how old she was, but I knew she was younger than my mother, Amy. I speculated she was in her early 40's, but the last 24 hours had taken a toll on her. My heart ached for her. She was living through my biggest fear, and I had no words for her.

Sherriff Mitchell and Mr. Cameron joined us. Mr. Cameron looked like he had been through hell and back and was now simply trying to survive the aftermath.

"Mr. Marshall," The Sherriff cleared his throat loud enough to draw attention. "I need to speak with you, your son, and your son-in-law about last night."

"Shall we step outside?" David stepped forward.

"No need," Mrs. Cameron said in a voice that was barely audible. "Everyone present is well aware of what transpired here last evening."

"Just the same," Mr. Cameron interjected leading the men to the front door.

"Let me get some fresh tea." Maggie said awkwardly moving towards the kitchen.

"I will help you." I followed.

The kitchen was, for once, empty. Maggie picked up the kettle and took it to the water pump out the back door. I turned at the sound of approaching footsteps. The Cameron's eldest daughter, Carolanne, walked into the kitchen and lifted the tin of tea off the shelf.

"Thank you, Carolanne." She set the tin on the large table in the center of the kitchen.

"It was sweet of you all to come by." She smiled softly.

"I am so sorry for all you and your family are going through." I had no idea what to say to her.

"Mother refuses to allow any of the slaves near the house, even the house slaves who were not part of what happened and who fought for our family and put the fires out." Carolanne rambled twisting the linen cloth lying on the table.

"That is understandable." Maggie returned, setting the kettle on the hook above the fire in the hearth. "This tragedy has made me nervous all morning." My eyes met hers. "You are not the only one." She confessed.

"I feel bad that I have been so," I couldn't use the word anxious or hypervigilant since they did not exist yet and my mind blanked on a substitute.

"I know," Maggie nodded solemnly.

"I heard Sherriff Mitchell say the men involved will hang before suppertime." Carolanne fidgeted with the tea bags dropping one in the kettle. "Things have been on lockdown since father regained control." Her voice was small.

"My father sent over our overseer, Harley and our ranch handler, Mac before he went to bed last night." Maggie leaned against the table clearly uncomfortable.

"Yes," Carolanne nodded. "I saw them this morning when Evelyn and I brought out breakfast for all those here to help restore order. Several of our neighbors also sent their overseers and ranch handlers. The place has been in a constant state of frenzy since this started last night."

"Did they catch the person responsible for this?" I asked.

"Yes," Carolanne nodded towards the back door. "The Sherriff finally learned his name and where he escaped from right before you arrived. He is from some plantation in Georgia. He has already sent a couple of Deputy's to inform them."

"So, he will not be hung with the others?" I asked.

"Legally, the Sherriff cannot hang him since he is the legal property of someone else. He must be returned to his rightful owner who will decide his fate."

"That does not seem right since he is responsible for all this. He should be executed with the others." I declared.

"Do you know what a strong field hand costs?" Maggie asked without any malice in her voice.

"No," I shook my head feeling ignorant and out of place.

"A healthy adult male field hand slave costs about two thousand dollars." Maggie replied. "If the Sherriff hangs this man on behalf of his actions on Mr. Cameron's plantation, then Mr. Cameron would be responsible for paying his owner."

"But if he is a runaway," I objected.

"Inconsequential." Carolanne shrugged. "Property is property."

I wanted to say, 'they are people, not property', but I couldn't bring myself to say it. Not after seeing the violence, death, destruction and devastation left behind in the wake of this person and those others responsible for it, I could not bring myself to feel any sympathy for them. Instead, I simply nodded in understanding.

"Is everything all right in here?" Angelina approached the kitchen doorway.

"Yes," Maggie answered with a slight smile. "We were just talking about property rights."

"I see," Angelina pursed her lips. "Where is the tea set?"

"Um," Carolanne looked around. "I believe it is over here." She walked across the kitchen and began searching through the shelves.

It did not take long for a flustered Carolanne to employ the three of us to help her in her search. I noted but failed to mention the irony of the fact that she, nor these other two ladies, knew how their kitchen was organized.

~

The day passed slowly, and I felt incredibly out of place. I had never felt so invisible. Listening to them discuss everything, including all the little things about their Southern culture, lifestyle, world that I never learned about in any college lecture or textbook. It was enlightening, disheartening, and mystifying.

Witnessing this part of their world through their eyes felt like walking on Mars. Despite the months I had spent in Savannah, I had purposely avoided the slave quarters, talking to any of the slaves outside of the house slaves — all of whom were kind and compassionate. From what I have observed, my husband's family treated their slaves exceptionally well.

Still, I was not naïve enough to think that there weren't things going on around me that I was not aware of. Who knows the real story. I knew I didn't. And if I was being honest with myself, I didn't want to know.

I felt so torn between the knowledge that I held from my twenty-first century life and this seemingly provincial life in the nineteenth century. Nothing felt real anymore. Watching both my worlds fall apart in real time was so overwhelming I felt numb inside.

As the afternoon sun descended across the sky, the men stayed out of the house. I had no idea what was going on beyond the parlor doors, and I was too scared to ask. Neighbors and family members dropped by with food, offering comfort and condolences, and condemning the actions that had transpired. I observed quietly from the periphery, listening to all the gossip, plans, and fears from the women in our social circle.

Keifer, Thad, and David reappeared shortly before supper time. Their faces were solum and drawn. David expressed his condolences briefly to Mrs. Cameron and her daughters before escorting his family back home. No one spoke on the ride home.

Keifer climbed into bed after the house had gone silent. My nerves were frazzled, and I found myself jumping at every little noise. I curled up to my husband and rested my head upon his chest. The strong steady rhythm of his heart soothed my aching soul.

"I am ready to go home." His voice was barely a whisper.

"Me too," I agreed biting my lip. "What happened today?"

"Ten men were hung and a dozen more were disciplined." His voice was stoic.

"Disciplined?" I squeaked.

"Fifty lashes each." I bit my bottom lip hard enough to draw blood after hearing his words.

I thought Keifer had drifted off because he was quiet for a while. His arm tightened around me, and his breathing was even. I closed my eyes and tried to turn off the thoughts in my head.

"Thirteen days." Keifer's voice was soft and soothing. "Thirteen days and we will be sailing North."

"Are you sure you want to leave?" My heart felt torn.

"I love my family, Sidney. I do. But Terrace Falls is my home." He squeezed my shoulder. "You are my home."

29

WEDNESDAY, AUGUST 12, 2020

I ROLLED OVER TO FIND THE pillow empty beside me. Landon, and everyone else, was already up and dressed before I opened my eyes. I sat up and rubbed my eyes wishing I could sleep for a few more hours. The sun was shining brightly through the thin blinds. I could hear the chatter and laughter from the others gathered on the makeshift patio under the RV awning.

My bare feet touched the thin carpet, and I could feel the remanence of the beach scattered across the floor. I walked into the small washroom and brushed my feet in the tiny sink. This closet of a bathroom had no room to move around. I tried my best to make myself presentable before joining the others, but it was not easy.

"Good morning, sleepy head." Emily was the first to greet me and everyone followed with various choruses of 'morning'.

"We saved you some breakfast. Are you hungry?" Jocelyn handed me a plate with ham, pancakes, and scrambled eggs.

As I took the plate, my eyes rested on the small campfire surrounded by stones in the middle of their seating arrangement. Emily had the small skillet and griddle off to the side, already cleaned and ready to pack up.

"Coffee?" Robert offered, reaching for the kettle.

"Yes, please." It sounded heavenly.

I sat down in the empty lawn chair between Jackson and Landon. It felt too early for everyone to be so bright and cheerful. Even the sun seemed to be mocking me by blazing down upon us at this early hour. The dilemma between my two worlds weighed heavily on me. The tension in my chest left me feeling nauseated and confused.

"What is on the agenda today?" I picked at the food on my plate with no desire to eat anything.

"Well, there are a couple of properties in the panhandle Emily, and I would like to look at. We have an appointment with the realtor tomorrow." Robert explained.

"Tomorrow?" I inquired.

"We thought we could travel this afternoon and make it there before sundown. It would give us a chance to look around, check out the local cuisine and," Emily's voice trailed off as Jocelyn cut in.

"Snoop around." I couldn't help but smile at the look on my little sister's face.

"I did not say that." Emily chuckled.

"No. No. I agree." Jackson cut in. "Relocating to a new state, new community is difficult. You never know how people will receive or perceive you." He looked over at his wife. "If I remember correctly, you were less than hospitable when we first met."

"Oh, come on." Jocelyn's jaw hung open. "That is no fair." Jackson's smile widened as he smirked at her, knowing full well she could not say anything in front of Landon.

"What?" Landon's brow furled in confusion.

"It was — complicated." My sister glared at her husband.

"Anyway," Jackson pushed forward. "Moving across the country and trying to acclimate to a new community is challenging at best."

"But you will not be doing it alone this time." I noted. "Safety in numbers and all that." I tried to join the conversation.

"That's right." Jocelyn looked over at me and smiled gratefully.

"Okay," Landon took a swig of his coffee. "We survived the move from Chicago to Boston, right?" He looked around at all of us. "And our relationships and bonds only grew stronger as a result."

"Yes," Jackson agreed.

"So, the way I see it is as long as we all stick together, there is nothing we cannot overcome." Landon reached for my hand.

"I agree." Emily beamed. "We are indestructible."

"Amen," Jocelyn cooed causing everyone to erupt in laughter.

We cleaned up our area around the RV and packed everything up. It did not take us long to get on the road. Spirits were high and the teasing, and laughter came easily. For the first time in days, I felt relaxed and began to believe that everything might be okay. I wanted to believe it in my heart. I wanted to hold onto the belief that despite all the insanity in both my worlds, that kindness, love, and compassion still existed.

The miles slipped by with the hum of the tires on the Southern highway. Jackson and Landon bantered about sports and football statistics. Jocelyn, Emily and I flopped down across the large bed in back of the RV to relax and talk.

The luxury master suite was more elaborate than most hotels. My eyes scanned the room, and it was almost humorous how an RV could be fancier than our apartment. When most luxury RV's that I have seen seemed to be somewhat tacky with golds, grey, and black. True to Emily's nature, the colors were earth tones with subtle blues, browns, and green. It felt cozy and homey in a way that most RVs failed.

"Quick question," Jocelyn was lying on her back, staring up at the ceiling and kicking her feet off the edge of the bed like a restless little kid. "Am I the only one who finds it beyond weird that I am lying here beside you — my sister, in the twenty-first century, and yet in few weeks you are heading to Chicago to be there when I am born in the nineteenth century?" Jocelyn waved her arms around dramatically.

"I admit, it is a bit odd?" Emily laughed.

"Odd?" I turned my head towards her and rolled my eyes with sarcasm. "Next month I am sailing with my husband and six-month-old son up to the coast to board a train to Chicago. No air conditioning. No fans. Just humid, miserable September Southern weather with the bonus of a full gown, petticoat, and corset." I complained.

"Ugh," my sister groaned. "You realize my time isn't exactly a spa day, either." She looked towards Emily for confirmation.

"Hey now, I've experienced both and twenty-five years in the nineteenth century heat and humidity does not make much of a difference." Emily shrugged.

"True," I sighed heavily. "Isn't it funny how, if you consider say how much changed between 1965 and 1990, it seems monumental in comparison to 1865 to 1890."

"Um, not really." Emily protested. "There is a reason that time was called the Industrial Revolution." She smirked. "You should pay more attention in history class." She nudged me playfully.

"Okay, you may have a point." I conceded. "It's just that the others — the advances in technology, seem more significant."

"We would not have technology if it were not for the inventions created in the nineteenth century." Jocelyn pointed out.

"All right," I chuckled with exasperation. "I give up."

We stopped for late lunch around three at some small roadside dinner in the middle of nowhere. The booths were held together with duct tape, and the floor had more grease on it than the griddle, but the food smelled fabulous. We filed into a corner booth and picked up the laminated menus.

"They have fried mushrooms." Jackson's eyes lit up like a child on Christmas morning.

"Oh, I love those." Jocelyn chimed in.

"That's sick." Landon muttered giving me the side-eye.

"I agree," I grinned at him before glancing over the menu. "Look at this." I pointed at the appetizer list. "They have fried okra too."

"What is that?" Landon asked.

"I do not know." I pursed my lips. "And I do not plan on finding out."

"Fried okra is good." Jackson smirked.

"Damn skippy, it's good." The waitress appeared with water glasses. "But more important, we have the best chocolate malts, and peach cobbler this side of the Mississippi." The perky blond placed a glass down in front of each of us.

"What else would you recommend?" Robert asked, picking up his water glass.

"The double bacon cheeseburger is a favorite and the Cajan pepperjack chicken sandwich is mighty tasty too." She smiled.

"Then let's split it." Jocelyn reasoned. "We'll take three double bacon cheeseburgers, three Cajan pepperjack chicken sandwiches, six orders of seasoned wedge fries, six chocolate malts, six peach cobblers, two orders of fried pickles and two orders of fried mushrooms."

"Wow. You're hungry." I stared blankly at my sister.

"It's for all of us." She smacked me on the head with her menu.

"Well, thanks for asking us what we wanted." I smirked.

"I think it's a great idea." Emily smiled tilting her water glass towards my sister.

"I agree," Robert nodded.

"Very well," The perky waitress literally bounced away from the table causing all of us to burst out laughing.

"Is everyone in the South so chipper?" I said quietly.

"I believe it is mandatory." Jackson rolled his eyes with a smirk.

I spent the rest of our meal quietly observing my surroundings while my companions chattered between bites. It was strange and rather ironic how despite the vast difference of time, some things truly never change. People in the Southern region still maintain an overall more jovial persona whereas individuals residing in the North have the tendency, then as well as now, to be more reserved in their hospitality.

It was almost comical in an amusing sort of way. I knew I was more reserved and introverted in nature, as was Emily and Robert. Overall, Jackson, Jocelyn, and Landon were more extroverted. From what I understood of my family members behavior in their *other* lives, their personalities were almost mirror images of their current selves.

The six of us stuffed ourselves, laughed together and felt completely carefree like none of us had since the dawn of this year. It was wonderful. The food was magnificent. The company superb. We talked about stopping to look at a couple of properties in Arkansas that just came on the market that Emily had found. She appeared to be on a mission.

Jocelyn's phone rang in her purse, but she ignored it. Two seconds later my own phone rang. I glanced quizzically at my sister and reached for my purse. I fished my phone out after noticing our father's picture displayed on my screen.

"Hi Dad," I greeted him cheerfully.

"Sidney," his voice choked. "Is your sister with you?"

"Yes," I furrowed my brow at Jocelyn. "What's wrong?"

"It's my brother," I heard him sob deeply. "Nicholas was in a car accident this morning. I just got off the phone with the hospital."

"Is he alright? Where is he?" My voice caught in my throat.

"What's going on?" Jocelyn demanded, but I held up my hand.

"He was taken to Boston Medical Center, where he was pronounced dead." Shane sobbed.

I went numb. The air was sucked out of the room. I could not catch my breath as silent tears poured down my cheeks. Landon took hold of my hand, his face full of concern, but I could not register any of it. I handed the phone to Robert without another word and ran out of the diner.

I didn't even register the blinding afternoon sun nor heat that hit my face as soon as I stepped outside. I ran across the parking lot to the grassy area and got sick. I wiped my mouth with the back of my hand and slowly walked around the side of the building where we had parked the RV. I leaned against the wall and looked up at the sky.

"Why?" I muttered to no one.

I slid down the wall, drawing my knees up and burying my face. My uncle Nicholas' face flashed in my mind's eye. His bright eyes, kind smile, and gentle baritone voice. His patience with my never-ending questions about *E.V.E.* and his offering wisdom to my often-conflicted heart about my feelings between my two worlds. He was such a source of great comfort in my life that the notion of never seeing him again shattered my heart.

"Sidney?" Landon's voice was soft as he knelt beside me and put his hand on my shoulder. "I am so sorry." I kept my head down but nodded. "Jackson and Emily are with your sister. Robert is still on the phone with your dad."

"How is Jocelyn?" I met his eye.

"Not good," he said softly. "Emily has offered to fly us all home, but I think we should stay together."

"No," I shook my head. "I do not want to mess with airports and such. I would feel better if we all stayed together. Jocelyn and I need all of you more. Besides, my dad," I looked up at Landon. "Oh, God, my dad, I," my voice trailed off.

"Don't worry, you can call him back when you are ready and coordinate your plans." Landon reassured me, wrapping his around my shoulders and pulling me to him.

My family walked around the corner slowly. Landon and I shielded our eyes against the blinding afternoon sun. Robert and

Emily both had tear-filled eyes, and my sister was supported by her husband. Jocelyn's face was grief stricken. Her eyes were red and puffy.

"Your dad is going to meet us in Boston. Ethan and Liang are going to drive out with him." I nodded. "Apparently, he has taken a leave of absence from the hospital." Robert held out his hand to me helping me to my feet.

"Good." I muttered as Landon rose to his feet.

"Here," Emily handed me a large Styrofoam cup. "I got you a chocolate malt for the road." She put her arms around my shoulder in a motherly manner.

"Thank you," I whispered through my tears.

"I am so sorry for your loss. Your uncle was a good man." Emily squeezed me gently as the six of us walked towards the RV.

"The best." I agreed.

The miles drifted behind us as twilight settled over us. Jocelyn and I continued to fight back tears that seemed to fall relentlessly. Landon stayed beside me offering a shoulder to cry on and ears to listen. He knew Jocelyn and I were close to our uncle, but he was the only one aboard that did not fully understand how close we were or the depths of what he meant to my sister and me.

While my sister and I dearly loved our father and the Chandler's, Uncle Nicholas had been a light in the storm. He was our only blood tie to both of us in both our lives. He was our connection, our sounding board, our compass. Without him, we both felt adrift having been severed of our true anchor. In a strange way, my sister and I had just been orphaned.

30

WEDNESDAY, AUGUST 15, 1860

THE SOUND OF THUNDER STARTLED me from sleep. I propped myself up on my elbows peering towards the bassinet in hopes that the sudden noise did not awaken my son. The peaceful snores from the pillow next to mine assured me that my husband was left unbothered. I held my breath for another second anticipating my son's morning cries, but they never came.

I slowly crept from my bed and wandered towards the window. The thin curtain moved lazily in the light breeze. I pulled it aside and gazed out over the vast fields. I choked back a sob as I recalled the vivid details of my uncle's death in my *other* life. I rested my head against the window and covered my mouth with my hand. Tears rolled down my cheeks unabashed.

Dawn was slowly creeping over the tree line when the rain started. It felt perfect to me. I wanted to crawl back in bed and cry the rest of the day, but I knew that wasn't an option. It was impossible for me to explain the reason behind my tears. I wished my grandmother were here. At least it would give me someone to confide in. As it stood, I was alone and at this moment, I truly felt it.

My son finally stirred under the clatter of thunder to let me know of his displeasure at being awoken from his slumber. I swiftly changed his diaper. I had become an expert with cloth diapers and found them much more agreeable than the disposable ones. I carried him over to our bed and began feeding him. Keifer stirred a bit and rolled over. Within seconds, he was snoring once again.

The rain left the members of the household restless. The women and small children had gathered in the parlor. Angelina and I worked on Caroline's wedding gown. Angelina was a beautiful seamstress, and I was merely following her careful instructions. The light ivory satin cloth had a slight entrechat pattern when shown in a certain light. It was obviously very expensive material that I was certain had come from Europe — Paris perhaps. But I did not ask. Maggie was creating the most elaborate delicate lace veil for her younger sister. Her elegant talent raveled any I had ever seen before.

Caroline fluttered about anxiously watching over our work. Her pacing around the downstairs corridors was enough to make any sane individual lash out irrationally. She fretted about the bouquet she would carry, whether Phillip was having second thoughts, and listed numerous things that could go wrong during the reception following the ceremony at the church.

Trixie and Edith were most helpful in wrangling their little nephew. My chubby little son was determined to explore every corner of his surroundings. The young girls laughed as they chased him, joined him on the parlor floor, and crawled around with him. He was enjoying all the attention and the laughter of the three of them filled the room with warmth.

Looking around the room filled with the ladies I was related to by marriage; I felt a kinship with them that brought about my fierce protective nature. Angelina had become a loving mother figure to me as our bond grew over the long summer months.

The men had made themselves scarce. They left right after breakfast for the Cameron's plantation. Keifer told me men from neighboring plantations were gathering to restore the front rooms of the Cameron's home and rebuild their barn. Families around the area had gifted various livestock to the family as most of theirs were killed or stolen in the insurrection.

It was heartwarming to witness how the entire community and all of Savannah had rallied around the Cameron's. The overwhelming sense of community was demonstrated daily by both men and women who came together to comfort, support, and restore the broken family.

"Mother," Caroline's voice broke my train of thought. "Can you bring in the sides another half inch each? It hangs loose." She pinched the fabric on each side to demonstrate.

"Darling, you do not want it that tight." Angelina stood up and gathered the sides carefully. "I will take it in another quarter of an inch, but that is all."

"Thank you," her daughter beamed with satisfaction.

"You need to calm down." Maggie did not look up from her task. "You are going to work yourself into hysteria before you ever make it to the church."

"Hush now, Maggie." Angelina glanced over her shoulder at her eldest daughter. "You were worse before your wedding." A sly smile of remembrance spread across her lips. "Much worse."

"I was not," Maggie said defensively, but shot me a smirk before looking back at her work.

"I believe all brides are nervous before their wedding." I said with assurance. "I know, I was."

"Your wedding was most beautiful." Angelina sighed. "Your grandmother made your gown, did she not."

"No." I blushed. "My mother did. She made it for herself when she married my father. It was her gown that I wore."

"I am sure she would have been honored to have you wear her gown on your wedding day." Angelina took my hand and squeezed it gently.

"Do you still have it?" Caroline asked.

"Yes," I nodded. "I have saved it for my own daughter on her wedding day if your brother and I are so blessed. If not, then perhaps our future daughter-in-law or another female relative may want to wear it."

"Did you bring it with you?" Edith asked.

"Oh, are you planning on borrowing it?" Maggie teased her 13-year-old sister.

"Edith is going to marry Phillip's little brother, Josiah." Trixie chimed in. "She wishes they could have a double wedding on Saturday." She giggled, causing Edith to toss a pillow at her little sister.

"Shut up," Edith glared at Trixie. "I do not." But the blush on her cheeks betrayed her.

The adults in the room all smiled but said nothing to the young girl.

"I saw Josiah at the engagement announcement," I smiled at Edith. "He is very handsome." And he was. He bore a striking resemblance to his older brother, Phillip.

"Yes, he is." Edith said quietly.

"Perhaps in a few years." Angelina smiled at her daughter.

"Pappa said we have to be eighteen." Trixie pointed out still smirking. "That's five years."

"I can count." Edith fired back, narrowing her eyes.

"Girls," Angelina's tone hushed both her younger daughters, but they continued to glare at each other.

The remainder of the day passed with little disturbance. Before nightfall Caroline's wedding gown was perfect and Maggie had finished her exquisite veil. Angelina held dinner until the men returned shortly after dusk. They were bone tired, filthy, but looking content with the day's progress.

I felt perfectly at ease once Keifer and I settled into our chambers. I had grown to love Gable Gardens and its inhabitants. His family had proven themselves to be loving, bonded, and compassionate despite my continued reservations about Eugenia and Victoria. Both of whom continued to ignore me as I did them. There would never be any love lost between us. Still, I remained baffled how the two of them were related to the rest of the Marshall's. They were different in both their traits and core aspects of their being.

31

SATURDAY, AUGUST 15, 2020

MY FATHER WAS BESIDE HIMSELF BY the time he arrived at Emily and Robert's midday. My brother and his girlfriend stood awkwardly in the foyer while my enraged father screamed about the injustice brought about by these ridiculous lockdowns and quarantine mandates.

It appeared he had not gotten past the visitor's desk at the hospital. Instead, they had sent someone down to talk with him regarding his brother's remains. Citywide quarantines and lockdowns had suspended all funerals. The hospital refused to release my uncle's body due to Covid restrictions. My father was forced to have his brother cremated at a local funeral home and the remains sent to Robert and Emily's home.

Emily, ever the gracious soul, had spent the last several days holding my sister and I together. She moved in and embraced my father in the foyer. His rage quickly gave way to sobs. He lowered his head to her shoulder and wept for the brother he had spent more than a decade estranged from, only to reconnect and build a stronger bond with.

I recalled the impact of my dad's brother, Monte's death from my youth. Uncle Nicholas had tried in vain at the time to explain the truth behind *E.V.E.* to his older brother. But my father would have none of it and in his anger and grief, turned his back on his youngest brother. It had been Jocelyn who had reached out to Uncle Nicholas and brought him back into our lives.

Looking at how uncomfortable my brother and his girlfriend looked, I moved towards them. I wrapped my arms around Ethan and Liang, trying to fight back my own tears. I noticed Ethan wore the same expression as Landon. They understood we lost a family member, but they lacked the depth of our despair. Their lack of knowledge about *E.V.E.* left them somewhat bewildered to our consuming grief.

"Can I get you some tea?" Emily guided my father to the couch in the front parlor.

Ethan and Liang slowly followed. Their faces were masks of uncertainty and confusion. The relationship between Ethan and Jackson had never truly mended after Jackson and Jocelyn's surprise marriage. I had hoped that time and distance would have healed those wounds, especially after our father had made peace with the young couple. But the tension between Ethan and our sister and her husband remained evident.

"I will put the kettle on." I told Emily and tugged on my brother's arm to make him follow me into the kitchen.

"What?" the annoyance in his voice was clear.

"First off, hello." I picked up the kettle and carried it over to the sink. "Secondly, why do you look so irritated?" I turned on the facet and began filling the kettle.

Ethan leaned against the side of the island like he was considering his words carefully. He had grown into a striking young man with our father's good looks and height. His hair was tasseled, and a bit longer than it should be. His athletic build served to enhance his natural features.

"Liang and I came because I did not want Dad driving this far on his own." My little brother sighed audibly. "I just fail to understand why Dad seems almost inconsolable when he hasn't been close to his brother in years." He rubbed his hand over his face.

"Can't you?" I set the kettle back on the stove and turned on the gas burner. "You and Jocelyn were inseparable growing up. I often found myself jealous of the bond you shared. But now you two rarely speak." I turned towards him and put my hand on his arm.

"Your point?" he stated not hiding his distain.

"Tell me," I met his eye. "How would you react if something happened to her?" I watched as his face softened.

"I would be devastated." Ethan admitted.

"You know she misses you." I squeezed his arm gently.

"I miss her too." He glanced towards the parlor. "But her life is here now and mine is in Chicago."

"And what does that have to do with the price of eggs?" I glared at him pointedly. "There was this marvelous invention about a century and a half ago called a telephone. It works quite well. It even allows me to talk with our dad about once a week even from Boston to Chicago."

"Fine," he huffed. "I get it. I am a terrible brother to both of you." Ethan rolled his eyes. "But my phone hasn't exactly been ringing nonstop either." He countered.

"Well, after reaching out for months without a response, I guess we both sort of gave up." I shrugged. "We just started calling Liang instead. She answers."

"Fair enough." He straightened up to his full height. "I will try to do better."

I brought out the silver serving tray from the walk-in pantry and set it on the island. I started arranging the cups and saucers adding a small dish for the lemons and a sugar dish. I took two lemons out of the crisper in the island and placed them on the chopping block. Without thinking, I began slicing them into small wedges and adding them to the small dish. Ethan watched me with a curious expression.

"Aren't you domesticated," he chuckled. "And here I thought you were going to be a career woman like our mother."

"I am nothing like our mother." I arranged everything on the tray with precision.

"I guess you've changed." Ethan shrugged casually.

"No," I paused looking straight at him. "I simply grew up and got my priorities straight. I realized that family is more important than a paycheck."

"You know she's getting remarried." He picked up a blueberry scone I was adding to the tray.

"So, I've heard." I playfully smacked his hand as he took a bite.

"This is fabulous," he mumbled with his mouth full. I guess some things never change.

"Emily made them." I turned back to the stove and transferred the hot water to the silver serving kettle with fresh tea leaves.

"She should start a bakery." My little brother took another large bite failing to wipe the crumps scattered across the front of his shirt or the island.

"She enjoys baking for her family." I picked up the tray and carried it to the parlor. Ethan and his trail of crumbs followed me.

The afternoon faded into evening. The Chandler's insisted Shane, Ethan, and Liang stay with them. They saw no reason to waste funds on hotels when they had plenty of spare rooms where everyone could stay comfortably and well fed. Shane resisted initially, but Emily was persistent about the importance of family and support during times like this.

Ethan and Liang brought in their luggage and Emily showed them to their rooms. After Emily had everyone settled, she, Robert and Jackson started dinner. My sister and I took our father out on a walk under the premises of getting some fresh air. His eyes were still red and held a weariness that was troubling.

My father centered himself between us as we strolled towards the small park at the edge of the neighborhood. For the first half of our journey, not a word was spoken. The evening air was warm carrying a gentle breeze that embraced us. The expression on Shane's face said that although his body was here, his mind was elsewhere. I was sure he had spent many hours after receiving that dreadful call thinking about his childhood and the two brothers he had lost.

"Can I ask you both something?" Shane asked as we turned the corner into the park.

"Of course," I responded immediately.

"Yes," Jocelyn added.

"How are my brother's doing?" He paused for a moment looking between us. "I mean, in your *other* lives." He said in a lower voice.

"Well," my sister began. "I saw him yesterday at my parent's house. He came by with his son, Tristen who was suffering from an ear infection."

"How many sons does he have there?"

"Five," she took our father's hand and squeezed it.

"Five?" Shane chuckled softly. "Really? How wonderful." He said more to himself than to us.

"Yes. There is Oliver who is the eldest. Followed by Ashton, Quinten, Tristen, and Jeremiah is the youngest." She explained.

"And what is his wife's name?" Shane inquired.

"Lydia. She is a lovely woman from Tennessee. He met her on his way home after the war. He collapsed on her parent's property, and she kindly nursed him back to health." Jocelyn grinned. "She truly was a Godsend."

"I wish I could meet her." Our father said softly. "I am so jealous that you both will see him again and Monte too."

"I am sorry, daddy." Jocelyn said in a small voice. A tear ran down our father's face as he nodded and hastily brushed it aside.

"And what about you?" Shane looked over at me. "Are you close with my brothers in your time *there* as well."

"No." I looked at him grimly. "Not exactly."

"But I thought," his voice trailed off.

"Patrick, Monte, and Nicholas are my younger brothers in my *other* time." I sat down beside him on the bench. "My mother passed away in childbirth and my father remarried shortly after to their mother. She does not care much for me as I look like my mother. After they were wed and relocated to Chicago, I stayed with my grandparents in Braintree, Massachusetts." I explained briefly. "Because of that, I really do not know my brothers at all. If it were not for Patrick's wife, Annabelle, I would know nothing of them."

"So, Nicholas is younger than you?" Shane looked confused.

"Yes, I believe he is six or seven years younger."

"If I understand this correctly, when you wake up tomorrow, you will be the same age you are now, but in a different time. Am I right?" I nodded and he turned towards my sister. "I know, for you it's the 1880s. But for you," he met my eye filled with questions.

"When I wake up, I will be at my husband's family plantation on the outskirts of Savannah, Georgia in August 1860. We are visiting his family to introduce them to our son." I smiled warmly. "Although I lost my son *here*, he was born in March 1860 *there*."

"You're a mother," he beamed. "I have a grandson."

"Yes, in a way." I laughed.

"What did you name him?" he asked.

"Keifer Lee Marshall, II, after his father." Shane nodded.

"And you?" he looked at my sister.

"Is due to arrive shortly after I arrive in Chicago," I said quickly, playfully rolling my eyes at my sister.

"What?" Shane laughed fully. "Are you serious?"

"Unfortunately," Jocelyn muttered with a smirk.

"We are heading to Chicago at the end of September to visit our family there through the holidays." I told him.

"And will Monte and Nicholas be *there*?" he looked hopeful.

"Monte is there now, but Nicholas is up at Westpoint Military Academy. But he will be home for Christmas." I grinned.

"So, he must be," Shane chewed on his bottom lip causing me to realize where I'd picked up the trait. "About what, 19 — 20?"

"I believe so," I held his hand. "I cannot wait to see him so young. It is hard for me to fathom."

"The lives you both lead." His eyes turned sorrowful again. "It is truly amazing. To see what you both have seen, endured, witnessed. I wish I had been so blessed."

"Dad," Jocelyn patted him arm drawing his attention back to her. "At times it is a blessing, but at other times it isn't." My sister's eye met mine. "Look at what Sidney is walking into. She has a young son, a husband who will travel with the Union Army as a surgeon throughout the duration of the war, and she will be alone at her estate to care for her son and elderly grandmother for the next four years."

"My goodness," his voice was barely a whisper. "I had not realized."

"I will be fine." I assured him. "Besides, I am hoping I can talk Patrick's wife, Annabelle and Emily to join me with their children at Terrace Falls."

"That would be good for all of you." My father agreed. "I would sleep much better knowing Emily was there with you too."

"You are forgetting something, Dad." I smiled coyly at him. "I am actually older than Emily there."

"Good Lord," My father ran his hands through his hair. "I will never get this straight."

"That's alright, Dad." Jocelyn chuckled. "We're still working on it too."

Shane nodded but looked back down at his hands. His shoulders slumped forward and shook slightly. Silent tears rolled down his cheeks and crashed on his folded hands. I wrapped my arm around his shoulder and pulled him to me. He buried his head in my shoulder and sobbed. Jocelyn covered his hands in hers and offered words of comfort. She pulled a handkerchief from her pocket and dabbed his cheeks.

"What is this?" Shane reached for her wrist with a slight smile. "You carry a handkerchief?" I couldn't help it; I laughed out loud.

"Yes," my sister looked almost embarrassed. "I know they are outdated, but still," she shrugged with a blush in her cheeks.

"Fine," I rolled my eyes and pulled a handkerchief out of my back pocket. "You are not alone."

"And what other traits have followed you two across time?" My father laughed genuinely through his tears.

"Oh, I don't know." Jocelyn eyed me carefully. "I suppose our grammar is more proper, although not as proper as my husband and his family."

"I suppose our manner of dressing. I guess I dress more modestly since the barrier came down." I admitted.

"And I guess I dress more feminine since mine depleted." My sister confessed the obvious making our father laugh even harder.

"I would say so. Getting you into a dress when you were younger — well, let's just say I would have had better luck getting your brother in one." Considering how hypermasculine our little brother was, his words lightened the mood considerably.

The old saying that laughter through tears is the best medicine, understood the physical and emotional truth behind it. The moon was visible through the trees but was stunted by the numerous streetlights scattered about the park. I closed my eyes for just a moment thinking about how modernization and technology have stolen some of the most beautiful aspects of life.

"I think one of the things I miss the most in this time is the lack of peace, innocence, and the strong sense of family and community." I said softly. "I never understood that until I had it."

"I know exactly what you mean." An expression of deep understanding crossed my sister's face. "Growing up here I always believed our family was normal, a bit dysfunctional," she chuckled humorlessly. "But normal. We did not have a close relationship with our grandparents, our aunts, uncles, or cousins. There were not big holiday Christmas' spent with extended family." She shrugged. "And I truly believed we were like every other American family. Sadly, I was right about that." I nodded, but my dad looked at her as if she were speaking a foreign language. "But *there,*" she shook her head slightly. "I learned what the true meaning of family, honor, loyalty, and community is."

"I think it is horrific how in this age, most have lost the fundamental foundation of what made America so strong." I said with sorrow.

"I wish I could see the world through your eyes." Shane took each of our hands in his. "Both of yours. It must be truly remarkable."

"It is in many ways," Jocelyn agreed. "But it is difficult in others." She sighed heavily. "At first it was really hard. I had to constantly monitor everything I did, what I said, and how I reacted. It was mentally exhausting. For months I clung to Jackson and his family always in fear of making a mistake."

"I know what you mean." I agreed with a subtle nod. "I spent more time around my grandmother because she understood, even if it was only a little bit since even our times vary so greatly. In a way, I felt very much alone. I was so envious of you for having Jackson and his family with you wherever you were."

"I had not realized how challenging it was, especially for you." My father squeezed my hand lovingly.

"It is." I acknowledged. "But it is also incredibly rewarding. Not only the family and community, but the culture. Being able to witness a world I had only ever read about in history class is unlike anything I could have imagined." Jocelyn laughed softly.

"It is amazing, but also frustrating." My sister laughed. "Knowing what lies ahead and being powerless to do anything about it."

"Explain," Shane raised an eyebrow at her.

"Okay," she leaned back a bit. "Hitler will be born shortly in my *other* time. Should we take a trip to Europe and end his life before he commits mass genocide? What about Stalin or Mussolini?"

"Or the horrors of reconstruction that occurred after the assassination of President Lincoln? Should I travel to Fords Theater and prevent that?" I looked pointedly at my father. "What effects could we have on the future if we acted on what we know? The domino effect would directly impact life as we know it today, but would save thousands and in some cases, millions of lives. Would you chance it?"

"I hadn't thought of it that way." Our father pondered.

"We're damned if we do. Damned if we don't." I shrugged.

"We could potentially be trading one tyrannical leader for another and who knows — the end result could be much worse." Jocelyn pursed her lips.

"The proverbial catch 22." Shane chuckled humorlessly.

"Something like that," my sister shrugged.

"No. It is exactly like that." I said pointedly. "That is why *E.V.E.* is more of a curse than a blessing."

"Well, I suppose we best head back. I am sure your brother is most uncomfortable after the way he's treated Jackson in the past." My dad smirked.

"Serves him right." I said, getting to my feet. "Perhaps he'll realize what an ass he's been.

"I doubt it," Jocelyn muttered as she took my dad's arm and began walking back towards the house.

32

SATURDAY, AUGUST 18, 1860

THE CORIDOR WAS QUIET DESPITE THE frenzy of activity carrying on downstairs and about the grounds. My footsteps echoed on the hardwood floors. The air felt hot and still showing no signs of the upcoming season. I knocked on Caroline's bedroom door just after noon.

"Yes?" Caroline's voice was a bit shaky.

"It's me, Sidney. May I come in?"

"Please," her voice trailed off.

I found her sitting at her vanity table. She was wearing a blush pink robe with her dark blonde hair styled in curls that cascaded down her back. Small sprigs of baby breath adorned throughout her curls. Her wedding gown was laid out across her bed. Tallie fussed with the final touches to her hair.

"You look so beautiful." I assured her. "No bride has ever looked so lovely on her wedding day."

"You are too kind," she blushed anxiously.

"We have less than an hour before the ceremony. We should get you into your gown." I placed my hand on her shoulder.

"Yes, ma' lady." Tallie moved quickly, picking up the gown with great care.

"I feel so incredibly silly," Caroline slowly rose to her feet placing her hand on my arm with a nervous laugh. "I have dreamt of this day for so long and now that it has arrived, I feel like I cannot breathe."

"Any bride who does not confess as much on her wedding day is a foolish woman." I assured her.

"I am so happy you are here with me today," Caroline took both my hands in hers. "I want you to know I consider you as so much more than my sister-in-law. This summer I am so happy that I got to build a real sisterly bond with you." She reached out and hugged me tightly. "I shall miss you greatly." She whispered.

"And I you." I released her and wiped a tear off my cheek. "You realize, I have only brother's, you are my first true sister."

"And I shall be here with you always." Caroline beamed.

"Now we must get you dressed. It wouldn't be fitting for you to be married in your chemise." I laughed.

"Mother would surely faint away." She chuckled lightly.

"No. Your mother is made of heartier stock that that. Though I do believe it would be the shame of Eugenia and Victoria's existence." I reasoned.

"That would be reason enough for me to forego my gown if it would not bring shame upon Phillip's family." Caroline simpered.

"I believe both his parents would actually find humor rather than shame in it." I admitted. "You are marrying into a family with true grit — much like your own parents." I admitted, although I failed to mention that while I found both of Phillip's parents sharing equal distribution of strength and gumption, the distribution between her parents, I had observed throughout the summer was very unequal in her mother's rather than her father's favor. I understood clearly why Angelina so desperately wanted my husband to claim his birthright. Keifer had inherited both her gumption and tenacity alongside her personality.

"They are good people." She agreed with a slight tilt of her head. "I feel very fortunate."

"Phillip is the fortunate one." I picked up her dress and helped her with it.

It took Tallie and I about ten minutes to get the gown fastened, tied, and perfect. Caroline looked beautiful. A low knock on the door drew our attention away from the full-length mirror.

"Caroline, darling, tis mother." Angelina's voice was soft.

"Please, come in." Caroline ran her fingers nervously over the front of her gown before turning towards her mother. "How do I look?"

"Breathtaking," Tears glistened in her mother's eyes as her hand rose to her mouth while she stared at her daughter. "No bride has ever been more beautiful."

"Thank you, momma." Caroline's voice cracked as she reached for her mother's hands, pulling her into a tight embrace.

"Well," I said dabbing my eyes with my handkerchief. "Mother, would you help me with the bride's veil?" For once I was thankful, I was not wearing makeup.

"Yes, of course." Tallie carefully handed it to her.

With Angelina on one side and me on the other, we carefully placed the veil over Caroline's curls. Angelina's hands were steady as she placed each hairpin with precision artfully hidden beneath curls and baby breath.

"There," Angelina stood back forcing herself to smile. "You are ready." Tears spilled out silently and rolled down her cheeks. She patted her pockets in regret. "Oh, bother."

"Here," I handed her my handkerchief with a small smile.

"Thank you," she dabbed her eyes with care. "My mind is so scattered today." A small smile played on her lips.

"I understand." I patted her arm as we both stepped back and admired the bride.

The rest of the family milled about downstairs waiting for us to emerge. Everyone was dressed in their Sunday best. The younger ones were restless and constantly being chastised by their older siblings to sit still and not get dirty.

We were divided mostly by family into various carriages for our trip to the church. However, due to the number of my husband's siblings and Maggie's children, Edith and Trixie joined us. My son was excited to ride with his two favorite playmates. He babbled and cooed stretching his chubby little arms towards them. Finally, I relented and handed him over to Edith.

"I cannot believe how much he has grown since you arrived." Edith looked sorrowfully for a moment. "Do you really have to leave?"

"I am afraid so, my darling. My home is up North now, and I have patients to attend to." Keifer tried to explain.

"But your family is here." Trixie replied stubbornly, narrowing her eyes at her older brother.

"That is true as well." He tilted his head looking carefully at them. "I am surprised you two are giving me grief. You were younger than my son when I married Sidney." He told Edith with a sly smile. "I am surprised you of all people would be giving me grief."

"But surely ma and papa," Trixie began but was interrupted by her sister.

"Victoria said you refused your birthright." Edith looked pointedly at me. "Because of her." She added in a smaller voice.

"That is not true." Keifer objected. "I moved North before I ever met Sidney."

"But that was for school. You stayed because you married her." Edith proclaimed.

"Eugenia said if Sidney was a real loving and devoted wife, she would honor our family over hers." Trixie announced with a pout.

"Figures," I muttered only loud enough for my husband to hear.

"Trixie. Edith." Keifer took an exasperated sigh. "I want you both to listen to me very carefully." His little sisters nodded. "I fell in love with Sidney. That is why I married her. Our home, our life. Our land is in Braintree, Massachusetts. You ask Phillip before the ceremony today if he would not follow Caroline to the ends of the earth to be with her. If he says no, then Caroline should end their engagement immediately."

"But Phillip is a Southerner. He would never abandon his family and move north." Edith said defiantly.

"I did not abandon my family. The landscape of it simply changed." Keifer informed her.

The hooves pounding on the dry dirt road rang loudly in my ears. I looked out the side window watching the cloud of dust being kicked up in our wake. The hurt and betrayal of Trixie and Edith's words cut me more than I wanted to admit. I had grown so fond of each of them throughout the summer. I loved the way they played and cared for my son, but now it somehow felt like a farce.

My husband squeezed my hand. A soft reminder that I wasn't alone. Still, I knew his little sisters' words wounded him deeply. He had been so excited to get to know them during our visit, but now I knew he could see how Eugenia and Victoria had poisoned them against both of us. Their bitterness seemed to radiate from their pores, infecting all those we loved.

"Victoria said that when the war comes, our family and Sidney's will fight each other." Trixie huffed. "She said you will shoot at Thad and Phillip and our neighbors to steal our slaves from us." Edith narrowed her eyes at her older brother.

"If a war should happen between the Northern states and the Southern states, I will not fight. I am a physician. I heal people, not tear them apart. I will help all soldiers regardless of which side they are on." Keifer said with conviction.

"Why would you heal men who are trying to kill your kin?" Edith asked.

"Who said that?" the frustration in my husband's voice was evident.

"Eugenia," the young girls said in unison.

"Figures," I whispered.

Our carriage rounded the bend revealing the only local church in our area. It was a large one-room building with a tall steeple and an iron cross on the top. We spent many long hours here on Sunday morning listening to Pastor Malcom drone on in the suffocating heat. His services, unlike those given by our Pastor Elliot, felt more like a lecture than a sermon. I cannot say I took a liking to the man; a sentiment I kept to myself.

I took a deep breath and said a silent prayer that the ceremony conducted at the height of the heat of the day would be short and swift. However, a part of me knew it was wishful thinking. Pastor Malcom would conduct the wedding sermon with the inflated sense of fanfare he did everything else.

My fears were soon confirmed. The ceremony was long and tedious. But Caroline and Phillip were the pure image of love and happiness. They stood face to face with their hands intertwined and a look of peace and love on their faces. When they were finally announced husband and wife, the guests of family, friends, and neighbors erupted in glorious cheers.

The reception at Gable Gardens afterwards was a splendor unlike anything I had ever witnessed before. David and Angelina had spared no expense in celebrating the union between the Marshall's and the Rhoades. The joining of these two prominent families and their empires created a formidable foe for anyone attempting to corner the economic market.

The kitchen had been busy for several days creating enough food and desserts to feed an army. Now it was spread across half a dozen picnic tables in the shade under a row of mature trees. The house slaves were dressed in their finest uniforms carrying silver trays with goblets of wine or punch and little desserts.

I put my son down for his afternoon nap upstairs as soon as we returned home. He was already cranky and overstimulated. It took me the better part of an hour to get him fed, and asleep. Although I appreciated Tallie's offer to do it herself, I knew she was already struggling with a colic Tobias. He was an incredibly fussy baby who spent most of his time screaming, especially at night. Poor Tallie looked exhausted, and my heart went out to her.

Keifer was in his element. I found him sitting in the shade amongst a circle of his childhood friends. For a moment I got a glimpse of the boy he once was in the man laughing before me. Bonnie's husband Randall was the only man I immediately recognized. The small, but rowdy group of gentlemen were indulging themselves in wine and smoking cigars.

"No matter their age, when they get together, they act like they haven't a care in the world." Bonnie walked up beside me holding a goblet of punch.

"Some things never change," I smirked. "How are you feeling?"

"Good," She nodded with her hand rested on her visible baby bump.

"And Mr. Farwell?" I had noticed he and his wife were absent today which I expected.

"His recovery is slow and painful." Her voice dropped an octave. "As you said it would be." I nodded. "My father-in-law is quite frustrated. It is difficult to keep pushing him, but I know it is best for him."

"It is," I agreed. "I know it is difficult for you, but you must remain strong, or his muscles will weaken permanently."

"When are you heading to Chicago?" Bonnie started wandering slowly across the grounds, and I followed.

"The end of September."

"Are you going by train?" she asked, pausing to take a little cake off the tray of a passing house slave. "Would you like one?"

"No, thank you." I smiled. "Eventually. We are going to take a ship from Savannah up to Boston where we will pick up my grandmother, Marissa. She is going to travel with us to Chicago."

"I envy you," she placed her hand on my arm with a heavy sigh. "I have never been out of Georgia except for once when Randall took me to Charlestown, South Carolina before our children were born."

"All the more reason for you to come visit me up North." I patted her arm gently.

"Tell me, what is it like?" she tilted her head eyeing me carefully. "Is it as bad as what we have been told?"

"Bad?" I swallowed back the bile in my throat. "How do you mean bad?"

"No. No. Not like that." Bonnie gushed. "I did not mean like that." She lowered her voice. "Do people up North hate us and want to destroy us?" I frowned. "I overheard Randall and his brothers talking on the porch the other night."

"The abolitionists are making a lot of noise," I said carefully. "They are projecting a lot of exaggerations and falsehoods about Southern life and slavery. Most people that live in the North have never been on a plantation, so they believe the worst. *Uncle Tom's Cabin* ignited a fire that will be difficult to extinguish." I admitted.

"Randall said state officials are pushing towards secession." I nodded biting my lower lip. "I fear that if any of the Southern states leave the Union, it will spark a war, especially if Mr. Lincoln is elected to office."

"I agree," I said simply because I didn't know what else to say.

"But he reassured his brothers that since the Southern states had removed Lincoln from the ballots, it would be impossible for him to be elected." Bonnie visibly let out a sigh of relief as I smiled tightly.

I wanted to ask her if her husband had also mentioned that the Democrat party had also split basically dividing the vote with all Democrats nationwide and in doing so, was almost guaranteeing a

Republican victory before the first vote was cast. But I didn't. I couldn't. And it made me sick.

My eyes absorbed my surroundings. These people that I spent the summer with, and learned about their lives, had accepted me as one of their own. I recalled their initial hesitation, reluctance even, at befriending someone born and raised up North. The skepticism of anyone from a Northern state was not unfounded. But their unwavering faith in my husband and their trust in his judgement won them over more than anything else.

Rumors and gossip of my skills as a nurse and caregiver circulated, especially after Mr. Farwell's stroke. His slow but steady recovery and progress had endeared me to many. Still, their newfound respect and affection for me, did not quelch their desire for Southern independence from the suffocating and over-reaching federal government. Their fervent belief of states' rights over federal stranglehold remained steadfast.

My time in the South had greatly altered my previous notions of many things I thought about the South and its inhabitants. I realized my unique circumstances having fallen in love with a Southern man. Most Northerners had no direct knowledge of the South and only knew what they were told in newspapers. Of which, I now understood to be greatly misconstrued and heavily biased. However, I learned that sentiment worked in both directions depending on which side of the Mason-Dixon line one stood.

It saddened me to realize that nothing has changed in more than a century and a half. Racial tension and discrimination fueled by those supposed leaders in Washington was disheartening. Time has proven mute to the disparities and almost futile in good men's intention to change things.

"Sidney?" Bonnie's voice cut through my thoughts. "Are you alright? You look pale." Her voice was thick with concern.

"My apologies," I smiled weakly. "My thoughts were elsewhere."

"I know I should not speak of the election." She chuckled lightly. "Randall reminds me constantly not to be so outspoken." She waved her hand dismissively. "But my father always encouraged me to read and expand my knowledge."

"My grandfather taught me the same." I looped her arm through mine. "Randall should encourage you as well. This is our country too and we should know what is going on as it affects us as well."

"My father believed the same." Bonnie said with a sly grin. "He was very supportive of my education and even wanted to send me to a finishing school up North, but my mother and grandparents fought ardently against it."

"Why?" I asked although I already suspected her answer.

"They did not want me to be influenced by Northern culture and nonsense." She laughed. "If they could only see me now." She squeezed my arm affectionately. "I consider you one of my dearest friends and you're a damn Yankee." She whispered with a smirk.

"And proud of it to boot." I chuckled.

"They look so happy." Bonnie looked towards the newlyweds.

"That's not happiness. That's naivete." I scoffed, trying not to laugh.

"Ah, but it's the ignorance of blissful naivete." She sighed heavily. "Do you recall it?" I nodded. "When we believed that marriage would be fun."

"And then we were confronted with their snoring, belching, and flatulence. And the dream evaporated on the wind." I snorted with laughter.

"But those first months of marriage," she looked over at Randall with a soft expression. "They were wonderful."

"Yes, they were." I agreed. "Where is your family?" I turned towards her. "You never mentioned where you were from."

"My family has a small plantation near Atlanta."

"I see," my eyes fell on my own husband who remained laughing and drinking with his childhood friends.

"Have you ever been?" Bonnie tilted her head.

"No, I have not." Not in this lifetime anyway. I was sure the Atlanta she was referring to did not exist in the one I vividly recalled.

"It is a beautiful place. It has grown a great deal since they built the train depot." She considered her words. "I fear the lack of railroads throughout the South may be troublesome if our country does divide."

"I agree," I wanted to tell her how significant the difference would be, but I held my tongue.

"Do you believe a war is coming?" Bonnie leaned closer to me and whispered in a low voice.

"Yes," I whispered keeping a smile on my face as Keifer looked over at me and smiled. "I believe the war will commence in less than a year.

"Oh, my goodness," her eyes widened, and she instinctively put her hand on her prominent baby bump. "It is going to be bad, isn't it?"

"Yes," I could see the fear in her eyes as her bottom lip trembled. "Let's walk," I guided her away from the reception.

Bonnie and I walked a while in silence. I knew her mind was reeling with ominous thoughts of war and what it would mean for her family. The fear of what could happen was evident on her face as she kept one hand protectively on her baby bump. I wanted so desperately to reassure her that everything would be alright, but I could not bring myself to lie to my dear friend.

"Are you sure?" she choked out the words trying to stifle a sob.

"Unfortunately, I am." My lips pursed in a frown.

"What can I do?" Tears rolled down her cheeks, but she did not brush them away.

"Sit down," I lead her over to a large tree covered in Spanish moss that had a small wooden bench beneath it. "You should not be standing so long in the sun." I tried to keep my voice light.

I looked around making sure we were a good distance from the rest of the party members. I did not want anyone to accidentally or purposely eavesdrop on our conversation. I knew I was dancing on a thin line that I could not cross, but my love for Bonnie and her family outweighed my doubts.

"So, you believe the country will split?" Bonnie fidgeted with her hands nervously.

"It will and soon." I placed my hands over hers to stop her fidgeting as it was making me nervous. "You said earlier that the South had removed Lincoln from the ballots, right?" she nodded. "What the Democrats are not considering is that by splitting their party essentially into two camps and having one candidate on the ticket in the North and another in the South, they are dividing their votes as well. They believe by removing Lincoln in the South, they are ensuring a victory for themselves. However, there are more people living in the North where Lincoln is the primary and favored candidate." I chose my words carefully.

"You think Lincoln will win the election?" Her voice was skeptical.

"I do," I nodded.

"And you think that will start the divide?" Bonnie looked down at our hands.

"Yes," I whispered reluctantly.

"What can I do?" her eyes looked at me pleadingly.

"Is there somewhere on the property that you can hide things?" She raised an eyebrow looking at me intently.

"Not really," she mused. "Perhaps I can have a storage unit built." Her voice trailed off, but I interrupted her.

"No. No. That will not work." I squeezed her hand to make her meet my eye. "No one. And I mean no one can know about it." I exhaled audibly. "Bonnie, this is very important. If, or rather when this war comes, it will not be long before the South is put under siege. That means the ports will be closed and no goods will be shipped out or in." Her eyes visibly widened with fear. "You need to store as much food that will not spoil, fabric, candles, and medical supplies."

"You are scaring me, Sidney." Her voice was barely a whisper.

"Darling, I am not trying to scare you. I only want to make sure you and your family are taken care of." I reassured her. "This war will be long and dreadful. Thousands of men will lose their lives and families will be torn apart. The South does not have the industries that the North does, and gunpowder, rifles, clothes, food, and medicine will quickly run out."

"Sidney," she squeaked.

"I simply want you to be prepared." I wrapped my arm around her shoulder and pulled her close to me. "I love you as if you were my own sister."

"I feel the same for you." She offered me a weary smile.

"If you can," I met her eye. "Make your way to Boston. Our estate is in Braintree just outside the city."

"You mean abandon our home, the South?" She sounded offended. "I cannot do that." She insisted.

"That is not what I meant." I said quickly. "I simply want you to know that you are always welcome at my home."

"I appreciate that, Sidney. I truly do. But I could never leave the South, especially if something as critical as a war breaks out." Bonnie offered me a weary grin.

"I understand and admire your loyalty and honor." I hugged her tightly. "I will always be here if you should ever need me."

"Thank you," she whispered.

We sat in silence on the perimeter of the reception. A closely bonded community laughing together, sharing food, and celebrating the new union with love and support. I had become a part of this world. I had been accepted by them, loved by them, and wanted desperately to protect them from the dark years that loomed ahead.

I brushed a tear off my cheek and reached for Bonnie's hand. She accepted mine with love and solidarity. My heart wanted to protect her and her family — to take them to Terrace Falls to keep them safe through the duration of the war. But I knew in my heart that I could not save everyone. My knowledge of the fate of the South in the next decade felt like a curse.

During the wedding and reception, Tallie and Sadie had carefully packed Caroline's suite. Her clothes, books, vanity, and trinkets were placed carefully in multiple trunks and loaded on a wagon. I watched silently as Otis passed under the row of mature trees and Spanish moss on his way to Bella Ridge. I was not sure if anyone even noticed the significance of his departure.

"Sidney," Bonnie's eyes lingered on the back of the wagon as it passed through the stone pilers at the entrance of Gable Gardens. "I value our friendship and appreciate your words. I truly pray that what you believe lies ahead will not come to pass."

"As do I," my voice was barely above a whisper.

"Still, I will heed your warning and take precautionary measures to ensure our survival." I nodded as she turned to look at me. "In my heart, I want to believe you are wrong. But my mind hears the truth in your words."

"Bonnie," I started but she held up her hand.

"Keifer told Randall that he has friends with relatives in government positions up North. Therefore, I can only conclude that you know more about what is coming than what is written about in our newspapers." My heart leapt at her rational and logical conclusion to my warnings.

Words caught in the back of my throat, and I struggled to swallow them down. I closed my eyes for a moment saying a silent prayer for strength and guidance. I inhaled the thick humid air that felt like soup being tossed into my lungs. My chemise stuck to my skin like a second layer suffocated beneath my thick corset. Despite my time in the South, I do not believe I would ever be able to acclimate to Southern humidity.

"I understand this must be difficult to hear. I only ask that you take a few extra precautions." I purposely kept my words vague.

"I will. I promise." Her smile was tight, but still warm.

Shortly thereafter Bonnie and I rejoined the festivities. Caroline and Phillip stood arm in arm with bright faces full of smiles and love. Their affection for each other was endearing and everyone could see their love was genuine.

33

THURSDAY, AUGUST 27, 2020

EMILY STARTED A FRESH POT OF coffee. It was the fourth one made in the last three hours. Everyone had gathered at Robert and Emily's before eight in the morning. Our dad, Ethan, and Liang had been staying with them for almost two weeks. The Covid-19 global pandemic had slowed government bureaucracy down to a standstill. We had only received Uncle Nicholas' ashes the day before. And thanks to our overreaching governor, we were prohibited from holding any sort of funeral or celebration of life honoring the man we all dearly loved.

"What time is the meeting?" Ethan picked up a homemade scone off the island.

"Ten o'clock," Jocelyn absentmindedly stirred her coffee.

The house had been solemn since our return to Boston, and the initial shock had worn off. Our two families remained huddled together in our grief and outrage. I tried my best not to be alone with Ethan if possible. I understood why my father brought him along, but his lack of empathy for the rest of us left me feeling cold towards him. Even Liang displayed more compassion for our family than my own brother could muster.

"It is ridiculous we have to do it over Zoom." Ethan took another bite and rolled his eyes.

"Your Uncle's estate attorney is in Bloomington, Indiana." Alex said with slight annoyance.

"That's stupid. In a family full of lawyer's, why didn't one of you handle it." Ethan scoffed without consideration.

"Because none of us are estate attorney's." Alex shot me a pointed look.

"Would you go to an OBGYN?" I leaned against the island and asked my brother.

"No," Ethan huffed. "I'm a man."

"Then why would you have a criminal defense attorney or corporate attorneys, or a family law attorney handle your estate?" I questioned him.

"Okay," he rolled his eyes at me.

"Attorneys specialize the same as physician's do." I informed him.

"Alright," Ethan shrugged. "Sorry." He turned his attention back to his scone.

I turned towards my father who was lingering next to the coffee maker paying no attention to his children or anyone else around him. He had been consumed by grief and regret. Each day my sister and I together or individually had been forcing him to take walks with us just to get him out of the house into the fresh air. Ethan had done nothing to help us or support our father in his grief. At this point, everyone in the house was tired of his behavior.

The rest of us exchanged various looks of discontent but remained silent. It was not worth upsetting our father over his son's selfish actions. The reading of our uncle's last will and testament was less than ten minutes away and no one had the desire to make this more difficult than needed.

Jocelyn, Jackson, Landon, and I had speculated the final wishes of our uncle last evening. They had stopped by our apartment for a nightcap after we all departed Robert and Emily's giving us the chance to speak freely. We quickly reached the consensus given that our uncle was unmarried with no children in this life, that he would leave everything to his last living brother in this time — our father.

Uncle Nicholas lived a very modest life. He loved his gardens, living a healthy life, enjoyed teaching, and thrived on research. He was kind, intellectually gifted, and loved his family beyond all else. His unwavering support and guidance for my sister and me throughout the depletion of the barrier of consciousness between our two worlds had been invaluable to both of us.

"Alright everyone, we should probably get logged in and set up before this starts." Robert's voice was steady.

Shane, Robert, Ethan, Jocelyn, and I grabbed our tablets or laptops and pulled up our email. We clicked on the link and waited impatiently as each of our faces showed up in a little window on the screen. We looked like the opening credits of the *Muppet Show* — a joke someone made during happier times.

"Good morning, everyone. My name is Erik Dove." A man in his sixties with silver hair and sharp features appeared before us. "I am sorry to meet you all under such heartbreaking circumstances." The lot of us nodded or muttered a soft good morning to him. "Mr. Chandler, did you receive the package I sent you by courier?"

"Yes, it arrived Tuesday." Robert replied. "I have it here, unopened as you requested."

"I know handling such matters over a Zoom call feels rather cold and impersonal. I apologize for that." Mr. Dove appeared genuine in his words. "I knew Nicholas for thirty years. He was a dear friend. I am sincerely saddened by his sudden death."

"Thank you." Shane was the first to speak.

"Are you Mr. Shane Timmons, his brother?" Our father nodded. "And these are your children?" Mr. Dove's eyes scanned over the rest of us.

"Yes, these are my daughter's Sidney and Jocelyn, and my son, Ethan." Shane introduced each of us as we each nodded as our names were called.

"Very well. Everyone is present as your brother requested." Mr. Dove looked down at the papers before him. "Let's begin."

My father took a deep breath with downcast eyes. I glanced away from my laptop to where my father was seated across the room. He had prominent dark circles under his eyes, and his hair needed a trim. His hands were fidgeting in his lap. His leg was bouncing nervously. Mr. Dove's voice broke my attention, and I looked back at my computer.

"I, Nicholas Tyrone Timmons, a resident of Boston, Massachusetts, with sound and disposing mind and memory hereby make, publish, and declare this to be my Last Will and Testament." Mr. Dove paused. "I guess his funeral and burial wishes are mute." He muttered in a soft voice as he scanned the document. "Okay. I hereby appoint my friend and attorney, Robert Abraham Chandler, as the Executor of this Will. If Robert is unable, I appoint my eldest brother, Shane Douglas Timmons, as the alternate Executor. My Executor shall have all powers allowable under law and shall serve without bond." Mr. Dove cleared his throat. "Does anyone have any questions?"

"No," the five of us answered in unison.

"Good." Mr. Dove's eyes dropped back to the document before him. "I bequeath my property in Boston to my brother Shane to sell or use as he sees fit. My personal property within the home is to be distributed or sold as Shane wishes. In addition, I bequeath my personal checking account ending in 6448 to Shane so that he may fully enjoy his retirement." The sound of rustling papers came through the speaker. "Let me see here, okay." Mr. Dove pulled out a paper from beneath the pile of documents. "Mr. Timmons, as of yesterday, Nicholas' checking account at Chase Morgan is $278, 651.33."

"What?" my father looked up with clear confusion in his eyes. "How is that possible?" He looked towards me without letting Mr.

Dove respond. "Did you know your uncle had that kind of money in his checking account?"

"No," I was just as surprised as he was.

"Neither did I," Jocelyn chimed in from across the table.

"Nicholas made some wise investments early on in his career." Robert said quietly.

"Indeed, he did," there was an obvious smirk on Mr. Dove's lips. "Shall we continue?"

"Yes," Shane responded still stunned by this revelation.

"I hereby bequeath to my nephew, Ethan Jude Timmons a trust in the amount of $150,000 to be managed by his father Shane Douglas Timmons until my nephew's thirty-fifth birthday." Shane nodded and Ethan looked almost pleased. I could tell by his expression he was not happy that Shane would be managing the trust for the next decade. "Any questions?"

"No," Shane answered, but Ethan spoke up.

"Does this mean that I have to ask my dad permission to touch this trust?" Ethan was not happy.

"Yes, until your thirty-fifth birthday." Mr. Dove answered.

"That's ridiculous." Ethan scoffed. "I'm an adult. I don't need a babysitter overseeing my inheritance."

"Uncle Nicholas clearly thought you did." I replied, earning an instant glare from my brother across the room.

"Let's continue," Mr. Dove ignored the last few comments like a seasoned attorney who was accustomed to such statements during a will reading. "Um," he paused again looking a bit hesitant. "This next section is in regard to his nieces. Ethan, you can log out now." Our brother looked puzzled but closed his laptop clearly still agitated and now looked almost insulted by being asked to leave the reading.

"My apologies," Mr. Dove spoke to our father. "Nicholas, from what I understand, was much closer to your daughters than your son and this is reflected in the next portion of the will."

"I understand," Shane nodded grimly barely listening to the attorney.

"All right." Mr. Dove looked back down at his papers. "I bequeath to my nieces Jocelyn Alyssa Timmons-Chandler and Sidney Harper Timmons the entirety of my investment portfolio whose dividends will be divided equally each quarter. Mr. Robert Chandler is to act as an overseer and advisor to each of my nieces for the investment portfolio. In addition, my savings account at National Teachers Credit Union ending in 5262 is to be divided equally between them to assist them with their futures and allow them to follow their dreams. Now let me see here," Mr. Dove shuffled some more papers. "As of yesterday, the savings account is $68,729,168.87."

"Excuse me?" Shane's head shot up.

"How is that possible?" If I wasn't so stunned, I would have laughed at the look on my sister's face.

"As I mentioned earlier, your brother made some wise investments early in his career." Mr. Dove noted.

"But to obtain that kind of wealth," Shane muttered. "I made investments also, but nothing remotely close to this." He ran his hands through his hair. "Nicholas lived so frugally. Did any of you know about this?" My sister and I instantly shook our heads.

"Yes, I did." Robert admitted as all heads turned towards him.

"Mr. Chandler, am I correct in assuming Nicholas went over his investment portfolio with you?"

"Yes, he did after he relocated to Boston. He asked me if I would help the girls with the investments just in case." Shane seemed more surprised with this than Jocelyn or me.

"Mr. Chandler, in the certified package I sent you, you will find all the information regarding Nicholas' investments. Would you like me to explain everything to Sidney and Jocelyn, or would you like to do it later in private?"

"I believe I should do it in private with them and their father." Robert looked towards my sister and me, and we both nodded back.

"Very well. If there are any questions, please do not hesitate to reach out. My phone and email address are enclosed in the email my assistant sent you all. Mr. Chandler, can you please distribute the personal letters Nicholas left to his family members?" Mr. Dove asked.

"Of course," Robert tore open the package on camera pulling out the first manilla envelope and holding three white sealed envelopes for Mr. Dove to see.

"Good," Mr. Dove acknowledged.

"Emily, would you pass these out please." Robert passed the small envelopes to his wife.

"Please read them later at your discretion. Do you have any other questions?" Mr. Dove asked.

"No, I do not believe so." Shane responded first. "Thank you for your time today."

"You are welcome. Again, I am sorry for your loss. Your brother was one of the best men I knew." Mr. Dove's voice was much softer now.

"Thank you. I appreciate that." Shane smiled gently then left the group. The rest of us followed.

Thankfully, Ethan had stepped outside after being excused. I had correctly assumed he was sitting on the back deck venting his frustration about the conditions of his new trust to Liang. I hated to think what the fallout would be when he found out about the inheritance Jocelyn, and I received. The meltdown would be catastrophic.

Thus far, Emily was the only one who knew outside the four of us the amount of money Jocelyn and I just inherited. I felt a strange mixture of fear and excitement over the news. Only a couple of weeks ago, Landon and I were tightening our belts, worried about student loans, the costs of our final year of school, and living paycheck to paycheck.

Now, my sister and I were multi-millionaires. It did not feel real. The idea was beyond my imagination and comprehension. I closed my laptop and just stared at the wall dumbfounded turning the sealed envelope over in my hands.

"Can you believe this?" My sister's voice rang out from the doorway.

"No," I looked up at her baffled face which I was certain mirrored my own.

"Sidney. Jocelyn. Would you please join your father, Emily, and I in my study?" Robert appeared behind my sister in the doorway.

I stood up quietly and followed them all down the hall. The house was too quiet. Emily had ushered everyone outside to provide privacy during the reading of the will, but that silence now felt heavy. The four of us took seats. Jocelyn and I sat together on the loveseat, while Emily, Robert, and our dad sat on the couch opposite us. The three of us were still awkwardly holding onto our sealed envelopes.

"Are you two all right?" Emily was the first to speak.

"No," I spoke before Jocelyn could. "I am not all right." I leaned forward and rested my elbows on my knees. "I am at a loss for words."

"Me too," Jocelyn met our father's gaze. "I mean, I just had no clue Uncle Nicholas had invested so well." She shook her head with a baffled look on her face.

"My brother was always private about his finances, but I admit, I had no idea either." Shane confessed.

"Okay, bigger issue." Jocelyn shook her head as if trying to gather her thoughts. "What do we tell Ethan? He's going to go absolutely ballistic. You saw the look on his face when Mr. Dove said that his trust would be overseen by dad until he's thirty-five."

"We don't tell him." I said quickly. "Seriously," I looked around at all the faces staring back at me. "What good would come of it?" I turned towards my sister. "Do you really want to tell him he got a hundred and fifty thousand dollars while we inherited millions."

"No," she admitted in a whisper. "Can't we just give him a larger portion out of our inheritance?"

"How?" my father asked. "He heard what he received."

"Can't we say the attorney made a mistake and that was left too," she paused. "I don't know, Robert and that his real inheritance was a couple million — like five." Jocelyn turned towards me. "Two and a half from each of us and," her voice trailed off.

"Jocelyn," Shane spoke softly. "I love that you have such good intentions and love your brother so much, but I do not believe that would be what your uncle wanted."

"But dad," Jocelyn looked surprised.

"Sweetheart, this is not about what is fair, but what is right." Shane looked tired. "I spoke with your uncle a great deal over this last year as we rebuilt our relationship. I know how much he loved both of you and treasured sharing such a special gift with you. He was not a reckless man. I am sure he gave a great deal of thought before he made any permanent decisions."

"So, we're supposed to keep this from our brother for the rest of our lives?" Jocelyn looked indignant.

"Not necessarily the rest of your lives. We can always say later that you both have expanded your investment portfolios and done very well. There is no reason to expand it with further details." Shane argued, but my sister clearly looked uncomfortable.

"Fine, but what about Landon?" Jocelyn pursed her lips.

"Same thing," Shane answered without hesitation. "I understand he is your live-in boyfriend." His eyes rested on me. "But he is not your husband. Not yet." I nodded.

"I understand." And I did. Even though I knew Landon and I would eventually become husband and wife I understood my father's concerns.

"We can sit down and go over the investments when you two are ready." Robert said leaning forward. Jocelyn and I both nodded but said nothing.

"Do you have any questions?" Shane asked.

"No," I rose to my feet. "I think I am going to go for a walk just to clear my head."

"Okay, darling. Can I get you anything?" Emily asked.

"No, thank you. I shall return shortly." I left them all sitting there.

I went straight out the front door without saying a word to anyone. The last thirty minutes had flipped my world upside down. Last week I was worried about student loans, rent, and covering utilities. Now, I would never have those concerns again. It was an odd sensation. Uncle Nicholas' letter felt like a lead weight in my hand.

The midday air was sticky and heavy. The sun held steady overhead in the cloudless sky. I wished I had grabbed my sunglasses on my way out, but in my haste, I had forgotten them on the kitchen counter where I'd left my purse. I stared at the sidewalk listening to the faint sound of birds chirping off somewhere in the distance. I soon found myself standing beside the bench I had once occupied with my uncle by the pond.

It felt like the perfect place to read his final words — at least his final words to me in this life. I sat down feeling the heat of the sunbaked wood through my jean shorts. I tore open the envelope and pulled out the letter. Tears stung my eyes. I rubbed them gently with the back of my hand to clear my vision.

My Dear Sidney,

I am sure you feel I have a lot to explain by the contents of my will and the inheritance I bequeathed to you. First, I want you to know that I am so very grateful for all the joy you and your sister brought to my life. I would like to think that if I had ever been blessed with a daughter, she would have been like you or Jocelyn. I know my brother is proud of you both.

Secondly, it will probably make you laugh to know how much I paid attention to your sarcastic remarks. After my release from Andersonville, the quickest and safest journey North was by ship. I landed in Boston harbor and found my way to Terrace Falls. The war had taken its toll, but you, your son, and our family were a delight to see. You welcomed me with open arms and insisted on overseeing my recovery before you would allow me to continue my journey to Chicago. You nursed me back to health as I was a mere skeleton in rags who appeared on your doorstep.

The barrier in my consciousness was steadily thinning. My mind was riddled with confusion and hysteria. You spent countless hours nursing my mind and body with love, care, and understanding. One night I had awakened from a terrible nightmare, and you had rushed to my bedside. After I calmed down you and I engaged in a conversation about the 20th and 21st centuries. You made a sarcastic remark about investing in Microsoft, Starbucks, IBM, and Apple. After you went to bed, I wrote those words down and committed them to memory. The following day, in the 20th century I invested and over the years, I kept an ear to the ground and kept investing.

I told myself it was simple clever positioning. I convinced myself it was to secure the future for my family, you, Jocelyn, and your families. At the time I had not realized that I would never be married here or that Monte would leave this time long before me. Still, as time revealed more I continued living modestly, enduring, researching, and waiting. I felt isolated and alone. My estrangement from Shane and him taking his children out of my life after losing Monte was more devastating and heartbreaking than anything I had endured. However, I believed that despite everything, I could make life a bit easier for you and Jocelyn.

Finally, I cannot express to you the joy I felt upon learning about you, Jocelyn, and the Chandlers. My heart nearly burst with joy. I finally felt grounded again in a way I had not since losing my brothers. My life had purpose, laughter, and family. Thank you for that.

You are a beautiful, kind, and intelligent young lady. I wish you all the best in your endeavors in life. I love you, my dear niece. I look forward to a very interesting discussion with you somewhere far away from this life.

Until we meet again.

All my love,

Uncle Nicholas

Tears rolled down my face. Nicholas must have composed this letter before his reconciliation with my father. He wrote of things that had yet come to pass — dangerous, but safe in the knowledge that I would always take care of him regardless of when or where. I brushed the tears off my cheeks and smiled at his heartfelt words.

"I suppose my sarcasm finally pays off." I whispered to no one.

"And you're surprised by that?" The sound of my sister's voice made me jump.

"Jocelyn?" I turned around suddenly. "I did not hear you."

"Sorry," she sat down beside me without asking. "I figured this was where you went."

"Did you read your letter?" She nodded still holding the folded letter in her hands. "You can read it if you want." She offered it to me.

"No. That's okay. He meant that for you." Jocelyn nodded still looking down at the letter in her hands.

"I feel horrible for Dad," she said in a low voice. "At least we still have Nicholas in our other lives, but Dad's lost both his brothers now."

"I know. It feels so unfair." My sister nodded in agreement.

"I guess I have you to thank for my financial future." She laughed without humor.

"He mentioned our conversation after the war," I stated with a slight smirk.

"Yes," Jocelyn finally met my eye. "You realize how careless that was, don't you?"

"Are you seriously reprimanding me for something I have not done yet?" I raised a brow. "How ironic considering," I left the thought dangling.

"I am just surprised you agreed with Dad and Robert about not telling Ethan and Landon about the money." Her lips pursed.

"I know it may be difficult to understand because you two were so close growing up, but if he knew he would be devastated. How could we explain to him that we were left a substantial sum and by comparison he was bequeathed pennies?" I reasoned. "Ethan knows nothing about *E.V.E.* and cannot understand the bond that we shared with Uncle Nicholas because of it." Jocelyn nodded slowly.

"I get it. I do. I just feel bad."

"I never said I felt good about it. But I do believe it is the best and most practical way to protect him."

"And Landon?"

"When Landon and I are married, I will tell him." I explained. "Until then, I will tell him I inherited some money and investments."

"You don't feel that is dishonest?" My sister tilted her head.

"Am I happy about it?" I shrugged. "No. I am not." I sighed heavily. "But it's not exactly dishonest."

"That's a thin line." I nodded. "I don't think I could do that with Jackson." Her voice was soft.

"That's different." I defended my decision. "One, you and Jackson are already married and happily at that. Two, Jackson couldn't care less about money — he has generational wealth and his own successful career. And finally, you and Jackson share your lives in both times like Robert and Emily. That creates a bond I will always be envious of. I will never share that with Keifer or Landon just as Phoebe and Alex won't. Our circumstances are not the same."

"I see your point." She conceded. "And I am sorry that you will never have that, but Landon and Keifer are both good men."

"Yes, they are. They share many characteristics beyond their careers." I admitted. "Yet they are distinctly different in others." I snorted.

"If you had to choose," her voice trailed off.

"Thankfully, I do not have to." I chuckled.

"Fine, but you cannot tell me they are equals in every way." The gleam in her eye made me roll my eyes.

"Of course not," I smirked but failed to elaborate. "Come on," I rose to my feet. We need to get back before lunch.

Ethan was in a foul mood when we returned. He stayed out on the back deck pouting about our father's control over his trust. I could only imagine what conversations and insights Nicholas must have picked up over the years to realize Ethan's frivolous and self-centered nature. Strangely, as children I was more like our mother whilst Jocelyn and Ethan favored our father's characteristics. But as we grew into adulthood, Ethan turned out to be more like our mother in many ways, and I more like our father. I never would have believed it a decade ago.

I found Landon in the family room watching *Lucifer* on Netflix with Jackson and Alex. They were sprawled out across the sectional couch surrounded by pizza boxes and empty beer cans. My sister and I stood in the entry way exchanging looks waiting to see if they would notice us.

They didn't.

We turned away and found Emily, Leslie, and Phoebe in the parlor. Phoebe was rocking Audry and my heart leapt missing my own sweet baby boy. I pushed the thoughts to the back of my mind and sat down beside her. She handed her daughter over to me with a loving grin.

"Hey, baby girl. Why don't you see your auntie for a bit." Phoebe's once polished style and perfect hair had been reduced to gym shorts and a tank top with a messy bun. She had dark circles beneath her eyes.

"She's still not sleeping through the night?" I offered a sympathetic look as Jocelyn sat down beside Leslie on the chaise lounge.

"That obvious, huh?" Phoebe laughed.

"Just a smidgen," I smirked.

Liang appeared in the doorway looking exhausted. She was wearing a pale-yellow sundress and sandals with her hair pulled up in a ponytail. She looked tired from the drama, and I could not help but wonder how much nonsense she was dealing with because of my brother that she did not speak about.

"Is he still pouting?" Jocelyn looked up at her.

"Of course," Liang rolled her eyes and sat down beside my sister. "He is in a mood." She rubbed her temples as if trying to rid herself of a terrible headache.

"I am guessing he told you about his inheritance?" I watched her carefully even though I pretended to be paying attention to the baby.

"Oh, I heard all about it." Liang shifted uncomfortably. "He has been itching to find out exactly what you two got." Jocelyn and I exchanged a look.

"Well, he should not worry about such things." Emily said softly.

"He's convinced you two received more than he did." Liang said dryly.

"It is none of his business what or how much we received." Jocelyn shrugged.

"Is that so?" All of us turned towards the doorway where Ethan was standing looking furious.

"Yes. That is so." Jocelyn repeated. "Why should you care?" she shrugged casually.

"Because I have a right to know." Ethan shouted, making Emily flinch, but the rest of us expected his reaction.

"Ethan," our father's voice carried down the hall followed by the sound of heavy footsteps. "Enough."

"No. It's not." My brother said, through gritted teeth, his eyes were blazing.

"Son," Shane's voice took on a dangerous tone. "You are a guest in this house. You will lower your voice and show some respect."

For a moment, their eyes locked in heated fury. The tension was palpable. The muscles were locked in Ethan's jaw as he stood there facing his father, fuming. His hands were locked in fists by his side, but he remained silent. Ethan turned slowly towards Emily, but his face did not soften.

"My apologies for my outburst." Ethan's voice was harsh and insincere. "Please excuse me." He turned away from us with loud footsteps on the hardwood floor. A moment later we heard the back door open and close behind him.

"Emily. Robert." Shane's voice was much softer. "My apologies for my son's inexcusable behavior."

"Please, Shane," Robert stepped up next to my father. "Think nothing of it. We understand, Ethan is hurting."

"Thank you, Robert," my dad placed a hand on Robert's shoulder. "My son is not hurting. He's ungrateful." He sighed heavily and stepped into the room. "Ethan should feel fortunate my brother left him anything. Clearly the will was written before he and I reconciled, but after he rekindled his relationship with my daughters. Ethan, however, never tried to have a relationship with Nicholas. He even mocked his sisters for establishing one."

"Ethan is still young, and rather impulsive." Emily smiled in a motherly way. "He will learn the importance of family bonds once he matures."

"No," Shane shook his head solemnly. "Unfortunately, my son is nothing short of entitled and selfish." He paused for a moment as if collecting his thoughts. "He wasn't like that before. I noticed the change in him become more prominent as his time at the university continued."

"That seems to be common trend with the liberal mindset of universities, particularly in Democrat controlled cities." Phoebe noted. "Still, I would have thought better of Notre Dame. It is a shame to see the destruction of education, history, and common sense."

"I've heard the same." Leslie spoke up for the first time. "I am seeing more liberal hatred spewed every day across social media and local news outlets. It's gotten to the point where I don't even bother anymore."

Robert and Shane sat down in chairs beside the hearth. There was a new understanding between them. I knew they had spent the last couple of hours going over the packet Mr. Dove had sent. My father now knew more about my sister and my investment portfolio than we did. The thought was more comforting than unnerving knowing we would be able to ask for his input and advice when necessary.

"When are you heading back to Chicago?" Emily asked my dad.

"Tomorrow morning. I think it's time we returned." Shane focused on Jocelyn and me. "Robert was telling me about your property hunt in Southern states and the reasons why."

"Are you thinking of moving?" I asked in a hopeful voice.

"You're not going to sell the house, are you?" Jocelyn jumped in before our father could respond.

"Given its unfortunate location, I fear I should have too." Shane pursed his lips. Despite being on the outskirts of the city we too are greatly affected by the rampant criminal activity and liberal ideology enforced by Beetlejuice. I believe I must sell while the market value is still inflated."

"But that is our ancestral home, daddy. You fought so hard to get it back in our family. If you feel you must leave, can't you rent it out. Just please don't sell it." Jocelyn looked towards me with pleading eyes.

"Jocelyn is right, dad. You shouldn't sell the house. It holds our history." I agreed.

"I wish there was another way, but after buying your mother out of her half in the divorce I need the money a sell would bring to purchase another home." Shane explained.

"In that case, let me buy it so it stays in the family. I can rent it out or whatever. But I won't let you let it out of the family." Jocelyn reasoned.

"Can you afford to do that?" Liang's eyes widened. My sister had momentarily forgotten she was in here.

"We'll talk about it later." My father said quickly as the room ignored Liang's question.

Jocelyn and I nodded at our father, while the room fell into an awkward silence. Liang shifted uncomfortably in her seat. I knew she could feel the unspoken words about financial matters but respected our wishes by not inquiring further.

"I will let Ethan know we are leaving in the morning. Excuse me," Liang rose to her feet and quietly left the room.

The room remained silent. The only sound was that of Liang's footsteps on the hardwood floor followed by the opening and closing of the back door. I eyed my sister carefully. Her eyes dropped. She knew she had said too much in front of Liang.

Dinner was tense that evening. The conversation was awkward touching on surface level topics. Liang had clearly mentioned something to Ethan about Jocelyn offering to purchase our family home from our father to assist him in his ability to move out of

Chicago. Ethan cut his roast with more force than necessary shooting Jocelyn and I glaring looks with every bite.

"What is your problem?" Jocelyn put down her fork with a clatter. "I am sick of your condescending looks."

"You offered to buy dad's house?" Our brother's eyes narrowed. "How much did Uncle Nicholas leave you?" Liang focused on the food on her plate. In that moment, I knew my sister and I would never look at our relationship with her in the same way again.

"Why do you care? You didn't even know him. You should be grateful he left you anything." Jocelyn spat.

"You mean I should be grateful for the crumbs after he apparently left you and Sidney a full meal? Yeah, whatever." The venom in his voice was the unmistakable on of an entitled brat.

"Wow," I muttered looking towards my dad. "Unbelievable."

"Ethan, that's enough." Our dad's voice held that edge and tone we all knew meant business.

"No, it's not." Ethan set his silverware down and huffed. "I can't believe everyone is okay with this unequal distribution. None of you care about me or my future at all."

Robert, Emily, and their entire extended family along with Landon and Liang were all sitting in the middle of a nasty family dispute. At least Liang had the decency to look ashamed considering this would not be happening if she had only kept her big mouth shut. My sister and I shot her dirty looks making sure she saw us. Her eyes immediately dropped back to her plate as she picked at her dinner.

"Explain to me little brother, why you believe you should have an equal share of Uncle Nicholas' estate." I leaned forward and folded my hands resting my chin on them. "Enlighten me." I dared. "You have not spoken to or even seen our uncle since you were what five, maybe six years old." I raised my eyebrows questioning him. "While Jocelyn and I have built a loving relationship with him. We spent time with him. We talked to him. We learned about his life. You do nothing and expect a reward?" I scoffed. "You are pathetic."

"Sidney," Shane's voice warned.

"You are a bitch." Ethan spat across the table with narrow eyes.

"Maybe, but I'm a rich bitch." I smirked.

"I hate you." Ethan retorted in a low menacing voice.

"Well, good. I'm not exactly a fan of yours right now either." I informed him.

"Me neither." Jocelyn added. "And I am also disappointed in some people's inability to respect family privacy and instead blab about something that is none of their business."

"Subtle," Liang finally found her voice looking up at Jocelyn. "I don't keep secrets from my boyfriend."

"Boyfriend. Meaning you are not part of this family." Jocelyn hit Liang where she knew it would hurt.

"You mean like Landon." Liang glared at me.

"Landon is more a part of this family than you will ever be. He has never betrayed anyone." I said with a confidence that made her visibly wince.

"How dare you," Ethan's voice rose an octave.

"If the shoe fits," Jocelyn eyed them both carefully across the table.

"After this trip," Ethan rose to his feet and dropped his napkin on the table. "I don't want to ever hear from either of you again." He pointed to Jocelyn and me.

"At least we can agree on one thing," Jocelyn chuckled and I nodded in agreement.

"Okay, that's enough." Shane jumped back in. "Let's all cool off before we say something we will regret later."

"I meant everything I said," Ethan's breath was heavy as he stared at my sister and me.

"Ditto," I chimed in.

"I'm good." A small smile played in the corners of my sister's mouth.

My dad looked like he was struggling to maintain his composure. He took a deep breath and looked between his three children. I was not sure which of us he was more surprised by. Somehow, I thought it was more my sister and my behavior. From the crease in his brow, it appeared Ethan's behavior was nothing new to him.

"Robert. Emily. I apologize for my children's behavior." Shane shook his head in disappointment.

"I'm outta here," Ethan mumbled walking out of the room. Liang followed not meeting anyone's eyes as she left.

"This should be a fun ride home." Our dad mumbled, rolling his eyes.

No one knew what to say. No one seemed surprised by Ethan's outburst or our responses. After two weeks of him walking around like he owned the place and was entitled to everything under the sun, no one had expected anything else. In fact, it simply reaffirmed Robert and Shane's insistence on leaving Ethan in the dark about our inheritance.

34

THURSDAY, AUGUST 30, 1860

I STARTED NOTICING AN ABUNDANCE of activity that felt off around the house. After the wedding, every evening after dinner men from around the county would arrive and gather in the barn. By Wednesday, they had started shooting at targets off in the distance set up on the fence posts. It was clear that they were forming a county militia.

Keifer had noticed but did not participate. But Thad was out there with David running drills — sometimes on horseback, sometimes on foot. They practiced marching, shooting, and hand to hand with bayonets. It was strange and unnerving. Keifer, nor anyone in his household spoke about it. At least not with me. Although I knew all of them realized and understood what was going on.

I could hear them from the parlor or the front porch. I had a habit of bringing my son outside in the evenings to play on a blanket under the big oak tree. Trixie typically came with us, always eager to spend time with her favorite nephew. The sound of them put my teeth on edge as the reality of what was coming hit harder than ever before.

Keifer joined me on the porch just after dinner. The men had disappeared behind the barn per usual. The sun was slowly drifting across the sky setting it ablaze with orange, pink, and gold hues. The trees faded into a silhouette backdrop. Trixie was giggling with my son rolling a small ball between them. I smiled to myself watching the genuine love between them.

"You've been quiet since the wedding." My husband observed. "Is everything all right?" I nodded but remained silent. "I did not expect my father to lead the county militia." His hand gestured to the barn off in the distance. "I keep hoping our leaders in Washington will be able to resolve this mess, but it doesn't seem likely."

"Lines are being drawn," I commented in a low voice.

"Appears so," Keifer's voice trailed off. "My father is upset with me. So, is Thad." He sighed heavily. "I have repeatedly tried to explain, but they are insistent that I stand with the South even if it's only as a physician. They cannot understand the oath I made as a physician and that I attend to soldier's care on both sides."

The wind whispered through the trees. But even the cheerful sounds of Trixie and our son's giggles could not drown out the military chants off in the distance. I saw my husband flinch each time one of the men shouted, "kill all those damn Yankees." My stomach knotted a little bit more each time and I found myself praying for our departure day.

"Darling," my husband reached for my hand. "Please do not take it personally." I looked at him as if I was seeing him for the first time.

"How can I not?" I scoffed.

"You know my family loves you." His voice sounded defeated.

"As they chant about killing my brothers and our friends?" I chuckled without humor. "That is a strange way to show it."

"Sidney," Keifer said with no conviction. "This is our home. Our culture. Our way of life. And the North is taxing us out of it because they do not approve." I simply nodded. "How would you feel if the federal government were threatening Terrace Falls?"

"I would do everything I could to protect it." I answered honestly and he squeezed my hand thoughtfully.

"My family is just doing the same." He explained.

"I know," And I did. But it did not make me feel any better about it.

The faded chants continued as a blade to my heart. Sadly, I could see both sides. I did understand why both sides believed they were right. I began to wonder what the landscape of North America in the twenty-first century would look like if the South had been victorious. The differences would be stark and unrecognizable.

"I do not want to argue with you, Sidney." Keifer's voice sounded tired. "I just want you to understand."

"I do understand, Keifer." I looked over at my husband. "That is what makes it so difficult."

"I don't want this bickering between the North and the South to affect us and our families." My husband squeezed my hand again.

"You realize that is not possible. This situation is only going to get worse before it gets better." I rationalized. "Listen to them," I leaned forward and gestured towards the barn. "They actually want a war they cannot win."

"They may," Keifer's voice sounded hopeful.

"No. They cannot." I said more forcefully than I intended. "How, Keifer, how?"

"These men are fighting for what they believe in." He swallowed hard. "For the right to live their life without federal overreach."

"Keifer, you have listened to our friends and neighbors for the last decade. Do you believe they too, are not fighting for what they believe in?"

"I believe they would say they are." He admitted.

"And how is the South going to win?" I sat back in the rocking chair and shook my head in disbelief. "Superior industries? No. Superior infrastructure? No. Superior training? No. Superior equipment? No." I leaned forward again. "So, explain to me how they are going to defeat the North?"

"Be reasonable," my husband smiled at his little sister tickling our son who was laughing uncontrollably.

"What am I being unreasonable about?" I raised an eyebrow at him.

"The inflated ego of the North." Keifer's words hit me like a physical blow. I bit my lip to keep from saying something I would regret.

Instead, I rose to my feet without looking back. I walked down the steps slowly and crossed the lawn. Trixie looked up with a face still full of smiles. I knelt beside my son and began putting my son's toys in the little basket.

"Hey little man," I picked up my son balancing him on my hip. "It is getting late." I picked up the basket before turning towards Trixie. "Would you mind carrying in the blanket for me please?"

"Of course," My little sister-in-law gathered up the patch-work quilt and followed me into the house.

I passed by my husband without saying a word. I didn't say anything to anyone who was bustling around the house as I made my way up to our chambers. I changed my son and cleaned him up. I took my time, humming softly to myself just to drown out the chanting I could still hear faintly from our bedroom window.

After I cleaned myself up and brushed my teeth, I climbed up onto the bed and leaned against the mountain of pillows holding my son in my arms. I adjusted him and began feeding him his evening snack. I gazed down at his chubby little face and traced my finger lightly over his cheek. My son reached up and wrapped his little fingers around mine. My heart swelled with pride and joy.

I knew my husband would be downstairs with his family for a while longer. I had known long ago that the political division between the states had the potential to cause tension, disagreements, or worse in my marriage. But I wanted to believe that our love and marriage were strong and could endure any possible conflicts that this political turmoil would lay on our doorstep.

Now I wasn't so sure.

I held my son long after he finished nursing. He fell asleep in my arms as I watched the sky outside the window grow darker. I closed my eyes and noticed the voices outside had finally ceased. It was replaced by voices below floating up the stairs. I couldn't make out what was said. It was just a blur of muffled voices. But being the only Northerner in the family, I found myself being more self-conscious than what I had felt when we arrived.

It was an uneasy feeling. I had wanted to believe that we had made progress over the summer and that my in-laws had come to accept me as their son's wife, their grandson's mother, and a part of their family. Now, I was beginning to doubt everything.

My mind replayed all those long conversations with Angelina on the porch, my time spent with Maggie sewing in the parlor, and lively dinner discussions. Had I imagined it all? Did I crave their acceptance so badly that these relationships only existed in my mind?

I felt pathetic.

I drifted off long before Keifer came to bed.

35

MONDAY, SEPTEMBER 14, 2020

LANDON WAS LOUNGING ON the couch, browsing through the streaming catalog selection on HBO MAX munching on kettle corn. He looked bored out of his mind. Beside him, on the coffee table lay a stack of unpaid bills. He had spent the morning fretting over his bank statements, his portion of our rent, cell phone, and utilities, and his med school tuition that was now overdue. I had approached him twice trying to figure out how to discuss our finances. Each time I got cold feet and ended up asking him if he wanted more coffee.

I cleaned the apartment again — third time in the last five days. When I was stressed, I cleaned. It was my coping mechanism and one that Landon appreciated because it relieved him from having to do anything. I put the pledge and dust rag under the kitchen counter. I brushed some strands of hair that had escaped my messy bun out of my face and took a deep breath.

"Landon?" I walked over and sat on the edge of the couch near his feet. "Can we talk?"

"About what?" his eyes never left the television screen as he continued scrolling.

"Look," I grabbed the remote from him and placed it on the table. "I know you are stressed." I began choosing my words carefully. "We talked about getting married." I started but he quickly interrupted.

"Guess we'll put that off for a while," he snorted. "Life has been put on hold or haven't you noticed?"

"I've noticed." I swallowed trying to ignore the sarcasm in his voice. "Unfortunately, creditors haven't." Landon scoffed but remained quiet. "Do you still want to marry me?" It was a loaded question, and I knew it.

"What kind of question is that?" He sat up straighter facing me. "You know I do." He reached for my hand. "I just thought we had agreed to wait until we finished our residencies and were in a better financial position."

"I know," I looked into his beautiful eyes and the little freckles sprinkled around his nose. Landon was a strikingly handsome man. "And we can wait until this pandemic nonsense ends because I want to do this right."

"Me too," he agreed with a slight tilt of his head. "I want to have our families and friends there with us."

"I know we agreed to keep our finances separate until we get married, but I am worried about you. You have been so stressed lately about bills." Landon shrugged nonchalantly, but the worry lines around his eyes were prominent. "My uncle left me a healthy inheritance. It is enough to get us through whatever life throws at us during this global insanity."

"Sidney, I don't want to know how much your uncle left you because your brother's meltdown tells me it was life changing for you and your sister, but not him." Landon raised his eyebrows at me. "Am I right?"

"Yes," I shrugged. "Uncle Nicholas left Ethan a hundred and fifty thousand in a trust to be managed by our father until he's thirty-five."

"That's not exactly spare change," He looked disgusted at my brother's ungrateful behavior.

"No. It's not." I pursed my lips in thought. "I think he should be grateful he got anything instead of acting like a brat because our dad is the trustee."

"Is your dad the trustee of Jocelyn's inheritance? She's only eleven months older than Ethan."

"Jocelyn is married and a lot more responsible than Ethan. She doesn't spend her evenings running around with buddies drinking beer and wasting our dad's money." I pointed out.

"Isn't Ethan engaged to Liang?"

"I don't know," I shrugged. "We have never been close. He used to be close to Jocelyn before she and Jackson got married. He has pretty much ignored her since."

"But you and your sister got close after she got married. You don't find that strange?" The lines on his forehead displayed his confusion.

"Why is that strange?" I questioned trying to sound innocent. "We grew up. Ethan didn't." I shrugged casually.

"You're not wrong. Still, I don't like the idea of you paying for everything regardless of what you inherited." Landon shifted uncomfortably. "It's just not right."

"Are you seriously going to be misogynistic about male pride?" I playfully slapped his arm and giggled. "Look, we know that it is not a matter of if we're going to get married, but a matter of when, right?" He nodded. "We're a team and we take care of each other."

"But not like this." His voice was low.

"Landon, the entire world has shut down. People are losing their businesses, homes, families, and jobs because a corrupt political party is obsessed with taking power." I flopped back against the cushions. "And I believe Robert and my uncle are right — the Democrats are going to do anything to take the White House and with it control of the government. If they do, we are so screwed."

"The world has gone insane," he agreed. "I can tell you the sooner we move out of this blue hellhole, the happier I'll be."

My phone buzzed on the kitchen counter where I'd left it on the charger. I rolled my eyes and pushed myself up. I walked over to the kitchen counter and saw my brother's name flashing on my phone screen. Dread formed in the pit of my stomach, and I considered declining the call or sending it to voicemail. But I knew he wouldn't give up that easily. I swallowed the bile in my throat and picked up the phone.

"Hello?" I tried to keep my voice polite.

"Can we talk?" I could tell by the sound of his voice he was trying to contain his anger.

"What about?" I glanced over at Landon and mouthed, 'it's my brother.' I held a finger up to my lips. He nodded as I placed the call on speaker.

"You know what about," Ethan's voice was strained. "I do not appreciate the way you and Jocelyn spoke to Liang. You owe her an apology."

"Ethan," I sat back down beside Landon. "I will not apologize, but I will thank her." I said evenly.

"What?" the confusion was evident in his voice. "What are you talking about?"

"For years, all of us considered Liang as family. But she proved to every one of us she's not and never will be."

"Why? Because she told me about the house?" his voice was angry.

"She repeated information that was not hers to share." I told him.

"You're being ridiculous," my brother scoffed. "It's not like Liang told me how much you two got, just that Jocelyn offered to buy the house so dad could move out of Chicago and keep the house in the family. Am I wrong?"

"It's not about whether you are wrong or right. It's about confidential information that she had no right to share." I explained.

"Confidential information. You are full of shit. You guys were sitting in the front room bullshitting." Ethan's tone was indignant.

"First of all, we were sitting in the parlor — not the front room. Secondly, Liang was not a participant in the conversation, just an eavesdropper. Finally, she is only upset because she got called out. I, nor Jocelyn, will apologize."

"And I suppose you agree with dad having control over my trust."

"I think Uncle Nicholas didn't know you. He didn't know whether you were financially responsible or not. He didn't know anything about your dreams, or your life goals. But either way, you were his nephew, and he wanted to do something to help make your life a bit easier. So, he left you a substantial trust fund and not knowing anything about you, he set it up in a way that he felt comfortable. And because you decided to be an ungrateful ass, you caused undue tension around family who were grieving the loss of a beloved family member." I lectured.

"You don't get it," My little brother spat with venom.

"You're right. I don't."

"You and Jocelyn obviously got a lot more than I did."

"So," I scoffed. "That is our business, not yours." I insisted.

"We are family. It is my business." His voice rose an octave.

"If you have an issue, why aren't you talking to dad?" I was quickly becoming exasperated with him.

"I have. He said if I wanted more information, I should speak with you or Jocelyn." His voice was tight.

"What did Jocelyn have to say?" I was sick of talking in circles.

Landon reached over and took my hand in his. His eyes held a kindness that I desperately needed. He knew my relationship with my younger brother was challenging on a good day, but I still loved him. The dynamics of Landon's relationship with his brother made it easy for him to sympathize. He frequently joked that I was fortunate to only be dealing with an entitled selfish brat while his brother was a liberal nutjob. Between the two, I had the better deal.

"I haven't spoken to her." Ethan admitted.

"You should," I sighed heavily rolling my eyes. "You two used to be thick as thieves. Now you barely acknowledge each other. When are you going to get over yourself?"

"Over myself," he sounded indignant.

"Did I stutter?" I smirked at Landon. "Yeah, over yourself. If you got your head out of your ass and treated her like your sister and friend, perhaps this conversation wouldn't be necessary."

"What is that supposed to mean?" He huffed.

"Take it for what you will, but this conversation is going nowhere. You should call Jocelyn." I ran my hand through my hair.

"I don't want to talk to her and Liang refuses to speak with either of you until you apologize for humiliating her at dinner." Ethan admitted.

"Well, the apology is not going to happen by either one of us. And the fact that you refuse to speak directly with the one sister you used to be closest to, says a lot, Ethan." I leaned forward with my elbows on my knees.

"To much time has passed." My little brother's voice softened. "I was horrible to her and Jackson."

"Yes, you were." I agreed, not willing to sugarcoat his behavior. "You were horrible, childish, and ruthless about something you couldn't understand."

"Wow, you're sweet." He muttered. "Why don't you tell me how you really feel?"

"You know I am right."

"You know what I don't understand."

"What?" I was getting bored and wanted to get off the phone so I could continue my conversation with Landon.

"Ever since you went to New Orleans with them over Spring Break it's like a switch flipped and you changed. Suddenly you were spending more time with Jocelyn and Jackson's family. You, the Chandler's, Uncle Nicholas, and even dad all seemed to be in on something that the rest of us were only on the periphery of — some secret club that I am deliberately left out of." My stomach dropped and I swallowed hard looking at Landon and rolling my eyes trying to act like his accurate depiction of the last few years was absurd.

"Do you hear yourself?" I chuckled lightly trying to keep the tension buried behind my words.

"Are you telling me I'm wrong?"

"Yes," I ran a hand through my hair. "Look. When Landon and I transferred to Boston we didn't know anyone. It was only natural that we got close to Jocelyn and her family. And yeah, at the time, Uncle Nicholas was still estranged from dad, so when he followed us here later, it was because we were his only family. Why are you trying to read more into it than the obvious?"

"I went from having a family to suddenly it just being me and dad alone in that big house. Then he makes up with his brother and suddenly, he's visiting Boston every chance he gets when he's not on the phone with one of you." Ethan's voice was cold.

"You sound bitter." I noted.

"Maybe I am," he confessed. "But you would be too. You all left me behind."

"No one left you behind. We were living our lives."

"In Boston," he said it with the same venom as if he said we had all moved to the fourth level of hell.

"Good Lord," I muttered. "What did you expect us to do?"

"I just wish the Chandler's never moved in across the street. All of this is their fault."

"Seriously? How do you figure?" I scoffed.

"If they had never moved in, Jocelyn would have never met Jackson. She never would have had a falling out with me or mom. She would be in med school like her original plan. Mom and dad would still be married." Ethan laid it out methodically.

"Ethan, Jocelyn never wanted to be a doctor. That was mom's dream, not hers. And our parents were miserably married. They couldn't stand each other. They didn't talk. They had outgrown each other." I told him. "No one should be forced to live a life they don't want."

"No one thought about how all of it affected me." He almost shouted.

"Ethan, you are not a child. Stop acting like one." I shouted back and disconnected the call.

"Damn," Landon smirked. "That was harsh."

"Reality usually is." I shrugged.

Our earlier conversation was not brought up again that day, neither were our finances. I waited to see if Landon would say something, but he didn't. I didn't want to push. My mind was still reeling from Ethan's tantrum. I knew he wouldn't have the stones to call Jocelyn. Jocelyn would listen to about thirty seconds of his crap before hanging up on him. I don't believe she would ever forgive him for what he put her and Jackson through.

The family we had once shared had been reshaped and we all knew Ethan really wasn't a part of it anymore. His recent behavior and disrespect had proven as much.

36

MONDAY, SEPTEMBER 17, 1860

KEIFER WAS UP AND DRESSED BEFORE I awoke. I reached for him before I opened my eyes but found the pillow beside me empty. Just as it had been since our heated discussion on the porch a couple of weeks ago. I didn't know how to breach this wall between us. I feared his family had finally broken through his armor and convinced him to stay and serve as a physician in the Confederate army.

I stared up at the cornflower blue curtains draped over the canopy bed above me. I felt so alone. However, my son's morning murmurs quickly informed me otherwise. I pushed the covers aside and stepped down onto the hardwood floor. My bare feet could feel the warmth of the wood seeping into the balls of my feet. I leaned over my son's bassinet and his face instantly lit up.

His smile was contagious. I found myself smiling down at him as his little hands held onto his little toes. He squealed, breaking into a full smile showing off his dimples.

"Good morning, sunshine." He laughed, letting go of his toes and reaching for me. "How is my little man doing today?" I picked him up and laid him down on my bed unpinning his diaper. "What is this?" I reached up and pulled his bottom lip out just enough to see two little teeth buds breaking through his lower gums. "You got two teefer's coming through." My son squealed again with excitement. "That explains your constant drooling lately." He laughed.

I cleaned him up and covered his little bottom with a fresh diaper. My son was cooing as I climbed back onto the bed and settled against the pillows to give him his breakfast. The early morning sun was breaking through the clouds, sending washed-out rays across the room. I could hear the faded sounds from below as the house slowly came to life. I wasn't sure how much longer I could stand this uncomfortable politeness that I found myself an unwilling participant in.

Tallie knocked on the door while I was dressing my son. She moved with graceful efficiency and only spoke when spoken too. I felt like I was existing in a vacuum, and I couldn't help but wonder what was being said about me behind closed doors.

I skipped breakfast not wanting to intrude on the lively conversation that recently always appeared to cease whenever I entered a room. Instead, I went to the parlor and picked up the quilt and his basket of toys. I had no idea where my husband was but didn't care. He hadn't had more than a perfunctory conversation with me in weeks. I could feel the bridge between us smoldering and wasn't sure if it was going to be steady enough to carry us to Chicago together.

"Are you not hungry or avoiding the family?" Angelina's voice asked as she approached our blanket under the tree.

"I was not hungry." I said without looking up.

"You missed supper last evening as well." She sat down uninvited with a raised eyebrow. "I suppose my husband's attempt at being inconspicuous was fruitless."

"Why was he trying to be inconspicuous?" I found it strange.

"He was not sure how you would feel about it." My mother-in-law said as if that was supposed to explain everything. "Keifer said he thought it really bothered you despite your reassurance that you understood." I nodded looking down and adjusting my skirt just to give me something to do with my hands. "That feels like quite the contradiction." Angelina's eyebrow rose as she picked up a toy and handed it to my eager son who was reaching happily for it.

"I do understand. I know I would do anything to defend our home." I exhaled tiredly. "But it is not that simple when I see Southern men training to kill my brothers, my friends and neighbors." I met her eyes briefly. "Still, I have grown to love so many in this community and it breaks my heart to think of them fighting my Northern kin."

"I sincerely pray it does not come to that." My mother-in-law gave me a small smile and stroked my son's cheek.

"Me too," I answered honestly.

"This election will determine what comes next." She said without meeting my eye.

"I believe so," I spoke softly.

"Are you excited to see your family?" I was grateful for the subject change.

"Excited and a bit nervous," I admitted.

"Why nervous?" Angelina continued rolling the ball back and forth with my son.

"I have not seen my father's family since my brother Patrick's wedding almost a decade ago. Patrick and his wife, Annabelle have had four boys since and are expecting their fifth child next month." I explained.

"I would imagine she is praying for a daughter after so many sons." My mother-in-law chuckled softly. "I was blessed with both and feel fortunate for it."

"I am thrilled our first child was a son to carry on Keifer's name, but I do pray our next child is a girl." I confessed.

"As a mother, you love all your children unconditionally. But there is a special unbreakable bond between father's and daughters just as there is between mothers and their sons, especially their first born." She gently brushed my son's soft blond hair away from his face with her fingers. "I admit I was very hurt and upset when Keifer informed us of your upcoming marriage and his intention to remain up North at Terrace Falls." I nodded recalling the harsh words she had written to him before our wedding day. "I was certain he would return home after school and marry a Southern lady that understood his place as the heir to Gable Gardens. But he made his choice." She shrugged with a smile. "And I reluctantly had to accept it."

"Begrudgingly," I smirked.

"Yes, that to." She laughed. "But this trip has shown me and David," she added. "That not only do you understand your husband's place in our family, but you also respect our culture. That has meant a great deal to us. Our son chose a good wife, and we are proud to call you our daughter as well."

"Thank you. I appreciate that." And I truly did. "Keifer has built his career in Boston and Braintree. He is a well-respected physician and has a reputation as a good honest man within our community. It has not always been easy for him. Many of our neighbors were reluctant to trust him because he is a Southerner, but they soon saw what I already knew from the moment I met him — his integrity, skills, and kindness are unmatched. He is a brilliant physician." I said proudly.

"Yes, he is." Angelina's eyes shone with obvious pride.

"I truly hope you and your family will join us in March for our son's first birthday and stay for a good long visit so we may introduce you all to the world we have built in Braintree." I placed my hand over hers and squeezed it with genuine affection.

"I am looking forward to it." Her eyes lit up with love.

37

SATURDAY, SEPTEMBER 26, 2020

THE NUMBNESS AND BOREDOM OF the global pandemic felt surreal. Thousands of people were doing the same thing, binging on various streaming services, driving each other insane, and twiddling their thumbs. Landon and I were exhausted from the long hours at the hospital and had no energy left over for anything else. We found ourselves spending most of our days off with my sister and her husband hanging out at their place or ours. Jocelyn and I combed over real estate listings hoping to find something that roughly fit the description we were seeking.

The lockdown had brought out the best and the worst in people. The division within our country seemed to be growing at a rapid pace. It was insane. Stores that remained open suffered shortages in toilet paper, soap, disinfectants, hand sanitizers, and most meat products. For some unexplainable reason the Northern states were more impacted by shortages than the Southern states, especially Southwestern states. Still, no one was entirely immune from the financial pain and frustration.

Small businesses and mom n' pop companies were permanently closing their doors in record numbers. They could not sustain the loss of customers or the inability to continue to pay workers who could no longer show up. I watched businesses that had thrived for decades collapse under the strain of the prolonged lockdown. President Trump approved stipends attempting to help struggling Americans, but it was a drop in the bucket after months of lost wages.

America was falling apart. Large companies were able to shift to online — their staff working from home offices, dining room tables, corners of their living room or bedrooms. It was better than nothing, but hosting Zoom meetings with small children running around in the background proved challenging for many working parents. Still, people pushed through. They endured the financial and relationship hardships while watching major cities throughout the country being looted, burned to the ground, and decorated with racial slurs. I wasn't sure how much longer this powder keg would last until it exploded.

Landon and I pulled into the driveway beside Jackson's SUV. I figured Phoebe and Alex, and their families would be around shortly. Our tightknit family had grown even closer during this worldwide shutdown. The loss of regular community events and activities had greatly shrunk our social lives to almost nonexistent outside of our family.

The afternoon sun shined brightly in the sky but did little to warm the day. Fall was creeping up behind us ready to burst into the season. The edges of the leaves hinted at the spectacular display just waiting to blossom with the upcoming season. A soft breeze moved the leaves slightly but was not heavy enough to impact anything.

We barely got our car doors open when a woman with a severe bob haircut wearing dark grey yoga pants, a black tank top, and running shoes started walking up the driveway. She was pulling a little yappy lap dog with a fiercely pink leash behind her. Her stance reeked of arrogance and entitlement. She stood there with her hand on her hip and the pint-sized furball yapping at her feet.

"Excuse me," she hurried towards us but stopped just outside the requisite six feet perimeter. "Excuse me." She said louder through her cotton nonmedical facemask. "Do you live here?"

I met Landon's eyes over the hood of his car. An unspoken message passed between us. This woman had all the earmarks of a typical liberal Karen down to the yoga pants, little dog, and unfortunate angled bob. We knew it wouldn't matter how we responded, she was here to voice her unsolicited and inconsequential opinion.

"Yes," I said closing my door a little harder than necessary. "My parents own this house." Considering Robert and Emily were basically my second parents and we were related – distantly by marriage, it wasn't technically a lie.

"Your flag," Karen pointed to the 3′ X 4′.5″ American flay displayed on a pole attached to one of the front porch columns. "It needs to be taken down. I understand how people like you find it necessary to hang it up for Memorial Day, July 4th, and Labor Day, but summer is over, and its constant appearance is well," she removed her oversized sunglasses with a flourish. "It's offensive."

"People like me?" I raised my eyebrows. "What do you mean by people like me?"

"Trump supporters." She spat the words like it was something vile in her mouth and I couldn't help but giggle.

"Are you asking if we support President Trump?" I put extra emphasis on the word president just for maximum effect, but before she could respond Landon joined in.

"How exactly is the American flag offensive?" Landon smirked. I knew how much he enjoyed screwing with Karen's.

"It is oppressive." Karen's words were curt.

"Is there a problem here?" Robert stepped out onto the porch with a face full of concern.

"Is this your house?" Karen fixed her glare on Robert.

"Yes. Why?" Robert folded his arms and leaned against the porch column by the steps.

"I was just telling your daughter that the holidays are over, and your daily display of this flag is offensive." Karen stepped towards the porch but remained mindful of her six-foot perimeter from Landon and me, she stepped into the yard to get closer to Robert. Landon and I leaned against the side of his car ready to watch the show.

"You find the American flag offensive?" Robert scoffed. "Are you serious lady?"

"I do not like your tone." Karen placed her hand on her hip facing off with Robert.

"Lady, I fought for this country and the right to tell you to go to hell and get off my property because I couldn't care less about your opinion." Years of squaring off with entitled Karen's in the courtroom had taught Robert how to control his voice and speak with a sincere sounding tone even when insulting someone. It was beautiful.

"That flag," Karen pointed once again with exaggerated emphasis towards Robert's American flag. "It's creating a hostile environment in our neighborhood. I demand you remove it immediately or I will." She took a step towards the flag, but Robert took two steps down from his porch causing her to pause.

"Ma'am, before you take another step, I feel it is my responsibility to inform you that I am an attorney and therefore, an officer of the court. If you touch my property I will unleash everything within my power to bring hellfire down upon you." Robert's voice was calm and smooth, but his words caused Karen's face to visibly pale. She inhaled sharply.

"This isn't over," Karen spat as she yanked the leash stomping off across the lawn pulling the little mop behind her.

"Have a nice day." I hollered after her, but she only turned and flipped me off for my troubles.

Landon and I burst into laughter at the sight of her storming off on her crusade to make someone else's life miserable. Robert shook his head with an exaggerated smirk on his lips. The entire scene was hilarious and was the best thing we had seen in weeks. The internet was full of people posting similar encounters with Karens around the country and their arrogant entitlement. My only regret was that I forgot to record the encounter.

"Damn, that was ridiculous." Landon shook his head and climbed up the front steps. Emily was standing in the open doorway with my sister beside her.

"I wish I would have filmed it." I followed Landon up the steps placing a hand on Robert's arm. "You were brilliant. The look on her face was priceless." I giggled and he just smiled but said nothing.

"Not to worry, I got the whole encounter." My sister held up her phone with a devious grin. "I'm posting it on Instagram."

"Good." I nodded on my way into the house.

Emily, Jocelyn, and I made lunch for everyone. The atmosphere was light and comfortable. We discussed various real estate listings in Southern red states that came up this week. A few held some promise with their acreage and proximity to desirable towns. We fixed ham, scrambled eggs, toast, and fresh fruit. The men were sitting around the table waiting on us adding their two cents to our conversation before we got the chance to place the food on the table.

"So, are we in agreement that we need a minimum of fifty acres, but ideally a hundred would be best." Jackson put a dollop of scrambled eggs on his plate.

"Ideally," Robert agreed. "Do you ladies have any other provisions I need to consider?" A sly smile played on the corners of his lips as he passed the ham after putting a slice on his plate.

"As long as we live somewhere there's at least three seasons." Jocelyn scraped butter across her toast. "I can't live without Fall but would be happy to never have to shovel snow again."

"Agreed," I chimed in.

"What timeframe are we looking at here?" Landon asked Robert.

"That depends on what we find." Robert shrugged.

"Most likely a year." Emily speculated.

"But if we can find property that already has access to utilities that would speed up things." Jackson stated casually, drawing attention from his father.

"Have you been studying real estate or construction?" Robert teased his son.

"I have been doing a bit of research just trying to figure out our best options." Jackson smirked back at his dad.

"Fine," Jocelyn waved her hand dismissively holding her fork. "I will put together a spreadsheet of what is available with all pertinent information. That way we can narrow down our options to locations that meet all our requirements."

"Spoken like a true lawyer." Landon laughed.

"You are lucky my sister loves you." My sister playfully stuck her tongue out at him.

"Believe me, I know it." Landon nudged me.

After dinner I helped Emily clear the table and carry everything into the kitchen. Jocelyn brought in the last of the dishes while the men went out on the back deck to enjoy the beautiful weather with their coffee. I wrapped up the leftovers and placed them in the refrigerator knowing they would not be there long. Emily's leftovers never were.

My sister and Emily started handwashing and rinsing the dishes. I climbed up on a barstool at the island and rested my head on my folded arms closing my eyes for a moment. Physically, I felt fine. Mentally, I was drained. The baggage from my *other* life was weighing heavily on me. My conversation with my mother-in-law repeatedly played through my mind. The sounds of the militia drilling behind the barn haunted me.

"Sidney," Emily half turned towards me. "Are you alright?"

"I do not know which is worse — sitting on the edge of a Civil War you know is coming or watching your country implode from within on the verge of another that could happen at any time." I lifted my head and looked at them.

"I've noticed how badly the division has deepened. Today's encounter only solidified that no one is immune from this insanity." Emily shook her head slightly.

"I miss normal." Jocelyn stacked the last of the clean dishes in the strainer.

"Normal ended around the time you were born." Emily chuckled. "I pray we can turn this country around if not for our sake but for your generation and your children's."

"It scares me," I said honestly. "We're in a war that will never end — one we were drug into under fallacies and deception. Young soldiers are dying and the corruption within the Democrat party and amongst spineless RINOS is destroying our country and they are getting wealthier in the process. If true Americans don't take back control, we will lose everything our founding fathers fought for."

"If we haven't already." My sister said glumly.

"I know things look bad now." Emily said softly. "And I fear it is only going to get worse before it gets better. But we survived before," she took ahold of my hand and squeezed it gently. "We will survive this."

"I know," I smiled slightly. "I just hope I have the strength this time around. I feel so doom and gloom all the time." I chuckled trying to lighten the mood.

"I understand." Emily admitted. "I hate losing the home I love and the city we've built our lives in because it has become so liberal and left leaning with criminals are running rampant in the streets. I don't feel safe going to the store or shopping by myself. Robert must accompany me every time I leave the house."

"I know," Jocelyn leaned against the island. "I don't feel safe going anywhere without Jackson."

"I am thinking about getting a concealed carry permit." I confessed. "Landon thinks I should."

"I've been thinking the same thing." My sister shrugged slightly. "It isn't safe to be female and unarmed anymore. Carrying mace, pepper spray, or even a taser isn't enough anymore."

"Come with me," Emily headed towards the stairway and with us behind her. She walked into her room and opened the armoire pulling out her purse. She set it on the bed and pulled out a sleek handgun. "I bought this three weeks ago. It's a 9mm Hellcat. The recoil is a little stronger than I would like, but the high capacity of rounds makes it an easy trade-off." The sly smile across her lips made me laugh. She was the last person I would have expected this from. "Robert has been taking me to the range to practice, and I took all the classes."

"And you feel comfortable carrying it with you?" Jocelyn asked.

"I do not leave home without it." Emily paused. "Not with these liberal judges letting dangerous criminals out on the streets without so much as posting bail."

"May I join you at the range? I would like to learn too." I told her.

"I believe it would be a good idea for both of you to take the classes and then we can get your permits as well." Emily placed the Hellcat back into her purse. "You can never be too careful these days."

The rest of the clan arrived early in the afternoon. The house soon became alive with the sound of little feet running around and Phoebe yelling at them to keep it down before they wake the baby. Once upon a time I would have found it maddening, but now it was the comforting sounds of family.

We grilled out that evening and watched the older children running around the yard trying to catch lightening bugs. The simplicity warmed my heart. This life. These people. This bond. This was the life I wanted for my children. I reached over and slipped my hand into Landon's. His eyes met mine with a gentle smile. An unspoken understanding passed between us.

The sun was fading behind the horizon. Alex and Jackson started a bonfire in the pit. Emily brought out a tray filled with chocolate bars, large marshmallows, and graham crackers. The kids bounced around inpatient as their parents' loaded marshmallows on the long skewers. Their enthusiasm was contagious and soon all of us were eating roasted and burnt marshmallows.

38

SATURDAY, SEPTEMBER 29, 1860

MY STAYS WERE SO TIGHT I could barely breathe. Tallie had been fierce when pulling the strings, but I had to admit it made my figure look fabulous. I held my arms up as Tallie helped me into the heavy light cornflower blue gown. It was trimmed in cream colored lace along the bodice with a pale silver silk ribbon that tied in the back. It was very garden party Sheek, I thought as I twirled in front of the mirror. The colors accented my blue eyes in a flattering way while the lace highlighted my blond hair. It was Keifer's favorite gown on me. The summer fabric was thin, but the layers were suffocating.

"Do we have to attend?" I complained, straightening my gown and looking at my husband's eye in the mirror.

"Yes." Keifer leaned over and kissed me on the cheek. "You have no choice."

"I know," I muttered.

"Plus, it will give you the chance to say goodbye to everyone." He kissed me on the cheek once more before heading downstairs.

"Ken ah's git ya any thang lse?" Tallie stood by the end of the bed.

"No, thank you very much for your help, Tallie." I smiled at the sweet young girl who nodded without a word and left closing the door behind her.

I looked over at myself in the mirror and took a deep breath. The last month had been difficult. We attended Ronnie's funeral. We mourned with his family. I spent time with Bonnie and helped with Mr. Farwell's recovery. I had spread myself thin physically and emotionally.

My little family was set to leave early Monday morning from the seaport in Savannah. We were sailing North towards Boston where my grandmother would be waiting for us to take the train to Chicago.

I was anxious to see my family but realized that I would also dearly miss the family that I was leaving behind.

This trip had been such an eye-opening experience that words failed to convey. I had no idea how I was going to explain this life to my twenty-first century family. We had all learned the basics of American History in school since we were children. Most of us have witnessed Civil War reenactments and walked the historic battlegrounds. But this . . .

Living in this world. Witnessing it firsthand. Absorbing everything I could, and learning the Southern culture from their perspective offered insight that I never anticipated. It showed me more about how passionate Southerners were or rather are, about maintaining their individual culture from the Northern region of the country. Strangely, most people I met over the last several months agreed that slavery was an outdated notion that needed to die out. They simply did not have an agreed upon solution of how to replace the workforce.

But most importantly it appeared that the extremely high and unbalanced federal taxes and the notion of approximately five million uneducated, illiterate, homeless Africans being free to roam aimlessly terrified them to their core. Southerners knew if slaves were freed, they would have no homes, no land, no money, no means to support or provide for themselves or their families. Their concerns mirrored the same ones that Ned had expressed to me earlier. It seemed to be a concern that both Northerners and Southerners could agree upon.

I picked up my son and walked over to the window. I gazed out over the vast fields and the beautiful tree line bordering the distant edge. A few puffy white clouds floated across the robin blue sky. It was a perfect day for an outdoor barbeque.

My son giggled in my arms and his chubby little hand reached towards the window. His fingers smudged the thick glass window. His light blond hair appeared almost white in the sunlight. He cooed, and squirmed, eager to join the gathering of people that were beginning to spread out the picnic tables, chairs, and food.

I could hear hooves, wagons, and carriages approaching the house. I took a deep breath and sighed heavily. I could not stop the heavy feeling in my chest and the dread of saying farewell to all those

I had come to care so dearly for. It was going to be difficult to leave them behind and then worrying about them for the next four and a half years.

I stood on the landing at the top of the grand staircase peering down at the bustling scene below me. Neighbors, old friends, and distant family members floated about smiling and greeting each other. The ladies adorned in their wide hoop gowns fashioned for garden parties such as this. The gentlemen wore slacks, jackets, and ties holding their various style caps tucked safely beneath their arms once they crossed the threshold. It was a sight to behold.

I bit my tongue trying not to giggle as my mind flashed back on the barbeque scene at *Twelve Oakes* at the beginning of *Gone with the Wind*. It felt surreal in an odd yet somehow comforting way. There was something peaceful and majestic about this culture, this lifestyle that I never expected nor experienced in all my years living up North. I could understand why Southerners were so passionate about their culture holding it dearly in their hearts and cherished it as their lifeblood.

My little man screeched loudly when he saw his father enter the foyer, drawing the eyes of our guests. Many chuckled watching my little man squirm in my arms as he stretched his arms out towards his father.

"It appears my son is demanding my attention." Keifer ascended the stairs towards us.

"He is not one to remain silent." I smiled at my approaching husband.

"I suppose I shall keep that in mind in the future." Keifer lifted our son from my arms. "And how is my mischief maker today?"

"In good spirits," I stated the obvious with a little smirk. "He is anxious to greet everyone."

"I see that." My husband jostled him in his arms and headed back down the staircase.

"Miss Sidney," Bonnie's voice rose before I made it halfway down the stairs. "Remus is asking to see you." She gently took my arm in hers. "I made sure he followed your instructions to the letter, and you will be delighted. He insisted that I not say anything to you." There was a glint in her eyes as she steered me towards the porch. "He wanted to show you himself."

I followed her through the hordes of people trapsing in and out of the house to the wide front porch. Remus and Mariam were sitting together in the rocking chairs as if waiting for me to arrive. Remus had a beautifully carved cane resting against his knee. His face lit up with a broad smile when he saw me.

"I found her." Bonnie proudly announced.

"I see that." Remus beamed.

"Good day, Miss Sidney." Mariam greeted me with a heartwarming gentle smile. She looked picturesque in her pale deep lavender gown and her greying hair pulled back neatly in a bun at the nap of her neck.

"Good afternoon, Ms. Mariam. You look lovely today." I took her hand lightly and gave it a gentle squeeze.

"Thank you, my dear." Her pale blue eyes sparkled up at me before she turned her attention to her husband. "This one has been working so hard. He could not wait to show you."

Remus set his glass of lemonade on the small table between him and his wife. His right hand gripped the curve of his cane while the left hand steadied himself with the arm of the rocking chair. He slowly rose to his feet, carefully watching his balance. He let go of the chair and stood up straight. A proud smile spread across his lips as he took a step towards me. His gait was slow, but steady. He reached out with his free hand and took my hand in his.

"Thank you," Remus leaned over and wrapped his arm around my neck. "I cannot tell you how much I appreciate all you have done to restore my health and strength." He hugged me tightly.

"You did all the hard work yourself." I beamed letting go of the embrace but still holding his hand. "I am so proud of you."

"You, my dear, are my angel. I do not know what we would have done without you." His speech was still a bit slurred, but I could easily understand him. His recovery was nothing short of a miracle.

"Thank you," tears stung the corners of my eyes. "That means a lot to me."

"We are going to miss you so much." Mariam stood up and patted my arm.

"I am going to miss you all as well. This feels like home to me now." I confessed.

"Angelina told us you will spend your holidays in Chicago with your brother's family before returning to Boston." Bonnie mentioned. "I have often wondered what Chicago looks like."

"It has a lot of tall buildings, people, and crime." Strange how some things never change, I thought to myself. "My brother is a physician also and has a home on the northside just outside the city."

"Angelina said your whole family lives there, yet you reside in Boston." She raised her brow inquisitively.

"Yes," I inhaled deeply. "My mother passed in childbirth and my grandparents took me in while my father grieved. When he remarried, his new wife was not very fond of having a stepdaughter who resembled his first wife so much." I shrugged casually. "So, when my father took a position in Chicago, I remained under the care of my grandparents." I explained briefly.

"So, this brother you will be staying with is your half-brother?" Remus inquired.

"Yes," I nodded with a graceful smile. "I have three half-brothers through my father's second marriage. We will be staying with the eldest. While I do not know him well, his lovely wife and I have become close. She is an extraordinary lady. She is expecting her fifth child next month and is praying for a little girl." I laughed nonchalantly. "Her first four children are boys."

"That poor thing," Mariam exclaimed politely. "Four boys — my Lord. I pray she is blessed with a daughter this time."

People continued to crowd around, bustling in and out of the house. Tallie, Nala, and Maddie hurried about carrying drinks on trays and handing them politely out to our guests.

"I suppose we should make our way to the tables off yonder if we hope to grab one in the shade." Remus gestured across the lawn.

"Yes, they appear to be filling up fast." Mariam squeezed my hand tightly. "I will find you again before we leave."

"I would like that." I hugged her tightly.

I was going to miss them all dearly. Over the last several months her family has become dear to me. I thought about inviting them to join us for my son's birthday celebration in March, thinking certainly a few more people would not make such a big difference. I leaned against the porch railing and realized it was impossible. If I were hosting my in-laws, nieces, and nephews, plus my family in Chicago, there was no practical way our estate could house them all on such short notice. Even now it was going to be a stretch to get the additions completed before everyone arrived.

I walked down the front steps, plastering a fake smile on my face trying not to think about how the lives of each of these people I had grown to care about so much were about to unravel. A sea of faces blurred past me as I walked towards the tables. Each step felt like walking through quicksand. I tried to push the thoughts from my mind and focus on the joy that surrounded me. But it was difficult. I wanted to help. I wanted to save them. I wanted to protect them from the years of harshness, death, and devastation waiting for us all just off the horizon.

As the sun faded behind the tree line, Ottis lit bonfires about the grounds. The ballroom glowed with dozens of lit candles hanging in the chandeliers about the vast room. A group of musicians, consisting of individuals from local families, had gathered in the corner and began tuning their instruments. Angelina and Maggie with the help of the household had decorated the room with fire lilies, violets, and greenery. It appeared magical.

The table in the far corner held a large punch bowl and small iced cakes on little paper doilies. I was amazed by the beauty and wholesome simplicity of it all while stunned by its brilliance. I had attended many dances up North, but nothing compared to the pure extravagance and elegance of this.

The younger children had all retired upstairs for the ball. It was a strict rule apparently that no one under the age of fourteen could attend. Various nannies from multiple plantations had disappeared as the sun began its descent. It was strange to me as such guidelines and traditions did not exist where I grew up.

"Admit it, you will miss this." Maggie joined me picking up a small teacup with saucer of punch.

"Yes," I smiled gently. "Very much."

"You know I had not realized how much I missed my brother until he returned." Her eyes looked soft. "Life carried on, as you know. The daily grind seldom leaves us time to contemplate such things."

"I understand. I feel bad for keeping him away for so long." I sighed heavily and touched her arm lightly. "Keifer is different here. I can see it in his face, his walk, his shoulders. He is at peace here. This land," I scanned the room with admiration. "All of this is a part of him, an important part." I smiled gently. "I never realized how much."

"I know you do not approve of our way of life." I noticed the muscles in her jaw tense. "But I appreciate you not making a scene whilst you've been here."

"We may have different beliefs on certain things, but you are my kin. I love you all. I will always stand beside you." I squeezed her hand.

"Do you think this secession talk will come to anything?" Maggie lowered her voice.

"Yes," I nodded. "I believe it will happen right after the election and before the inauguration of the next President of the United States, a President of the Confederate States will be sworn in." I bit my lip realizing I had said to much as Maggie's eyes widened.

"Oh, my Lord," her hand went up to her chest. "If that happens, a Civil War will be inevitable."

"I agree." My voice was barely audible.

"I fear what that would bring." She choked out the words.

"As do I." I admitted.

"I suppose it would put us on opposite sides." Maggie had tears in her eyes.

"No," I confessed. "We will never be on opposite sides. As long as we have love and faith in our family bonds, we shall never stand against each other." I reassured her.

"Politicians in Washington are going to tear this country apart." Anger flashed in her eyes. "They are responsible for all this."

"That is because it is not their children nor their loved ones on the front lines risking their lives. Politicians do not care about their constituents. They never have, and they never will." A disgusting fact that never changed regardless of time.

Keifer walked over with a smile on his lips. He looked stunning in his grey slacks and jacket, crisp white button-down dress shirt, and black tie. His dirty blond hair was combed back in a messy stylish manner that enhanced his chiseled features.

"How is my beautiful wife?" He leaned over and kissed me on the cheek.

"I am well." I offered him a half-hearted smile. "I am going to miss everyone." I said sadly. "It is harder to leave than I expected."

"I know," he draped his arm around my waist.

"Does that mean you are going to miss me big brother." Maggie smirked.

"Perhaps not you personally, but I will miss your family." Keifer chuckled at himself. "Thad is good man, and I am quite fond of your children."

"I am going to miss your lovely wife, and my sweet little nephew too." Maggie dished back to her brother with a coy smile.

"Would you care to dance?" My husband smiled sweetly at his sister taking my hand.

"I would love too." I shook my head with a giggle and let him lead me to the center of the dance floor.

"Are you sorry to be leaving?" he asked.

"Yes. I daresay I am." I admitted. "Your family is wonderful. I am going to miss them and all my new friends terribly."

"But you shall see them soon." He brushed a strand of loose hair behind my ear. "My parents are so excited about coming North for our son's first birthday. I truly hope we have a mild Spring, or they are going to lynch you." He raised his eyebrows with a coy smile playing on his lips.

"Perhaps," I laughed. "Can you imagine if they saw their first snow?"

"That would be an experience." I imagined their faces. "But I am sure your younger siblings would love it."

"True," he twirled me around gracefully.

As the evening wound to a close, friends and neighbors embraced Keifer and I, shed tears, and wished us well. I never would have imagined it would be so difficult to leave. Bonnie promised to write often and keep me updated on all the juicy gossip I was going to miss. She had become a dear friend, and I hated missing the birth of her child. Her fiery passion for life and shear stubbornness encompassed the spirit of the South in my heart. She was the embodiment of a true Southern Belle.

39

SUNDAY, OCTOBER 11, 2020

THE PRESSURE COOKER THAT HAD become the norm in our country felt ready to blow at any moment. The presidential campaigns were bombarding every aspect of our lives. I had never paid much attention to politics, but even I could not deny what was at stake. The Democrat party, especially the extreme liberal left was running amuck unchecked by anyone. I hated to think what would become of the United States if that moronic puppet Joe Biden and his comrades managed to steal the election.

Social media had become a landmine of political nonsense. Friends from high school and college, even some extended family members who I was connected with on social media but rarely saw in real life, surprised me by some of their political views. I watched as people, friends, and family members tore each other to shreds because of differing opinions. It was beyond absurd. Still, I refused to engage in any political discussions with anyone outside my immediate family.

Thousands of new Covid-19 cases were diagnosed daily. The Spanish government had implemented a partial lockdown while the Italian Prime Minister was asking parliament to extend Italy's state of emergency through the holidays. Earlier this month, even President Trump and First Lady, Melania had tested positive for Covid -19. President Trump had spent several nights at the Walter Reed National Military Medical Center before returning to the White House. Travel restrictions throughout the country and globally remained in place.

"Are you hungry?" I leaned against the side of the couch and nudged Landon.

"Sorta," he barely looked up from the television.

"Are you going to veg here all day watching old movies?" I exhaled loudly.

"Old movie?" He scoffed, pretending I deeply offended him. "*True Grit* is a classic. John Wayne, Glen Campbell, and Kim Darby — it's one of my favorites."

"Uncle Nicholas loved this movie." I sat down beside him. "I miss him."

"I know," Landon put his arm around my shoulder pulling me closer to him and kissing my forehead.

A knock on the door broke my train of thought. "Are you expecting anyone?" I rose to my feet.

"No," he shook his head. "It's probably your sister." He turned his focus back to the movie before I reached the door.

"Hello darling," Phoebe stood on my doorstep holding little Audry in a carrier as Carson chased Wally down the hallway. "We were going stir crazy." She turned towards her son and husband running towards the far end of the hall. "Just pick him up."

"Gotcha," Carson laughed as he lifted a shrieking Wally and tossed him over his shoulder. "Little man is getting faster." He said approaching us.

"Are we interrupting anything?" Phoebe looked apologetically at me.

"I wish," I chuckled, stepping back and letting them in.

"Oh, hey," Landon spun around and stood up to greet our guest. "What are you guys doing out?"

"Nothing," Carson set Wally down on his feet.

"Hi Uncle Landon," Wally hugged Landon before running towards me. "Aunt Sidney," he grabbed my waist and looked up at me. "Do you have any cookies?"

"Sure," I led him over to the kitchen. "Let's see what we've got."

"Only one." Phoebe set the baby carrier down on the island and sat down on a barstool. "I never thought I would say this, but I really miss going to the office."

"I know exactly what you mean," I sympathized pulling out a chocolate chip cookie from the cookie jar on the counter.

"Thanks!" Wally said excitedly before taking a bite.

When Phoebe turned to adjust Audry's blanket, I handed Wally a second cookie while placing a finger over my closed lips. He smiled broadly and quickly ran off into the living room before Phoebe noticed. When Phoebe turned her attention back to me, she was none the wiser about the extra cookie I had slipped her son. I smiled at my best friend considering my actions justified as my role of aunt for her children whom I adored.

Phoebe and I chatted in the kitchen whilst fixing some sour cream chicken enchiladas and Spanish rice for dinner. The men had absorbed themselves in classic western movies with Wally coloring at the end table in the living room. It was one of the few times I had seen him so focused. His new obsession was superheroes and comic book characters. He was concentrating hard on remaining in the lines so he could do the characters justice.

"Did you see the governor of New York ordered the closing of schools throughout the state including all non-essential businesses and religious institutions?" Phoebe asked, shredding the chicken.

"France, Iceland, and Spain are enforcing similar protocols as well." I remarked stirring the rice. "Your dad was right when he said things are going to get much worse before it gets better."

"It certainly appears so," she muttered.

"Is it me or does this whole thing seem orchestrated?" Phoebe turned towards me with a crease in her brow.

"By who? That moron, Fauci?" I shrugged. "Supposedly, this virus was released from some laboratory in China."

"One of my friends in the DA office told me it was an American lab in North Carolina." Phoebe rolled her eyes. "Who knows which is true."

"Did you see they charged Derek Chauvin for George Floyd's death?"

"I am not surprised." She scoffed. "They need a scapegoat to blame."

"One of the nurses I worked with, Brandy, her husband is an officer, and she told me that technique Chauvin used was textbook — taught to every cadet at the academy. Floyd was a violent criminal and a drug addict. He died from an overdose, not from anything

Chauvin did." I leaned against the counter facing her. "I cannot believe how suddenly half the country has gone completely mental."

"That we can agree on," Phoebe shook her head slightly. "I truly hate to think of the world I brought my children into." Her voice dropped an octave. "This one anyway." She whispered before returning to her normal voice. "I just want to keep them safe and healthy."

"And you will," I reached out and squeezed her shoulder. "They will have wonderful childhoods — on both planes." I started rolling up the enchiladas and placing them into the baking dish.

"I hope so," she muttered just loud enough for me to hear.

"You know how they say history repeats itself?" I nodded. "I cannot help but think of the correlation between John Brown and George Floyd." Phoebe tilted her head and raised an eyebrow. "Is it me, or is there a strong similarity between the two?"

"No, it is not just you. I noticed that as well." I turned to face her. "Two known violent felons with a sordid criminal past who lost their lives due to their own actions, who are martyred by half the country, and appropriately villainized by the other half causing racial tension and divide people even after their deaths." I rolled my eyes. "I guess history does repeat itself.

My heart went out to Phoebe and to all the parents who were now faced with an uncertainty we had never experienced before in our lifetime. I leaned against the counter and thought of Bonnie who was already the mother of several young children and due to give birth again five months before our nation collapsed into a devastating civil war. I had briefly searched different record bases on the internet and could not find anything about her, her children, or the Farwell's in Savannah past 1863. It was like they all somehow disappeared, and it left me feeling so apprehensive and scared.

"Sidney? Did you hear me?" Landon's voice cut through my thoughts.

"I am sorry, what?" I turned towards the family room.

"Would you and Phoebe like to vote on the next movie?" I glanced at Phoebe who rolled her eyes and shook her head with a smirk.

"We're good. Watch whatever." I told him.

"Okay," he smiled back.

"Dinner smells good." Carson grinned from the couch.

"Thanks," I chuckled giving Phoebe a knowing grin.

"Some things never change." She checked the heat on the refried beans, lowering the temperature a smidge. "What were you thinking about?"

"I was trying to find some information on a friend of mine," I lowered my voice. "In Savannah." She nodded. "But I haven't been able to find anything after the war."

"Have you checked the city records or the newspaper archives for Savannah?" Phoebe put the pan of enchiladas in the oven.

"I will check."

Phoebe and I joined the guys. Audry stirred a bit in her carrier wanting her own dinner. Phoebe discretely adjusted herself and nursed Audry while the enchiladas cooked. They men had decided upon *The Great Escape* with Steve McQueen and James Garner.

"This is one of my dad's favorite movies." I said curling up with Landon.

"You know it's based on true story." Carson leaned over towards me.

"Seriously?" I hadn't realized that.

"Yeah, it raised quite a stink when it released, especially in Europe. Many people were pissed about the realism of the prisoner camp, it being shot in Bulgaria I think, and the use of American actors portraying Polish and Englishmen who died in real life for Hollywood theatrics." He explained. "It was banned in most of Europe."

"I can understand why. This released in the sixties, didn't it." I looked over at Landon.

"1963, I believe." Landon thought about it, looking at Carson for confirmation.

"Yeah, I believe so."

"So, Hollywood thought it was a good idea to release this less than twenty years after the end of the war?" I scoffed. "I can see why they were so upset. Talk about insensitive."

The four of us spent the next half hour watching the movie and only commenting on the commentary. Wally continued coloring with an intense look of concentration on his little face. He immersed himself in his coloring and ignored the adults around him. He chewed on his bottom lip doing his best to stay in the lines.

By the time we gathered around the dinner table, my stomach was growling in anticipation. The sour cream enchiladas smelled heavenly. Carson pulled over one of the taller bar stools from the breakfast bar for Wally to sit on, making it easier for him to reach the table. He beamed with pride, being at the same level as the rest of us without sitting in a booster seat which he insisted was only for babies and stating he was now a big boy. The child was adorable.

We passed around the refried beans and Spanish rice while Landon scooped out the enchiladas onto everyone's plate. We barely got through grace before everyone started digging in. Everything tasted phenomenal. I was impressed by how well it turned out, considering only a short while ago I was almost as incompetent as my mother in the kitchen. Thankfully, Emily took the time to teach me how to cook and bake.

"You know this is nothing new in Hollywood. They push a narrative, and the world is just supposed to suck it up without questioning it." Carson shrugged adding some sour cream to his refried beans. "Walt is probably spinning in his grave watching his dream turn into every parent's nightmare."

"Walt had some," Landon wrinkled his forehead and pursed his lips for a moment. "Peculiarities. There is no dispute about that. But at least the man had the decency to be subtle, if not inconspicuous in his beliefs."

"This woke crap coming out of all corners of Hollywood is disturbing. I hate that I must monitor everything now between books and cartoons because it goes against everything, we believe in." Phoebe explained. "It has gotten to the point that we canceled our Disney and Hulu subscriptions last month."

"There are very few celebrities that aren't corrupt in some way or another." I added.

"All for the price of fame," Landon smirked.

"I never understood the appeal." I added some cheddar cheese and sour cream to my refried beans. "I never wanted camera's following me everywhere, taking pictures, invading my privacy."

"That is because you have self-esteem." Phoebe grinned. "Most of the people who spend their lives in front of a camera don't. That's why they crave the validation."

"It's sad, really." Landon concluded. "The way the media and Hollywood twist reality and focus solely on a warped agenda."

"Want to hear something odd?" Carson grinned knowingly. "I was reading an article the other day about the link between John F. Kennedy and Abraham Lincoln. It was weird."

"Weird how?" I was curious.

"Well, Lincoln was elected to congress in 1846, and Kennedy was elected to congress a hundred years later in 1946. Same with their presidencies — 1860 and 1960." Carson recalled.

"Huh, I never realized." Landon raised an eyebrow.

"Me neither," I shrugged.

"Also, they were both advocates for Civil Rights. Both of their wives lost a child during their presidential terms, and obviously they were both shot in the head, but did you know they were both shot on a Friday?" Landon asked.

"No, I didn't know that." Landon looked at Phoebe and me, and we both shook our heads. "That's weird."

"Oh, it gets better." Carson seemed almost giddy. "Lincoln's secretary was named Kennedy and Kennedy's secretary was named Lincoln. Both Presidents were assassinated by Southern men, and both were succeeded by Southern men named Johnson. Andrew Johnson, the man who succeeded Lincoln was born in 1808, and Lyndon Johnson, Kennedy's successor, was born in 1908." He was on a roll. Plus, their assassins are known by their full names, each containing fifteen letters each, and were born a hundred years apart — 1839 and 1939. President Lincoln was assassinated in a theater named Ford while President Kennedy was assassinated in a Lincoln made by Ford. And the strangest coincidence is that Lincoln was murdered in a theater whose assassin ran to a warehouse to hide from authorities and Kennedy was killed from a warehouse whose killer hid out in a theater."

"That was a lot of information," I muttered stunned.

"Yeah," Phoebe looked at her husband as if seeing him for the first time, but with a look that reflected something more along the lines of pity than pride.

"Interesting," Landon took a bite thinking carefully. "I had not realized they were so closely related."

"Me neither," Carson looked pleased with himself. "I just thought it was cool."

Landon and I exchanged a look — one of those looks that couples who have been together for a long time and experienced more than most — where an entire conversation takes place by just locking your eyes briefly. Carson missed it completely, but Phoebe caught it. She pretended she didn't as her eyes dropped back on her plate.

"Like I said earlier, history repeats itself." I glanced at Phoebe. "I just hope the Democrats remember enough history not to start another civil war."

The conversation shifted to the canceled second debate and Joe Biden hiding out in his basement. The consensus was Biden was a pathetic contender who couldn't win without rigging the election. Carson, always the optimist, refused to believe that a party of governmental officials would ever do something so dishonest. He insisted that people when into politics with good intentions and genuinely wanted to make a difference in the lives of their constituents. I felt almost bad for him and his naivety.

Later that evening after our company had gone home, I turned off our bedroom light and curled up with Landon. He was streaming *Castle* on the Roku channel leaning against a pile of pillows. I rested my head upon his chest and draped my arm across him.

"I am going to need to call Phoebe tomorrow and apologize." I glanced up at his silhouette.

"For what?"

"She caught that look between us after Carson finished his Lincoln Kennedy spiel."

"Ouch," Landon winced. "Sorry."

"I feel bad," I admitted.

"Come on, Sid." He snorted. "She clearly didn't marry him for his brains. I'm honestly surprised he can tie his shoes."

"Granted, I have heard Phoebe refer to him as a glorified trophy husband." I admitted. "But I feel bad. I don't want her to think we were mocking him."

"He clearly memorized the points in that article to impress us."

"Landon, even though he never says anything, I am sure it does bother him at times that he doesn't have the same educational background as the rest of us." I propped myself up on my folded hands on his chest. "All of us have advanced degrees."

"Ah, bullshit Sid." Landon rolled his eyes. "Carson and his little associate's degree from community college. Leslie doesn't have an advanced degree, and she doesn't talk like a moron."

"Leslie has a bachelor's in science from an Ivy League university — Brown, I think."

"Whatever," Landon huffed.

"I thought you liked Carson. You two always seem to get along so well."

"I do. We do," he waved his free hand dismissively. "I just don't like it when someone pretends to be something they're not."

"Landon, I think he was trying to impress you." I looked at him sympathetically.

"Alright. Alright." He sighed heavily. "I'll call Phoebe tomorrow too and apologize."

"I love you," I reached up and kissed his soft lips.

"I love you, too."

40

SUNDAY, OCTOBER 14, 1860

ANNABELLE MOVED KEIFER AND I into what would be — in another life, my sister, Jocelyn's bedroom and put my grandmother in what would be Ethan's room. The overwhelming sense of deja'vu was almost unbearable. It was the first time I had been confronted so personally with a connection between my two parallel lives. I suddenly understood what my sister had been talking about for so long when her barrier began to disintegrate.

There were times I struggled to breathe, especially in the family room or front parlor. I am sure my brother, Patrick and Annabelle thought his older sister had mental problems or something. Thankfully, Marissa explained it off as exhaustion from our long journey. I do not believe they fully believed her, but my anxiety lessened after the first week and I got better at hiding the flashes that plagued me between my two worlds.

My sister-in-law looked like she was ready to deliver any day. Still, I knew she had some time to go before Jocelyn made her appearance. Plus, I finally got to meet the infamous Mimi that had played such a crucial role in my sister's life. She was a stout, lively woman who could wrangle all four of my nephews into shape in thirty seconds' flat. I smiled as she would mutter under her breathe about the boys' behavior after she gave them a verbal lashing. It was clear how much she adored each of them. I loved her character and infectious personality immediately.

We were there less than a week before my father, Walter and the contemptuous woman he had married, Bethany joined us for Sunday dinner after church services. I watched them carefully throughout the long-winded sermon. I knew my grandmother was anxious and excited to see her son and I tried my best to put myself in her shoes

— truly I did. But seeing the woman who my father allowed to discard me as yesterday's trash filled my heart with silent rage. I jostled my restless son on my lap trying to remember what era I was in and not confront her. I figured my best option was to avoid her as much as possible.

"My goodness, Sidney," Walter cornered me as soon as services concluded and gave me a perfunctory side hug. "Is this my new grandson?" My son was fussy and buried his face on my shoulder.

"Hello," I purposely left off the title. "Yes, this is my son, Keifer Lee."

"He is a brute." Walter tried to touch my son playfully, but lil' Keifer was having none of it.

"My apologies. He is hungry and ready for his nap." I patted my son's back and moved towards the door.

"We will see you at supper." He called after me, but I did not turn around.

I hurried towards the carriage before I could answer any more awkward questions. A few minutes later, Keifer and my grandmother joined us, and Eddie, my brother's stableman, and Mimi's husband drove the carriage back towards my brother's home.

"That was rude," my grandmother looked at me with annoyance.

"How so?" my son continued to fuss, and I handed him over to his father. "I was perfectly pleasant."

"You were cold." Marissa scolded me. "I raised you better than that."

"That very statement is why I was perfectly pleasant and not warm or loving." I shrugged.

"When are you going to forgive him? He was young and made mistakes." She looked at me with disappointment.

"When are you going to stop making excuses for him?" I huffed.

"Ladies," Keifer was patting our cranky son on his lap. "I understand this is a sensitive subject for both of you. Can we please just enjoy ourselves and each other or this is going to be a miserable holiday season for him. Is that what you want?"

"No," I looked out the window.

"Of course not." My grandmother turned her gaze to the opposite one.

I watched the houses float by and thought about our second evening here. The four of us had finally got some decent sleep and were feeling mostly human again. During a lively dinner discussion where Patrick and Keifer talked about their medical practices and patients. Marissa, Annabelle, and I half listened to the men but mainly talked about family and our children.

While we were enjoying coffee and dessert in the parlor there was a knock on the front door interrupting our conversations. I didn't think much about it when I saw Eddie pass the parlor door to answer it. Then I heard their familiar voices. They were unmistakable and I felt my breath catch in my throat. Before my brain could fully process it, there they stood — a very young Robert and Emily with their three children. I was struck again by how much Jackson resembled his father, especially when Robert was young. My grandmother saw the color drain from my face and placed her hand on my arm trying to steady me.

"Robert. Emily," Annabelle scurried awkwardly to her feet. "I am so happy you made it." She walked over to them and embraced them warmly.

"Sidney," Annabelle turned and led her guests into the parlor. "I would like to introduce you to the Chandlers, our dear friends and neighbors. This is Robert, his wife, Emily, and their children, Alexander, Phoebe, and Jackson." She smiled warmly as I rose to my feet followed by my husband and grandmother. "Robert, Emily — this is Patrick's older sister, Sidney from Boston, her husband, Dr. Keifer Marshall, and Patrick's grandmother, Marissa." We all shook hands and exchanged pleasantries.

"I am pleased to meet you." I kept searching their eyes for some recognition but there was none.

"Are you a physician too?" Keifer asked Robert as he joined them for a brandy near the hearth.

"Worse," Patrick jumped in before Robert could answer. "He is an attorney."

Everyone found a seat and the children disappeared off with my nephews. The atmosphere was jovial. Robert and Emily were as pleasant and easy to talk to as I recalled from my *other* life. I tried not to stare at them, but I could not help it. They both looked so young. I was trying to do the math in my head and figured they had to be a couple years younger than me.

The evening had left me visibly shaken. My grandmother knew the significance of the Chandler's in my *other* life and tried her best to keep me grounded. I was failing miserably. Finally, I had to excuse myself and retire early because I could not get my barrens. When my grandmother had checked on me later, she held me while I cried and tried to make sense of this bizarre situation, I found myself in.

As soon as we arrived at my brother's home, I went upstairs and fed my son before everyone else returned. He was still nursing and was slowly starting to eat soft foods. He had six teeth now and was getting up on all fours rocking back and forth trying to figure out what to do next. I knew it wouldn't be long before he was crawling everywhere. His determination and stubbornness told me he was definitely Keifer's son.

I settled back into the rocking chair by the window and gazed out over front lawn. The Chandler's new house stood across the street with its freshly painted shutters and newly laid cobblestone walkway. There were only a few scattered mature trees, but most of the landscaping appeared new. Emily had been busy planting flowers and shrubs along the walkway. She was every bit as meticulous in this era as she was in her *other*.

I heard voices downstairs as the house filled up with family members. I felt torn. I wanted to see my Uncle Monte — to meet him in this world. He was young and not yet married to Vivian. The memories of him from my *other* world were faded and few. I was curious about the man whose death had caused a decade long estrangement between Shane and Nicholas.

But my spineless father and evil step-monster were down there also. I thought I was prepared for this. Now I wasn't so sure. I traced my fingers lightly through my son's soft hair brushing it away from his beautiful hazel eyes that were so much like his father's. A smile played at the corners of his mouth as my precious son drifted off to sleep.

I laid him down gently in the crib beside our bed. I stood over him, thinking of how much he was a blessing in my life and how I could never imagine loving anyone as much as I loved him. He was my angel.

I looked around the room and struggled with the flashes that showed my sister's room as I had seen it countless times in the twenty-first century. It was unsettling on the senses. I had no idea I would have such a reaction to my childhood home. I was newly built with the smell of fresh paint still lingering in the air. I had noticed last night in the parlor that the nails for our Christmas stockings — a lifelong staple in my childhood home, were absent from the fireplace mantel. They were yet to be placed there for the first time this upcoming Christmas. A small detail with timeless memories.

I smoothed out my dress and headed down the stairs. My palms were sweaty. My steps were slow. I gripped the handrail harder than necessary. I wished I could confront the two of them for just five minutes in the twenty-first century. I knew exactly what I would say to both of them. I wanted my father to understand how badly he had hurt me, how betrayed I felt. I wanted to tell Bethany what a horrible, cruel, and heartless woman she was for turning her back on a small child simply because I looked like my mother. I wanted to tell her how she had destroyed any possible relationship me or my son would have with Walter now or in the future.

But I couldn't. The social restrictions and conventions did not allow me to voice anything beyond politeness. It was times such as this that I felt truly suffocated simply because I happened to be born female. Voices drifted up the stairs. It appeared the families were enjoying lively discussions. Jackson and James ran around the corner with two-year-old William toddling behind with his stubby little legs. Mimi scooped him up as he resisted her.

"Settle down, chil. You's time ol' come." Mimi carried the reluctant toddler into another room.

I entered the parlor and noticed how everyone had broken into smaller clusters. Robert, Keifer, and Patrick were huddled near the decanters holding a brandy in one hand and a cigar in the other. My grandmother was talking with Walter, Bethany, and Monte. Annabelle, Vivian, and Emily were standing near the bay windows with the afternoon sunlight casting their faces in a warm glow. They were a picturesque image.

Vivian was a comely young lady with bright, kind, blue eyes and ash-blonde hair that cascaded in curls across her shoulders and down her back. She had delicate features and a tiny waist that immediately made me jealous. She was wearing a burgundy gown trimmed in ivory lace that heightened the feelings of Fall in the air.

Walter tried to make eye contact with me as soon as he noticed me in the parlor archway. I approached the ladies deliberately avoiding his eyes. I knew I could not avoid him throughout the entirety of our visit, but I felt determined to minimize our interactions as much as possible.

"Is your angel asleep?" Emily kindly asked.

"Yes, thank you." I smiled warmly accepting a glass of lemonade from one of the housekeepers, Missy.

"He is a beautiful child," Vivian added. "He looks so much like his father."

"Yes, he does." I agreed and Emily nodded.

"I do not mean to pry, but you looked upset when Walter spoke with you after services." Emily appeared confused.

"Our relationship is complicated." I said softly.

"Bethany is watching you," Annabelle's voice was low. "What happened between the two of you?" I was surprised Patrick had not told her.

"I thought you knew," I was surprised Patrick had not told her.

"No," Annabelle shook her head. "Patrick is more about peace and harmony. Anything disagreeable — he simply sweeps under the rug and pretends it doesn't exist." She whispered, gesturing softly with her hands.

"My mother, Julia passed away during childbirth. Walter remarried Bethany a few years later and together they had Patrick, Monte, and Nicholas. Bethany was always very cold towards me and hated how much I resembled my mother. Shortly after they were married, Walter accepted a position with Bethany's uncle in Chicago. They moved and left me with my grandparents in Boston," I shrugged nonchalantly. "Well, Braintree just outside of Boston. We have an estate there called Terrace Falls."

"I had no idea." Annabelle looked horrified placing her hand on my arm and squeezing it gently. "I am so sorry, Sidney."

"I appreciate that." I grinned through the embarrassment of being abandoned. "As you can imagine, being raised by my grandparents, I am very close to them and unfortunately, I cannot say the same about Walter."

"Annabelle mentioned you traveled here from Savannah," Vivian cleared her throat and graciously changed the subject. "Your husband is from the South, is that right?"

"Yes, Keifer was born and raised on their family plantation, Gable Gardens just outside of Savannah." I shifted my weight uneasily trying to gauge their feelings about the South and Southerners.

"I have never been to a Southern plantation." Emily stated.

"Me neither," Annabelle admitted. "But I have always wanted to see the South."

"I had visited once briefly after we were married, but this was my first extended stay. We spent the summer, and it was lovely. His family hosted the most elaborate barbeques and balls I have ever seen. Everyone in their community was so warm and kind. I hated saying goodbye to his family and all the friends I had made."

"That seems to be very contradictory to what we hear of Southern plantations up here." Vivian seemed surprised, but the other two ladies nodded in agreement.

"We have been told such horrors going on." Emily voice was barely above a whisper. "Beatings, assaults, and worse," her voice trailed off.

"I am sure it happens, but by who?" I lowered my voice a little so only the three of them could hear me. "There was a slave insurrection at a neighboring plantation. It was terrifying. Their young daughters were attacked, and their little boy was murdered for trying to defend his young sister."

"Oh, my goodness," Annabelle gasped.

"I had heard that was happening more often down there." Emily noted. "Ever since John Brown's raid on Harper's Ferry, the tension between the Northern and Southern states has intensified, even becoming hostile."

"I fear what will happen if the Southern states decide to secede." Vivian turned towards me. "Did you hear talk of secession while you were down there?"

"Yes, a lot of it." I nodded. "Sadly, everyone I spoke to agreed that slavery is an outdated and unsustainable system, but given the unbalanced taxes being placed on them by the federal government they cannot afford to pay workers."

"I do not know much about taxes — state or federal, but I guess I always assumed they were uniformed." Annabelle looked confused. "Patrick is mindful of me reading newspapers or other material about things outside of what he deems acceptable for ladies." She shrugged casually.

"Most husbands are," I was not surprised since Jocelyn had mentioned more than once how controlling Patrick was over what she was exposed to in her *other* life.

"Robert mentioned something about unequal taxation between the Northern and Southern states, and I had not thought much of it at the time." Emily looked a bit concerned.

"From what I understand, they are incredibly lopsided. The Southern states, especially wealthy plantation owners, are paying more than eighty-six percent taxes on all cotton, rice, and tobacco grown in the South. That's over three fourths of their income being paid out in federal taxes that are used to build Northern industries." I explained.

"Is that true?" Annabelle looked stunned.

"I believe so," Emily told her. "I have heard Robert discussing it with his colleagues."

Before I could comment further, Walter approached us. He stood awkwardly off to the side. He cleared his throat softly. When I did not turn around, he cleared his throat louder.

"Sidney, would you please join me on a walk before supper?" I closed my eyes and took a deep breath.

"Of course," I smiled at him before addressing Annabelle, Vivian, and Emily. "Please excuse me." They nodded without a word.

"Please," Walter gestured towards the door.

I grabbed my sunhat and parasol from the entryway and walked out onto the wrap-around front porch. The afternoon sun was fighting to break through the grey clouds lingering overhead. I paused for a moment on the porch steps looking out over the plush green lawn and the stunning array of colors singing from the tress. I thought of how different the landscape appeared from what I was accustomed to seeing from these steps and how strange it must be for Jocelyn to experience this daily.

I walked down the steps slowly. The sound of my heels on the cobblestone echoed loudly in my ears. I reached the gate and unlatched it, walking through without waiting for Walter to be a gentleman. I knew if he did, it was merely for social convention and nothing to do with him demonstrating any respect for me.

"Sidney," he walked up beside me matching my pace. "I understand why you are upset with me." I bit my lower lip struggling to remain silent. "I made some mistakes in the past. I honestly thought I was doing what was best for you." I nodded without responding. "You were happy at Terrace Falls and were attached to your grandparents."

"They provided me with a good life." I kept my eyes forward.

"I trusted they would." Walter kept his voice low.

We walked around the corner towards the park. Trees line the cobblestone walkway showing off their Fall brilliance. This was my favorite time of year, and I wished I was taking this walk with anyone else — well, almost anyone else.

"I know Bethany can be difficult." I knew he was expecting a reply, but I didn't offer one — I didn't trust myself, not to be brutally honest. "But she has been a good wife to me and mother to your brothers." Walter concluded.

"I am happy for you." It was the politest thing I could think of to say.

"Despite being a Southerner, your husband seems like a good man." Walter switched tactics. "I am sorry I did not make it to your wedding."

"Keifer is a good man." I simply sidestepped his remark.

"You seem happy."

"I am."

"Sidney," he exhaled loudly and stopped walking. "What do you want from me?"

"Nothing," I shrugged.

"Why do you insist on treating me this way?" Walter took off his hat and ran his fingers through his graying hair with exasperation. "I have apologized. What else do you want from me?" He put his hat back on and straightened his shoulders.

"I do not want anything from you." I said honestly. "Walter, I do not even know you. If it were not for the letters from Annabelle, I would not know my brothers or nephews. You, nor your wife, have ever made any effort to know me or anything about my life. I came for a visit to introduce my son to my brothers and their families, and you expect me to act like your loving daughter. Why?"

"You are my daughter," he raised his voice an octave.

"That never mattered to you before. Why should it matter now?" I tilted my head and eyed him carefully.

"Does your husband enjoy your insolence?" Walter's face twisted in indignation and flushed red.

"My husband does not expect me to be a wallflower." I lifted my chin in defiance.

"Only a Southern man would allow such behavior from his wife." Walter narrowed his eyes.

"Only a coward would abandon his child for a cheap woman." I retorted before I could stop myself.

Walter's face turned pale. I saw his fists clenched at his sides and before I realized what was happening his hand struck the side of my face with enough force that I hit the ground before I could catch myself. My hand immediately went to my face more from shock than pain.

"How dare you speak to me this way." Walter loomed over me shaking his index finger.

The sound of heavy footsteps drew louder and closer. I was glaring up at Walter's purple face when a fist from the corner of my eye connected with his jaw. I heard the scream from my grandmother before I realized what had happened.

Walter stumbled backwards almost losing his balance before catching himself on the picket fence to steadying himself. My eyes shifted to the man standing before me full expecting to see my husband attached to the fist. I inhaled sharply when the silhouette turned and I realized it was my brother, Patrick. He reached down, offering his hand to him and helped me to my feet.

My grandmother rushed up beside us holding the hem of her skirt up and gasping for breath. I grabbed her arms as she tried to slow down and catch her breath.

"How dare you raise your hand to me." Walter screamed rubbing his jaw.

"How dare you strike a lady," Patrick turned on him with fire in his eyes. "Your own daughter." His chest was heaving as she squared up to his father. "You haven't seen her in more than two decades. She travels here to introduce us to her husband and son. She makes the trip — the effort to get to know us after you took her entire family and moved across the country and left her behind."

"I have every right to strike my child if she disrespects me." Walter roared. "And she disrespected me and your mother."

"I do not care what she said," my grandmother rose to her full height with her chin stuck out proudly. "I did not raise you to put your hands on any lady."

"She disrespected me and my wife." Walter's face was a dangerous shade of purple, but his voice dropped back to a normal tone when confronted by his mother.

"Walter, I love you. You are my son. But you must understand how the decision you made shaped your relationship with your daughter. You abandoned her. She has a right to be upset." Marissa exhaled slowly.

"Sidney can be upset. She will not be disrespectful. No Northern man would tolerate a wife with a mouth like that." Walter turned his focus on me. "I did not raise you to . . ."

"You did not raise me at all." I said matter-of-factly. "You walked out on me and left me with your parents while you started another life in a different city with your replacement family." I struggled to keep my voice calm.

Walter looked like he had been punched again. His lips were pursed together in a tight line. His chest was heaving with indignation. I could see him flexing his fingers at his side, balling them into fists and then releasing them trying to control his temper.

"My wife sent us to let you know supper is ready." Patrick straightened his jacket, turning towards his father. "Keifer, Sidney, their son, and my grandmother are guests in my home. My wife is getting ready to deliver my child any day now. Respectfully, dad I must ask you and mother to skip dinner."

"As you wish, and we will not be back until she apologizes or returns to Boston." Walter pointed his finger in my direction.

"Walter," my grandmother cradled her son's face in her hands. "I am sorry you feel this way. I love you, son, but you are in the wrong here."

"She disrespected me and my wife." Walter said through gritted teeth.

"Father, you are fortunate it was me and not her husband that saw what you did."

"Like I care," Walter spit on the ground. "She's a traitor marrying a slave owner and bringing that ruffian here to embarrass our family."

"Son, I am ashamed of you." My grandmother's voice was small. "Dr. Keifer Marshall is one of the best men I have ever known. He is an honorable man."

I could see her words cut him sharper than any knife ever could. She patted Patrick's arm lightly, her lips pursed into a thin line. The slight tremble in her lower lip was the only outward sign of how much this betrayal was breaking her heart. Despite his numerous flaws and poor behavior, my grandmother loved her son as dearly as I loved my own. She suddenly looked frailer than I had ever seen her before. She reached for my hand without another word, and we walked back towards my brother's house in silence.

Family and friends were milling about between the parlor and dining room waiting for our return. I felt all eyes land on my grandmother and me as we made our way over to my husband. I watched his expression change as we drew closer and he saw the looks on our faces.

"What happened?" he whispered trying not to draw attention but immediately turned my face gently to see the raw red handprint that still stung my skin.

"Her father slapped her," my grandmother said softly putting a gentle hand on my husband's arm as his face went red with rage. "Patrick handled it."

"How?" Keifer whispered through gritted teeth.

"As you would have," she reassured him guiding him gently towards the dining room and away from prying eyes.

Thankfully, my husband let it go, but only for now. Patrick and Walter entered the foyer. Their shoulders were stiff and the tension between them was palpable. Patrick removed his hat and handed it to Eddie before turning towards Walter.

"Wait here. I will get mother." The coldness in Patrick's voice was noticed by everyone within distance as he headed towards the dining room.

I saw him lean in and whisper something to his mother. Bethany's jaw tightened as her lips pursed into a thin line. Her eyes narrowed in my direction, but she remained silent. Patrick took her elbow and guided her to the foyer. Everyone else stood in awkward silence in the dining room. No one spoke. No one sat down.

"Walter, what happened?" Bethany lost all pretense and her voice rose loud enough for everyone to hear.

"My daughter disrespected us." Walter snarled.

"Patrick, you are choosing your half-sister over your parents." Bethany scoffed. "If you do not immediately demand her to leave, I will never forgive you."

"Mother, this is not the time nor place. Please respect my wishes." With that, the sound of footsteps on the hardwood floor brought Patrick back into the dining room.

Moments later after we were all seated the front door opened and closed. A collective sigh could be felt by everyone and supper turned into pleasant conversation with delicious food.

When the children were all settled down for the night, everyone gathered in the parlor. No one had mentioned Walter, Bethany, or the details of our encounter in front of the children. But Monte was three brandy's in, and his cheeks were flushed from the glow of whiskey. The ladies had gathered amongst the lounges and couches sipping coffee whilst the gentlemen stood around near the hearth with easy access to the canisters.

"Is anyone going to explain what happened this afternoon?" Monte's words were not quite slurred but quickly moving in that direction. "Why did our parents leave before supper?"

Patrick shifted uncomfortably and took another shot of whiskey. He refilled his glass two fingers worth and looked towards his grandmother and me. I met his eyes carefully waiting for him to respond but Marissa spoke up first.

"Your father slapped Sidney across the face," she stated matter-of-factly meeting Patrick's eye. "Your brother reacted appropriately and asked them to leave."

"Why would he slap you?" Monte stared at me with a raised eyebrow. "He doesn't even know you."

"He did not appreciate me pointing out that fact to him," I shrugged casually. "Nor what I said about his abandonment."

"I see," Monte leaned against the mantel. "You know, we did not even know about you until Patrick got engaged." The casual way he said it cut deeply.

"How . . ." the words faltered in my throat as the depth of my father's betrayal went much deeper than I had realized. It became clear as to the real reason my own father had missed my wedding.

Our grandmother opened her mouth but closed it again trying to find the right words to make sense of such betrayal.

"I do not understand," Marissa's eyes searched between her two grandsons for explanation.

"I am afraid it came out while we were writing out wedding announcements." Annabelle said softly. "When I asked Bethany about mailing a letter to you. She said it was best to let sleeping dogs lie. I did not understand but assumed perhaps there had been a previous disagreement I was not aware of, so I wrote a letter to you. Bethany was extremely upset when she found out and humiliated me."

"Are you telling me he never once mentioned being married to my mother, Julia or having me?" I wasn't sure if I should laugh or cry.

"No," Patrick shook his head and downed the rest of his whiskey.

"What did he ever say about his family in Boston? His parents? His childhood?" my grandmother was indignant.

"Not much." Monte shrugged. "We knew he grew up on a farm outside Boston and his family still lived there."

"But he purposely kept you all from having a relationship with me or your grandfather to protect his lie?" Marissa seethed.

"It was not our father who decided to keep us away. It was our mother." Patrick poured himself another brandy and leaned against the mantel. "She gave him an ultimatum — her and his sons or his parents and Sidney."

"I knew it," I muttered under my breath.

"Our father admitted she monitored every letter he wrote back home and read everything sent to our house before he saw it." Monte confessed.

"I knew Bethany hated how much I resembled my mother, but to erase my existence," my voice felt small from the full scope of my father's betrayal.

"Patrick and I wanted to change that." Annabelle reached over gently taking my hand. "That was why I started writing to you. I wanted you to get to know your brothers, your family and for them to finally know you."

"I am so happy you did." I squeezed her hand. "I look forward to every one of your letters. They mean so much to me."

I excused myself to get some air. I grabbed my shawl from the tree stand in the foyer and walked out onto the porch. The cool evening air was a welcomed reprieve. I leaned against the railing staring out into the darkness. The stars overhead sparkled brightly across the sky.

"I had no idea," my grandmother's voice was barely a whisper.

"You know," I kept my eyes forward. "In all the times I have spoken to Jocelyn about her life here, never once has she ever mentioned Walter or Bethany being in her life." I turned my head slightly. "Am I the cause she never knew her grandparents?"

"No," but her voice lacked conviction as she stepped beside me. "That was the consequences of their own actions. You have nothing to blame yourself for."

"Perhaps," I glanced over at her profile. "But it does not make me feel very good about myself learning that my own father chose to erase me."

"Sidney," my grandmother wrapped her arm around my waist. "You are loved. You are cherished. You are not a mistake." She hugged me tightly. "Don't you know you are the light of my life? You have a wonderful husband and a beautiful son. You are smart. You are kind." She leaned her head against my shoulder. "You have been and always will be, my special girl."

An hour later I was lying in bed wrapped in my husband's arms. Silent tears ran down my face onto his chest. I no longer felt like the strong confident lady I had been in Boston or Savannah. I felt like a broken discarded shell of my former self. I replayed the days events over in my mind. I could not bring myself to regret what I had said to Walter, but I did regret that it appeared to be the catalyst for a permanent rift in our family.

41

TUESDAY, NOVEMBER 3, 2020

THE ELECTION UPDATES PLAYED OUT on the large television screen in the living room at Robert and Emily's. The family had gathered for dinner after a long and grueling day of morning classes and an afternoon shift at the hospital. I spent my lunch break in-between the two in line at the library to cast my vote in the presidential election.

Looking around at my neighbors and community members it became more obvious that the widely democrat city was something our family could not support. Perhaps Robert and Emily were right in wanting to relocate to a more right-leaning state where our rights and our children's future would be more protected.

Emily and Robert had laid out a spread of pizza, breadsticks, cheese dip, and other various snacks and desserts. It was a lavish spread for us, but typical of them. They loved to entertain and were born hosts. Emily explained that Phoebe and her family were staying home this evening. Carson's parents had arrived for a visit from Florida. I told them Landon was stuck at the hospital working a double shift.

The atmosphere was lively. Jocelyn brought along a bottle of peach wine to share, while the men drank Rolling Rock. It took the edge off of what was sure to be a very long night. Considering the various time zones, closing times of the poles, and how the results were tallied, we had no clue when a final winner would be declared.

Robert was flipping through the different networks trying to find the latest updates. He would listen for a few minutes, sigh heavily and scroll on. He landed briefly on MSNBC — a known liberal pseudo-network that despised President Trump twisting all his accomplishments and achievements to fit the leftist narrative.

Robert was standing in front of the television with his hand on his hip. The tension in his shoulders was palpable. The female broadcaster had a more masculine haircut than all the men in this household. Robert grunted his disapproval at the liberal drivel spewing from this moron's lips.

"This progressive liberal democrat bullshit is destroying our country." Robert sighed audibly, running his hands through his hair. "Can you believe this?"

"Pappa, why do the liberal democrats hate Oompa-Loompas?" The room fell silent as Charlie's small voice caught everyone off guard.

"What?" Robert looked down at his grandson standing beside him holding a breadstick in his hand.

"The lady on tv said the orange man is bad. Doesn't she know the Oompa-Loompas were good. Mr. Slugworth was the bad man, but he turned out to be good at the end." Charlie's voice sounded so pure and innocent.

The adults in the room looked at each other, stunned by the simplicity of a child's view of the world around them. Jocelyn slipped first with a slight snort. Jackson lost it. His laughter broke through the silence until every adult had tears rolling down their faces.

"The innocence and naivety of babes." Jocelyn wiped the tears off her cheeks.

"Well?" Charlie tugged on Robert's sleeve looking confused. "Why do they hate them?"

"Buddy, they aren't referring to Oompa-Loompas from the movie. They are saying 'orange man bad' as a derogatory statement against our President — President Trump." Robert explained. "They enjoy bullying people."

"That's not very nice." Charlie pursed his lips.

"No, Buddy. They aren't very nice."

"We watched *Willy Wonka and the Chocolate Factory* last weekend." Leslie broke the silence.

"New or old?" Jackson asked.

"Original one with Gene Wilder." Alex rolled his eyes at his brother. "We watched the other one once and couldn't even make it through it, it was so bad."

"Ditto," I added. "I don't know why they thought it would be a good idea to remake such a classic."

"The new one follows the book." Jackson turned towards me with a smirk.

"I don't care. If I wanted that version, I would have read it. The movie sucked." I concluded.

"Okay, I have a question." My younger sister leaned against the back of the couch facing us. "How do you believe the country would be different if the South had won the Civil War?" She raised an eyebrow at our uncle before taking a sip of her wine.

"The South had no chance of winning." Robert spoke before the rest of us. "They could have if the Southern states had worked together as the colonies did at the onset." He shrugged.

"Meaning?" Jackson tilted his head with intrigue.

"Well, if memory serves the Continental Congress sent Benjamin Franklin, Thomas Jefferson, and John Adams to France and," Alex took a swig of his beer. "Another European country. The Netherlands and Spain, I think." He shrugged. "The point is, they sent intelligent figures to European power-holds to establish the colonies as an independent country from Britian. I have never heard of the South doing so, with the exception of trying to get Queen Victoria, was it," he shook his head slightly. "I don't remember. Anyway, to recognize the Confederate States by embargoing their cotton or something to that effect."

"And you believe that would have made a difference?" Robert chimed in.

"Maybe," Alex shrugged.

"The Souths failure to unite is what resulted in their downfall." Jackson snorted.

"They did unite." Jocelyn objected. "They formed the Confederate States of America." She rolled her eyes at me.

"No. They really did not." Alex stated as my sister looked around at all of us shaking our heads. "They were more concerned with individual states rights rather than supporting each other for their mutual independence."

"Didn't the governors of Georgia and South Carolina refuse to send their state militia to join the regular army because they wanted them there to protect their states?" I asked.

"Yes, and that turned out to be another critical error. President Davis pleaded and begged for those troops, especially when confronted with Union troops marching into Atlanta. That old song and dance of state rights over federal rights came back to bite them in the ass." Robert chuckled.

"Fair enough." Jocelyn conceded. "But how different do you think our country would be if President Lincoln was never assassinated?"

"You could speculate a lot over that one." I chuckled. "The U.S. would be a very different country, that is for sure."

"Reconstruction would have never happened the way it did." Jackson noted. "Lincoln was all about restoring and unifying the country at the end of the war. Andrew Johnson was all about revenge for causing the war and holding the slaves accountable for causing it. He was a true Southerner"

"Do you think Lincoln would have sent all the Blacks back to Africa?" Jocelyn asked.

"He wanted to." I shrugged. "He said it on multiple occasions. He even had a plan on how to do it, didn't he?"

"Yes, he did." Robert admitted. "He knew what would befall them if they were freed in the South. And it was not any different in the North. Blacks were equally despised, and Lincoln knew they would suffer more after gaining their freedom regardless of which region they were in. He also talked about sending them out west to colonize themselves away from whites. His wife's family were slave owners too."

"You also have to consider, if reconstruction never happened the Southerners who fled west to either work on the railroad or to settle new territory would not have been motivated by their desire to escape the federal stranglehold over the Southern states." Alex explained.

"Think about how that alone would have impacted the federal government's relationship with Native Americans." Robert observed. "If our ancestors had not been so diligent in settling the west, who knows how the United States would have been redefined."

"The west — all the way to California had already, pretty much been claimed by the U.S. before then, right?" Jocelyn inquired.

"Yes, but they were not states. I do not believe Arizona became a state until the twentieth century." I tried to recall. "Either way, our ancestors were a dominate presence across the territories." I poured myself some more wine. "It is interesting to speculate." I said before taking another drink.

"And on that note, I am going to take these little ones upstairs." Leslie ushered Lucy and Charlie. "Give Daddy and your grandparents a kiss and say goodnight to everyone."

The conversation stalled momentarily while the children went around the room giving everyone kisses and hugs. Leslie told Alex she was going to read them a bedtime story and would be back shortly. I was guessing they were planning on spending the night here — something not out of the ordinary in this close-knit family. It was easier with young children, so their parents didn't have to worry about disrupting their schedules.

"If you look at various, seemingly small and perhaps even insignificant in appearance — events, they can alter the course of history." Alex proclaimed after the echo of footsteps on the stairs had disappeared. "Look at the General Lee's military orders, for instance that were intercepted by McClellan. That changed the entire war." He raised his eyebrow at Robert, running his fingers through his dark wavy hair.

"Wouldn't it be something to be able to change that." Robert laughed, shaking his head slightly. "It is a shame I was so young at that time and not privy to the information we have now." Robert said with thick sarcasm.

"Imagine if you had known." Alex had a specious twinkle in his eye.

"Weren't you the ones who had warned me, repeatedly — not to meddle with history." My little sister smirked.

"Yes," Emily, Robert, and Alex answered in unison with cocky grins.

"Obviously, there is no way we could do that because we would have no way of knowing." Robert chuckled.

"Unless," I raised my eyebrows at them. "I told you." Their eyes all turned to me. "I mean, I am in Chicago right now with you two." I looked at Robert and Emily.

"Hey now, I am there too." Jackson nudged me playfully. "Granted, I am what four?"

"Almost," his mother laughed.

"You are adorable," I teasingly pinched his cheek before turning towards Robert and Emily. "But I can't." I ran my hand over my face. "Neither of you know I have the gift of *E.V.E.* and supposedly, I do not know anything about either of you having it."

"You know what this sounds like?" Jocelyn snickered. "That episode of Friends where Rachel and Phoebe are grilling Joey about Monica and Chandler's secret relationship — 'they don't know we know, they know'."

"Very funny," I rolled my eyes at her with a smirk. "Only you."

"She's not wrong," Alex laughed. "Why can't you just say something in private?" he looked at me.

"We didn't know you inherited *E.V.E.* or that Monte and Nicholas did until Monte told us when Jackson and Jocelyn announced their engagement *there*." Robert looked confused.

"Monte knew about you all because I told him." I clarified. "I was concerned about Jocelyn getting pregnant and the effect it would have had on her life *here*."

"We never knew," Emily said softly with eyes full of what if's and what could have been . . .

"So, you are in Chicago right now with my family." My sister leaned against the breakfast bar. "Annabelle is still pregnant with me."

"She was when we arrived," I nodded. "You were born a couple weeks ago." I laughed. "You want to talk about chaos. The family went ballistic over your birth."

"No one can ever say I don't know how to make an entrance." Jocelyn smirked.

"You certainly did," Emily chuckled lightly. "The first girl amongst that horde of boys. Your mother was beside herself."

"She was elated." I told my little sister. "She barely let anyone hold you." The pride was evident in my voice. "You were such a beautiful baby. You looked like a porcelain doll."

"With a headful of dark auburn hair and big doe eyes." Emily smiled.

"Mimi had to wrangle the boys away from you. They were so excited wanting to hold you. Patrick Jr. sat beside Annabelle on the bed so serious and calm while the other three were bouncing around the room trying to get to you." I smiled.

"My eldest brother was always the stoic and studious one." I nodded. "He is a lot like his father," Jocelyn sighed. "He lacks the fire the others have. But he is kind in a more subtle way and absolutely brilliant. He is an incredible physician."

"Yes, he is." Robert agreed.

"What were my other brother's like as little kids?" my sister asked.

"Lively," I rolled my eyes towards Emily who chuckled. "Mimi has her hands full."

"Ah, Mimi. I miss her so much." Jocelyn's eyes glistened. "She was the heart of our home."

"I never realized how feisty she was." I chuckled. "She knows exactly how to handle them and keep them in check."

"It must be strange being there right before the war." My little sister speculated. "I forget sometimes how odd this must be for you."

"It has been an interesting education in family dynamics." My eyes grew wide with unspoken words.

"Sunday dinner," Emily whispered as her and Robert's facial expressions shifted from light-hearted to recognition.

"What?" Jocelyn looked at the three of us with confusion.

"Our first weekend in Chicago there was a nasty confrontation between Walter and me. Your dad asked him and Bethany to leave before supper." I summarized without elaborating.

"My grandparents were at my house?" Jocelyn's eyebrows furled. "They never came to Sunday dinners."

"They used to," Robert said quietly. "Before that Sunday."

"Okay, I need details." Jocelyn sipped her wine waiting for answers.

"Apparently Walter gave in to Bethany's ultimatum and erased me from existence." I shrugged casually downplaying the hurt and betrayal that still stung.

Emily recounted what happened from the abandonment, the walk, the exchange of words, the slap and subsequent punch to Patrick asking his parents to leave. It sounded even worse listening to it second-hand. I felt myself shrink against the island feeling rejected all over again.

"Your grandparents were never invited to a Sunday dinner or a family holiday since." Robert added when Emily finished. "Patrick never trusted his parents after that and had limited contact with them. Walter and Bethany moved to California after the war."

"I always wondered why they never came around. My parents wouldn't talk about them. My mother once said they had a falling out over secrets but would not say anything more than that." Jocelyn explained. "I never knew what happened."

The atmosphere shifted as a collective pause fell over the room with the latest election poll updates posted. We were optimistic about President Trump's chances of being reelected. Joe Biden's campaign had consisted mainly of him hiding out in his basement citing the pandemic as justification. He was a career politician who had managed to accomplish absolutely nothing in more than four decades in office. He was continuously mocked by former President Ronald Reagan for his ineptitude and incompetence.

The hours dragged on without any declaration of a winner. Still, nothing. I finally headed home around midnight. Landon was waiting up for me looking haggard. He had beat me home by mere minutes. I barely got him showered before we collapsed. We went to bed feeling comfortable with President Trump's comfortable lead in the results.

We could not have been more wrong.

Little did we know, the nightmare was just beginning.

42

TUESDAY, NOVEMBER 6, 1860

I **PACED AROUND OUR BEDROOM** trying to squash the knot in the pit of my stomach. Patrick, Monte, and Keifer had gone down to city hall to cast their vote for the Republican Party candidate, Abraham Lincoln. I hated not being able to vote, of having no say in anything political, or in any major part of my life. I recalled my sister raging over the limitations her family, Patrick in particular, in the nineteenth century put on her studies and opinions. Even knowing the outcome of this election did little to ease the tension I felt in my shoulders.

Lincoln had built his campaign on standing against expanding slavery into new territories and states, as settlers continued to push westward to the Pacific Ocean. He was an unlikely candidate who few believed would win. Lincoln was selected by the Republican party simply because he was somewhat known through his previous debates with Stephan Douglas and had not been in politics long enough to have earned an enemies list. His averageness was his main appeal for the nomination.

John Bell of Tennessee, the Constitutional Union Party (former Whig party) candidate, was favored to win on the platform with a single objective — preservation of the Union. His deliberate strategy was considered too soft by many voters, but his party used it as a way to simplify the multifaceted platforms of their opponents.

The Democrats had split into two factions across the border line between the Northern and Southern states. The Northern faction threw their support behind Stephan Douglas, and he became known as the Popular Sovereignty candidate. The Southern Democrats put their faith in John Breckinridge who pushed for the rights of slavery in new territories.

But Americans remained divided on what they wanted. The Northern states were heavily populated in comparison with the rural South. The large Southern plantation owners were the epitome of Southern aristocracy. The South maintained a social structure, held onto traditional values, and was far more conservative than their Northern counterparts. The two halves of the nation struggled to understand each other. The conclusion of the Dred Scott case and the Fugitive Slave Law only deepened the divide by the time election day came around.

Still, I dreaded the outcome of election. Lincoln would win with forty percent of the national votes and one hundred eighty electoral votes. Breckinridge would finish second, Bell third, and Douglas last with only securing one state, Missouri and splitting New Jersey with Lincoln. I knew his win would be the final catalyst for the Southern states to begin their secession from the Union.

"Sidney?" A knock on my bedroom door pulled me from my thoughts.

"Yes," I stood by the window looking out at the bare maple tree that was a mere shadow of what it would look like in my *other* life. "Come in."

"How are you, dear?" my grandmother entered my room and closed the door behind her.

"Worried." I said, turning to look out the window again. "I hate sitting idly by and remaining silent when I know what horrors are waiting on the horizon."

"I know," she walked over to the edge of my bed and sat down. "We knew this was coming. We have prepared for it." She exhaled softly. "That is all we can do."

"I understand, but the reality has already been written in our history books." A tear rolled down my cheek.

"Darling," she waited until I turned around to face her. "The next four years will be the closest we will ever be to hell on earth. Not a single family will escape the horrors of this war. Not one household will escape the grief of a life cut short. However, we know our loved ones — Patrick, Monte, Nicholas, Robert, and your loving husband will come home to us." She said gently. "They will survive."

"But at what cost to their humanity? The carnage Patrick and Keifer will witness firsthand with the mangled bodies of young soldiers. What price will their souls pay for Robert, Monte, and Nicholas when they are forced to kill their fellow countrymen?" I brushed the tears off my cheeks that were now flowing freely. "If Lincoln had agreed to the Crittenden Compromise, the civil war would have never occurred, and slavery would have died out if the federal government eased the tax burden on the South."

"You know, no one mentions the Crittenden Compromise anymore — at least no one in the North." My grandmother shook her head slightly. "They portray Lincoln as some great emancipator, but they fail authenticity."

"History is written by the victors," I muttered.

"You mean distorted." Her eyes narrowed.

"Exactly," I scoffed. "I never heard about the Crittenden Compromise in school, not even at Northwestern University. I had no idea that representatives from both sides tirelessly worked together to agree on a compromise to using the thirty-sixth thirty parallel marker from the Missouri Compromise keeping slavery in the South and none in the North in all existing and future territories and states." I began pacing again. "But Lincoln in all his arrogant wisdom outright refused it because he ran on the platform that penned slavery into existing states." I huffed with indignation. "His arrogance cost the lives of more Americans than every succeeding war combined."

"That is what the Republican's get for getting average elected." Marissa huffed.

"One stroke of the pen and that pompous ass could have stopped years of pure hell." I continued pacing.

"Sidney? Marissa?" Mimi knocked softly on the door. "Suppa's edy."

"Thank you," Marissa wiped her tears with a handkerchief. "We shall be down directly." She rose to her feet and approached me placing her hands on my shoulders. "Wipe your tears, my darling. They cannot see you have been crying, and we have no excuse for your tears."

"I just want to scream." I hastily brushed the tears off my cheeks.

"Darling," my grandmother guided me towards the door. "All we can do is pray. It is in God's hands now." She paused and kissed me on the cheek. "Let's enjoy supper with our family."

APPENDIX

2021

Chandler

- Robert Abraham – Corporate Attorney
- Emily Jade – Novelist
    - Alexander Nolan – Family Law Attorney
        - Leslie – Alexander's wife
            - Lucinda – Alexander & Leslie's Daughter
            - Charlie – Alexander & Leslie's Don
    - Phoebe Rochelle (Chandler) – Criminal Attorney in Boston
        - Carson Adler – Phoebe's Husband
            - Wallace Abraham – Phoebe & Carson's Son
            - Audry Jade Harper – Phoebe & Carson's Daughter
    - Jackson Wyatt – Corporate Attorney/Married to Jocelyn
        - Jocelyn Alyssa (Timmons) – Jackson's Wife

Timmons

- Shane Douglas – Hospital Compliance/Sidney, Jocelyn, & Ethan's Dad
    - Sidney Harper
        - Landon Addicus Harrison – Medical Student/Sidney's boyfriend
    - Jocelyn Alyssa – Sidney's Younger Sister
        - Jackson Wyatt Chandler – Corporate Attorney/Jocelyn's Husband
    - Ethan Jude – Sidney & Jocelyn's Younger Brother
        - Liang Chi – Ethan's Girlfriend
- Nicholas – Shane's Younger Brother

Harrison

- Jim – Security Specialist
- Diana – Teacher
    - Holden
        - Gabriella – Holden's Liberal Wife
    - Landon – Medical Student/Sidney's Boyfriend
    - Lizzy

Friends

- Erica Grant, MD – ER Physician
- Veronica – ER Nurse
- Brandy – ER Nurse
- Kevin – Boston PD/Brandy's Husband
- Erik Dove – Nicholas' Estate Attorney
- Tammy – ER Nurse
- Amy Timmons, MD – Sidney & Jocelyn's Mom/Engaged to Dane
- Dane Bailey, MD – Pediatric Surgeon/Engaged to Amy
- Darline – High School Teacher/Dane's Sister
- Jason – Firefighter/Darline's Husband

1860

Terrace Falls, Braintree, MA

- Keifer Lee Marshall, MD
- Sidney Harper (Timmons) Marshall – Keifer's wife, Jocelyn's sister
    - Keifer Lee Marshall, II. – Keifer and Sidney's son
- Marissa Simone Timmons – Sidney's Paternal Grandmother
- Ralph Miller Timmons – Sidney's Paternal Grandfather (Deceased)

Estate Workers

- Ned – Estate Foremen
- Duncan – Ned & Naomi's Son
- Naomi – Cook/Married to Ned/Duncan's Mom
- Marta – Housekeeper
- Preston – Grounds Keeper
- Wanda - Housekeeper

Neighbors

Morgan

- Evan
- Charlotte
    - Levi
    - Adelaide
- Kenzie - Nanny

Bennett

- Edmund – Braintree Banker
- Iris (deceased)

McKenzie

- Martin
- Molly
    - Nancy

McKendrick

- Stephan
- Judith – Sidney's Close Friend
    - George
    - Brian
    - Paul
    - Gabriel
    - Cameron – Courting Nadine Beeler

Howard

- Jerimah – Mercantile Owner in Braintree

Kirby

Beeler

- Fredrick
- Abigail
    - Jerold
    - Nadine – Courting Cameron McKendrick
    - Dalton Hindsley – Abigail's Nephew from South Carolina
    - Luke Hindsley – Abigail's Nephew from South Carolina

Petraits

- Raymond
- Paula
    - Caleb – Son
    - Harmond – Ranch Hand

Church

- Pastor Lawerance Belville

Gable Gardens, Savannah, GA

Marshall

- David
- Angelina
    - Keifer Lee
        - Sidney Harper (Timmons) – Keifer's Wife
            - Keifer Lee II – Keifer & Sidney's Son
    - Margaret "Maggie"
        - Thad Wooden – Maggie's Husband
            - Marina
            - Susanna
            - Milo
            - Oliver
            - Tobias

- Edmund – Deceased
- Eugenia
- Victoria
- Caroline
- Edith
- Beatrice "Trixie"
- Lucas

Plantation

- Harley – Overseer
- Mac – Ranch Handler
- Ottis - Stableman
- Leroy - Coachmen
- Maddie – Cook
- Polly – Cook
- Jerimiah – Overseer
- Tallie – Housemaid/Wet Nurse
- Nala – Housemaid
- Sadie – Housemaid

Farwell/Farwell Farms

- Remus
- Mariam
    - Randell - Bonnie's Husband
        - Bonnie – Married to Randell
            - Daniel
            - Mary
            - Elise
    - Adam
    - Lynn
    - Conrad
    - Molly
    - Melanie
- Franklin – Overseer

Cameron

- Nathen
- Francis
  - Carolanne
  - Sylvia
  - Evelyn
  - Ronnie

Rhoades/Bella Ridge

- Leo
- Alice
  - Phillip – Caroline's Husband
    - Caroline (Marshall) – Phillip's Wife/Keifer's Sister
  - Henry
  - Elizabeth
  - Josiah

Note from Author

When I embarked on creating the spin-off of my *E.V.E.* series, I decided to approach it from the perspective of someone living dual lives in both the nineteenth and twenty-first centuries. In doing so, the focus of the main character stood on traditional moral and ethical Christian family values.

I learned a great deal about both periods when researching material. Most, especially the historical elements, were never taught in either primary or a university setting. Which is upsetting considering how much misinformation, specifically historical misinformation has been posted on social media platforms.

I did my best to be true to my character(s) and the challenges each were facing in their respective periods. I look forward to continuing Sidney's journey through each and sharing her adventures with you.

References

Bierce, A. (1994). Civil war stories. Dover Publications, Inc. New York, New York.

Davis, W. C. & Wiley, B. L. (2000). Civil war: A complete photographic history. Tess Press. New York, New York.

Etcheson N. (2004). Bleeding Kansas: Contested liberty in the civil war era. University Press of Kansas. Lawrence, Kansas.

Faust, D. G. (2008). This republic of suffering: Death and the American civil war. Random House, Inc. New York, New York.

Freeman, J. B. (2018). *The field of blood: Violence in congress and the road to civil war.* Farrar, Straus and Girous. New York, New York.

Katcher, P. (2007). The civil war day by day. Chartwell Brooks, Inc. New York, New York.

Lanning, M. L. (2007). The civil war 100: The stories behind the most influential battles, people and events in the war between the states. Sourcebooks, Inc. Naperville, Illinois.

Potter, D. M. (1976). The impending crisis: America before the civil war 1848 – 1861. Haper Perennial. New York, New York.

Wright, M. (1996). What they didn't teach you about the civil war. Presidio. Novato, California.

Author Bio

A. L. Waddington has her master's in military psychology and is currently working on her dissertation for her doctorate. She is an avid researcher and reader, and when she is not lost in the world of her own creation, she is busy exploring the southern region of the country. She is slightly addicted to coffee, gardening, and cooking. She and her husband, Eric, reside in northeast Texas with their daughters and three very spoiled puppies.

Find out more about A. L. Waddington and her books at www.ScarlettInkPublishing.com.

DISCOVER WHERE IT ALL BEGAN:

~THE EVE SERIES~

ESSENCE, BOOK 1

Our minds often wander, but can our souls?

Jocelyn Timmons does not believe she is anything special — just an ordinary high school senior, living an ordinary life full of schoolwork, volleyball, and friends. She's about to find out how wrong she is. Jackson Chandler moved into the house across the street. His dark wavy hair, green eyes and charismatic personality drew everyone to him. Everyone, but Jocelyn. Whenever Jackson gets near Jocelyn, she feels ill and dizzy. When he touches her, she blacks out and has visions of another life, at another time. As the odd hallucinations evolve and become clearer, she feels a strong pull towards the people she sees there. Frightened, she watches her once stable life begin to crumble around her, and she begins to question her own sanity.

Could it be possible that these episodes are actually her own memories of a life she is living somehow, somewhere, somewhen? Maybe this is time-travel or some other paranormal mysticism? Our minds often wander, but can our souls?

ENLIGHTENED, BOOK 2

Time stands still cause time can't heal.

The barrier between Jocelyn Timmons consciousness continues to dissolve as she better understands the two lives she lives and enormity of her newly discovered inherited gift of *EVE* (Essence Voyager Era) which allows her to fall asleep on one plane of existence and awaken on another as her soul travels nightly. Present-day Jocelyn uncovers the vast wonderment of the Victorian era but soon learns that life during then was not as grand for women as she has read in the classics.

Still, she finds comfort in the support of family and friends; a bolstering contrast to her overly hectic, career-oriented family in the twenty-first century. Her love for Jackson Chandler strengthens over time and becomes the light she so desperately needs as the world she has always known no longer makes sense. Yet, the closer she is drawn to Jackson by their mutual ability, the more strain develops amongst those she loves in 2009.

On the other side of Jocelyn's consciousness in 1878, she remains ignorant of *EVE*. Her life is crumbling around her, yet she finds herself anxiously awaiting the images that invade her dreams. Jocelyn longs to be the woman she portrays in that world, yet her jealousy is unbearable.

Miscommunication, betrayal, and hidden agendas make trust nearly impossible. The clearer the visions become the more she questions the motives of her closest confidants and foregoes revealing the images that plague her perception. As her life seems to unravel, Jocelyn's two worlds collide, and she is enlightened as the pieces start to fall into place. But is she strong enough to survive the truth? Is Jackson really her destiny? And can their love transcend time?

PERCEPTION, BOOK 3

My hopes, my dreams, and most of all me...we will finally be, set free.

Questions, questions, and more questions . . . they consume Jocelyn Timmons' life—both of them. Questions that never seem to have an answer. They haunt her, eat at her, and dreams of a normal senior year of high school have finally floated away into nothingness. Inheriting the gift of *EVE* (Essence Voyager Era) has become both a gift and a curse. One that Jocelyn doesn't know if she wants or can accept.

The world she once knew and thrived in has all but disappeared in the last two months. And now she wonders if she can ever find her way home again. Her fiancé, Jackson Chandler, and his family seem to be the only ones who understand what she's going through besides her uncles, both of which she's grown very close to. But even they do not fully grasp how turbulent the situation at home has become. Will Jocelyn survive the torments of her mother and brother? Or will she find a hidden key to finally unlock her golden cage?

ILLUMINATION, BOOK 4

Can time predict the future?

In the gripping conclusion of the bestselling *EVE* series, Jocelyn and Jackson come face to face with the challenges of living combined lives on both planes. While Jackson struggles under the demands of his chosen profession, Jocelyn discovers hidden branches on the family tree. But the more she uncovers, the deeper she finds herself and her family in an uncharted realm that no one considered possible.

Can *EVE* not only skip around with family members but also switch branches? The happy couple soon learns that a branch, like time, has the tendency to bend in the most unexpected directions and occasionally even break. When that happens, lives are forever changed, the forces of destinies altered, and fates derailed. The fluidity of time begins to take on an obscure meaning as the barrier between the two worlds fades into darkness.

AND DON'T MISS WHERE IT ALL BEGAN:

~THE SPIRIT QUEST SERIES~

TRANSCENDENCE, BOOK 1

A storm is brewing . . .

Several years ago, Sidney learned that she, like her sister Jocelyn, has inherited the gift or curse of EVE — the ability to live parallel lives on two separate planes of existence two centuries apart as their soul travels nightly. A prospect she has yet to fully embrace.
Sidney's 21st century life consists of her boyfriend Landon, completing her residency and following her mothers' footsteps to becoming a doctor. She has worked hard and sacrificed much to get where she is, and she is proud of all she has accomplished.
But the actions of her 19th century self-threaten to jeopardize it all.

As the treat of the looming Civil War darkens her world, she is consumed with her limited abilities as a woman. Unrest and tension surround her Boston home as her neighbors speculate what the future holds. How can She remain silent in her knowledge when her husband Keifer, and all those dear to her will soon be in jeopardy?
Is losing the life of someone you love to save your future in another world selfish? Can she be so selfish?

The storm around her is brewing and she feels powerless to stop it.

www.ingramcontent.com/pod-product-compliance
Lightning Source LLC
LaVergne TN
LVHW041056080826
845145LV00007B/1598

* 9 7 8 1 9 4 8 1 4 3 3 0 1 *